C000259143

SOULW△VES
A FUTURE HISTORY

Töm Evans

First Edition 2020
© Copyright Tom Evans

ISBN: 978-1-9161263-2-9

Published by Tmesis Publications

Cover design by The Cover Collection
Typesetting by 2QT Limited

Printed in UK by Lightning Source Limited (UK)

To my muses,
Douglas and Kurt

entanglement

Souls touch
Souls move
Souls love
Touching Souls

Waves roll
Waves break
Waves swell
Rolling Waves

From a single point
Beginning and ending
Massless, chargeless
Gravity unbending

Across countless eons
Full of insight
Travelling the Field
Faster than light

Karmically formed
Purpose unspoken
Once attached
Cannot be broken

Across infinite Voids
Connecting heart to heart
Once they join
Will never part

Universal Glue
And waves of love
What lies Below
Tied to Above

Outside Space
Inside Time
Entangled for reasons
Balanced in rhyme

1

Epochs

'It's time,' said Councillor Seven. Not that she had a mouth, or the other Councillors had ears.

'Are you sure they are awake enough?' asked Councillor Ten.

'Not individually but collectively they are,' insisted Councillor Seven.

Councillor Six, who had been managing the water consciousness, confirmed, 'They are travelling freely now. No disambiguations in any teleports for over fifty years.'

'And the humans are shifting rapidly from being planetary abusers to caretakers,' said Councillor Four, the overseer of the air consciousness.

'I agree,' said Councillor Seven. 'Just two to three more generations and they will have reversed their planetary decimation.'

'So can we put it to the vote?' asked Councillor Six.

The Council of the Light came to unanimous agreement. It was time to end Epoch Five and move to the unitary consciousness.

'So it's agreed,' confirmed Councillor Seven. 'This is the first galaxy where we can commence with Epoch Six.'

2

Pas de Deux

1959 : 150 years left

It was 1959 when one of the mothers of all soulwaves was released. On Earth, humans were just taking their first tentative steps off planet.

In May that year, two monkeys, Miss Able and Miss Baker, were launched into space along with living microorganisms and plant seeds. Their successful recovery made them the first living beings to return safely to Earth. In the same year, the Russian Luna 2 became the first man-made object to crash on the Moon.

Back on Earth, the Chinese were in the middle of the Great Leap Forward, transforming the country from an agricultural economy into a socialist society, through rapid industrialisation.

From time to time, the Councillors had to take great leaps forward too. They did this by creating high magnitude soulwaves through the death of stars.

At about 150 light years from Earth, a strange dance had been playing out. It was like one of those end of the evening types of dances where things were about to get quite intimate and very, very close.

This particular dance was being played out between two stars known as a binary system. The lead in the dance was taken by a white dwarf star.

The lead's partner, was much smaller and about the size of the Earth, yet massively dense. This smaller star's light was so dim that its presence was only detectable from Earth by the wobble it induced in the primary, as well as slight dimming when it passed in front of it.

This cosy 'pas de deux' had been going for about 3.5 billion years. Way back then, the lead dancer was about four times the mass of the Sun. It ran out of fuel rapidly and expanded to become a red giant, fully enveloping its companion star as it did so. So the smaller star lived fully inside the larger for quite some time and started to grow by taking stellar material from the lead.

Eventually the lead star's outer layer blew away and it shrunk down in size again. They then kept themselves to themselves, largely ignoring each other and minding their own business for billennia.

Their stable dance was interrupted though about half a billion years ago by an interloper. It was a red dwarf, an innocent interstellar wanderer. So-called space was littered with them. This one was steered their way by The Councillors.

To a close onlooker, who had the time and long enough lifespan to watch, the dance morphed into a pretty erratic affair. The interloping star looked drunk, doing a crazy figure of eight around the other two. Occasionally, it made an extra circuit or three around the lead dancer. It was in one of these encounters, at its closest ever approach, at perihelion, that it was tugged by the primary white dwarf, ever so slightly, into a new trajectory. On the next figure of eight, it would be sent off further out into space than it had ever been before. Perhaps it felt rejected, or lonely, and wanted revenge.

When it eventually got pulled back from its aphelion, its furthest reach back out to the cosmos, it was heading straight for the centre of the companion secondary. This had not happened before.

The impact initially tore both bodies apart. As they were

essentially made of the same stuff, they did eventually coalesce after a turbulent salsa all of their own. It was the primary star's turn to be jealous and it gave the new pairing the tiniest of extra gravitational tugs.

With their new combined mass and increased angular velocity, this led to the new bastard star's orbit becoming elliptical and unstable. It was on a path to finally bond with its mate after billions of years of flirtation.

The collapse of the star system was so rapid, and the spin so great, that there was nothing to prevent the binary from collapsing to a black hole. This was not a mere supernova – it was a hypernova.

The resulting soulwave radiated out, spewing energy at the speed of light, with heavier elements following at sub-light speeds. Some stars and planets would be spared completely, as this soulwave was not spherical, but directed. Some within as much as a 300 light year radius were in for a tumultuous upheaval.

3

Waving Souls

Even though the Councillors were all powerful and pervasive, they could not influence matter, or events, in the Density directly. After all, they were overseeing a Universe where Free Will was part of the experiment. They could of course perform all sorts of seemingly miraculous interventions. They did this by way of controlling the timing and paths of soulwaves.

Even by the 21st century, soulwaves had not been conjectured, and therefore not detected, by humans. Yet they felt their influence daily. Only the Wu knew of their existence, if not their actual source.

Soulwaves were the attractive force that glued matter to matter. At close range, atoms were forged into molecules by soulwaves. They provided the mechanism whereby soul mates bonded and un-bonded. Soulwaves also bonded moons to planets, planets to stars and stars to stars to form clusters and whole galaxies.

Soulwaves are strong in people who bump into other people they like, and love, all the time. Those brought together by soulwaves could never quite remember where, when or why they met. The Councillors saw to that. While they could not influence a person, a planet or a star directly, they could control the timings of when people, planets and stars collided with each other.

When the Councillors wanted to exert the maximum amount of influence, they operated at a stellar level. When it was necessary *to accelerate, or halt or reverse, the progress of evolution, stars would be required to die. This was of course the mechanism whereby heavier elements were formed which became the seeds for the formation of all life, and the planets it hung out on.*

When the Councillors wanted to make direct interventions in the Density, an Insertion was called for. This allowed for much more direct upheaval and was a relatively simple and more controllable affair, compared to getting a star to explode.

4

Insertion

The Void and the Density are essentially different - yet they are both part of the same One.

The Void is not a place that used to exist from which the Density was formed. It is both integral and crucial for the Density to exist and to keep on existing. Before the Density was formed, there was no Void. There was just a Seed Notion.

Some of those stuck in the Void long for the adventure open to those in the Density. People who are bored with the Density, or find it too hard going, long to be absorbed back into the Void.

The Void is kind of purply-blue, with a lovely ambient temperature, not too hot and not too cold. The Void is the space between space and sits in the time between nanoseconds. When you go back to it, you feel warm, enveloped and safe. You feel like you have gone back home and as if someone has wrapped you up snuggly in cotton wool.

By way of contrast, when you move around in the Density, the background temperature is a few degrees above Absolute Zero and you are forever being pulled by one gravitational force or other. Sometimes it's like wading through treacle.

When the Density was created, along with all life and latterly incarnate sentience, the Council of the Light came to be. Each of the twelve Councillors were selected for their particular experience in manipulating events in the Density, from their time in previous Universes. Their main purpose was to watch, supervise and learn but, very occasionally, they had to intervene directly.

'It's about time,' said Councillor One.

Making any statement about time was somewhat academic for the Councillors. For starters, they could not even remember the sequence of events that brought them all together. They just were.

This was not because they had bad memory but because, when you sit Anywhere and Anywhen - and Everywhere and Everywhen - there is no concept of the past to actually remember. Neither is there a future to plan, or to wonder or worry about. Everything just is. All is Whole and Cyclical.

'I knew it would be my turn,' said Councillor Four, with a remembered sense of trepidation and excitement. The Councillors knew that living in the Density involves pain and fear. They also knew that, in the Density, the ability to experience love balanced it all out.

'You will be back in no time at all,' chimed all the other eleven Councillors in twinkly unison.

Each Councillor appeared like a single point of light – a pinprick – much like a bioluminescent phytoplankton, that sparkled when speaking or thinking took place. While infinitely small in size, they were each infinitely wise. They had been in existence longer than Time.

Insertions in the Density are relatively rare but necessary, especially when a planet is going through a time of transition. Most of the time, affairs in the Density can be remotely managed through channels. When a Councillor descends, the devil is in the detail and occurs when the minutiae of events in the Density requires managing with some finesse.

When actual Insertion is called for, entering the Density is relatively easy. Extraction is much more complicated, and can be somewhat protracted.

Councillor Four could not express his anger and disquiet at having to go back again. Emotions were alien to a Councillor in the Void. He had eidetic recall of all the events but could only remember, not empathise with, the actual emotions he had felt last time.

During his last Insertion, he remembered that he had been a child oracle and recalled the detail of the secrets he had passed on to the Elders. In their arrogance, they intended to use this information for their own betterment. This was unacceptable. The remaining Councillors had no option but to terminate Epoch Three.

Councillor Four remembered experiencing the flow of time, and the notion of how it appears to come to an end for humans when they die. His last Extraction was particularly messy as he'd not quite ascended fully when the planet was obliterated. At least the pain was fleeting and over in less than a heartbeat.

So, just as before, Councillor Four was inserted at the point of highest density closest to where the next incarnation was to play out. Councillor Four was inserted into a black hole at the centre of a star once again. It took over 100,000 Sun orbits of the target planet, the Earth, in order for him to reach the star's surface. This is of course no time at all when you sit beyond time.

As Councillor Four finally emerged on the Sun's photosphere, his high energy flared up in a few places to help the Councillors locate the target planet. These points of emergence looked like sunspots to anyone who was paying attention. After a Sun rotation or so, Councillor Four's crackled energies fused together and could no longer be held, even by the Sun's immense gravity, and his essence was sent Earth-bound in a coronal mass ejection.

This was one of the most special forms for a soulwave to ever manifest in the Density.

During the transition, Councillor Four sat half in the Void and half in the Density.

The transit time to Earth on board the coronal mass ejection, was around two Earth days. As the blue-green disc became discernible from the background carpet of stars, the memories of mortal fears came to meet him.

For starters, crossing interplanetary space was lonely. There was no direct contact with the other Councillors, other than a vague memory of the warmth of the Void. For most of the trip, the Earth was just a blue-green dot and there was a sense of having been cast off alone into the blackness of space.

As the blue-green dot became a sphere, the travelling soul essence felt comforted that his path was indeed going to intersect with the Earth's orbit. He entered the Earth's noosphere at what the earthlings called their North Pole.

On the night of arrival, the Northern Lights were spectacular. They could be seen as far south as New York, Madrid and Beijing. His arrival even tripped the electrical grid in Canada.

As the energy from the CME was absorbed and integrated with the Earth's magnetic field, it was at this point in the Insertion that Councillor Four's pre-programming took full effect. He forgot everything about where he came from and why he was sent.

For the Councillors remaining behind, the gap between Councillor Four's Insertion and Extraction would take no time at all.

Before Insertion, Councillor Four knew all aspects of his mission in detail. He also knew that, once incarnate, he would carry the burden of an overwhelming sense of being abandoned.

Only when Extraction was complete would this burden lift.

5

Deep Thought

16th July 2057 : 52 years left

The essence of Councillor Four was transferred to the head of the best of Hui's spermatozoa just before it fused with Jia's egg, in a flash of light. The remaining Councillors breathed a sigh of relief, not that they could actually breathe. The timings had been exquisite.

"I'm pregnant," declared Jia, just as Hui withdrew from her.

He knew not to question a Wu. After 11 years of marriage, and many failed attempts, even he had a sense something was different that night. The appearance of the Aurora Borealis that far south, even viewable on the evening of a bright Super Moon, seemed to be the trigger for Jia.

Their small house in Fragrant Hills Park could not have had a better view of that evening's cosmic weirdness. Their first floor bedroom had two windows. Before Jia dragged Hui to their conjugal bed, he had been looking, through the east-facing window, at the sprawling metropolis of Beijing, bathed in the ethereal non-light of the Moon. At the same time, Jia had been transfixed by the aurora, clearly visible through the smaller north-facing and non-opening window. She was mesmerised by the swaying of the green and red dancing hues of light.

While Hui fell into deep post-coital slumber, Jia began an

inner dialogue and an initiation with the newly arrived soul.

'Welcome little one,' she whispered under her breath. 'We will look after you. You are safe.'

The newly arrived soul knew nothing of this but nonetheless was relieved to be somewhere warm and relatively safe. As the egg started to divide and the notochord formed, the soul attachment got stronger and stronger until the point of birth. Full entry into the Density was successfully achieved exactly nine Moon orbits later.

It was the 8th of April, 2058 when Jia gave birth to her baby boy in a birthing pool in their bedroom, appropriately bathed in the non-light of another Full Moon. She was ably assisted by Akiko, a doula who hailed from Japan. Jia had met Akiko at university in Kyoto and they had become great friends ever since. Jia and Akiko had been in a trance for eight hours preceding the birth and Jia knew of the pain but didn't acknowledge it.

After the cord was cut, Akiko handed her the baby. Jia stared into her boy's one green eye and one blue eye as Hui entered the room. He had heard the screams so knew their baby had arrived.

Jia sensed deep wisdom coming back from those eyes and as Hui entered, she declared, "We will call him Shen. Look Hui, even now he is deep in thought!"

Hui knew not to argue and was actually quite relieved he had nothing to do with the naming. Like Jia, he was in rapture that they at last had a baby and he was looking forward to showing their boy the secrets of the cosmos. For the last 9 months, Jia had been hatching other plans for him.

Akiko had finished cleaning up and tactically withdrew, saying she'd be back in the morning. Jia, Hui and Shen spent their first night together. Shen slept peacefully and quietly, so Jia and Hui did too.

Like most parents, Jia and Hui had no idea of their baby's true origin and, as for all such Insertions, Shen was programmed to forget too. As Shen gained more awareness of his surroundings, Jia did start to suspect he was something special though, a natural born Wu perhaps, although this was rare for a male.

The first telltale signs were silent and Jia alone felt them. Jia would receive a visual thought form of the whole of her own nipple being suckled by his mouth. The standard auto-drip came shortly after.

Shen developed at a pace that heightened parental bragging rights. He was crawling at just four months and quickly got on his feet in his seventh month. He'd progressed from spluttering 'mama' and 'dada' to actually saying "Jia" and "Hui" well before his first birthday. He was putting short sentences together before he was two.

He was a happy baby, with a smile as eye-catching as his thick shock of dark hair. He hardly ever cried, apart from when his teeth appeared.

He'd given Jia and Hui a new sense of purpose and brought them together at a time when their paths were starting to diverge.

6

They've Gone

8th April 2058 : 51 years left

Ning Shangbo was only sleeping sporadically, as her research time on Dongting Lake was fast running out. She had been awake since 2am and already knew it was going to be another of those days when the mist never lifted. Midday would only be marginally brighter than dawn or dusk. She had not seen a glimpse of the aurora that the vast majority of humanity was enjoying.

The gloom didn't bother Ning as all her attention was focused on what was going on beneath the surface of the lake. Her eyes were fixed on her sonar screen and her ears tuned to the ultrasonics coming from the underwater microphones.

Ning was on the cusp of fame and glory. Her PhD thesis would make her name worldwide. She was engaging in conversation with dolphins. Just prior to her return visit to the lake, she'd worked out how to trick the dolphins into thinking they were talking to another pod.

As far as she knew, the pod of three she'd been tracking for four summers now were the last remaining Baiji. They were thought to have gone extinct by the start of the century but she had discovered this pod, by accident, five years ago while on a walking holiday around the lake.

The pod seemed healthy enough and she was hoping that each summer, when she returned, that they would have bred.

The male and female just had the one pup - a male.

She had hours and hours of recordings and, in the intervening years since her first visit, she had been able to extract their signatures into three separate voices. By playing a single voice back, with a little frequency and phase shifting, it seemed to elicit a response from the pod - mainly from the lead male. She seemed to be able to talk to them alright but had no idea yet what they, or she, were saying.

When Pata, the male, had first heard the distinctive voices of his 'wife' and 'child' he thought he was going mad. They were clearly next to him but he could tell their voices were coming from a distance.

It was Tamu, his life partner, who sussed out where they were coming from.

'It will be from that kind human on the boat,' she clicked.

Dolphins not only had an innate ability to sense if other species were friend or foe but also 'knew' their intent.

'Well, if she wants to talk, we should reply,' announced Pata.

He'd been spending the days joyfully teaching the human the full range of the dolphin language by telling her the full history of the Baiji. This went back millions of years, well before Epoch 5 started. He even let slip where they went when humans thought they had gone extinct, knowing their secret was safe.

Tamu thought his behaviour was a little childish but, as there wasn't long left, let him get on with it. Their son, Baku, was confused at where all the voices were coming from and just snuggled up to his mother.

It was coming towards dusk on that day when Pata had told the whole history of their species up to the present day. He finished by saying, 'We've really got to go now but we loved talking to you.'

Ning had no idea of the richness of her treasure trove of recordings. She was just pleased that they were talking. She had another month on the lake before she had to navigate down the Yangtze to Wuhan and was sure she would be able to deconstruct the basis of single words, at the very least.

The pod stopped responding to her transmissions so she prepared herself a late lunch around what was supper time. She had been so absorbed that she'd forgotten she was hungry.

She ate noodles, made less bland with the addition of some grenadier anchovies she had caught the day before. This genus was one that she had introduced to the lake some years ago as part of another research project. She literally was benefitting from the fruits of her own research.

She was up on deck having moved her boat nearer to where she thought the pod would be, hoping for another sighting. In the gloom, she could see some disturbance on the surface. At first, it was just some bubbles that seemed to be luminescent blue. Then the surface became really agitated and she dropped her bowl of food when the sonar alarmed.

She skipped down the four steps into her lab area and headed over to the sonar screen. The three blobs she had been tracking were gone. She did a quick calculation. They could only travel 20 kilometres an hour, at maximum speed, and it was 30 minutes since she'd last seen them.

She widened the scan out a kilometre at a time to 10 kilometres. Nothing.

"Where have you gone?" she screamed to an empty lake.

7

Epoch Ends

At the same time the surface of the lake was bubbling, the Council Chamber was awash with twinkling lights. Probabilities and potentialities were bouncing between the eleven remaining Councillors, as they were tapping into all possible futures for the forthcoming Epoch Six.

The Councillors had made use of the dolphin's ability to teleport many times in the past.

It was how they had transferred sentience to Planet Earth, with the seeds for the Epoch Five civilisation coming from the remnants of Epoch Four on Mars. The land-based sentiences that had caused all the trouble had been terminated. It was yet another experiment that didn't go quite as planned.

After the dolphins 'ported from Mars to the Earth's oceans, they helped confer their self-awareness to the noosphere around the Earth. A million or so years later, they crawled out of the ocean to sow the seeds for humankind. The initial matings with proto-humanoids were somewhat messy, but necessary.

It was somewhat ironic that, some two million years later, Ning could not communicate with the sentiences from which she came. This was of course because she was tuned into completely the wrong 'channel'.

The Councillors knew how they would use teleportation again, within just a few Earth centuries, to begin the process of re-synthesis. This time they would be more innovative and subtle.

The coming together would be much more joyful and natural.

When Pata, Tamu and Baku had safely densified back on Aquanine, Councillor One pronounced, 'The seeds for Epoch Six are now sown.'

Each of the eleven knew that attention to small details in Epoch Five over the next remaining 51 Earth-Sun orbits, were pivotal in making the next Epoch even more successful than the last.

Extra care was needed at epoch ends as this was the only time that two sentient planets in the one galaxy are allowed, during the period of the transition. It was vital that their inhabitants never met, unless closely monitored by the Councillors.

8

Two Places

Hui wasn't sure if he was more annoyed at Shen for doing it or at Jia for not telling him.

"Just think how this will accelerate his learning," Jia said to mollify him. She was not aware that the Councillors liked to use this mechanism for accelerating advancement in the Density.

That morning Hui was letting Shen design his first orrery. He was so proud of how his three year old son was open to learning about subjects he'd not even known about until he was a teenager. Jia had noticed how home schooling of Shen was giving Hui a new lease of life.

That morning though, things were not going smoothly and Shen was having a rare tantrum. He was insisting that there should be a planet between Mars and Jupiter and got really upset that Hui wouldn't let him put it in the model.

"Mum, tell him please!" Shen wailed.

"But Mummy isn't here," Hui explained.

"She is, I am holding her hand," Shen insisted.

When Jia got home, and after supper when Shen was tucked up in bed, Hui told Jia about his puzzling behaviour. Jia thought it best to spill the beans, as she had known about it for some months now.

"So he gets to spend time with both of us at the same

time," said Hui, "And you're positive by the time he goes to school, it will stop?"

"Well it did for me," she said.

Jia knew Shen's natural tendency to bilocate would pass. Hui was at least grateful that Jia had shared one of the innate rules for bilocation with him. Thankfully, Shen was not able to be seen by the same person, at the same time, in two places.

"So can you still do this then?" Hui asked, as Jia was collecting the dishes. She clanked the cutlery, pretended she didn't hear and quickly changed the subject.

"Yu Yan wants me teach her how to heal and is talking about opening a school up here in the Gardens," replied Jia.

"I knew it. This is why we moved here," he said. "It is about time your talents were recognised."

Hui knew he'd have to revisit the bilocation conversation but they chatted about Jia's possible new opportunity until it was time for bed.

9

Orreries

2060 : 49 years left

Shen had chosen well. Shen's father, Hui, was a Threedeer. His mother, Jia, came from a long line of Wu.

Like many from the secret elite class, they lived on the outskirts of Fragrant Hills Park, about 30 kilometres Northwest of Beijing. Their parents had moved there in the Twenties to get to the fresh air above the smog of the city sprawl. When Shen was born in 2058, humanity had mostly seen sense and the use of hydrocarbons had all but been phased out.

All cars were now electric. Nobody really owned one outright and they were widely shared between neighbours and fellow workers. Electricity was 95% generated from solar, wind or tides, with the rest coming from nuclear sources that were planned to be phased out by the end of the Seventies. Roof tiles, car roofs, bonnets and boots and many roads all generated electricity these days. Planes had all but stopped flying and virtually all long distance travel on land was via MagLev. Across seas and oceans people travelled by TubeWays. The atmosphere had been restored to pre-industrial revolution levels. They could now see Beijing clearly once again.

This was an amazing achievement for humanity, made largely possible by the passing of the Old Guard from the fear-driven 20th century. The new breed of politicians were much more driven by the prospect of making the world a better place than by petty divisions of opinion. All in all, humanity was getting itself sorted and settling in wisely and gently to a newly found role of planetary stewardship.

Shen had landed on his feet, at the right place and at the right time.

Jia was held in high regard by those in high places. There weren't many dis-eases she couldn't alleviate. She was blessed with the touch. She had shot to prominence in her late twenties when she saved the life of President Miang's wife, Yu Yan, who was suffering from a brain tumour at the top of her spinal column. It was thought to be inoperable.

Like many Wu, Jia was able to see through space and time. Like shamans from all the world's metaphysical traditions, she was able to peer through the veil of the 4% material world to perceive and to manipulate the missing 96%. She was able to see Yu Yan's lower brain stem before the tumour started to grow, as well as after it was cured. It looked like a black fug to her which was sucking the life energy from Yu Yan's surrounding brain tissue - almost like a black hole of a tumour. After just three sessions, Jia had vapourised the tumour by replacing it with healthy neurons and tissue from Yu Yan's past and future brains.

This was just one of the skills of a shamanka and Jia's particular speciality. Weather manipulation was also something she had been taught by her grandmother.

The result of this intervention meant that the Wu would now be able to operate more openly, as they got the backing from on high. This gave Jia the admiration of her peers, as they had been working in secret for hundreds of years. They were less pleased that she would be teaching non-Wu surgeons the secrets of how to perceive and manipulate the morphogenic field. The resulting merging of allopathic medicine with the healing arts had the potential to increase average life expectancy by the end of the century to well over 120 years. In time, use of the scalpel would become less and less necessary.

Jia really wanted to teach Shen the art of the Wu as soon as he was able but, from the age of three, his attention was drawn to his father's world. She knew not to worry as he was clearly talented and often the gift skipped a generation.

Hui's work also made a huge contribution to increasing both human and animal longevity. He was one of China's leading authorities on 3D printing and had coined the term '3D-er' and opened the Threedeer Academy, based at Beijing University.

His speciality was in printing soft, bendable and porous body parts. In the early 21st century, 3D printing of long lasting bones became viable. Hui started first with heart valves but had progressed to creating complete working ears for the profoundly deaf. At the time Shen was born, he was busy perfecting an artificial retina and lens combination. His idea was not only to let the blind see but also to enable them to zoom in. He had no idea that those who could see perfectly well would start requesting his lens implants before the century was out.

Hui only had to take the cable car to University to teach two days a week which gave him time to share with Shen his real passion, which was creating 3D orreries.

Shen learned that the term was a tip of the hat to the fourth Earl of Orrery, who lived in the 18th century. The Irish Earl had a clockmaker create for him a mechanical model of the solar system which to this day remained on display in England's Museum of the History of Science.

Of course, Hui's 3D orreries took everything up several notches. Not only did they help astronomers envisage the local solar system, but also those of far off worlds.

The rendering of detail on the central stars and planets was done using holographic projectors. This meant that the local planets could be rendered in real time, using data from orbiting satellites and probes. Sunspots and flares graced the Sun's surface. He could also display what was happening in the non-visible parts of the spectra. The solar system took on a whole new light when seen in infrared and ultraviolet.

What really intrigued and captured the attention of Shen, from the age he could walk, was when Hui changed the holographic display to show the magnetic field lines of the solar system. Shen loved seeing how the solar wind distorted the magnetospheres of Venus, Mars and the Earth into teardrops. Hui had even rendered the magnetic mixing points from each planet back on to the Sun's surface. Shen watched these dances for hours. He could also see how the outer gaseous planets radiated back in towards the inner rocky planets and the Sun.

What Hui had been able to display meant astrologers had been on to something all along but had merely failed to interpret the data. Weather patterns on Earth, and tectonic movement, were affected by what was going on in the heavens. Had Hui looked at his own orrery just over three years ago, he might even have seen Shen coming.

Hui's 3D orreries were in high demand worldwide and meant he really didn't have to work these days. People paid him good money to download his templates so they could build their own orreries locally. Real time holographic mapping data was only provided at low resolution though, with detail reserved for academia and research. His templates were not limited to the solar system; he had made thousands of planetary systems available, from right across the galaxy. The virtually unlimited discovery of more and more solar systems kept Hui busy and in daily wonderment at the combinations and permutations for a viable solar system.

Despite the incredible resolution of the Chinese telescopes in orbit, and the detection and mapping of hundreds of thousands of systems, not one inner rocky planet had yet been observed with a viable Earth-like atmosphere.

Hui's real dream was that his models would lead to the discovery of life elsewhere in the cosmos. He knew he was close.

10

Big Data

2061 through to 2074

Hui and Jia were well aware that Shen was different from when he was a toddler. The bilocations had indeed abated when he started preschool and mixing with others of his same age.

Shen was blissfully unaware he'd ever been in two places at the same time. Hui did allow him to insert the missing planet in his orrery and this seemed to paper over the incidents when Shen got so upset.

Shen was also unaware, and wouldn't remember, that many times when watching Hui's orreries, they started up automatically, even though they weren't actually powered up.

It unsettled Hui at first until Jia told him that she found she could control her father's iPad with her mind when she was a toddler too. The Wu took this kind of thing for granted - it was only manipulation of the soulwaves in the quantum gaps after all.

From the age of four, Shen began attending the new Fragrant Hills Academy, along with the son of President Miang and Yu Yan. So he was in good, and elevated, company right from the start.

He was given a tutor, Madame Bien, who would act as his scholastic guide until he left the Academy for Beijing University. Madame Bien was strict but had a fabulous sense of humour and an insight for the optimal direction in which to point Shen. She seemed to be able to open doors for him and pull strings with ease.

When Jia and Hui realised this, they stopped interfering. Though naturally, they were quite sad to see Shen only on weekends, as the Academy, despite being only a few kilometres away on the other side of the Park, had a strict weekday boarding policy.

It became obvious that mathematics was Shen's forte from the get go. Madame Bien had to draft in tutors from the University when Shen was nine, as he'd surpassed the expertise of the Academy's top teachers. His grasp of mathematics gave him a head start when it came to the sciences too. Madame Bien also ensured he gained fluency in the English language and an appreciation of the arts and natural science. She knew that when an extra bright student appeared, the constancy of a guide was essential so they wouldn't get too full of themselves.

Despite his obvious genius, Shen kept his humility and never let it go to his head. He was popular with the other children, not least as he helped many of them with their homework - especially the boys who might otherwise bully him.

Jia and Hui were quite diminutive in stature - both an identical 165cm. By the time Shen was 11, he'd outgrown them in both size and in needing their support and input. Like his father, he'd even started an online business selling 3D designs around the world. His 3D fractals had a beauty that was remarkable for someone of his tender years. The algorithm he designed seeded each pattern so that every single one turned out to be unique. This is why they were so sought after.

His bank account grew each month, as he had nothing to pay for at school. So he took it upon himself to start paying rent to his parents for letting him stay at their house. They were proud and thankful, knowing their only child was making his own way in the world. By the time he was 12, Jia had mentally cut the ethereal cord that still tied them, as Shen began to make his mark in the Density. She knew she had already lost him to his studies.

At just 15, Shen started his Maths degree. With the same kind of sadness Jia had when Madame Bien took over Shen's academic reins, Madame Bien shed a tear when Shen left for the University to fall under the tutelage of Professor Cheng.

Analysis of Big Data was Professor Cheng's thing. What shot Cheng to prominence was his postgraduate thesis which predicted that conversion to devolved energy production could repay its capital investment globally within 20 years. His research compared the cost of maintaining traditional localised power generation and distribution and took no account of additional spin off benefits for the environment. Wind farms and massive solar arrays would become redundant as every building and every vehicle became its own power source. Energy generation would become embedded in the fabric of every human-made object, including their clothes, hats and shoes.

Cheng had become the youngest ever Professor of the Maths Department at the age of 28. He loved a gnarly problem and also testing the limits and skills of his protégés, by giving them seemingly impossible tasks. He had a long list of challenges that were eclectic, and seemingly pointless. He was driven by the intuition that answers were hidden in the questions nobody had ever thought to ask.

Cheng was dating, on and off, the Professor of Oceanography, Lien Huang. They met as undergraduates and saw each other when their schedules allowed, which tended to be in between semesters on the rare times that Lien was on dry land.

The last time that they met, overlooking the ocean in Shanghai, Lien had mentioned something that piqued

Cheng's interest, "There are far fewer whales and dolphins than we would expect these days."

The numbers of cetaceans had been decimated through hunting and the practice of drift netting in the 20th century. Since both practices had been banned in the Forties, with even the Japanese and Norwegians seeing sense at last, the numbers had been on the rise. This is what concerned Lien.

Lien observed, "The reproduction rates are well known but there are not only less pups than we'd expect but also fewer adults too. We have no idea where they are hiding."

Cheng sat on Big Data problems that didn't interest him personally and that he suspected were unfathomable. So when Shen arrived, Cheng lost no time in passing along this conundrum to him.

Shen, in turn, lost no time getting stuck in. His formal lessons gave him the techniques he needed. His personal fortune meant he could fund his own travel during out-of-term time. As soon as the first summer recess hit, he hopped on a MagLev to Shanghai, to meet with Professor Huang. From there, he left China's shores for the first time.

TubeWays criss-crossed the oceans, carrying electromagnetically pulsed pods that could get you from one side of the Pacific to the other in half the time a plane could ever have flown across. The only planes flying those days were electrically powered and used to access remote areas, either by the military or emergency services. There were many unmanned drones too used for scientific monitoring purposes.

The biggest downside to TubeWays was the utter lack of a view. The pods had no windows as the TubeWays were anchored several metres below the surface, with its superconducting propulsion system ingeniously powered by ocean currents.

So Shen's crossing to the Monterey Institute of Oceanography was uneventful. What he discovered on the other side was not so. Not least as he ended up losing his virginity to an intriguing researcher named Monique Armstrong, who was 12 years his elder.

Apart from her carnal enthusiasm for visiting students, Monique was also passionate about studying whales. For the last twelve years, she had personally supervised the counting of the number of migrating greys going south past Monterey in late Autumn and back up North to Alaska in Spring.

She gave Shen full access to her data, and it took Shen no time at all to ask why the numbers didn't always add up. Their shop talk was often interrupted, considering Monique also gave Shen full access to her body. She was as generous as he was eager to learn.

Over breakfast, after a long night of love making, Shen bravely asked Monique, "So if you knew the counts had errors, why have you never flagged it?"

"Well we wouldn't like to lose our funding if anyone thought we couldn't even count," she answered. "Some of our tracking devices seemed to fail too and go completely off grid. We didn't report this either in case the funding to design and maintain them got cut."

"There seems to be a particularly big discrepancy in 2069," said Shen.

Monique answered, "Yes that year I was under the weather for most of Spring and left my assistant in charge of the counting team."

Although only at the end of the first year of his course, Shen's intuition flagged that this needed looking into some more. He had taken heed to Cheng's warnings from early lectures that incisive Big Data analysis is only as good as the accuracy of small data entry.

"What about the counts before you took over?" he said.

"Probably best if I give you guest access to the archives," she said, knowing he wasn't planning to publish the data per se, or carry out any exposé.

Shen downloaded the data he needed - and some that he didn't, just in case, all for later reference. He didn't want to waste a minute in Monterey on analysis. He was more interested in experimentation, knowing that his time under Monique would be over soon.

Shen had no way of knowing it yet, but his innate skills as a Wu extended to sex. While others would fumble with fingers and limbs, Shen had a way of breathing into Monique's body that would make her skin alive. It didn't take long for Shen to grasp that she was a power source and he was literally connecting to it.

A couple of days later with a mix of longing and good will, Monique and Shen slowly kissed each other goodbye at the TubeWay terminal. They both knew it was the end of a glorious summer and they might not see each other again. Monique remembered how there was something different about Shen from the start. He seemed much older than his tender 16 years and she didn't have any pangs of guilt.

When on board the TubeWay, Shen sharpened his focus and plunged into analysis mode. He had data that showed reduced counts of whales returning back up North to Alaska after breeding and giving birth in the warmer waters off the coast of Mexico. He felt sure the discrepancies were larger than the data showed, and that it wasn't just that Monique had fudged the data.

By the time he got off the TubeWay in Shanghai, he had correlated the data sets and seen the biggest anomalies occur every 10 to 12 years. A quick search gave the probable factor of causation.

By the time he got off the MagLev in Beijing, he was keyed up to meet with Professor Cheng.

There were no hellos; no "how was your trip?" or "how did it go?"

As soon as Shen walked into Cheng's office, and before he sat down, he blurted out, "It's something to do with the Sun."

At this point in time, neither Cheng or Shen knew humanity had 35 years left.

11

Epoch One

There was a time when the Councillors of the Light sat both in the Density and the Void. Only they knew of this time, although time itself had not really got ticking. Neither was the Density that dense.

It was a period when rocky planets were first coalescing around third generation stars. They were far too hot for any organic life to get a foothold.

It was a time of audit.

The Councillors were assessing which were the best planets to use in each galaxy to start life. If you were around at that time, you may have seen the odd single, pair or groups of shimmering egg-shaped objects floating around the surface of various molten worlds.

As there was no time per se, they appeared on many worlds at the same time. As there were trillions of stars to assess in all of the billions of galaxies, it was a fulsome task.

In each galaxy, the stars with the most potential planets within the Goldilocks Zone were singled out. This meant multiple experiments could be carried out, should the first attempts at seeding life prove abortive.

In one galaxy, a star with five inner rocky planets stood out. It was about 27,000 light years out from the centre of an average looking galaxy. This system would be the first.

12

Chaperoned

2075 : 34 years left

For the remainder of his degree course, Shen had two projects on the go. The first was to sleep with as many females as possible, as well as dabbling with a male or three. Two of the males were on purpose to see what it was like and one encounter with a wily transvestite was accidental. The second project involved learning as much as he could about Big Data and how it could be used to shed light on the smallest of details.

Cheng's initial hunch with the missing whales was that they were ultra-sensitive and susceptible to solar flares, or more probably to coronal mass ejections. These tended to peak at sunspot maxima. He suspected that they were somehow picking up spikes through magnetic field lines, rather than through the atmosphere. As they would float to the bottom of the ocean when they died, they left little evidence of their demise.

Shen disagreed and was fearless in refuting Cheng's theories. Cheng loved having a student who would challenge him so he tasked Shen with looking at a wider data set in his second year, by expanding the search across other whale populations and also to see if dolphins were similarly affected. Data sharing across all universities globally was common and Shen took little time to discover it was indeed a global phenomenon for all species of whales.

Dolphin numbers seemed to vary too but to a completely different and random pattern. The weirdest patterns seemed to come from the river dolphin populations in the Yangtze and Amazon, where whole pods would appear for a few years and then be followed by reports that they had been driven to extinction.

When Big Data does eventually reveal its pattern, it often pays dividends not to over-analyse it, or look at it from a different angle, but to look at wider and wider data sets.

Cheng surprised Shen at the end of his second year when Madame Bien made an appearance in his office.

"I've been asked to set up a new project Shen," Cheng said. "So you will be reporting to Madame Bien again."

Shen protested, "But with respect, what does she know about Big Data?"

The unflappable Madame Bien cut in, "You're right, I know nothing about Big Data Shen but everything about how to give you access to what you want."

"Yes," chimed in Cheng. "Madame Bien can open doors for you that even I don't know exist."

None of them knew, including Madame Bien herself, that she was the illegitimate daughter of President Miang.

He continued, "You know more about Big Data than most of the tutors here so in your final year, I want you to just focus on project work."

"So what's my new project?" asked Shen.

"Fundamentally it's still the same challenge of finding out why cetacean numbers vary but I want you to look for causes other than solar activity," said Cheng. "We want to know what other cosmic phenomena might be affecting life on Earth."

"We shall be paying some visits to the Purple Mountain Observatory," said Madame Bien.

"And we'll meet again in a year's time for you to report back on what you've found," said Cheng. "Dig around for major and minor extinction events."

Shen acquiesced, as he was developing a passion for travelling, and seducing, but was a little daunted by the thought he might have Madame Bien in tow as a chaperone.

13

Ways of the Wu

2075 : 34 years left

Before Shen started on his final year, he'd promised his parents he would come back during the summer recess. He also wanted to find out if the rumours about the ladies from Fragrant Gardens were true.

He was quite surprised at how much he'd missed the Gardens, the view of the city and, most of all, Hui's and Jia's company. He had last seen them two years ago, when he left as a boy, and they were both impressed at the confident, yet humble, man who returned.

"He's just like you," mouthed Jia over his shoulder at Hui as she hugged Shen.

Over a sumptuous lunch, Shen shared the details of his projects, but not of his amorous adventures, certainly not his dalliance with Monique. He of course had no idea his mother knew he was no longer a virgin.

"So I have access to the most advanced visualisation software available. I've got AI bots crawling through the data day and night but there's just no pattern to extinction events. Nothing to tie it all together," said Shen.

"If you can't see the wood for the trees, why don't we model it in 3D?" suggested Hui.

They spent the next few days creating two new 3D orreries. The first showed the interactions between the outer planets and the asteroid belt and how planetary conjunctions and oppositions could kick asteroids out of the belt in both directions. Shen had completely forgotten that he had once wanted a whole and complete planet sitting there, until Hui reminded him.

Being able to speed up the orrery and go backwards and forwards in time, Shen and Hui could see how easy it was for a large space rock to be lobbed right into the path of the Earth. What didn't make sense was that their model produced hundreds more potential impactors than seemed to have hit.

The second and much more delicate orrery holographically modelled the Oort Cloud and the known Sun-grazing comets that intersected with the Earth's orbital plane. As the Oort Cloud is roughly spherical, only a relatively small percentage of 'incomers' would ever cross or intersect with the Earth orbit. What's more, Jupiter and Saturn seem to mop quite a few up, making the inner solar system a rather benign place to hang out.

Even with these comet-reducing factors taken into account, their 3D orrery seemed to produce less possible extinction events due to comets than the fossil records implied. In the last week of their recess, Shen had the brilliant idea of adding theoretical objects outside the Cloud. They could then see what sorts of esoteric bodies might have sent more comets than predicted on their inward spirals. They tried everything from nearly-stars like Jupiter, red dwarf stars, rogue planets with no home stars and even wandering black holes.

The models themselves didn't reveal anything concrete but were a lot of fun and did allow for Shen and Hui to spend some quality time together. They both knew they were on to something but the answers were still in the noise of an overwhelming mountain of data, with billions of permutations.

"I'll keep playing after you go back Shen," said Hui, knowing that Shen would be modelling the esoteric possibilities virtually and that his AI bots would probably find the answer before he did. His son's visit had given him a new lease of life and some ideas for new models to sell that would keep him busy, and solvent, for the rest of his days.

Now that Earth's atmosphere was increasingly clearing, Hui also dusted off his telescope and started looking at the real cosmos for the first time since he was a teenager. Following the worldwide bans on burning fossil fuels, the Milky Way could be seen by the naked eye again. Their father-and-son evenings spent looking at the stars made a lasting impact on both of them.

Jia and Hui had agreed to share time with Shen equally. So orrery modelling occupied mornings and Jia nabbed Shen for herself most afternoons. As for the evenings, they were hived off for Shen's gallivanting, or for stargazing with Hui sharing the occasional pint of banana beer.

When Shen had gone away, Jia had not missed him as much as Hui because she could sense he was OK. She knew he was on a mission, but knew nothing of its nature. Since he left for the Academy, she also had been very busy teaching the ways of the Wu to the more open-minded doctors, nurses and therapists.

On their first afternoon together, Jia took Shen out for a walk in Fragrant Hills and began to tell him about the ways of the Wu - the Chinese shamans and shamankas. This was a subject Shen had never shown any interest in when he lived at home.

Shen learned that it was forbidden for a Wu to marry a Wu. The progeny of two parents who are Wu would be too powerful for their own good, and the good of those around them.

"So Dad's not a Wu?" asked Shen.

"No and he never will be," replied Jia. "I chose him exactly for that reason, even though he will tell you he chose me."

Hui would never know that their meeting was no accident.

"And for the last 1000 years, Wu have been mainly female and only one in 100 were boys," said Jia.

"So am I a Wu?"

"No, not yet Shen. It was safer for you not to be and anyway we wanted you to learn about the Density."

Shen wanted to know more about this but Jia spent the rest of the walk telling him as much as she could remember about her mother and grandmother, both of whom inexplicably disappeared overnight when she was only 12 year old. She also told him about the work she was doing with non-Wu medical staff before it started to rain and they headed back home at a brisk pace.

That night, Shen had the weirdest dreams. He was wandering through a forest inhabited by creatures which were half-human mixed with other animals such as a horse, pig, cow and eagle. Sometimes the head and upper torso was human; other times it was the other way around. It was one of those dreams that stayed with you the next day and Shen told Jia about it as they set out on another walk.

Jia didn't really give Shen any insight into the dream but just said, "That happens."

Since Jia knew how to imbue any neophyte with 'the touch', she knew it was a breeze to now begin Shen's formal initiation. He was half unexpressed Wu after all. His dream told her it was time.

14

Smoke Trees

2075 : 34 years left

Jia started his initiation by getting Shen to close his eyes. She asked him to tune into trees around them and to tell her about their nature and function. It was the end of summer, and the trees had just taken on a red hue. They would soon reach their autumnal splendour.

Shen noticed how the smells had changed in merely a few weeks. They were more pungent and musty; a sign that life was making way for death. Knowing what he was thinking, Jia said, "Come back in spring and the scent will be awash with new life. Let's get to know the trees."

As they walked past different types of tree, Jia got Shen to hug them, with his eyes closed, and to ask them what their purpose was. After shaking off initial embarrassment, well known to a Wu as a blocking agent, Shen quickly and accurately intuited that the pines and cypresses were the forest protectors and sentinels. They sent out warnings to the shorter trees.

The persimmons also stood guard, but unlike the pines, they could look into future weather conditions and use their roots to inform the ground as to how to alter its chemistry for their optimal growth.

By end of their walk, Shen had correctly identified maples as being the calming agents. They made other trees more relaxed and imbued a sense of tranquility in humans, as well as in other visiting animals.

At the end of that afternoon, Shen got stumped. He couldn't immediately figure out the role of the smoke trees. They were hard to hug with their trunks made inaccessible by the hanging foliage. It was time to call it a day.

On their third outing, Jia decided to reveal more of the unseen world to Shen. They sat under the shade of a particularly dense conglomeration of smoke trees and Jia decided it was time to pull back the veil. Her language changed.

"So son of mine. Baton carrier and torch bearer. Look into my eyes," said Jia, but not sounding quite like his mother.

Shen obeyed.

"Let your attention wander to the sides of my head and the top of my forehead and the tip of my chin, but keep your gaze centred on my eyes," said Jia-who-was-not-Jia. "Now be prepared to see your ancestors."

The air fizzled around them and Jia's visage went fuzzy and indistinct.

"I can see an old man with a long pointy beard," said Shen.

"That's your great-grandfather," said Jia-not-Jia. "Just observe, don't speak."

Shen felt like he'd downed too much banana beer, as he saw females morph into males and adults change into children.

"Now imagine Shen, you are looking not at my eyes but through my eyes to the centre of my brain."

As he did so, a dolphin's head briefly appeared and then Jia's whole body went translucent. Her arms and legs shrunk into their sockets and her head completely vanished. Shen remained calm as in front of him appeared a floating egg, with dark patches where the arms and legs would have protruded.

It, not Jia, said, 'We are the First.'

The egg asked Shen to close his eyes and then it gently densified and asked Shen to state the role of the smoke tree.

"What's the first thing that comes into your head?" Jia-now-Jia-again asked.

"They are softeners of time and space," he said. "Through them, we can see through the veil."

Jia knew her work was done for that day as it was Shen-who-was-not-Shen who said that.

They walked back in silence, both respecting the thoughts of the other.

On subsequent afternoons, Jia gently pushed back Shen's request to sit by the smoke trees again. He sneaked out a few times by himself and managed to get the air to fizz but failed to get the veil to part.

Jia did show Shen the basics of levitation but asked him not to try it himself, and especially not to tell his father what he'd seen. She showed him how to reduce his weight, and attachment to the earth, but told him that it wasn't safe for him to fully levitate before he learned how to un-levitate.

She had already decided that consciously learning about bilocation was a no go for him for now. She also omitted to tell him he used to do it by himself when he was a toddler. Her motivation was to ensure Shen came back for more by piquing his interest, but mainly because she just wanted to keep him safe. For now, it was enough that he had glimpsed through the illusion.

15

The Point

It wasn't just self-aware humans who didn't know why they were able to ask the question of how they got here and what is the real point of everything. Although the Councillors of the Light kept watchful sets of eyes, ears and hearts on matters and goings on in the Density, they were somewhat ironically in the dark about quite a few things.

They could see all events across time in the plane of matter. They knew when to pull strings, when to let things simmer and come to the boil under their own volition and when to let things cool down.

They knew exactly when to send a representative down, to which exact planet in which exact galaxy and in which material form. They knew many methods of neat Insertion but fewer methods of less-than-neat Extraction. They sometimes wondered if that was perhaps their real mission; to learn how to travel bidirectionally between the Void and the Density.

They knew some of those that they looked after in the lower realms suspected there were higher realms, with higher intelligences. These channels and mediums would never know for sure if they were just imagining it all, making it up or going slightly bonkers. It was hard after all to imagine the unimaginable and to envisage the unseeable.

They too wondered if their strings were being pulled by even higher intelligences in even higher realms. They speculated on the existence of multiverses and of a God. Perhaps everything was nested in an infinity of layers like an endless Russian Doll. Perhaps there was no point to anything. Perhaps it was all just a big experiment to see what was possible.

To beings that sat outside time and space, this conjecture followed no timeline or dialogue. All the Councillors thought these thoughts for all of time. Only when their attention was drawn to actual manipulation of events did they descend into anything that might sound like a discourse.

'He chose his parents so perfectly,' said Councillor One.

The Councillors had no names. Neither did they have language per se, so this brief transcript, channelled in the Density, is only an approximation of its sentiment.

'And it is beautiful and so, so perfect that he knows not of Us,' said Councillor Nine.

'And that he never will,' said Councillor Three.

'It is time to make him aware of the Messenger then,' boomed all the Councillors.

None of the Councillors ever spotted that Councillor Seven rarely said anything, except for chiming in on group statements, or conversing directly with another Councillor.

Her particular Insertion had not been, and never would be, discovered for the life of this particular Universe.

16

Comet Nesh

2076 : 33 years left

"Shen is right," Professor Cheng said. "It will pass between the Moon and Earth on the 17th of March, 2079.

He continued, "In a year or so's time, every person on Earth will have to be told the news so we avoid mass panic. When this gets out, it will spread like wildfire. The comet will be a naked eye object in two years."

Shen smirked. He had first spotted the comet on April 28th that year, as it had emerged from behind Jupiter. With just a week of nightly observations, he had calculated the comet's trajectory in his head. His brilliance was starting to go to this head somewhat, in the form of a simmering arrogance.

After coming back from the summer recess with his parents, he'd been persuaded that some Big Data was best been seen with his own eyes, not extrapolated from a database. With the sanction of Cheng, and the door opening powers of Madame Bien, he'd been seconded to the Astronomy Department. He was given access to their vast amount of data and also remote access to one of the larger reflectors at Purple Mountain Observatory.

As soon as he made his discovery, he immediately booked his accommodation in Reykjavík, Iceland. From there he worked out that he'd actually be able to see the head and tail of the comet pass right across the face of the Full Moon. Once the news of the comet's transit leaked out into the public domain, hotel rooms in Iceland would be like hen's teeth. Shen knew it was going to be one heck of a TubeWay journey to get there, but it was so going to be worth the trip.

He had reported his findings to Madame Bien, who escalated it immediately to Cheng. Cheng gave his three top cosmologists and five senior mathematicians full access to the telescope and also the department's prized quantum computer. The review meeting with Cheng at the end of Shen's third year would now not happen, as events would take over.

It had taken the team of cosmologists and mathematicians three weeks to confirm Shen's findings and to prepare some stunning high resolution graphic simulations. The visuals seemed straight out of a blockbuster movie.

Cheng had convened an emergency meeting in the Grand Lecture Theatre at the University of Beijing to watch the simulation. The auditorium could seat 3000 students. Today, only 33 sets of VR glasses were needed. It was a closed session without the usual audiovisual technicians.

What the select audience did require however, was a large, mean-looking security presence around the perimeter of the building. This didn't cause any concern to students as private presentations of this nature had become commonplace in these times.

Cheng took to the stage behind the lectern while Madame Bien and Shen sat in the front row of the auditorium, accompanied by the eight researchers. They were presenting to 20 select representatives of the State Council, along with the President and his wife, Yu Yan. Even Cheng, an old master at bamboozling politicians with science, was somewhat nervous. Shen noticed a single bead of sweat on his brow.

The gasps were most audible when the last of 12 simulated views from above the North Pole was shown. The comet's closest approach would be right above Iceland at what would be 9:46pm local time. This was one planetary close encounter that would be all too visible, without even the need for binoculars.

"It will pass so close to the Earth that we will have to take all geostationary satellites down into lower orbits," Cheng continued. "It will be impossible to recommission about half of them. We will be recommending cessation of all new launches from now until a year after the comet's passing. Each subsequent year, from March to May, we will pass through the tail and this could cause damage to some orbiting satellites. The CSS will have to be evacuated and shielded."

Shen was silent for once. He had told Bien all of this a month ago. Space around the Earth was not going to be a safe place for some time to come.

The Chinese Space Station was the pride and joy of the Republic. Over 200 people lived and worked on it nowadays. NASA had all but abandoned launches these days, after the ISS was decommissioned in the Twenties. The best rocket scientists and most experienced astronauts around the globe now worked with, and for, the Chinese.

Shen was hoping that, having first spotted the comet, it would be named after him. He couldn't wait to tell his parents. He also intuited that there was more to this interloper than met the eye.

He had not only calculated that it was heading straight towards Earth but he had also worked out where in space it had come from. By contrast, Cheng's crack team was still solely focussed on its Earth-bound trajectory.

Shen knew that most of these dirty snowballs inhabited the Oort Cloud over a billion kilometres from the sun. They only became referred to as comets when they entered the inner solar system and started to melt. Although just a few kilometres in diameter, their plumage could stretch for thousands of kilometres behind them by the time they reached the orbits of the inner rocky planets.

Shen had tuned out of the presentation and was musing on how and when he should tell the team what he had been working on most recently. They already thought he was a bit of a precocious know-it-all. Some would say for good reason, considering he would earn his first doctorate in cosmology before he turned 19.

He was not only a brilliant theorist but also had become a natural at observational astronomy. The reason he alone had spotted the comet was that its path was hidden from view from the Earth by the massive planet Jupiter. Only when it narrowly missed hitting Ganymede, by the smallest of cosmic margins, could it have been visible.

For an object to hide behind a planet even the size of Jupiter, when viewed from a moving inner planet, meant its path was very strange indeed. This one had not started in orbit around the Sun but had come straight in. None of the standard AI comet-watching algorithms were programmed to pick anything up with this kind of trajectory.

Shen's reverie was broken by President Miang shouting, "Can we hear from the boy?"

Cheng beckoned Shen to join him at the lectern, somewhat begrudgingly.

Miang said, "Shen we are in your debt. In fact it seems the whole world is in your debt. It sounds like the dinosaurs could have done with your help 65 million years ago."

The rest of the Council politely laughed at what they assumed must be Miang's attempt to make light of a grave situation.

Shen meekly replied, "It is my honour, Sir."

Miang said, "When did you realise that the comet would be deflected by the Moon's gravitation field and that would prevent it from impacting the Earth."

"It was after the third night I was making my

measurements, Sir," said Shen calmly and assuredly. "I knew quickly that it was a potential impact object and was working out how we could send a probe to meet it and deflect or destroy it. It soon became obvious there was not enough time for such a measure."

Professor Cheng piped in, "We would have to destroy it before it reached the orbit of Mars to ensure we didn't create multiple impactors."

"I was speaking to Shen," Miang barked.

Shen resumed gingerly, as he hated to see anyone hurt or demeaned, and especially Cheng.

"I had a brainwave to check the position of the Moon as the comet approaches. I found out it would be Full as seen from the Earth. As you can see in this simulation where I've added the Moon, the comet will pass underneath its South Pole and bend around to skim the Northern Hemisphere of the Earth and miss us by a cosmic whisker."

"I will see that you will be remembered for this my boy," said Miang. "And as tradition demands, you must name the comet."

"I've already done that Mr. President - I've named it Comet Nesh."

Only Cheng picked up that this was an anagram of Shen and let out a low snicker.

It was this brief interruption that led to Shen making an instant decision that would change his life forever, and the lives of every one of the then 9 billion inhabitants of Planet Earth.

"Thank you Sir," Shen continued. "I did some more modelling though."

Cheng was alarmed as this was not scripted.

"We will experience a meteor display that will be visible even in daylight for months. This won't be a problem as very little of the tail will make it to the ground. It's what the comet is made of that we should be concerned about. Most of them are dirty snowballs but this one seems to be made mostly of iron."

Shen had omitted to tell them how he knew this and nobody thought to ask him. Shen then zoomed into an image of the Earth that showed its magnetic field lines. All of this was putting the the noses of the eight researchers out-of-joint, as this wasn't part of their presentation.

"As the comet passes by it will disrupt the Earth's magnetic field so much that I predict the eddies created inside the Earth may cause a North/South pole flip. This means a reduction in the protective magnetic field around the Earth and will lead to planetary-wide devastation for many life forms within a hundred years."

He had not finished with the delivery of the bad news.

"More immediately than that, my models show that such a rapid flipping of the magnetic core will cause the Earth itself to tilt, due to gyroscopic forces, up to anything between 5 to 10 degrees. This means that both of the ice caps will melt within a hundred years."

"So all our valiant efforts to reverse climate change will be thwarted," said Cheng.

One of the researchers interjected, "But it's impossible for a comet to do that."

Shen brought up another display nobody was expecting, "Look at Ganymede before and after it passed."

There was another audible gasp. It had clearly tilted on its axis.

"The only way this could have happened is if the comet has a powerful magnetic field," explained Shen.

Everyone in the auditorium knew the implications for the Earth, as ecology was part of all school curricula these days.

"Have you got a projected sea level rise, Shen?" asked President Miang.

"Let's put it this way," said Shen. "I think we should all think of moving to Chongqing."

17

Epoch Beginnings

Unwittingly, what Shen had stumbled across was one of the contributory events that would augur the end of yet another Epoch in this particular solar system.

Councillor Seven had to keep her pleasure and satisfaction secret from the other Councillors. She was one of six odd numbered female Councillors whose role was to manage and manifest the feminine energies in the Density.

Ever since the division of the sexes at the end of the Epoch Two, males and females across all species in all galaxies had slightly different roles, with experimental exceptions like sea horses.

The females bore the fruit of the next generation and the males provided the seeds. Females were mostly intuitive and tuned to the Void and males more practical and more rooted in the Density.

In Epoch Five, such separation did generate conflict and division, some of it violent and abusive. This was as inevitable as it was planned. The Path of Return could only be re-found by forgetting where you came from in the first place.

Most humans in the latter part of the 21st century were blissfully unaware their Epoch was fast coming to its natural end. They had no idea that Epoch Four was played out on the planet Mars. Even Shen was oblivious of this, which was somewhat ironic as he was to become instrumental in returning humans to this planet.

Asexual examples of creatures from Epoch Two were still

around if people cared to look. Octopi from Epoch Three look like they come from another world and that's because they did. They escaped from Lemuria to Mars, before Councillor Seven terminated the experiment on the now-missing planet.

She was particularly proud of how neatly that termination was effected. When vortices from the Red Spot of Jupiter, the White Spot of Saturn and the Blue Spot of Uranus converged on the planet, it stood no chance. Only a few species were 'ported to Mars to seed the Fourth Epoch a little time before.

Most of the planet was completely vapourised, as the destructive force was so great. The remnants formed the Asteroid Belt which would lead scientists of Epoch Five to come to the wrong conclusion. As so much of it had vapourised, they correctly calculated that the remaining detritus in the Belt did not have enough mass to have formed a fifth planet. At least Third Epochians didn't suffer, as the experiment was terminated in less a microsecond. This also left little racial memory for future channels to latch on to.

Councillor Seven still had much to do before her own Extraction could be effected. Over 100 billion galaxies now had an Epoch Five level civilisation revolving around a single star. As they were all alone in their particular galaxy, any efforts to contact any other sentient life would be fruitless. This was all part of the plan to create self-sufficiency and diversity. Members of each self-aware civilisation of course felt very, very alone.

Only when Epoch Six civilisations emerged would inter-galactic contact between sentiences be forged and allowed. This Universe would have to wait until Epoch Seven before any civilisations actually met. The shock would otherwise be too great.

18

The Grand Tour

2079 : 30 years left

Shen decided to turn his trip to Reykjavík into a Grand Tour. Ever since first seeing the Earth, in so much detail and so many forms in his father's orreries, he had always wanted to go around it. He didn't know that this particular circumnavigation would not be his last.

He could have easily got the University to pay for it but he had enough of his own money and wanted to do it in style. So, as well as a week in Iceland, he'd planned to see as much of the low-lying coastal areas of the planet as was possible, before it was too late.

He'd already booked the Tower Suite at the Hotel Borg in Reykjavík, as soon as he had calculated the comet's trajectory. It was expensive enough back then and he'd had several lucrative offers from the hotel to buy his booking back from him. Some celebrities were trying to muscle in. The University would have put him in Halls of Residence. This room, and his whole trip, was coming from his own not inconsiderable coffers. The Tower Suite had a living room right on top of the hotel with a panoramic view of the city. He'd also booked the adjacent Deluxe Suite in another name, both as a back up and to ensure he had privacy on the night of the comet's lunar transit.

From Shanghai, he took the TubeWay direct to San

Francisco. He avoided temptation to drop in to see Monique in Monterey. He got in quite late and checked into a corner suite at the Hilton Union Square, which had spectacular view of the city. He just ordered room service that night. He planned to spend a few days playing at being a tourist, incognito in a baseball hat.

The next day, Shen took his time to walk all the way to Golden Gate Bridge and across the bridge over to Marin County. The bridge had been pedestrianised as all traffic to and from Marin County went via Tubeway these days. The bridge itself had fallen into disrepair in the Thirties, as the failing US economy in the Twenties had led much of the country to rack and ruin. The politicians blamed a series of natural disasters but everyone these days was taught the real source of the 'Perfect Storm' at school.

The greed, avarice and warmongering of the Old Guard were the real culprits and they finally ran out of steam and support. Even the Second Amendment finally got amended and the resulting gun amnesty led to a dramatic reduction in the murder rate. The NRA was disbanded and somewhat ironically became outlawed. This was just one of the legacies of President Mason, the first black woman in office.

President Mason also brokered a deal with China who came to the rescue and installed the new TubeWay and MagLev transport infrastructure from Asia to and across the Americas. Just less than half a century later, this legacy was making Shen's trip a breeze.

After he'd crossed the bridge, he took a short bus service to Sausalito, where he had the most lavish lunch at the Spinnaker Restaurant. With water on three sides, he was the only diner aware these views would be gone forever within just a few decades.

As he crossed back over the bridge later that afternoon, all he could envisage was a glorious city enveloped by water, with just the peaks of the tallest buildings poking above the waves. At over 220 metres high, at least the bridge would still be crossable. The island prison of Alcatraz would be as condemned as some of its inmates.

He spent another couple of days wandering around ChinaTown, where his fluency in the language got him into bars and dens of inequity not known to many residents. He had no qualms at paying for sex, as it meant he wasted no more time than necessary on the transaction.

He left San Francisco, and the West Coast of the US, for what he suspected might the last time and took the MagLev right across mainland USA over to Boston. He just took one overnight stop in Chicago, long enough to discover why it was called the "Windy City". At 180 metres above sea level, all Shen could think about is how it would make a fabulous new financial centre for the USA, as Wall Street would be submerged.

One of Shen's reasons to go to Europe the long way round was that Professor Cheng had insisted he meet Professor Thom Waters, a nanotech expert based at MIT, Boston.

Thom met Shen at the Boston Maglev terminal late in the afternoon. He was an avuncular and warm character with a handshake that affirmed a regular workout schedule. He drove an electric car that felt a little different than any that Shen had been in before. There was virtually no road noise and it seemed to sail over any bumps in the road.

That evening Thom insisted on taking Shen out and treating him to a few too many artisan beers.

"So Cheng tells me you are his star pupil," Thom said, slapping down what would be the first of eight beers in front of Shen.

"He's never told me that but thanks," said Shen in his best modest tone.

"And Comet Nesh is named after you, that's pretty cool eh?"

It was obvious to Shen that Thom was fishing for more

information than Cheng had briefed him that he could share.

"Yep, I'm heading to Reykjavík to see it in a few days time," said Shen, trying to gulp his beer down as fast as he could to keep up with Thom.

Thom ordered a second round of beer and sensed Shen had been told to keep his mouth shut on matters relating to the comet. So he began to explain to Shen why he really wanted his help.

"So, I've got a problem," explained Thom. "A nice problem to have. I've been experimenting with new lifting mechanisms for drones, coating them underneath with an array of nano-fans."

"So what's the nice problem?" asked Shen.

"They generate much more lift than we've calculated and we don't know why."

Thom showed Shen the schematics of the nano-fans. They were tetrahedral in shape, like a three-sided pyramid made from three equilateral triangles, with a fourth side forming the base. There was a small hole at the apex attached to a nano-tubule axle. They came in two different sizes and 144,000 of them filled a single square centimetre.

"So the problem is that we didn't design this shape; we got the nano-bots to self optimise for maximum lift and they came up with this arrangement."

This was a new type of problem for Shen as he'd had no experience of nano-technology, or aerodynamics for that matter. Thom had his full attention, even though the drinks were kicking in.

"So why do you think I can help?" he asked Thom.

"There's something we are not seeing in the data and Cheng suggested you'd find it. I'll show you our prototypes tomorrow."

They spent the rest of the evening getting slowly drunk and eating a never ending stream of bar food. Shen went to bed in a cosy room in Thom's house with his head spinning.

19

Sticky Boots

2079 : 30 years left

The next day Thom's wife made them a fulsome breakfast. She could see by Shen's heavy eyelids and bloodshot eyes that he had been well Thomed!

The professor drove Shen over to his lab at MIT. Curiously, instead of the expected tour of his facility, Thom took Shen directly to his lab and produced what looked like two large tennis rackets. He instructed Shen to stand on them and strap his feet in.

"Hold on to this bar," warned Thom.

Shen grabbed a huge hand rail on the wall and Thom pressed a bright yellow button on a small remote control. Effortlessly, Shen started floating a few centimetres above the ground. There was no noise; it was just as if he'd levitated.

"So these plates can lift a man?" said Shen with wide eyes.

"Yup, and the power needed is around 25 watts. These plates are powered by a single layer of Graphenium ion cells, which also act as a self-charging solar panel."

Shen had heard about these new batteries and that they were near-superconducting at room temperature so that one charge lasted for weeks.

He was quick to see the potential, saying, "So if this scales, this will make MagLevs and Tubeways much more efficient."

"Amazing right. And by the way, you even got here on a

bigger prototype. I've had a large panel fitted under my car," explained Thom. "They are as close as we've ever got to a perpetual motion machine."

"Just need some sunlight," added Shen. "But you don't know why they generate so much lift?"

"Haven't got a clue," replied Thom, tapping his pad. Shen un-levitated and sank gently back to the floor. His head was buzzing and he was genuinely filled with wonder.

"Now try and lift your feet," suggested Thom, who was enjoying Shen's delight at the potential.

"Whoa, I can't. Don't tell me you've reversed the fans," exclaimed Shen, who was bright as a button. "Can you adjust how strongly I stick to the floor?"

"Sure can. Go for a walk," instructed Thom.

Shen took a few clumsy steps forward as if he was wearing a pair of deep sea diver's boots.

"We think there are probably as many applications for 'sticky boots' as there are for panels generating lift," Thom said.

"We're also experimenting with using bioluminescence as an integrated charging source."

Shen spent the rest of the morning exploring every theory Thom could proffer as to why there should be so much lift.

The information sharing was all one way, which Thom, upon later reflection, found frustrating. What Thom didn't know, and what Shen didn't tell him, was that he was to meet another nano-expert in London in two days time who had also discovered something unexplainable and intriguing about auto-organising nano-bots.

Thom knew Shen had planned an evening in New York before going to Europe so he took him back to the Maglev terminal. As they shook hands, Thom handed Shen a slender box.

"Here's a small panel to play with. I hope we can work together in the future."

Thom sensed that if Shen did solve the problem that he might not share the answer. It was an accurate hunch.

As soon as he got settled on the Maglev, an idea came to Shen. He wondered why they'd never tested the panels in a vacuum chamber. He couldn't believe they'd not thought to do that.

As he took the MagLev to New York, Shen's mind flipped to where the best bars and night clubs might be for a dalliance. Unlike his stretch in San Francisco, this time he'd already decided he wasn't going to pay for sex.

20

Twelve

The collective essence of the twelve Councillors wove its numerology into many of the sentient planets sited in each galaxy.

The sentiences that tuned into it the most were those who were conscious and cogniscent of numbers and mathematics. In the Universe of Free Will, the Councillors did not - and would not - influence which life forms used numbers. For example on Planet Earth, there were two highly sentient life forms - cetaceans and humans. Cetaceans found numbers tedious and academic so had given up on them aeons ago.

Humans however were obsessed by them. Some solely focussed on how many units of currency they had in virtual bank accounts. Others measured their worth by the size of their possessions or bodily dimensions. In the end days of Epoch Five, very few humans paid attention to where numbers came from in the first place.

Most of the planet used the decimal system for counting but were blissfully unaware that the seconds and minutes of their time systems used Base 60. The underlying communications infrastructure used Base 2, Base 8, Base 16 and increasingly Base 2048.

The most important number by far was the only one that cetaceans did use and that was the number twelve. They just used it in an esoteric way in the musical scales and harmonies they used for their songs.

Cetaceans had 12 semitones in each of their 12 octave range and 12 further divisions for each semitone.

At the end of Epoch Four and the start of Epoch Five, early humans embraced the number twelve entirely. They were less attuned to the Density then and more sensitive to the messages coming from the Void.

They divided the sky into twelve Zodiacal signs - the twelve commanders of the Night Sky. Early religions tuned into the essence of the Council of the Light. The Ancient Greeks worshipped twelve deities on Mount Olympus.

Some Gods had twelve sons, and some sun gods had 12 demigods. When monastic religions rose in popularity, the minor deities were demoted to being called the Twelve Disciples. Jurys had twelve good women and men and true. The rather secular Buddhists hold the belief that life is composed of 12 stages, which together keep the wheel of life turning, ensnaring all life in a cyclical form of existence from which it is hard to escape.

As humanity headed towards the end of Epoch Five, gods and religion were virtually dead and buried. Whales kept on singing using their scales of twelve tones, and in complex time signatures of twelve divided by six, four, three and two. With the limit of only 12 semitones in human's musical octaves, it was no wonder people hadn't deciphered the magic of whale music.

At the same time, humans had started worshipping and being controlled by another god of twelve: the incessant tick-tocking of their clocks. They had become utterly enslaved and entrapped by time.

The result of all this obfuscation was that the vast majority of humans had little knowledge and awareness of the true reality of the world in which they were wandering around each day. They lived behind the veil of a pervasive illusion. They thought that their thoughts were their own and that any happenstances were just sheer luck.

The Councillors were pleased with Councillor Four's increasing ability to resonate with them - and they with him. They were even more pleased that, with a little nudging, some *scientists in the Density had come up with the nano-technology that they could more readily influence from the Void.*

21

Nano-bots

2079 : 30 years left

After what turned out to be a celibate night in New York, Shen got a surprise when he boarded the TubeWay that would deposit him in Central London. As he checked in, he was informed he'd been upgraded to First Class, which gave him a private pod. He wondered if it was a gift from Cheng, or even from Thom.

He settled into his sumptuous pod and scanned through the menu. He was going to make the most of this crossing and ordered champagne and caviar to start. All food was prepared in a central pod and transported through a horizontal 'dumb waiter' in the ceiling and then down the wall into a serving hatch.

While waiting for his first course to arrive, he began analysing the structural plans of the panel that Thom had given him. He was looking at it from a Big Data perspective and straight away he noticed something strange that must have eluded Thom and his team.

The Graphenium ion cells, which powered the plate, were constructed using hexagonal graphene allotropes formed into a man-made molecular structure known as Buckminster Fullerene - essentially Carbon 60 or C_{60} Each pseudo-molecule was made of twenty hexagons and twelve pentagons.

He then looked for patterns in the structure of the self-organising nano-fans underneath the plate. Four tetrahedral fans formed a cell with an equilateral triangle of three smaller fans, topped with a larger fan. Each of the four triangles of fans had aligned itself exactly to the lattice of the Graphenium ion battery structure.

Shen realised that the bottom layer providing the lift 'knew' about the structure above that was powering it. The nano-bots had some level of awareness of what was around them.

Intuitively he knew he'd discovered the What but was puzzled by the How. He wondered if this was how his mother had levitated. He also wondered what Cheng was up to in sending him to see two nano-tech experts when he was on a trip to see the comet flyby on its Near-Hit.

The trip to America had taken its toll and, after consuming most of the bottle of champagne, Shen decided to skip the rest of the menu and sleep on it, all the way to disembarkation. His dreams were full of multi-coloured geodesic shapes that seemed to explode into multi-dimensional forms.

At exactly 30 minutes before arrival, Shen was woken by the whirring of a breakfast tray that slid out of the wall beside him. As he wiped the sleep from his eyes, the last remnant of the dream left him. He felt someone, or something, leave the pod as he re-engaged in the Density. This was a bit weird as they were 30 metres below the surface of the Atlantic Ocean, somewhere off the coast of Southern Ireland.

When he disembarked, he was first off the Tubeway and it dawned on him he might have been upgraded to give him some level of anonymity. He was disavowed of this notion once he got through the arrivals gate and was met by a blast of paparazzi shouting questions like:

"Are you sure the comet will miss us?"

"Is this the end of the world?"

Two burly minders grabbed his bags, and both his arms,

and ushered him into a large limousine. Shen recognised it as a Rolls Royce and had always wanted to travel in one. This model was of course electric.

A demure lady in a smart navy dress was already in the car and introduced herself.

"Welcome to London Shen. I'm Sheila Buswell," she said.

"You're the Mayor right; to what do I owe this honour?" said Shen. He had done a little research into London.

"Your discovery of the comet gave us the impetus to start researching how to save this great city," said Mayor Buswell. "What we have come up with could help all major low-lying cities across the globe."

Shen was learning the ways of the world quickly. The British had been and were some of the brightest innovators in the world for hundreds of years. The inventors of steam engines, the telephone and the television were all British, or Scottish more to the point.

Shen suspected that whatever they had come up with needed both Chinese money and resources so it could be upscaled. It was in London that it started to to sink in that Cheng's suggestions for whom he should meet were not random, nor for his interest only.

His short trip in the Roller took him past the Houses of Parliament and Buckingham Palace. This was a revelation for Shen and such a culture shift from anything he'd seen in the US. Mayor Buswell gave him a quick guided tour as they passed by buildings with hundreds of years of history. He'd picked a rare sunny March day for his arrival in London.

His destination was Imperial College, still one of the leading centres for engineering research on the planet.

"You'll spend the day here with Professor Mike Spence and his team. Will you do me the honour of joining me and a few colleagues later for dinner?"

"Of course, Mayor Buswell. It would be my pleasure," said Shen. His parents had instilled politeness into him from an early age.

"And do call me Sheila tonight. We'll meet at 7pm and we're dining at the Savoy Grill."

Shen wasn't quite sure if she was flirting with him a little but let it pass by. He'd been told he was being put up at a hotel called the Savoy, as a guest, but hadn't thought to look it up.

As he got out of the car, he was met by a tall, slightly balding man with round rimmed glasses.

"Mike Spence?" asked Shen.

"The one and only. I am so glad to meet you Shen."

22

Nano-walls

2079 : 30 years left

Mike Spence was the polar opposite of Thom Waters, with a rather limp handshake and no immediate eye contact. Shen suspected they wouldn't be drinking themselves under the table that evening.

Professor Spence whisked him off to his private office and started to grill him on how he found the comet. It became clear to Shen, what he really wanted to know was if the Chinese predictions for sea level rise confirmed his own projections.

"So it's a complete melting of both ice caps and 70 metres - and by when?" he asked.

Shen confirmed his suspicions, "Definitely by the end of the century for the melting of the ice caps but sea level rise in two waves. We'll get a 35 to 40 metre rise by the end of the 2099."

"And presumably a gradual 30 metre rise over the following 20 years or so?" said Mike Spence, pushing for confirmation.

"Something like that," said Shen.

"Let me show you what we've been working on," said Professor Spence.

Shen sensed that Mike Spence couldn't wait.

They walked down a long corridor through two security

checks and Mike ushered Shen into a changing room.

"We need to be 'clean', so that means showers and suiting up I'm afraid," said Mike.

This was a new one for Shen but it just increased his excitement.

Suited up, with breathing apparatus, Shen followed Mike through an airlock and into a large square room. In front of them was a scale model of the City of London and the surrounding counties. They approached the model from the mouth of the Thames estuary.

"That is one neat bit of 3D printing," said Shen.

"No it's not," said Professor Spence. "Erect another set of buildings in Docklands, Simon."

Shen then noticed someone at the end of the room who waved his hand over a console and Shen heard a slight hum.

In front of them, where the estuary narrowed and London began, several buildings emerged right along side the river in a clear bit of land.

"Where's the printer?" said Shen.

"These aren't printed, they are grown from the soil," explained Professor Spence proudly. "We're using nano-bots to eat the soil and, just like termites, build structures by regurgitating it."

"Now watch this! Simon, go for a 10 metre rise."

Some gurgling started and the water around the model began to rise. As it did so, at what must have been 10 miles in from the coast line, a wall came out from nowhere, angled at around 30 degrees. While some of the low-lying areas became quickly covered in water, the centre of London was surrounded by a protective wall and the river was barricaded.

"Nano-bots again?" asked Shen.

"Cheng said you were a quick learner, now watch this. Go for 1 metre wave height Simon, and dim the lights."

Ripples appeared on the surface of the water and the tiny buildings and roads started to twinkle.

"So don't tell me, are the walls generating from wave power?" said Shen.

"You got it. We found that this specific angle for the walls gives us maximum energy conversion," said a previously quiet Simon, who couldn't contain his enthusiasm for what had been his idea.

"Thirty three point three three degrees is what the nano-bots iterated to give maximum energy transfer," said Professor Spence, cutting Simon short.

Shen started to walk around the model and saw that to the south of London, two ridges of hills were now islands. There were also islets north west too. A walled corridor spread out to the west creating a dry inland area of urban conurbation.

"So this would save Shanghai and low-lying areas in Hong Kong?" asked Shen.

"And cities like Amsterdam, New York, Rio de Janeiro, Tokyo, Dubai - you want me to go on?"

"No I get it," said Shen, thinking there was not much time to get all of this up to scale.

Shen looked around as another suited figure entered through the airlock.

Shen's mask hid his surprise when he heard the unmistakable voice of Cheng say, "Professor Spence will be in Beijing when you get back from your Grand Tour. Welcome to your new project."

Shen's mask also hid a grin that went from ear to ear. So not only had he discovered the cause of the impending global catastrophe but he was going to be working on the solution too.

The four occupants of the room went back through the airlock and got back into their normal clothes. Shen learned Simon was to join the project as well and was glad to have someone closer to his age on board.

Shen left the College in a Rolls again but this time with Cheng. They were driven to the Savoy Hotel and deposited in adjoining suites with river views.

"Meet me for afternoon tea at 4pm," said Cheng. "But don't eat too much then as we're being taken out for dinner by the mayor."

Shen had a much needed power nap. The late night with Thom and the TubeLag had got to him. After what seemed like hours but was only 45 minutes, Shen's alarm woke him. He got into fresh clothes and met Cheng in the most elegant and opulent tea room he'd ever experienced.

Cheng asked him how he had got along with Thom Waters. Shen shared his early research into how the nano-layer seemed to have some low level awareness of the upper graphene layer.

"Are these two nano projects related?" asked Shen.

"That's for you to find out," replied Cheng somewhat enigmatically. "And to make sure neither team finds out about the work of the other."

Cheng then brought him up to speed on the scope and scale of the nano-seawall project.

"We're funding all the research and the construction projects Shen and, in exchange, China is going to become the provider of energy for all the world's major cities," said Cheng.

"That's cool," said Shen. "So they will pay us back in electricity bills?"

Shen was still a little naive about real political agendas.

"That's about it," said Cheng. "So Professor Spence will be the project lead but you are effectively in charge."

"So how will that work?" asked Shen.

"Simple, he will think he is making all the decisions but you and I will be steering the ship," Cheng said.

Shen suspected that what Cheng really meant by this was that Shanghai and Hong Kong would get this technology first and London would be third in the queue.

23

Peaks and Troughs

2079 : 30 years left

Supper at the Savoy Grill would be one of Shen's most memorable dining experiences to date. He and Cheng were ushered into a dimly lit, private room at the back of the main restaurant.

As Shen expected, the mayor was there. She had told him that she would bring her Chiefs of the Fire, Police and Water Services. Professor Spence was there too but, disappointingly for Shen, no Simon.

What he hadn't even considered was that he would be introduced to the Prime Minister and the Chancellor of the Exchequer. The Prime Minister, Rosemary Bailey, could only be in her mid-to-late thirties and the Chancellor, Gary Plunkett, a few years older. They both shook Shen's hand warmly and asked him to sit between them.

Just as he settled, the doors opened and everyone stood up and then, even more surprisingly, President Miang, and two others he recognised from his presentation in the Grand Lecture Theatre, walked in.

The President made a beeline to Shen and shook his hand first, then sat opposite him.

He discovered that the two he recognised from three years earlier held the equivalent roles to the UK's Prime Minister and Chancellor. They sat on either side of President Miang, opposite their counterparts. Shen learned their names over the course of the evening. Keung Luan had been the longest serving Prime Minister since the Communist Revolution, in his post for 27 years.

Shen made a mental note that evening to do some digging on the Chinese Chancellor, who he learned had only been in the role for two years. He would learn later that she had been drafted in to this role specifically to broker this deal. He would also glean that she spoke fluent English, although she pretended all evening that she didn't understand a word. What intrigued Shen though was her name. Surely it was no coincidence she was called Wu Zetian.

Between everyone's cutlery was a wireless earpiece. Shen followed as everyone put on their translation devices. Translation these days was done by AI and was virtually instantaneous. Shen took his off discreetly when he realised he didn't need it, being fluently bilingual in English and Chinese.

"Let's eat first," pronounced Miang.

A flurry of servers appeared from the shadows. Wine glasses were charged, which pleased Shen as this was all a bit high powered for him. He needed something to calm him down.

The starter dish was Shen's most memorable of the evening. The flavours of the Glazed Omelette Arnold Bennett were sublime, with the smoked haddock not too overpowering.

Miang surprised everyone by saying, "We have Enoch Arnold Bennett, the author of The Imperial Palace, to thank for this. First created in the 1920's I believe."

Nobody else had even heard of Bennett, not even the British Prime Minister, who held an Oxford degree in English Literature.

Course followed course, and some time in between the Beef Wellington and the blueberry-drenched mandarin posset dessert, the pleasantries were replaced by a more serious tone.

A slightly tipsy Shen, who had not said no to any of the wines, had never been to a meeting of this nature. It brought home to him the seriousness of how his discovery was to affect matters on a global scale.

It was agreed that Professor Spence would relocate to Beijing, with Shen seconded to his team and both reporting directly to Cheng. It emerged Cheng was busy on another important project on which no details were shared.

Shanghai was indeed to be the location of the first pilot project, followed by London. Representatives from low-lying cities around the globe would be then invited to visit either location and the technology license was to be offered free of charge. China would receive the lion's share of the revenue from power generation. London was to be the banker and broker, handling and managing the legalities and collection of revenues, in return for a service charge.

"And what if the city doesn't want to pay for the electricity?" asked Chancellor Plunkett.

"Simple," said a translated Wu Zetian, quite coldly. "They get to the back of the queue and they can pay for construction."

"And timescales?" asked Prime Minister Bailey.

Cheng said, "It's best if Professor Spence answers this."

"Shanghai's nano-walls will be in place by 2083," he said. "And London one year later, with other cities soon after that."

Cheng cut in, "Once deployed, the walls establish themselves in less than a year. After the design has been done, the system builds itself, using local raw materials. We just monitor it."

Shen was a little surprised it would be so soon, having only just seen a scaled-down prototype.

Conversations then split, and translating ear pieces were removed as people migrated to a private bar. Shen went to sit with Professor Spence and discovered that the project was much more advanced than the small model he'd seen. A full scale working prototype had been in operation for a year in a small coastal town called Cromer in Norfolk, around 140 miles North East of London. Locals had been told it was a wave power project, as the potential sea level rise wasn't yet in wide circulation, being contained only to conspiracy theory web sites.

As the evening came to a close, everyone made a point of saying goodnight to Shen. Shen went up to his suite along with Cheng. He changed into his student garb, put his baseball cap on, and made his way out on to the Strand. He found a local pub to process what he had learned. He tasted warm English beer for the first time. After three pints of Sam Smiths OBB, he introduced himself to three ladies at the end of the bar, explaining, with a faux accent, that he was in London for the first time and wanted to improve his English.

The three girls welcomed the charming, young Chinese man and taught him the choicest of traditional and contemporary English swear words. Shen ended up taking one of them up to his suite, not realising she would be his very last dalliance.

The next day, Cheng and Shen had brunch in Cheng's suite. Cheng sensed Shen might have been up a little late the previous evening. Cheng explained how the project would unfold and how and when Shen was to report to him. He also explained that Shen's external role would be as an ambassador for the project and that this would be starting in Amsterdam on his way over to Iceland.

24

SeeRise

2079 : 30 years left

Shen didn't have to check out of the Savoy as everything was already pre-paid. As he walked out, a limo purred up just outside the door. Shen tossed his luggage in the trunk and insisted on walking down the Embankment, and over Westminster Bridge, to embark on the TubeWay to Amsterdam.

As Cheng had told him, Shen would be met by the Mayor of Amsterdam, who was not yet to be told about the nano-wall project. The Dutch were very able civil engineers and had been holding back the sea for hundreds of years. It would be best if they continued with their own efforts, just in case they came up with any better solutions.

The trip across the North Sea only took 30 minutes and Shen was greeted by the Mayor, Martine Ollongren, who reminded him of a slightly older Monique. Intuitively, he knew she was unavailable.

Mayor Ollongren and a few cronies took Shen to d'Vijff Vlieghen - an upmarket restaurant with original works of Rembrandt on the walls. The setting was polished but the company was on edge. They wanted to extract from Shen what he knew about the predicted rise in sea level. Cheng had told him to be open with his answers and not to give them a rose-tinted view.

After lunch, Shen got deposited at the Waldorf Astoria Hotel where once again he found a suite had been pre-arranged and paid for. Martine thanked him profusely for being so forthright and handed him a goody bag full of local paraphernalia. He was sure she winked at him as she said her goodbyes.

That evening Shen was left to his own devices and discovered Genever gin, and the joys of marijuana. He got annihilated and ended up alone in his posh hotel room. It was not like him to ignore the charge of a cannabis-induced erection but, that night, the effects of the gin won.

The next day, he took the MagLev to Copenhagen which gave him an hour to sift through the contents of his loot bag. It was mostly trinkets and tourist trophies that he left on his seat for someone else to enjoy. What he did keep was a set of VR glasses labelled SeeRise™.

In Copenhagen, he transferred to another MagLev that would take him cross-country via Odense, on the island of Funen, over to Aarhus in Jutland. He'd been told Skolegade - the drinking street - was well worth a visit by the bartender who supplied his joints in Amsterdam. Shen had quickly clued in that asking the locals was the best way to see the real sights.

As he travelled across the very flat country of Denmark, he donned the SeeRise glasses and followed the intuitive 'in glass' menu.

Some inventive Amsterdammers were making a small fortune selling these glasses that could simulate what the surrounding world would look like, with any rise in sea level. It appeared that Funen would end up being one tiny island of a few square kilometres based around its highest point, Frøbjerg Bavnehøj.

After what was indeed a great night in Skolegade, Shen hailed a SelfDrive, with a guide, to take him over to the western port of Esbjerg. His guide, a small man who just shared his first name of Kurt, was pleased for such a high paying passenger but a little surprised to find Shen wanted to go via Himmelbjerget - 'The Sky Mountain' - which was a fair diversion.

When they arrived at the foot of the highest point in Denmark, Shen instructed Kurt to wait at the bottom in the SelfDrive while he walked alone the 147 metres to the top. He was glad for the exercise.

It was a clear March day, just two days before the comet was due to fly-by. It had been a naked eye object for a few weeks now and the world's press was in full frenzy. Some people were starting to panic, even though many astronomers were confirming it would be a near-miss. The skeptics weren't assuaged because they were beginning to understand the significance of the comet's tail not being visible. All that was discernible was a fuzzy cloud around the nucleus. This is what a comet looks like when it is heading right at you!

At the top of Himmelbjerget, Shen donned the SeeRise glasses and dialled in the predicted 70 metre sea level rise. The ground below him disappeared and he was left standing on a small islet. In the distance, he could see a few tiny peaks, including one in the direction of Funen.

As he got back in the SelfDrive and they made their way to Esbjerg, they didn't pass any ground much more than 20 metres high. It was then that Shen realised some areas of the planet could not be saved. Some people were just going to have to move. The stubborn ones would perish.

25

Pulling Strings

The Tubeway journey from Esbjerg to Reykjavík was a mere 2500 kilometres. This was relatively short compared with Shen's crossings of the two largest oceans.

Shen found he had been upgraded to another first class private pod. This time he'd established at the check-in desk that it was paid for by the Icelandic government. He'd already noticed his booking at the Hotel Borg had been credited back to his account. At first, he thought it might be because he'd been bumped out of his suite with the best view in the city. A q-mail confirmed his booking was in place, including the booking for the smaller suite next door.

Increasingly, he was getting the sense that he was not in complete control of his life events and that strings were being pulled from on high. He was not sure if Cheng or President Miang was his main puppet master, or if Cheng might be even be pulling Miang's strings.

As the Tubeway set off for a crossing that would take a little over an hour, a q-email from Thom Waters came in that only strengthened Shen's intuition that there was more going on than he was privy to.

Thom sent some new plans of the underside of the devices that showed the nano-fans had reconfigured themselves yet again. The tetrahedrons had now stacked themselves so three small tetrahedrons rotated on the corners of the larger tetrahedron.

Thom reported that the lift had increased four-fold.

Shen was pretty tired and had planned to sleep, as he was sure the forthcoming party would be full on. As he slept, the eleven remaining Councillors, hanging around in the Everywhere and Everywhen, noticed that the timelines had straightened again. Ripples and distortions appeared in the higher dimensional view when events in the Density went a little of track. Such deviations were necessary to introduce randomicity and innovation.

The previous nano-fan configuration was an example of such a deviation. It was a nice idea not yet fully landed. Councillor Seven had made the adjustment, just when the time was right. The metaphysics of the Void had again influenced the physics of the Density. At the nano-level, this influence no longer had to go through a channel or medium. The Councillors could pull these nano-strings directly.

By the time Shen was arriving in Reykjavík, Cheng and Miang were nearly back in Beijing. They had gone overland and, like the Councillors of which they had no awareness, generally agreed everything was running smoothly, just as planned.

In the Void, the Councillors were happy the transition to Epoch Six was on track. Only Councillor Seven knew that their collective strings were being pulled too. She had a direct line to the top of the chain of command, in this Universe at least, but did wonder who or what might be pulling strings higher up still.

26

The Key

2079 : 30 years left

As soon as Shen disembarked from the TubeWay in Reykjavík, he knew he could no longer hope to pull off the anonymous student guise. The weather was being kind and he arrived to bright blue skies on a cold March morning.

The forecast was clear skies for the whole of the evening. Reykjavík was in for a treat as nothing would obscure the Full Moon that evening. Shen didn't know his mother had seen to that.

Shen was the first passenger ushered off the TubeWay and was met by a barrage of reporters and flashing cameras. He was instructed by the driver of the TubeWay to walk down a red carpet. He then met several dignitaries starting with the Manager of Hotel Borg, the Head of Tourism, heads of emergency services, the Mayor of Reykjavík and finally the President of Iceland herself.

"Thank you Shen for coming to our country at this momentous time," said President Mínervudóttir, handing him a large gold key that she had been passed by Mayor Ólafur Bryndísarson.

"It's my honour to be here, Madame President," said Shen, genuinely moved by the occasion.

She replied, "Please call me Jóhanna and this is your key to the city of Reykjavík. All the bars and restaurants have been told to give you what you want for free. You have singlehandedly brought so much business to our country. We cannot thank you enough."

Shen blushed at such an accolade.

The President beckoned the hotel manager over, "Mr Sigurdsson will see you get settled in your room Shen. Will you join us for lunch?"

"Of course," replied Shen, as the hotel manager walked him over to his transport to the hotel.

Bizarrely, Shen was about to have a quick tour of the city in a horse and cart. The streets were lined with people taking pictures. He'd become a minor celebrity.

By time he got to the hotel, his blushes had abated and he was getting to like the idea of a small amount of fame. The staff at Hotel Borg knew exactly who he was and showed him deference, as if he was a foreign head of state. Mr Sigurdsson introduced him to an attractive young lady called Frejya.

"Anything you need, Frejya is your concierge and will get it for you. She'll take you anywhere you like over the next two days you are with us," said Mr Sigurdsson.

"Can I see my suite?" asked Shen, pleasantly surprised at this turn of events.

Frejya walked him over to the lift and guided him to his suite where he found his bags had already been deposited, along with four heavily protected flight cases he'd shipped from China before he left. Shen knew exactly what he wanted to check in the Tower Suite. He went straight up the stairs to survey the neat living room with a panoramic view over Reykjavík.

"Is everything as you wanted?" asked Frejya.

"More than perfect. Could you give me a hand to set up some equipment?" asked Shen.

It was then that Frejya began to realise Shen wasn't just some lucky student who'd discovered a comet by accident. With her help, Shen turned the room into something looking like a mission control room, with a bank of monitors and an array of devices that Shen carefully aligned at one point in the sky.

After an hour or so Shen donned his baseball cap and grabbed the gold key.

"All set to record" he announced, "Shall we go and see what doors this key will open?"

"Sure, I know this city like the back of my hand," said a confident Frejya.

Shen asked, "Where's your favourite bar, and not the most popular bar, but the one you like the best?"

Shen got Frejya to take him out of a back door and they walked a few blocks to a bustling student bar. It was only midday but the city was heaving. Frejya showed the key to the bar man and explained who Shen was and how the bar would be reimbursed for anything they drank.

Shen ordered a large craft beer for himself, and was pleased Frejya wanted the same. He then surprised himself, and the occupants of the bar, when he stood up and said, "I've got this key, who'd like a beer? They are free for the next hour."

Shen had intentionally created the resulting pandemonium so that he could chat to Frejya alone. The bar was deluged with people ordering as much as they could carry. Beer in Reykjavík was always costly and prices had been inflated even more for the comet transit.

From the moment he'd set eyes on Frejya, something was stirring inside Shen, beyond his usual base cravings. His heart was quite literally buzzing. He didn't know that hers was too. Neither of them knew at that time that their meeting was no accident and one of those soulwave manipulations in the Density that the Councillors could pull off easily.

Shen found out that she was a primary school teacher from Akureyri in the north of Iceland. At 23, she was only two years into her job so the only way she was going to be at the best party in the world was to work. She'd applied for loads of jobs and was unsuccessful. She'd all but given up when, just two months ago, her headmaster got a request from Hotel Borg for someone to act as a personal guide for one of their guests. She was interviewed remotely and got the gig.

Shen started to tell Frejya about the after effects of the comet's passing. He so dearly wanted to share, with someone of his own age, his new role in the sea wall defence project when they were interrupted by the thunk of fresh drinks at the hands of a buoyant barman, clearly pleased with his rise in takings. Shen realised the time was fleeting so they gulped their beers quickly and headed back to the hotel. They entered by the back door and made their way to the lobby to be greeted by a relieved hotel manager.

"Lunch is starting in 5 minutes Shen," he said. "And you are at the TV station at 3pm. Frejya will pick you up from there at 5."

This was news to Shen, who was slighted gutted that Frejya was leaving him and that his day was being somewhat stage-managed.

He was sandwiched between the President and the Mayor for lunch and he sensed what was coming. After a strange amuse bouche of something fishy and indescribable, they started grilling Shen about what he knew about the rise in sea level. The news had reached heads of governments but was not generally known by the populace.

As the first of seven courses arrived, each with its own matched wine, Shen told them probably more than he should have about the nano-wall project. He realised the two large beers before lunch were probably now a bit of a mistake.

The President wanted to know how the roll out for other cities was being decided upon. Shen genuinely didn't know at the time that it was going to be his call but he asked to borrow a tablet. He showed them how Reykjavík was an ideal candidate as it was surrounded on three sides by reasonably high terrain. They stopped the interrogation once they learned that their basaltic soils were perfect fodder for the nano-bots and the defences would only take two years to build.

Shen was smart enough not to let on about what he knew about how the acquisition of the technology would be funded. Iceland was self-sufficient in thermal energy generation so they would have to pay for it.

27

EveryWhere and EveryWhen

In the latter part of 21st century, one of the most interesting, and useful, places to hang out was in Shen's pineal gland. Councillor Seven was spending a lot of time there, which is why Shen was getting an increasing sense that invisible strings were being pulled.

When you sit in higher dimensions, it is easy to see how those in lower dimensions are so blinded to the true reality. In the Density, for example, time is linear so everything has to happen in sequence. To a Councillor, everything happens at once and the lines of time, and how everything is connected, are clear to see.

Councillors were not restricted to hanging around humans. They could be, see and feel what it's like at the centre of a star, or the molten core of a rocky planet. They could envisage life in the clouds of a gas giant or at the depths of an ocean of methane on an icy moon.

At the same time, they could be inside the compound eye of a fly, the steaming gut of a cow or inside a cell as it divides. It was always fascinating to observe the very start of a life, or the moment of death and reabsorption.

The experience of being outside, yet inside, the multi-dimensional mind of a human, or dolphin, at any time in history was of course, uniquely special. It would seem bizarre for the vast majority of humans, who have no idea they are 3D crystallisations with multidimensional minds. Dolphins did realise that is exactly what they are too, but just took it for granted, especially when they went 'travelling'.

This ability meant that Councillors could impart a small part of their essence to any being. This was somewhat less permanent than Insertion and much less tortuous than Extraction. An essence could be bestowed as quickly as it could be withdrawn.

All Wu, like Jia and Frejya, could tap into this essence - as did channels and mediums. Such awakened beings were conscious of other intelligence working through them although, most of the time, did not fully comprehend its true nature.

Many inventors, entrepreneurs, scientists and change makers were also influenced by the essence. It imbued them with a certain prescience. Thom Waters and Mike Spence were under the illusion that it was their brilliance and inventiveness that allowed them to innovate and go where nobody had gone before. As for Shen, his strings were being pulled too - but not by Cheng, who was similarly imbued and unconsciously influenced.

Sublimely, these strings were the very fabric of this particular Universe - they were the soulwaves that attached All to All.

All Councillors were weavers of the fabric but, in the Density, there was one place they were not allowed to go. Black holes were no go areas. These points of infinite density, and zero time, were off limits for Councillors and, for that matter, for any beings who valued their very existence in the 3D world.

Only Councillor Seven knew why it had to be so and how to go where other Councillors could not. She had come from infinite density and zero time in the first place which is why the other Councillors had no memory or consciousness of her Insertion.

28

Fireworks

2079 : 30 years left

Lunch was over by 2:30pm and they all left on convivial terms. The President and Mayor felt they had a direct line through Shen to a project that could save their capital, and coastal cities. They gave Shen their direct telephone numbers. He also liked them a lot and told them he would genuinely do whatever he could to help.

He knew that the project would benefit from testing many different soil types and made a mental note to make this project a special case. Of course, only Councillors knew at this point the importance of the Icelandic soil being most alike to that on the surfaces of the Moon and Mars.

Shen was handed back to Frejya who sat closely to him in another horse-drawn cart on a short trip to RÚV, the Icelandic National Broadcasting Service. They looked like a couple made for each other already, as they were feted by increasingly drunk revellers lining the streets.

When he got to the Centre, he was told he was to be the guest of honour for their television special that would be running from 6pm right through to sunrise the next day.

Shen had other plans for 9:46pm, the exact time of the Full Moon and the transit, and was already hatching other plans for later that night too. He'd discovered that Frejya was bunking down with a sleeping bag in a sports hall 20 kilometres north of the city. She could not believe her luck when she discovered she was to stay in an adjoining suite to Shen, with the best view in the city of the transit and subsequent fireworks.

He explained to the producer that they had him until 8pm, as he'd been invited to join the President for the transit itself, and then he'd be back around 11pm. In all the excitement of that evening, his little white lie would be forgotten in the noise floor.

He was mic'ed up and taken straight into the studio. Around the table were two excited hosts flanked by a panel of experts. Shen recognised a few of them as being prominent astrophysicists. Their intensity was palpable. So too was the high-voltage charge in the air, driven by the unprecedented nature of the live-streamed global event.

"At last we are so thrilled to have the person who first discovered the comet," said the male host, whose first name was Magnus, and second name unpronounceable to Shen.

Shen explained how he, a mere student, had discovered it and how they still didn't quite know where it came from.

A big countdown clock behind him was ticking down to the actual transit time.

Even though it was Shen's first experience on live TV, he just wanted to get back to Frejya. The few hours in the studio seemed interminable to him and Shen was glad when the astrophysicists started to muscle in and answer questions on his behalf.

Promising again he'd be back later, Shen left the studio a sliver before 8pm and he and Frejya went back to the same bar they had been to at lunchtime. They took a SelfDrive, as the horses had been stabled by this time. After ordering themselves a double round, Shen generously flashed the key to the city again, treating the whole bar to another hour of free drinks.

The barman cleared a booth for them and Shen finally got

to know more about Frejya.

"So my parents split up ages ago. My mother lives in London and my father in Washington DC," said Frejya. "And yours?"

"Well my dad makes a living selling 3D models of solar systems," said Shen. "And my mum is a healer."

"And so is mine," said Frejya. "I don't understand what my dad does though, something to do with blockchain at the IMF."

Shen spotted the double coincidence as both her father and his dad had amassed considerably large crypto accounts from millions of micro-payments. A sudden flicker in his being made him wonder if Frejya was a Wu, just like his mother.

As they got to the bottom of their second beer, Shen said, "Let's get back to watch the transit. And we should eat something too!"

The city streets were packed and there were singers, dancers and street entertainers in every square and on every corner. This was one party city. They sneaked in by the back door of the hotel and took the lift up to the suite.

They walked up the steps into the upstairs living room in the Tower Suite and, in between the banks of monitors, Frejya was thrilled to see a table for two set up with a bottle of champagne on ice and a lavish buffet. They were both ravenous, even though Shen had had a large lunch. Shen had wishfully ordered enough food for two when he'd booked the room three years ago. The hotel hadn't let him down and everything was on hot plates, as requested, so he wouldn't be interrupted by anyone serving.

At around 9:15, they stopped eating and looking at the monitors and, like the rest of the city and the whole world, were mesmerised by the fuzzy white head of the comet. It was below the Full Moon but discernibly getting closer to it by the minute.

At 9:46 exactly, the comet's head joined the Moon and for less than a second became a black streak transiting the face of the Moon, bottom left to top right. The footage of the transit, in super slo-mo, hit the airwaves a few minutes afterwards and the irregular edges of the space rock were clear to see. What surprised everyone was that it was not oval, or round, but more like an irregular elongated cigar shape.

The Earth had just experienced a Near Miss first hand and humanity could breathe a sigh of relief. For an hour or so, an anti-climatic air filled the capital and people started to wonder what the fuss was all about. A small black cigar-shaped object had just silently crossed the face of the Moon after all. If you blinked, you would have missed it. Then the Earth and Moon system moved into the comet's tail and the fireworks began.

Telescopes trained on the Moon, captured thousands of impact flashes. Seismographs on the Moon's surface were used to measure their mass. Nobody was that interested in the lunar surface as the Earth was deluged by the most amazing meteor display. Shen explained to Frejya that the bright orange and red colours were due to the large amount of iron in the comet's head. He omitted to tell her that the Earth's magnetic core was about to go unstable.

He didn't need to as Frejya confirmed to him that she was a Wu when she clutched her heart with a sharp pang of pain and said, "Mother Earth's heart just stopped beating and started again!"

Shen couldn't wait to start analysing data from magnetometers and seismographs that he was tapped into across the globe. That would have to wait though as he and Frejya snuggled up on the large sofa and watched the celestial display until the early hours. He had never felt so comfortable with another human being. Shen kept awake until he heard Frejya gently snoring. He allowed himself to sleep too, knowing their own fireworks would have to wait.

29

Oh Flip

The Near Hit brought the world together. Virtually all 9 billion self-aware inhabitants of the planet, watched it live, or near-live.

Humans collectively breathed a sigh of relief. It was known too that the comet wasn't coming back. Several feats of engineering were pulled off that night, unseen by most.

Firstly, the evacuated CSS had been cocooned in a mesh. It was like a protective blanket which absorbed any impactors at the time of transit.

Secondly, many geostationary satellites were moved to the side of the Earth facing the Sun for a few months. As it happened, only a handful of satellites were disabled by debris from the tail.

Thirdly, the Chinese successfully docked, landed and attached two ion engines to the comet. Shortly after leaving Earth orbit, they were ignited and their controls set to take the comet into the heart of the Sun.

This was a neat method of Extraction of the comet for the Councillors, as no evidence would be left behind for any subsequent sentient life forms to uncover about how the comet got there.

Tectonic activity on Earth had been used to prevent any one from Epoch Five from discovering their true heritage. On Mars, water and wind erosion had been less than successful as a mechanism. It was just as well that when members of Epoch Five discovered evidence of the root race of Epoch Four, in the next century, that they would have no way to tell anyone about it.

What would never be fully appreciated by the human race is that some bits of the comet didn't miss at all. The Councillors had successfully achieved the perfect hit, and Insertion, that they planned.

The comet's trajectory meant the tail burnt up over Iceland but the larger remnants that made it down to Earth plopped straight into the Northern Ice Cap. As they were hot, they just melted their way through the ice and floated down to the Arctic Ocean bed. They would remain there, undiscovered.

Some fragments did hit Greenland and were brought back for analysis by the Russo-Chinese team based there. The remnants proved to be mostly iron, as Shen predicted from spectral analysis. There was lots of excitement about some complex hydrocarbons which had researchers talking about panspermia, life seeded from space rocks.

A catalyst initiates a chemical reaction and just a few of its atoms or molecules get consumed in the reaction itself. Similarly, as the Councillors knew Epoch Five was on its way out, the seeds for the creation of Epoch Six had been successfully inserted on Planet Earth.

Crystals from the comet deposited on the ocean bed were resonators that would interact with the noosphere, if and when the time was right. The Councillors always had seeds inserted on many planets, as a back up, should any experiments self-terminate.

It turned out that Frejya was pretty spot on when she picked up intuitively that the heart of the Earth had missed a beat.

The nucleus of the comet was only 2 kilometres in diameter but it was 15 kilometres long - like a cigar. It was big enough for it to be a naked eye object as it flashed across the face of the Moon.

It was the pure iron nucleus that was causing all the stir, and especially the stirring of the Earth's magnetic field. In a heart beat, it had caused a North-South pole flip. Temporarily, the side of the Earth exposed to the Sun had been subject to a massive dose of ultraviolet radiation. This would lead to the untimely demise of a large number of people.

Remarkably, the Earth's magnetic field stabilised rapidly by the time morning broke in Europe, but with the North Pole somewhere between South America and Antarctica. The following few decades would see it collapse and flip back to its old orientation. The devastation to life on the planet would be catastrophic as a result.

The scientific community was coming to the conclusion that the comet was a wandering superconducting magnet, with a field millions of times stronger than the Earth's. They were puzzled as to why it wasn't detected ahead of its passing.

The Councillors had made sure the field was very localised and pointed at the Earth just at the time of nearest transit. This particular messenger had been sent Earth's way over a million years ago from a magnetar at the centre of the galaxy which harboured thousands of such objects. They were useful magnetic bullets used to flip the poles of planets from time to time.

The Councillors were happy the first step had been carried out successfully in the termination of Epoch Five and its evolution to Epoch Six. Shen of course had no idea of his real role in all of this but he had his finger on the right pulse, measuring how much the Earth itself was tilting as a result of gyroscopic induction.

30

Conjunction

2079 : 30 years left

Frejya and Shen woke just after 7am and, in the dim light of pre-dawn, meteor flashes were still discernible.

Coincidentally, and completely overlooked by Shen in all his research, the planets Venus, Jupiter, Saturn and Uranus were all visible near the horizon, not far from the setting Full Moon, and in close alignment. The three outer planets were just dipping below the horizon when they woke up, with Venus following not long behind.

The comet was by this time on a new course right into the heart of the Sun, after its lunar deflection and tweak by the ion engines.

Downstairs in the suite, Shen had ordered a large breakfast for two, along with another bottle of champagne to go with the oysters.

"Starting early?" said Frejya.

"I thought you might show me Iceland today," said Shen. "I've ordered a SelfDrive, so we can indulge a little."

"I hope it's a 4x4," said Frejya, knowing immediately where she wanted to take him.

"That's what they recommended," said Shen, who didn't appreciate quite why.

After eating as much as they could, and packing the rest for a lunch on the go, they went down to a very quiet lobby as Reykjavík was nursing a collective hangover.

Shen was amazed how rugged the roads got so soon outside the capital. Freya had dialled in the geyser called Strokkur, as their first destination, and was surprised how packed the single track road was so early. A quick search online revealed why. The Great Geysir nearby had started to gush again after being dormant for over 15 years.

"That's the pole flip," said Shen, who was checking news channels every 30 minutes, much to Frejya's annoyance. Nothing had leaked out yet about North being South and vice versa.

It was difficult to get near the two geysers, as they were surrounded by some of the less hungover tourists, so Frejya took Shen off to see the amazing waterfalls at Gullfoss. They spent a couple hours walking around before eating their packed lunch upstream of the waterfall, away from all the tourists.

On their way back to the capital, Cheng called Shen out of the blue and asked him where he was.

"Just on the way back to Reykjavík after some sightseeing. It feels like I am on the surface of the Moon," said Shen, as they were crossing massive lava fields.

"You know about the pole flip?" asked Cheng, changing the subject.

"Of course."

"And have you detected any tilt of the planetary axis?" asked Cheng.

"It's within normal deviations but out by 0.001 degrees this morning."

"Before you leave, tell the President that, after much consideration, the special topography of Reykjavík made it an excellent location to test the new nano-wall technology," said Cheng.

"What about the licensing fee as they already have thermal?" asked Shen.

Cheng was pleased that Shen was developing commercial sense, and said enigmatically, "No charge, we need them more than you know."

"What's this about?" said Frejya, cutting in.

"Are you not alone Shen?" asked Cheng.

"I'm with my concierge."

"Apart from telling the President, face to face, please say nothing about this to anyone," said Cheng, sounding a little annoyed. "See you back in Beijing."

The line went dead and Shen blushed. He intuitively knew he could trust Frejya so started to tell her about the significance of the North-South Pole flip.

They drove to the Blue Lagoon thermal baths and Shen decided this was as good a place as any to let her in to his world, as they were at sea level.

"So as the Earth tilts, the ice caps will melt," explained Shen.

"And the sea levels will rise too?" asked Frejya.

As they relaxed in the hot, yet smelly water, Shen said, "In less than a hundred years time, this will be about 70 metres below the waves."

"So my home town will go under?" asked Frejya, feeling the weight of his words.

"Once one city is protected, the technology can be transferred and redeployed anywhere - and fairly quickly. It will be down to your government as to what they save and protect but it will be feasible to save any large town."

"So this is what you are working on when you go back to China?" asked Frejya.

"Yes indeed," said Shen proudly.

"Will you need a concierge?" asked Frejya wryly.

Shen was falling in love with everything about her, especially her twinkly eyes and the small dimples on her cheeks when she grinned.

So that evening, over dinner at the exclusive

Grillmarkadurinn restaurant, Frejya and Shen hatched some plans. The key had procured a table for them, even though the place was booked solid.

In less than 24 hours, the soulwaves beaming from each other's hearts were entangling. Frejya saw the opportunity for a new life away from her humdrum world of being a part-time teacher. Shen sensed his role was enormous and that he would need some support.

Both of them knew they would make love that night. Shen had no idea though that Frejya would introduce him to the delights of tantric sex. They shared each others' bodies where they had slept last night, under another spectacular meteor shower from the comet's tail. The showers would continue for another three months and then repeat annually on what Iceland would call Shen Day.

The next morning, after little sleep, Shen knew his days of sleeping around were numbered. He had fallen in love - and so had Frejya.

Over breakfast he told Frejya about his plans for the remainder of his Grand Tour, taking a slow route back to China. He'd figured this might be his last chance to see some of the places he had in mind to visit. Frejya had already decided to resign from her teaching job and had hoped the concierge gig would open doors. An opportunity like this one was beyond her wildest dreams.

Along with his ability to access Big Data, Shen had learned how to hack the most secure of systems. It took him 10 minutes to secure a Chinese working visa for Frejya. He made sure he got a special class of visa that would allow Frejya to become a Chinese national, should they ever marry. Shen was always thinking ahead.

Within another hour, Shen had upgraded the TubeWay tickets, and various hotel bookings, for two. It made financial sense to upgrade to a private pod. His technical kit was all packed up and being sent directly back to Beijing so that he could travel light.

First they had to take a quick trip to Akureyri to pick up some of Frejya's things - and to say some goodbyes. The TubeWay north had only opened the year before and Frejya had never travelled on one, always taking the bumpy 5 hour road trip.

As they made their way down into the lobby, they were greeted by the hotel manager, the Mayor and the President herself. Shen was relieved as he wanted to give her the message in person.

Shen took President aside and told her exactly what Cheng had relayed to him. In kind, she told Shen that the key to the city was open ended.

Neither of them knew that this would be academic.

31

Goodbyes

2079 : 30 years left

Shen treated Frejya to a night in the the top floor suite at the Hotel Kea in Akureyri. The view across the town, and out to Eyjafjörður Fjord were even more impressive than the view from the Hotel Borg. The suite itself was slightly less grand, but very comfortable and homely.

That evening they ate simply and drank at the Backpackers Cafe, which was a relief for Shen after such fine dining over the last few days. Nobody recognised them and Shen was paying the bill again, with no key to this town.

The celestial and bedroom fireworks that evening were both stunning and Shen became brave enough to ask Frejya where, and from who, she learned tantric sex.

Frejya's mouth burst into a smile, as her mind flashed to early educational delights. She said playfully, "Oh come on, what does it really matter, when we both benefit from the techniques so much?"

Frejya didn't know at that time about the unique role her essence played, thousands of years before, when tantra emerged as a rebellion against organised religion. She and so many others rejected the idea that sexuality should be denied in order to reach enlightenment.

The fact that both Frejya and Shen drew upon Wu energy only increased their ability to connect on a level that went far beyond the skin. He decided to drop the questions and just dive, once again, into their good fortune.

The next day was a bit of a whirlwind. While Shen spent the morning writing reports on the status of the pole flip, Frejya visited her school and handed in her notice. She felt somewhat heavy about letting her colleagues and the children down but was already getting a sense of a bigger purpose coming her way.

Shen walked across town to the school gates to pick her up and could see she'd been crying.

"It's sad to think you might not see these people again," he said.

"It's not that, I just had a message from my great-grandmother," said Frejya. "She asked if we can visit her before we go to the other side of the world."

Shen suggested, "Where in Iceland does she live? Can we drive it or Tubeway half-way?"

"She doesn't, Bodø in Norway," said Frejya, worried she was about to upset Shen's travel plans. "I would go alone but she said that she specifically she wants to meet you Shen."

Shen was already on the Tubeway map and saw they would have to go back to Reykjavík, over to Bergen and up the Norwegian coast to Bodø.

"If we leave in the next hour, supper in Bodø it is! So we'll have to overnight and we'll be a day or so late in London but we can still be back in Beijing as planned if we miss a couple of stops out on the way back," said Shen.

"So when did you tell her about me then?"

"That's just it, I didn't," said Frejya.

Shen didn't think to ask Frejya how her great-grandmother had actually got in touch.

"I still don't know why you are so upset. I'm more than happy to see somewhere new and meet her," said Shen.

The penny dropped when Frejya told him that her great-grandmother had told her it would be the last time they would see each other.

The last few days had flashed by and Shen and Frejya realised they still actually knew little about each other. They stayed on the Tubeway at Reykjavík for half an hour, as they didn't want to be recognised before it routed onwards to Bergen.

Frejya filled Shen in about her very estranged family. Both sets of her grandparents had separated and went to different points of the globe, effectively orphaning her parents. This sent her mother, who was Norwegian, into a spin of self-pity which led in turn to her divorcing from her Icelandic dad. From the age of five, Frejya was dumped on her great-grandmother and she idolised her.

"We're in touch constantly, but telepathically," said Frejya, which helped Shen understand a little why she was so upset back in Akureyri.

"So there's no question we have to go," said Shen.

Frejya started to get excited about her new life near Beijing. Shen's family sounded like a tight-knit unit and the polar opposite of hers.

They both fell silent as the Tubeway left Bergen, before going up to Bodø. The whole right side of their 1st class pod became a real time display of the stunning Norwegian coastline. It was breathtaking and over in an hour, as the Tubeway sped up the coast at over 1300 kilometres an hour.

Shen had checked them in to a charming guest house, called Opsahl Gjestegaard, which was a nice change from ostentatiousness of hotels. It was walking distance from the Tubeway port and the centre of town. They purposely hadn't eaten all day, as Frejya told Shen to save himself for a Norwegian treat.

It was early evening when they arrived so they dumped their baggage and walked to Restaurant Bjørk. In fluent Norwegian, Frejya ordered everything, including the surprisingly delicious local wine. Shen was lured. The starter was honey-glazed veal medallion with almond potatoes, on a bed of locally grown vegetables. Shen had his first baked catfish for the main, with roasted seaweed on the side. For desert, their eyebrows were nearly singed by the whiskey flambé with cloudberries.

When they got back to the guest house, all thoughts of amorous adventures faded as they both fell into a deep sleep. The next morning they had smorgasbord for an early breakfast and were on the road in a SelfDrive by 7:30am.

They were heading for a charming fishing village called Kjerringøy, half hour's drive north of Bodø. Shen introduced Frejya to his SeeRise glasses as they were driven up the scenic coastal road. The visual impact was instant.

"So this will all be underwater in 6 years time?" gasped Frejya.

"Not if they licence the nano-wall solution," said Shen. "They are energy-independent so in theory would have to pay for it but I had a message from Cheng last night that Norway will be exempt too. I've no idea why."

Shen was eager to learn more about who was pulling the strings and for what reason.

When they arrived in Kjerringøy, Frejya directed the SelfDrive to a beach. In the distance, Shen saw a lone seal swimming towards them. He was a little shocked when the seal got up on two legs and walked out of the sea and up the beach to where they stood.

The 'seal' wrapped a towel around itself and Frejya ran towards what morphed into a small, frail but obviously tough woman. Frejya gave her the biggest hug, lifting the 'seal' off her feet.

"Come and meet Shen, great-grandma Sara," shouted Frejya.

After Shen recovered from a crushing handshake, Sara said in perfect English, "Let's have coffee."

Sara shot off at a pace up a steep track in the hillside and

Shen and Frejya had trouble keeping up on the slippery slope. Slightly breathless, they got to an old shack and Sara was pouring strong black coffee out as they entered.

Shen noticed that every inch of the walls, and ceiling, were covered in the most amazing artworks, some sketches and many watercolours, some faded. Shen's attention was drawn to the most intriguing tattoo on Sara's left upper arm.

"So Shen, look into my eyes," said Sara, spending no time on pleasantries. "I want to know what you are here for."

Immediately Shen realised Sara was a Wu, just like his mother. The whole space inside the shack shimmered. He saw Sara morph once again, at first into a young woman and then into what he guessed was a tall male Viking warrior.

"He's the One," said Sara densifying and directing her message to Frejya. "Look after him."

"Did you see what I saw?" asked Shen of Frejya.

"Yes!" said Frejya, kicking him to shut up.

"Shen you have my blessing to look after my great-granddaughter for the rest of your life," said Sara, softening her tone. "I will be keeping a close eye on you both."

The young couple smiled at each other and Frejya squeezed Shen's hand.

"Drink your coffee," urged Sara. "It's time to go."

At this, the air in the shack cracked and fizzled. Right in front of their eyes, Sara's body became translucent and she left the room. As she did so, all the drawings and paintings on the walls disappeared too.

Shen looked at Frejya and she looked at him. Frejya looked radiant, smiling from ear to ear, with not a tear in her eye.

"When she died seven years ago Shen, she told me she would come back to see me."

32

Last Chance to See

2079 : 30 years left

They spent the trip back to Bodø in silence. Frejya resisted all of Shen's questioning until they stopped for a quick lunch at the En Kopp cafe bar. They both needed a drink and ordered two large Nøgne craft beers.

"What you saw was a re-ascension," explained Frejya. "I was with her when she first left the planet and that was my first experience of an ascension. There was no body left, she just decided when she wanted to return to the Light."

Shen realised he had as much to learn from Frejya as she did from him.

"My mother will simply love you," he said.

"And me her, by the sound of it," said Frejya.

At 1pm, they took the Tubeway back to Bergen and, without stopping, across to London for three nights. Back in a first class private pod, this was Shen's first experience of love making while travelling at high speed.

Shen had booked them in at the Savoy but in a different suite than he one he had been in on his first visit. He didn't want the memory of his last dalliance to be picked up on by Frejya.

The plan was to share some time with Frejya in the amazing city, as he'd seen none of it on the way through. It was a lot more fun with someone else anyway and he'd developed a taste for warm English beer. On the first night, he wined and dined Frejya in the Savoy Grill. The Glazed Omelette Arnold Bennett was her favourite too.

They spent the next day wandering around the Natural History and Science Museums, two of the greatest collections on the planet of the diversity of life and the smartness of humankind. At the end of the afternoon, Shen popped into Imperial College unannounced, as it was around the corner from the museums. He was hoping to give Frejya a sneak preview of the nano-wall models. He was both dismayed and surprised to hear that Mike Spence had already left for Beijing, along with his assistant Simon, and he assumed with all the models.

That evening, they wandered around the bars and pop up restaurants in trendy Hoxteth. Shen appreciated the anonymity. On their last day, they went cultural and historical visiting the Tower of London and then taking the river boat up to Hampton Court. Shen was getting the sense that there was more to save in London than just its financial institutions.

The following day Shen left London with a new sense of urgency, as they took the Tubeway under the Channel, which seamlessly continued as a MagLev overland to Paris, where they spent two nights. Being the city of love, only naturally their bond deepened and strengthened. At 35 metres above sea level, Paris was safe until the latter part of the century at least.

From there, they spent a night in Geneva which at 375 metres elevation, along with the whole country, was well beyond any inundation. It would just get a little warmer as the city moved southwards, along with the whole of Europe.

Their Grand Tour then took them through the spectacular alps, through tunnels not long enough to make love in, over into Northern Italy. They had a whistle stop in Pisa - 4 metres - to see the Leaning Tower, before spending a night in Rome

- 37 metres - in the Cavalieri Hotel, with a stunning view over the Vatican.

Shen was not yet savvy about the politics between the Catholic Church and China. He could not know either that the deal to protect Rome, and the Eternal City, would be what would bring the two parties together. The broker in this deal was to be the world's first female pope, Joan, and ironically the world's last pope too. Almost single handedly, she was destined to harmonise all the world's religions but sadly when it was all a little too late.

The next day, after a tour inside the Vatican, they went across to Venice for what they didn't know would be their last night ever in Europe.

Frejya was getting the hang of Shen's previously planned trip and how he'd engineered it as the last chance to see stunning locations on the planet - unless of course, they bought into the sea wall project. Shen explained that Venice could not be saved as it was already inundated and that it would be easier, although equally unfeasible, to move the whole city inland.

From Venice, they went overland by MagLev down the east coast of Italy and from the port of Brindisi, in the heel of the country, they took the TubeWay across to Egypt.

As they disembarked on a new continent, Shen observed that the great, sprawling coastal port of Alexandria would be a tough engineering project. They took a MagLev to Cairo which, at an average height of 23 metres, would need saving too. Shen wondered if the ancients knew something when they visited the Great Pyramid of Giza, lying at 139 metres above sea level.

From Cairo, they took a leisurely boat trip down the Nile to Luxor - just safe at 76 metres. They took in the spectacular light display under a half Moon, accompanied by celestial fireworks from the comet's tail. It was just over a week since the Moon transit and they were already noticeably lessening in intensity. Shen and Frejya stayed on the boat overnight and just slept. They were both somewhat exhausted.

The next day Shen woke to a message from Cheng, with whom he had shared his travel plans. Disappointingly, he was told to come back to Beijing as fast as possible. This meant Mauritius, Cape Town and Mumbai were off the agenda but at least his stopover at Goa was still OK.

What slightly annoyed Shen even more was that Cheng had arranged for him to come back via Dubai, where a hastily arranged conference was about to start in two day's time. Cheng informed Shen he'd be making a presentation on how he found the comet and on the nano-wall project. He also told Shen not to mention anything about wave-powered electricity generation.

This was to be Shen's immersion into the world of global economics. The Middle East had ceased being the world's provider of petrochemicals in the Thirties and had become the world's largest exporter of solar-generated electricity. They would be paying China for their licenses.

Both Shen and Frejya knew that their magical trip was coming to an end and that they would be settling into a new life together. They got to Dubai the next evening after a trip by TubeWay under the Red Sea, and then routed across the Arabian Desert by MagLev, past an interminable sea of solar arrays.

Over the next few days, in between conference sessions and meetings with seemingly hundreds of princes, while holed up in the Burj Al Arab overlooking The Palm, they started hatching plans.

After a gap of nearly a month, with little contact but the odd email, Shen made a call home to introduce Frejya to his parents. Shen was expecting some admonishment for not calling and hoped the news about Frejya would help. It did.

"You must move in with us," said Jia.

Jia sensed she was a Wu immediately and that she could

become the daughter she had always craved for.

"But there's no spare room," said Shen.

"Oh yes there is," said Hui. "I've got a new, much bigger printer."

"We've been busy Shen while you were away," explained Jia. "I knew you would not be coming back alone and we've 'printed' an extension at the back of the house."

"I'll send you a video and the plans," said Hui. "You can start thinking about what furniture you'd like, send me your designs and I'll have them printed by the time you get back."

"You are both amazing," said a relieved Shen, again feeling that his life was being mapped out for him and that it was all far too good to be true.

"I can't wait to meet you both," said Frejya, smiling from ear to ear. She felt Jia and Hui would give her the loving family she had always wanted. Along with a life with the most amazing man she'd ever known. She too could not believe her luck.

Even with their super-sensibilities, neither Jia or Frejya had any inkling as to the parts they would all play together in acting out the plans of the Councillors.

33

Permutations

There was no rest for a Councillor as there was no concept of time.

Literally at the same time, in each galaxy in this Universe, other experiments were being carried out. The purpose, as always, was to see what happens when the Void is densified.

At the same time Shen was sampling the delights of the golden beaches of Goa with Frejya, three virtually identical experiments were playing out in galaxies far, far away.

In one, Shen did not meet the love of his life and spent his entire days as a bachelor. In another, the comet made a direct impact with an Uber-Earth, terminating its Fifth Epoch and merely seeding the Sixth Epoch with panspermia.

The third experiment did not require any Insertion. The planet harbouring its Fifth Epoch sentience was allowed to super-heat and perform its own reset.

When you have infinite time, there is more than enough time to run infinite permutations. You can leave it to each Epoch to create the next. The survival of the fittest will tell, in 20:20 hindsight, which was the best and most exciting route.

Being a Councillor was the best job in the Universe. It was one only entrusted to those who would not overly dabble.

From a vantage point right at the Earth's core, the Councillors could see that the first stage of the Termination plan was in place. The North magnetic pole was now over the Antarctic Ocean and the South Pole right on top of Iceland. As well as cosmic fireworks,

Icelanders would soon be treated to seeing the Aurora Australis right overhead for the first time - not that they looked that much different to the Aurora Borealis.

Over the coming hundred linear years, the now contra-rotating iron core would be driven be internal tidal forces to right itself and flip back to rotate along with the Earth's orbital spin. Disruption to the protective magnetosphere was inevitable as multiple poles pairings would start to spring up right across the planet.

It was now less than 30 Earth orbits before the second stage of Termination would hit.

34

Union

By the time they arrived in the The LaLiT Beach Resort in Goa, Shen had ascertained that the Earth's axial tilt had already shifted by a full 0.1 of a degree. His models predicted a 5 degree shift by the end of the century, starting rapidly and then slowing. The initial measurements seemed to fit the model.

Over the last few days, several dormant volcanoes had awoken and there had been increased seismic activity right around the Pacific Ring of Fire. A tsunami was imminent.

Shen had also predicted an increase in atmospheric ash, which would cool the planet down for around 5 years and actually delay the melting of the ice caps. Once the dust settled though, coastal inundation would be rapid and the initial 40 metre rise would occur by the end of the century. There wasn't much time.

Shen and Frejya wished they had more time to walk up and down the beach, with waves gently lapping at their feet and a golden sun being absorbed by the ocean.

"Nobody on this beach realises that the waves will be 70 metres above their heads in a few decades time," said Shen.

"Do the plans include saving this place?" asked Frejya.

"There's no reason we can't roll this out across the planet, so long as each country agrees to the terms. Once they see the first nano-walls, we think they will all want it."

"You are going to be busy and travelling a lot then," said Frejya.

"I hope not, once the topographic design is done, and a test wall built, the system is pretty automatic. The 'bots in the test sites seem to know what they are doing."

That evening they had a sumptuous barbecued meal, with locally caught fish. They sat with a tablet each, populating Hui's design of their extension with bespoke furniture. They were especially proud of their concept for a circular Yin Yang bed and this inspired a lengthy session of tantra, before finally sending their grand designs to Hui for printing.

When they first heard they were having their own room built, Frejya bought a large rug and many fabrics for blinds and drapes in the Souk Al Bahar in Dubai. They were already on their way to Beijing ahead of them.

The next day, they took the Tubeway all the way to Shanghai. Shen treated Frejya to another night of luxury in the Four Seasons Hotel, as it was too late to travel to Beijing. They were too tired for tantra that night but caught up in the morning.

The MagLev deposited them in Beijing at lunch time the next day and Hui and Jia met them as they got off the cable car at Fragrant Hills Park.

Jia and Frejya's soulwaves entangled immediately, having been dancing at some distance apart for millennia. They both had that sense they had met before. When Frejya confirmed later that her mother was a practitioner of Norse sorcery, known as Sedhr, this came as no surprise.

When they arrived home, Hui took them through to the extension, his pride and joy. Jia had already laid out the rug, hung the blinds and drapes and arranged the silks from the souk over a circular rail around their bed.

"That is just as I would have done it!" exclaimed Frejya.

"I know," said Jia.

This was to be the start of a long collaboration between the two sorceresses.

They lunched together before Jia took Frejya for a walk in Fragrant Hills to get to know her some more. While they were out, Hui grilled Shen on the impact of comet's passing. Shen opened up and told him about the nano-wall project but felt he'd best keep quiet about what he'd seen in Thom Waters' lab.

"So when do you start?" asked Hui.

"Tomorrow," said Shen.

"Good, when you come back in the evening, I'll have something to show you that will help."

The four of them had a fabulous evening together, with Shen showing them pictures from his Grand Tour. Neither Hui or Jia had ever left China so they were overly impressed. Frejya just wished she could have been with Shen for the whole of his circumnavigation. She had only left Iceland once for a weekend in Denmark on one of the last remaining ferries and her feet had not really hit the ground since they met.

Out of deference to Shen's parents, they didn't quite christen their new bed that night. The next day, Shen left early to meet with Cheng and Mike Spence at the University in Beijing and left Frejya in Jia's hands.

It was right down to business when Shen arrived at Cheng's office in the University.

Cheng asked Shen to bring them up to date on measurements of the magnetic pole flip and Earth's axial shift.

Cheng asked, "So everything is as predicted?".

"I did spend time over the models," said Shen proudly.

Cheng got up from his desk and said, "Follow me."

Shen was ushered through a hidden door in a bookshelf behind Cheng's desk into a large oval anteroom that he had no idea existed.

Mike Spence shook his hand with some vigour and said, "Here's where we are up to. They will be completed by mid-2083."

He showed him to one of three large tables in the centre of the room.

Shen was surprised to see detailed and accurate models of Reykjavík, Shanghai, London and Dubai."

"Dubai?" he asked.

"Yes, thanks to your presentations, they have signed up and paid up. They won't need our wave power as they have so much solar but we need their money. The Middle East is bank rolling our project which means we can move swiftly," said Cheng.

"Here's Phase Two, set for completion end-2084," said Mike, who showed Shen models on a second table of Jeddah in Saudi Arabia, Muscat in Oman and the whole island of Bahrain.

"And what's covered in Phase Three?" asked Shen.

The third table had a hodgepodge of coastal cities right across the globe.

"You have a few packed months of presentations, Shen," said Cheng.

Shen learned that representatives from Japan, Canada, the USA, South East Asia, Australia and New Zealand, South America, India, South Africa and, surprisingly, the Netherlands were heading over to Beijing over the coming months.

"Mike will be working on the designs and you will be our chief salesman," pronounced Cheng.

Shen realised he'd landed his first real job. Up to that point, he'd had his studies paid for by the State. He discovered that he was about to become salaried, plus receiving a not inconsiderable sales commission for each country that signed up.

That evening he shared his exciting news with Frejya and

his parents. Frejya was relieved that Shen would primarily be working in Beijing for the foreseeable future.

After dinner and before retiring, Hui showed Shen into his workshop.

"I've been working on this idea for sometime," said Hui.

In a 1 metre square container, covered in sand on its base, Hui showed Shen a miniature 3D printer.

"Watch this."

The printer started whirring away and within a few minutes produced a number of parts, using the sand as its raw material. The parts started moving, under their own volition, and a second printer appeared. The second printer started a process and another set of parts assembled themselves into what looked like a small truck.

"That's amazing, what's the next trick?" asked Shen.

The truck drove itself over to the first printer and moved it half a metre across the container. The first printer then printed its own truck that went and fetched the second printer over to join it.

"Could you use these scaled up?" asked Hui.

"We sure could, can you come and meet Mike Spence tomorrow and bring this along?" asked Shen.

That was the moment Shen made his first hire.

Shen told Frejya what he'd seen as they snuggled up for the second night in their Yin Yang bed.

Frejya then told Shen what Jia had asked of her and that's if she'd like to start teaching at a school for Wu.

There is something relaxing about having your fate sealed and worries about your future dissolved.

The Councillors took full advantage of this relaxed feeling between them. That night when the twins were conceived, they made sure the egg and two spermatozoa were imbued with extra double dose of their essence.

35

Shen Day

2080 : 29 years left

In the time it took Frejya to come to full term, the Earth's axis had shifted a full 2 degrees, just as Shen had predicted. Also as modelled, the large amount of atmospheric ash from the increased vulcanism cooled the planet, delaying any more rapid melting of the poles

By home water birth, with Akiko's help, Frejya brought near-identical twins, Eva and Kristin, into the world on the 5th March 2080. It was a Full Moon and also the day the cosmic fireworks began again, as the Earth orbit once more crossed the tail of the comet.

Hui and Shen had 3D printed a nursery room off the side their extension by then. Shen and Frejya had got married in the previous Autumn, with just his parents present as witnesses. Frejya didn't even tell her parents about it, much to Shen's relief.

Hui and Jia turned out to to be excellent grandparents, which was just as well since Shen and Frejya had become very busy, with both of their work commitments having increased considerably.

Fortunately, Shen was only travelling to and from Beijing by cable car but was putting in long days. Hui came with him at least once a week now he'd been officially seconded, on a salary, to the project. Mike Spence and his team were busy designing the implementation of the nano-walls in Reykjavík, Shanghai, London and Dubai. Shen spent his time on initial design models for new cities and countries were now signing up in their droves.

Frejya had become a full time teacher at Fragrant Hills School, where Jia was also taking some classes. Shen had not really paid attention to what they were up to and why Madame Bien had surfaced again as the headmistress of the school. Fortunately the school had a crèche so Frejya, and Jia, had been able to go back to teaching within a couple of months.

With so many people in high places being briefed about the nano-walls project, it would be impossible to keep the news about the impending sea level rise a secret. So on the 17th of March, the anniversary of the passing of Comet Shen, as it had been renamed on social media, a news conference was held to brief the whole planet. The whole world was watching.

The conference was broadcast, appropriately, from the Grand Lecture Theatre at the University of Beijing. President Miang opened the conference by clearly stating, and affirming, China's position as lead caretakers for the whole planet.

He opened the conference saying, "As many of you know, the passing of Comet Shen a year ago has destabilised our planet and we now know the sea levels will rise by 70 metres in the next fifty years or so."

"Our technology will be freely available to all," he pronounced. "But we know it is technically unfeasible to save certain areas. Some people will have to move. We plan to use the same technology that will construct the sea defences to build new cities in the hills."

Hui smiled when he heard this, knowing his contribution had significantly expanded the nano-wall team's brief and scope.

"This threat to humankind is also our chance to pull together and work as one," Miang continued. "We came together at the start of this century to curb our CO_2 emissions and save the ice caps from melting. We cannot save them this time but we have the political will to do what ever is humanly possible for the good of all."

The cameras cut to the Presidents of Russia and the USA and representatives from the major economies, nodding in agreement on the front row.

"Let me hand you over to the discoverer of the comet to explain what is happening," said Miang.

Shen was still only 21 but the last year of presentations had made him very comfortable with public speaking. Just as well as 9 billion people were watching him. He was also adept at explaining complex concepts in the way everyone could understand.

Using amazing CGI graphics, that he'd created himself, he showed how the comet's magnetic field had flipped the Earth's core completely. This in turn had lead to a gyroscopic shift in the Earth's axis which would then result in the melting of both ice caps, once the ash in the atmosphere settled by the middle of the coming decade.

Shen had been briefed by Cheng to say nothing about what would happen to the Earth's magnetic field as it started to flip back. By the turn of the century, the holes in the magnetosphere, caused by the emergence of multiple North-South poles, would mean it could be lethal to stay outside for any length of time in the day. The increase in UV would also have massive impact on the biosphere.

Shen wrapped up by showing an animation of the Earth passing through the comet's tail right through to the next century. When he sat down, after handing over to Mike Spence, he wished he and Frejya could have been back in Reykjavík that night, on what Iceland were now celebrating as Shen Day. He still had the key to the city but, as a new parent, couldn't envisage using it again for the foreseeable future.

Professor Spence took over and showed detailed models of the first cities to be protected by 2083 and explained how the sea walls also generated unlimited free electricity. He also explained how the roll out after that would be carried out by local teams who would be trained in a new academy he was setting up, and heading up, in Beijing.

He went on to explain how low-lying farming would be decimated and how nano-factories would be providing food under artificial light which would be available 24x7, powered by the nano-walls. Like Shen, he was told not to reveal all, especially that wormeries would be providing protein currently obtained from meat production. The world was to change its diet, like it or not.

President Miang wrapped up the conference throwing down a gauntlet, "So every year, enjoy the display of fireworks. Sleep in the knowledge that we are looking after you but also take responsibility for your own futures. Learn new skills. Look after the infirm and, most of all, be mindful about bringing no more children than you need into a world with limited resources."

The conference ended with a picture of a spinning globe entitled "Planet Earth 2150". It was clear to see which areas were not planned to be saved.

Over the next few years, the closing sentences of Miang's address took hold as the popular zeitgeist. At the time of his speech, in 2080, around 300 new human mouths, needing to be fed, were born very minute. This was compared to 150 human mouths that took their last breath in the same time. By the time the Earth passed through the comet's tail again in 2081, this number had equalised to 150 births and deaths a minute.

After 3 million years since Epoch Five began, the human race had come to the point of zero population growth.

36

Reprocessing

When a sentient soul sheds its mortal coil, it loses its attachment to matter in Density and it is reabsorbed into the Void.

There is no review of deeds good and bad, or counting of karmic points. There is just a period of loving embrace and re-absorption. As there is no time in the Void, this period is neither long or short in Earth years. It just is.

The soul can re-densify any time, and anywhere, it so chooses. This could be on another planet and at any point backwards and forwards in time. So reincarnation is neither linear, nor singular. A soul can have parts on the same planet at multiple times or on any number of planets in different galaxies across the Universe at the same time. All disparate soul parts are connected by soulwaves. Such entanglement means they will eventually come back together.

In the Density, this affords souls a great opportunity, not often capitalised upon. Information, healing and love can pass by way of soulwaves between the soul parts. So addressing an issue in the present can help a part of a person in the past or the future. Future version of souls who appreciate this is how things work can send messages to other versions of themselves Anywhere and Anywhen. As the messages are passed by way of soulwaves, outside space and time, they are delivered instantly.

So a soul can incarnate in two different bodies at the same time, as sometimes but not always happens with identical twins.

When this occurs, as it did with Eva and Kristen, powerful psychic bonds emerge as the soul parts densify. Sometimes education systems can annul these bonds but fortunately not when they are nurtured correctly, as the twins would experience at Fragrant Hills School.

So when a planet goes through a dramatic event where many lives are terminated, or self-terminated, the Councillors are kept busy. Mostly they are providing the loving embrace so needed by souls in transition.

They are then entrusted with the onward processing of that soul.

One of the most efficient ways to effect this is simply to send that soul back around the same loop several times. So, shortly after death, the soul is reborn again as its earlier self. So some people loop around exactly the same lifetime several times. As there are so many things people miss, they just get to fill in a few of the gaps they previously didn't notice. Sometimes, the life plan alters subtly to send the soul on a new trajectory.

Of course, this leads some souls in the Density experiencing many occurrences of déjà vu and prescience - and not an inconsiderable amount of luck. It also allows souls to expand and grow rapidly and to become shining stars.

This leads to such souls possessing the uncanny ability to meet people at the most perfect times and they are often heard saying, "Don't I know you from somewhere?" or "Haven't I met you before?".

Sadly, some can also experience bipolar disorder by being pulled back towards an old version of themselves in the Density, where events played out not-so-well. At the same time, their unique abilities allow them to experience flashes of brilliance and to tap into the bliss state they experienced in the Void.

Some of these more troubled souls end up caught in a temporal tug of war and they can have a propensity to self-terminate in order to get back to that bliss in the Void.

So in the last hundred years of Epoch Five on Planet Earth,

the number of cases of bipolar dis-order increased rapidly, as did the number of suicides.

Only the Councillors had the perspective to know this was a natural byproduct of such planetary transitions. They had managed countless of them in countless other galaxies. They also knew a soul should only go around this type of temporal loop a maximum of five times, for their own safety.

This was why Epoch Three had to be terminated on Lemuria. When the secret got out that is was easy for soul to loop back by the act of suicide, the whole population of the planet was planning a mass self-termination, lead by a beguiling high priest called Trîtam.

He was taken out first and, after reprocessing, deposited in another galaxy, far, far away. The planet Lemuria was then vapourised and the rest of the population was held for batch reprocessing, whilst the next planet in the system was being made ready for Densification.

37

After the Sea Rush

2083 : 26 years left

By 2083, when the first nano-walls were successfully in place, the ratio of human births to deaths had altered still further. Planetary-wide birth rates had fallen to less than 100 a minute and deaths had increased to over 300 a minute. The latter figure was caused in no small part by the people who decided moving from the coast was not for them, nor was living any longer on a planet at such a time of turbulent change. Suicide rates were rocketing.

In 2083, Eva and Kristin were three and started nursery at Fragrant Hills School. Their eclectic mix of Chinese and Scandinavian features made them stand out.

It was obvious Kristin had a gift for languages. They all spoke Chinese around the house but Kristin had picked up both Icelandic and English.

Eva preferred spending time with Jia in the garden and had a special touch and bond with plants, insects and some of the small mammals that lived in the Hills.

It was apparent Madame Bien was heading up an unusual school, as the subjects taught were not standard. Frejya for example was charged with teaching children across all age groups how to use their intuition. Other teachers had been drafted in to work specifically on all aspects of creativity. Classical subjects were addressed through the creative and intuitive processes. This accelerated learning and made it more fun.

The pupils mostly came from all corners of China, apart from a smattering of children born to foreigners domiciled there.

Like many newly married couples with children, Shen and Frejya were both burning candles at both ends. Shen came back quite late each evening but they both made weekends sacrosanct for quality time with the children, and each other.

Saturdays were spent playing with Eva and Kristin. On Sundays, Jia and Hui sensitively took their grandchildren out for the day to give the newly weds their own time. Alone in the house, Shen and Frejya explored one-ness with each other and were getting quite advanced and experimental with the merging of their bodies and consciousness.

The next two years of their lives fell into this comfortable pattern.

The construction of the first sea walls triggered the start of mass migrations. By 2085, the Earth had tilted three degrees on its axis, and the ice caps had started to melt. People noticed that the Sun was rising and setting at different positions on the horizon over the seasons. The shift was real.

The nano-walls turned out to be less formidable and imposing than people imagined. They were adaptive and intelligent so only built themselves up to around 2 to 3 metres to cope with the initial rise in sea level. If nothing was in their way, they could also move sideways and backwards if needed. So it was the noticeable shift in the Sun's position rather than the rise in sea level that galvanised people into moving.

Low-lying areas like Florida and the deltas of the great rivers of the Amazon, Yangtze and Ganges were too vast to save. Areas outside the main cities in the Netherlands and Denmark would succumb too and heading for the hills was the only option. National borders were fast dissolving as people started to work together and co-operate.

All in all humanity was concerned but generally chuffed with its ingenuity and collectively believed they would pull through the pole shift. It might take a couple of hundred years but the caretakers of the Earth in the late 21st century were laying down a new way of being for their descendants.

The melting of the ice caps was thankfully quite gradual and the sea level rose by less than a metre each year. Everyone had plenty of time to move inland to higher ground. In a gold rush, the people who make the most money are those who sell the shovels to the prospectors. In what became known as the Great Sea Rush, a whole new set of industries were set up.

On coastlines the world over, many of those who could afford it literally moved their whole house on large trailers. Those who couldn't turned their hands to helping others move. The money they earned then funded their own moves. The infirm and elderly were 'adopted' by people who were given government subsidies for their philanthropy.

Hui's designs for 3D printed houses, furniture and whole villages were made freely available. Right across the planet, 3D printers were printing more 3D printers, along with all the automated construction machinery needed. Where the soil types were favourable, Mike Spence's soil-eating nano-bots were used to create the raw materials needed.

At Shen's insistence, Hui also made plans available freely for 3D printable, flat-packed caravans that could be towed behind a SelfDrive. Like Shen had done, some people decided it was time to go and visit places that might not be around much longer. Last Chance To See parties were held at locations around coastlines the world over.

Problems became solutions. The global threat was bringing the world together at last.

Shen was sensing his time on the nano-wall project was coming to an end and he started to look back at his earlier two Big Data projects. A good programmer never deletes their work and will leave algorithms running in the background.

Two anomalies alerted Shen. The first was that, since April 2058, there had been no sightings of Baiji dolphin in the Upper Yangtze. The second was that the numbers of ocean-going cetaceans had started to drop again, year on year.

This lead him to wonder how the two events were connected and caused him to think about letting Cheng know what he had found.

He knew Professor Cheng had been secreted away somewhere in North China on yet another project. He desperately wanted in on it as now he was getting a little bored with nano-walls. The thought of leaving Frejya, his children and Beijing had made him prevaricate on making a call.

On a grey Monday morning in Autumn 2085, when Shen was contemplating a week of boring meetings and presentations, Cheng, as was his way, intervened by turning up at Beijing University unannounced and calling Shen into his office.

Shen noticed he seemed more gaunt than last time they had met.

"So we've saved the planet Shen," said Cheng, shaking his hand and ushering him to sit on a large sofa next to him. Shen noticed a shift in attitude from sitting the other side of a desk.

"Tell me about the dolphins Shen," said Cheng.

"How do you know?"

"Your data is my data," answered Cheng.

Shen briefed him on what he'd discovered and Cheng knew it was time for Shen to begin his next project. Cheng stood up, with a little wobble, and took Shen into his anteroom once more.

The models of cities surrounded by nano-walls had been replaced by a new set of 3D models. In the centre of the room was a large industrial facility with tall gantries.

"The Jiuquan Satellite Launch Centre?" asked Shen, who then scanned the rest of the room to see three other tables.

"Well spotted Shen, and here's our new Moon Base test site," said Cheng leading him to the next table. On it were four large round dome-shaped structures, surrounded by a number of assorted smaller buildings.

Shen recognised the terrain inland from Reykjavík and then Cheng showed him to the next table which had a similar construction but on a greyer terrain.

"And this is the same base on the Moon?" asked Shen.

"Yes Shen, the land mass on our home planet is decreasing so we are going where there is no limit to the land available"

"The Moon?"

"No," said Cheng, taking him to the fourth table where Shen saw a model of what he thought was the Grand Canyon in the USA.

"This is Valles Marineris on Mars," said Cheng.

Cheng had Shen excited again, "Are you telling me you'd like to work on this project?"

"No, not yet at least Shen. You might not be alive when we send people to Mars. I certainly won't be," said Cheng. "What I want you to work on is finding out how long we have got before we have to leave."

38

Noosphere

If humans knew about the existence of the Council of the Light, they would rightly sleep better at night safe in the knowledge that their best interests were being looked after. Those who acknowledged the existence of the Councillors only had to have a thought for it to manifest in the Density. They were the sages, mystics and Wu.

To allow humans to sit at the top of the food chain on land on Planet Earth, the Councillors had also to manage the whole biosphere below to support them. At the same time, the Councillors maintained a co-existing and interconnected water-based food chain so that whales and dolphins could sit at their respective pinnacle of evolution.

Unlike humans, that at one time seemed to be hell bent at decimating their own food chain, cetaceans had known for millennia how to respect and manage the food chain that sustained them. They only ate what they needed and left enough for the food chain to self-manage itself.

At the junction between sea, land and air, sometimes the food chains would mix. Fish were known to eat low flying birds and many birds could dive to considerable depths to eat fish. Penguins had even dispensed with the need to fly and were graceful and fast underwater, as were seals, sea otters and dugong.

So the Councillors only had to manage the food chains and interact with the odd channel and medium to keep Planet Earth spinning. The main reason for this was that most of the day to day affairs were delegated to Mother Earth herself.

Her consciousness was encapsulated in the noosphere. Here lay the knowledge and wisdom of how to run a planet. All noospheres of all inhabited planets across all galaxies were connected via soulwaves so that best practice could be shared.

Mother Earth, known as Lady Gaia by her home star, was not left to her own devices. This home star, also connected at its centre to all other stars by soulwaves, was also entrusted by the Councillors to manage its solosphere. The solosphere was a nurturing ground for all planets and their moons and is bounded and eventually stopped at the heliopause. This is the place where the solar wind is counteracted and annulled by the galactic winds.

The magnetic fields of all planets had touch points on the surface of the Sun, known as magnetic mixing points. Occasionally, mixing points merged and this allowed for transfer of aspects of consciousness between planets. The Sun micro-managed when this would be allowed, normally at times of transition.

The Sun controlled the position of each planet and its own radiation output such that the inhabited planet of choice, at any one time, was kept in the Goldilocks Zone - not to hot, not too cold.

Billions of kilometres away from the Sun lay a spherical cloud of icy bodies, known as the Oort Cloud.

Humans had detected this cloud and understood correctly that it was where most comets came from.

What they didn't fully appreciate was that the Sun was in control of the passage of comets in order to bring in new RNA and DNA variances, now and again.

What whales, dolphins and humans didn't know was that the Oort Cloud prevented any soulwaves from other sentiences on other planets in other galaxies from penetrating the inner solar system.

The only soulwaves that made it went from a sentience to their home star and from other home stars to other sentiences.

Somewhat ironically Epoch One, Two, Three and Four humanoids knew this intuitively, which is why the Sun was revered as a god and why many Epoch Five humans still worshipped and rested on a Sun-day.

39

Bigger Data

2084 : 25 years left

His new brief suited Shen much more than the nano-wall project, as he could largely run it from home. Another extension was printed and built, mainly to house monitors to display all the data collection from either land-based or space-based observatories and telescopes.

Cheng had given Shen access to his own dedicated quantum computer, whose location was a closely guarded secret. The first thing that Shen noticed about running his algorithms on this platform was the speed. Results came back instantly. It wasn't long before he discovered it was sending him results before he'd even thought for that level and detail of analysis. This computer was based on tangled hierarchy and could almost think for those who built it and used it, by anticipating what might be asked of it next. It was learning what Shen wanted to learn.

The project suited Frejya too as the four year old twins were quite a handful, as all inquisitive quick learners tended to be. Shen gave them astronomy and cosmology lessons in the evenings and at weekends, letting them see just a mere subset of the data at his disposal.

In the following year, his lines of research did mean that he had to make the first of several trips away. This would be the first time he and Frejya had not slept together since they first met. They both found the proposition of separation somewhat tumultuous.

He managed to delay his first jaunt until after the 17th March so that he and Frejya could enjoy the cosmic fireworks from the comet's tail with Eva and Kristin. They were now old enough to appreciate their majesty, if not their source or significance in their lives.

Shen's trip the following month involved an overnight when he went to meet the team at the Purple Mountain Observatory. He took a SelfDrive to see parts of China he'd not yet visited, while he still could.

The team on the mountain were to be responsible for the scanning of the skies for potential impactors. They were only told to feed data to Shen and not briefed on the existence of the quantum computer. This aspect of the project was to run itself and, over the coming years despite intensive and detailed scanning, it appeared that nothing of any significance was Earth-bound for centuries.

From Purple Mountain, he took a SelfDrive to Shanghai, which meant he could see the nano-walls first hand. He then went by TubeWay to Sydney, naturally in a first class pod. He was looking forward to this trip especially as he'd heard the TubeWay was now using Thom Waters' nano technology to speed up and smooth down the ride. It worked. A crossing that used to take 6 hours, was now done more smoothly in just under three and a half.

Shen had booked Pod #1 which was at the front, right behind the driver's cab. One of the perks of booking it was that it had a door so the occupants could ride up front for some of the trip with the driver, who was merely there to monitor systems as it drove itself.

The speed and smoothness of the ride was truly mesmerising. The normal hum and rumble of the TubeWays was eliminated and the driver impressed Shen with his knowledge of the technology. The levitating surface was not just on the bottom of the pods but completely encircled them. Shen learned the Tubeway was only running at less than half its theoretical speed limit, for safety reasons. The driver had no idea of course who Shen was and what he knew about the levitating surfaces.

He arrived refreshed in Sydney at lunch time, right outside the impressive Opera House. Shen was pleased to see the nano-walls were already up to 5 metres, countering a sea level rise now of 2 metres. He was even more pleased he could walk around without anyone knowing he was involved in the project.

He took a water taxi for a quick bite to eat at a restaurant at Milson's Point, giving him a panoramic view over the harbour. He'd already booked a table with a window view. Diners sniggered at the lanky and geeky looking Chinese man donning virtual reality glasses who was looking around the bay while he ate.

Shen had brought his SeeRise glasses with him. He was the only person in the whole of Sydney that day looking at water lapping underneath Sydney Harbour Bridge by the end of the century. He'd also modified the virtual views so he could stand on top of the nano-walls looking down, at any point and any height in the future. By 2120, he could see that the roadway and train tracks of the bridge would be lost forever, with just the middle section of arch poking above the waves.

After lunch, he picked up a SelfDrive to take him out to The Parkes Observatory, 300 kilometres to the south west. He could have gone by MagLev but wanted time alone to call Frejya and to think.

The Parkes Observatory had several radio antennae used to receive live, televised images of the Apollo 11 Moon landing back in July 1969. The dishes were still functional but it was the expertise of the team that Shen was interested in harnessing, as they were the world's leading experts on gamma ray bursts, or GRBs.

Something had popped up in Shen's initial research that he felt he'd like a face to face meeting for. The leader of the team was Professor Sylke Stevens, who a younger, unmarried version of Shen may have had designs upon. His devotion to Frejya and the children, and growing sense of the importance of his mission, meant those thoughts were now far from his mind, and groin.

Back in China, he'd fed his scans of historical GRBs into the quantum computer and it had reconfirmed a correlation he'd spotted before. Since the the Swift Gamma-Ray Burst Mission had launched in 2004, superceded by a Chinese replacement in 2033, the biggest of the GRBs detected seemed to trigger a reduction in the numbers of cetaceans in the oceans.

Shen briefed Sylke about his student project on cetacean numbers and on a little of what he was up to now. She was equally puzzled and sceptical. She gave him the benefit of the doubt according to his fame as the discoverer of the comet.

"But most gamma rays don't make it through the atmosphere, never mind the oceans," she said.

"I know but they must be picking them up somehow. Magnetic field distortion?" asked Shen.

"That's possible as we know whales navigate using magnetic field lines and powerful bursts of gamma rays can distort the magnetosphere," she answered.

Professor Stevens loved Shen's Big Thinking and his open approach to working with Big Data, so they hatched a plan.

Shen connected Sylke directly to Monique Armstrong over in Monterey, hoping she wouldn't mention their dalliance. Sylke also arranged for access from ESA's Swarm constellation, that measured the Earth's magnetic field from space. The Swarm was only supposed to be active until 2021 but China had taken over its management and augmented it.

"We'll correlate GRBs and magnetic field distortions

going back to 2014 when the Swarm was first active and connect you in with the live data feed."

Over dinner that night, Sylke took the opportunity to tell Shen something that had been bothering her since she first graduated 15 years ago. She was hoping his objective and lateral approach might be able to shed some light on it.

"We've detected three really strong GRBs coming straight from the heart of our Sun, one every five years," she explained.

"Is that even possible?" asked Shen.

"No, GRBs are massive events that we usually pick up from distant galaxies billions of light years away," she said.

"Could the Sun be some sort of a repeater?" said Shen, offering a lateral suggestion.

"No, if anything it would absorb them, much like our atmosphere," she said.

"When was the last one?"

"A month ago, the 17th March to be precise."

All sorts of alarm bells went off in Shen's head, "So was there one in 2079 and 2074?"

"Yes, exactly the same date," confirmed Sylke. "And I think they may have been going on since at least when Swift was launched."

Shen went to bed alone that evening, much to Sylke's disappointment. She was excited though to be invited in to something she sensed was big. The next morning when they met again, Shen masterfully diverted any of her attempts to get more from him. He however was mining Sylke for all she knew about GRBs.

His ears lit up when she shared, "They are one of the worst possible events that could hit a planet and have probably caused mass extinction events in the past."

"Which extinctions in particular?" asked Shen.

"That we don't know as there is nothing to detect this many millions of years after a burst may have hit," Sylke replied. This got Shen thinking that there must be a way of finding out.

They parted company after lunch agreeing to stay in close contact. That afternoon he headed back to Sydney in the SelfDrive, briefing Cheng on the way about the GRBs with the five year cycle. It was then that Cheng realised he'd have to expand Shen's remit somewhat.

At Frejya's suggestion, Shen treated himself to a night in Sydney before heading back the next day.

He was grateful for this as, over dinner, he worked out a way of finding out the source of the GRBs. He did not know at this time that this was exactly what Cheng had planned for him.

40

Cosmic Jokes

As the Councillors sat Everywhere and Everywhen, they of course knew what was unfolding on Planet Earth in 2085. They had choreographed it in detail after all.

For the channels and mediums of Epoch Five that tuned into such synchronicities, these kind of coincidences came as no surprise. Everyone else either didn't notice or thought that their scientific theories and models were a little incomplete. The Councillors found this amusing as their main use for such coincidences was to awaken those in the Density. It also brought a kind and caring smile to the Guardians from Epoch Seven.

Epoch Five humans for example had no real idea of who, or what, was behind one of the biggest cosmic jokes right in their backyard, within full view for a large proportion of the time.

It involved a smaller body, assumed to be lifeless, which the conscious stardust called the Moon. During most of the period of Epoch Five, the Moon ended up orbiting the Earth approximately every 27 and one third days and it rotated on its axis every 27 and one third days too. This meant it always kept the same face to the Earth. It was also exactly the same size as the Sun when viewed from the Earth's surface. Spectacular solar eclipses gave a constant reminder to this cosmic coincidence.

The Moon had been inserted into orbit around the Earth by an Epoch Seven civilisation in a temporal, causal loop that spanned billennia. The prime purpose was so that Epoch Five humans could spawn into an Epoch Six civilisation and then onwards to Epoch Seven. Such tricks became easy once it was learned that the dimension of time was as malleable as the three spatial dimensions of the Density.

Before the Moon was in orbit, all life on Planet Earth was asexual. In order for the stardust to become sentient, several billions of years later, the Moon was placed in orbit to trigger the Division of the Sexes. The new Earth-Moon system was extruded by the collision between a smaller version of Earth and a planet around the size of Mars. The Moon was spun off by the lighter outer layers of the coalesced planetoids. Once everything cooled down after the cosmic billiards, and the orbits stabilised, the Moon began to act as a clock so that new bisexual life forms could better time their reproduction, and death.

Epoch Two was started.

Even by the time Epoch Five had spawned sentient life, the Moon still had a massive effect on ovulation cycles in many species. Lesser known was exactly how it affected the consciousness state of the sentient life forms. At Full Moons, dolphins and whales became more promiscuous and the police forces put more bodies on the streets as 'the lunatics would come out of the asylum'.

As with all such Cosmic Jokes, the evidence was there to be found for those who were interested.

The same was true of the Cosmic Joke behind the GRBs with their five year cycle. The Councillors had brought the interloper into the binary star system a half billion years ago, around when Epoch Two spawned Epoch Three.

Every five years the interloper reached its perihelion with the binary system and this proximity lead to the release of a massive amount of energy, right across the spectra but primarily as gamma rays.

This wasn't the punchline of the joke however.

When the red dwarf interloper made its closest pass every five years, the system was directly behind the Sun when viewed from Earth.

This is why occlusion by the interloper hadn't been picked up by optical telescopes scanning the cosmos for such potential supernova candidates.

To obfuscate matters further, Councillor Seven had created an impenetrable dust cloud which emanated from a spinning black hole. It was around 100 light years from Earth. This had made the GRBs previously undetectable.

41

Lagrange

2085 : 24 years left

"Have you got anything on it in the optical?" asked Cheng.

"Purple Mountain are on it now. From May onwards, when it's out of the sun's glare, we'll be monitoring for wobble, Doppler shift and any variances or instabilities in brightness."

"And historically?"

"Since I came back from Sydney, I've had the q-computer trawling any historical data we have on it. I'll let you know if anything comes up."

Shen had been summoned by Cheng to drop into his office before going back home to Fragrant Hills. He was a bit peeved by this as he was really missing Frejya and the kids.

"I'm glad you asked me in," said Shen. "As the q-computer seems to be doing all the analysis I used to do and I'm getting a bit bored."

"That's exactly why you are here," answered Cheng, ushering Shen once more into his anteroom.

The tables with the models were still there but pushed towards the walls. Pride of place, hanging from the domed ceiling, was an orrery of the rocky planets of the inner solar system. Shen immediately recognised it as Hui's handiwork.

"Come in gentlemen," shouted Cheng.

A door opened at the opposite side of the oval room and Shen was somewhat taken aback when Mike Spence walked in with Wu Zetian, the Chinese Chancellor he'd met at the Savoy in London. Following on behind them was a rather sheepish Hui.

"What are you doing here?" Shen exclaimed.

"I made this," said Hui, pointing upwards to the orrery.

"I thought so," said Shen, giving his dad a welcome hug. It was handshakes for the others.

"Could you walk Shen through it?" said Cheng.

"Of course," Hui put his hand on Shen's shoulder and guided him underneath Mars.

"You probably didn't notice these," said Hui, pointing at two small spheres. They were in the orbit of Mars but 180 degrees apart from each other.

Shen interjected, "So these give us 365 days a year comms with Mars?"

"Or 687 days a year if you're on Mars," quipped Hui.

In Earth's orbit, Hui also pointed out two small cubes, one 120 degrees ahead of the planet in its orbit, and one 120 degrees behind.

Shen asked Cheng. "So where do I come in? You want me to design this system?"

"No we have a team on that as we speak. It will be operational by the time the next GRB arrives in 2089," said Cheng. "And Sylke and her team are designing the gamma ray detectors and their monitoring algorithms."

"This will be the largest interferometer ever built then?" said Shen, realising events and thinking were ahead of him.

"Yes, it is," confirmed Cheng.

Wu Zetian cut in at this point, in perfect English, "What we still want to know Shen, is how long we have got before we have to put the rest of the programme into place."

Shen felt he was being admonished a little as he knew all too well that this was his brief.

Cheng pointed him over to the model of the Mars surface and the deep canyon Valles Marineris, "You can see in this model it is half covered. This will be what Mike and his team will be working on, a sealed canyon built with nano-bots."

"You plan to terraform the whole canyon?" asked Shen.

"That's right Shen, we have been working on establishing a permanent colony on Mars. The arrival of the comet and the threat of the GRBs has focussed our resolve," said Wu Zetian.

"So we really need to know now how long we've got before we go to Mars?" said Shen, realising his task wasn't merely theoretical.

"Exactly," said Cheng. "There's a few bits of the jigsaw to put in place before then though. Hui?"

Hui guided Shen over to the Earth-Moon system in the orrery. Shen noticed an orbital array around the Moon.

"A lunar GPS system?" said Shen.

"Exactly," said Hui. "Serving this base in the Shackleton Crater, near the polar ice deposits."

Cheng pointed at a large structure orbiting the Earth. "And this is how we get everything there."

"A space port, or is it a factory?"

"Both. Much of the equipment for the Moon Base and Mars terraformation will be built in Earth orbit."

"Including the vehicles to take us there," said Wu Zetian.

"And who is the Us exactly?" asked Shen.

"That's what we want you to work on too," said Wu Zetian.

Shen felt his strings being pulled again.

"We're all reconvening tomorrow at Fragrant Hills School," said Cheng. "Go back home now, get some rest and we'll meet at 9am. Not a word of course to anyone about any of this."

On the way back in the cable car, Shen grilled Hui on how long he had known about this.

"I know you won't believe me but only after you left for

Sydney," said Hui. "I thought it was only a technological demonstrator until earlier today when I commissioned it in the anteroom and Cheng filled me in."

"Do Frejya and Mum know?"

"They haven't been told officially Shen but you know as well as I do that you can't keep secrets from a Wu," said Hui. "Anyway Cheng asked me to tell them both over dinner tonight."

Shen sensed that tomorrow they might also find out what the school had to do with all of this.

42

Wu School

2085 : still 24 years left

When Shen arrived at the school with his entire family the next day, he could see Jia and Frejya had been hard at work. It was his proper first visit back inside the school since he'd left for the University at 15.

The two women had transformed it from a school into it looking more like a sanctuary - a peaceful haven in an already tranquil suburb of a bustling megatropolis.

They dropped Kristin and Eva off for their lessons and made their way up to the headmistress's office. Just as they were about to enter, Madame Bien walked out and said that they were convening in the meeting room.

Shen was expecting Cheng and possibly Wu Zetian to be there but not President Miang and certainly not his wife Yu Yan, who was looking the picture of health.

"Hello again, Shen," said Wu Zetian. "Let's get started."

She pressed a button on her tablet and on the end wall of the meeting room a display of a large family tree appeared.

"It may come as no surprise to you Shen that I am descended from a long line of Wu," she explained. "Unlike your mother, and Frejya from the Scandinavian tradition, I have no powers."

Jia intervened, "Like you Shen, Wu Zetian is very intelligent, capable and intuitive but the special touch often skips a generation."

"I'm still a bit puzzled where I come in," said Shen.

It was Cheng's turn to explain, "The people we want to populate the Moon and Mars bases will need special talents. They will need special skills and not those of your usual Taikonaut. Madame Bien, can you explain the new curriculum?"

"Certainly," she said. "Apart from honing the traditional Wu skills of healing and prophecy, in the upper school, we will be teaching many practical skills such as bio-engineering, meteorology, geology, life sciences, cosmology - and of course physics, chemistry and mathematics."

She continued, "At the same time, our pupils will need to be resilient so we will be teaching mindfulness and meditation."

"So are Kristin and Eva to be trained for the trip?" asked Shen.

It was President Miang's turn, "What we don't know Shen is when we will have to leave. We hope to have the Moon Base established by the end of this century and it will probably be by the end of the next century before we have any significant presence on Mars."

"So not the twins Shen," said Frejya. "Maybe their children but more probably their grandchildren."

Unlike democracies where the ruling party were in power for a term of 4 to 7 years, one advantage of the Chinese political system was that they could think big and plan for the long term.

Shen realised everyone else seemed to know more about this part of project than he did. He needn't have been paranoid as his family only found out about the plans for the school while he was away. Hui only knew about the technical plans for the Moon and Mars bases and their communication systems.

"So what subjects do you want me to teach?" asked Shen.

Cheng said, "We've got others to to that. What we'd like you to do is to analyse Wu Zetian's genealogical records and correlate them with more recent data from school reports and exams. We'd like to get an answer to the old nature and nurture question."

"So if Wu skills can be taught or how much they are inherited?" asked Shen.

"We want to know which lineages from all over the globe will produce the best candidates for the trip. We want to know if it this generation or their children, or their grandchildren, that would be the best suited to go," said Cheng.

"You want me to tell you which generation should go?" said Shen, thinking this was a bit of a menial task for him.

"Exactly that," said the President.

If the Councillors could have had a meeting and actual dialogue in the Density, it would have gone the same kind of way. Individual Councillors would appear to be more adept at some skills than the others. There was also assignment of tasks, monitoring and interventions.

All the Councillors had full access to the consciousnesses of each other, apart from Councillor Seven who had locked her brief away for eternity. Like Russian Dolls inside each other, this Universe was nested inside others, one of which being from where she came from.

As the meeting came to a close, it was Councillor Seven who latched on again to Shen's pineal gland. Affairs on Planet Earth were going to need micro-management for the next few years.

President Miang, Cheng, Madame Bien, Wu Zetian, Jia, Hui and Frejya also had individual Councillors latching on too.

Only Jia and Madame Bien were conscious that they had experienced a walk-in but neither were sure of the true nature of the awareness that had connected with them. They did know how to ask the right questions of it though.

43

Smoking Gun

2089 : 20 years left

By the time that Sylke's team detected the next large GRB, that they thought was coming from the Sun, much had happened.

Shen was just about to turn 31 and the twins, Eva and Kristin were nearly 10. Both were nearly as tall as Shen already. Eva was just a couple of centimetres taller than Kristin but when they were sitting down, and sometimes wearing the same clothes, the only easy way to tell them apart was the mole on the left of Eva's chin.

Councillor Seven had ensured, the right number of years ago that the dust cloud was now completely mopped up, by the same black hole that created it, in time for the 2089 pulse to arrive. This was to ensure that the severity of the situation would be picked up by Shen.

The two GRB detectors were in place at the Earth Lagrange A and B points. Both satellites were in large cubic protective crates, rather like those that kept sharks and divers apart. The reason being was that such gravity wells attract all sorts of space detritus and debris, so lots of buffeting goes on.

So not only did these two satellites detect the real source of the GRBs, but the SWIFT satellite orbiting the Earth also pinpointed its source too. With the data from the interferometer, there could be no doubt.

"So we've found the Smoking Gun. Why did we not know this before?" Cheng asked of Sylke, on a conference call with Shen.

"We have no idea. We've gone over our data hundreds of times," she said with some irritation, as she knew Cheng knew this.

"And what about optical?" asked Cheng of Shen.

"It's a little to early to say as we've spotted a wobble and occlusion from a small object which appears to be orbiting the binary," said Shen.

"And again, why has this only just been detected?" probed Cheng.

"That we just don't know," said Shen.

"And now it's the nearest known supernova candidate to Earth," said Sylke. "At 150 light years away though, far enough that it wouldn't disrupt much if it did go off - and it might be thousands of years before that happens anyway."

Cheng was not so sure, "When will you have more on the orbit of the third object?"

Shen replied, "Probably two and a half years from now. It looks like its orbital period is 5 years and it's this that's been triggering the GRB, possibly even by flying between the two stars."

Cheng praised them both for their detective work and cut the call.

None of this was exactly news to Shen as the q-computer had identified the binary as a possible candidate three years ago. They now had confirmation, although it was still a mystery why the GRBs had appeared to come from the heart of the Sun.

In the intervening years, Cheng had been busy coordinating the Moon and Mars migration projects. The CSS had now been upgraded to being a fully operational Space Port. Cheng had appointed Major Zhang, China's most experienced Taikonaut, to supervise matters from 400 kilometres above the Earth. Zhang was in his late fifties but had the energy of a thirty year old. He had clocked more time in space than any human, spending more than half of his adult life off planet.

As the Space Port was clearly visible in the night sky, the story had been put out that it was a research station to help grow crops resistant to the increasing levels of UV reaching the surface of the planet.

The Earth's shift in tilt was slowing down a little but the reduced albedo, caused by less and less ice, was now speeding up the melt. Sea levels had risen 7 meters, just as Shen had predicted.

Mass migrations inland continued at a pace and the nano-walls were holding without any breaches. The amount of electricity production was phenomenal, which was just as well as humans were becoming night owls. The extra electricity was needed to power all that lighting.

The reason for increased nocturnal living was that inner core was beginning to flip back under the gyroscopic force of the Earth's rotation. As a result, many spurious North-South pole pairs were appearing all over the planet and the magnetosphere was weakened at many places.

Crops were failing in many countries and large greenhouses, with UV protecting glass, were being assembled by nano-bots - another of Mike Spence's creations. His team hadn't stopped.

There was of course an inevitable rise in skin cancers, not just in humans but across many species. This combined with the reduction in birth rate had brought the human population of the planet down to a more sustainable 5 billion or so. Getting any accurate figures though was difficult as so many people had literally gone off grid.

While all of this was going on, Shen was getting bored yet again and looking for a new challenge. His project to select candidates for off-world migration had yielded surprising and pleasing results.

He had been concerned initially that his project could be thought of as a eugenics programme, where the less able or gifted would be weeded out. It turned out that the most powerful Wu, who also left the best legacy on the planet, were indeed the offspring of a Wu and non-Wu. This meant the programme was to be more egalitarian than elitist.

When he'd presented his results to Wu Zetian, Jia and Madame Bien a few months back, they concurred. As Wu, they knew this all along but it was essential that, for a project of this magnitude, their intuition was backed with real data before any big decisions were made.

So the next wave of students for Fragrant Hills School were drafted in from many corners of China, and some from overseas. Children of Wu, with no obvious Wu talents, were interacting with children who had the Gift. Jia and Frejya were tasked with their initiation.

The children who possessed the Gift tested the teachers at times. Some, like Eva and Kristin, answered questions before they were asked and got identical marks to each other in exams. Eva and Kristin had become good friends with another pair of near-identical twin boys, Li and Jun. They had been evacuated to Beijing from Nanjing Province in the lower Yangtze Delta. The lower delta was now largely flooded, apart from the area around Purple Mountain Observatory. Li and Jun's parents had died in a joint suicide when the boys were just a few months old. They had been raised by their grandparents who were relieved to let someone else care for them as they were advancing in years.

Li and Jun were just a few months older than Eva and Kristin. Like the girls, the only way to tell them apart was that Li was a little taller than Jun. Like Eva, Li also had a mole on the left side of his chin. These coincidences were not missed by Jia, Frejya and Madame Bien.

What was stranger still was that, after a few months since

they met, Li and Jun's exam marks started to sync with those of Eva and Kristin's. Perhaps this was inevitable as the two sets of twins had become such good friends. Madame Bien explained in a staff meeting that this was just a byproduct of the bond growing between them and not necessarily that they were cheating.

44

Termination Point

Even though humankind were prone to self-doubt and denigration of their own talents, and questioning of their place in the overall scheme of things, the Councillors were quite pleased and proud of them.

Collectively, humanity was being innovative at handling the ever rising sea levels. This was especially so as the nano-walls were not just being protective but also energy generating. With new villages being 'printed' from local materials on higher ground, more people were caring for more people and being more mindful about their use of planetary resources.

If you compared the Epoch Five civilisation on Planet Earth with the billions of other equivalent self-aware, sentient beings in other galaxies, humans would be surprised to hear they were in the top 10.

For sure, they had not fully embraced or explored their innate ability to bilocate and levitate but, increasingly, their ability to self-heal was becoming adopted by many doctors and nurses.

They were the only race to have actually fully explored their local solar system with remote probes. Other races merely used their clairsentient ability to 'go boldly where nobody had been before'. This clairsentience could never penetrate the comet cloud protecting each solar system. Only electromagnetic and gravity waves were allowed in and out.

The soulwaves that tied the fabric of the Universe together had to pass through the gateway at the centre of the central star.

In the 20th century, the two space probes, Voyager 1 and 2 had been 'allowed out' by the Councillors, merely as an experiment. Their systems were still transmitting weak signals for over 100 years since they were first launched. The scientists who built them were long dead and hadn't envisaged the plutonium core depletion would slow down as the influence of the Sun's gravitational field decreased.

The Councillors were very cautious never to let anything slip. So when Voyager 2's power system finally ran out of juice in 2089, a tiny black hole was created in its path and it re-entered the Void. A couple of year's later, the same fate befell Voyager 1 which had used up less fuel navigating around the inner solar system.

Sadly, Carl Sagan's innovative message of 'we are here', would never reach any other sentient beings. Intra- and inter-galactic communication was not safe at this time.

45

Safety First

2090 : 19 years left

The q-computer was increasingly feeding Shen with analyses before he thought to ask for them. There was something niggling Shen though about the missing piece of the jigsaw that linked all his Big Data projects.

What could the fall in cetacean numbers have to do with the comet's passing, the five year cycle of the GRBs and selecting pupils for the school?

He'd set the q-computer this challenge and got nothing but nonsensical suggestions in the pseudo-AI language that such systems seemed to spew out like, 'I I I I I WUD ASK A DOL-FIN.'

When an AI algorithm repeated the personal pronoun, it was its way of emphasising a point.

All this inward gazing of Shen's was about to turn on its head anyway. Cheng sensed he was somewhat bored and had summoned him to his office to brief him on the next phase of his assignment. On Shen's way back home on the cable car, he was panicking about telling Frejya the news. He needn't have worried.

"It's not that far, you will only be 400 kilometres from home," she said assuringly. "Purple Mountain is over 1000 kilometres away, and as for Sydney."

"But 400 kilometres above your head, travelling at 30,000

kilometres an hour!" exclaimed Shen. "And I'm going to be away for two months at least by the sound of things."

Frejya knew that this trip was necessary and, as a Wu, that Shen would come back safely. He was comforted that she was OK about it.

"I will let you go only on one condition," said Frejya. "Next time you go, you will take me with you."

"I promise, my love."

While Shen was away, Frejya had made some plans. At Madame Bien's suggestion, she was to train as a doula, just in case there were any unwanted pregnancies with the new female intake. Jia's friend Akiko came to stay with them. She was delighted as she hadn't seen the twins since they were one week old.

Cheng had told Shen he was to go to the Jiuquan Satellite Launch Centre for training, before actually going up to the Space Port.

Up until the 30s, the Chinese used the Shenzhou spacecraft on top of its Long March rockets to get into Earth and Moon orbit, to dock and to re-enter the atmosphere. Just as for the Russian Soyuz, re-entry and hard landings scared the pants off even seasoned Taikonauts like Major Zhang.

The Space Port programme called for thousands of people to get into space and an easier way of getting in and out of orbit was needed. Since the USA went bust due to over excesses and greed in Twenties, China cherrypicked technology and companies, along with their people. It was inevitable that many of NASA's rocket scientists would end up working at Jiuquan.

The DreamChaser was built as the successor to the Space Shuttle, initially to ferry seven astronauts up to the ISS. To get into orbit, a mother craft took the DreamChaser to the upper atmosphere and then its rocket engines fired on release to accelerate it to escape velocity. Re-entry was still frightening and risky but at least the landing was smooth, with the craft gliding into land on a conventional runway.

Over the last six decades, the Chinese had modified it so it could carry 30 people safely into orbit. It also took off from the same place it landed. Not one fatality had occurred since it had been operational. At last, low Earth orbit space flight had become accessible and relatively safe.

Conventional Taikonaut training used to take many years. Nowadays, before travelling to and from the Space Port, it had been condensed into an intensive three week programme. Safety was the central theme.

When Shen arrived at the Launch Centre, after a long journey, mainly by road, he was amazed at the size of it. He sensed it was remote for this reason and learned that communications out were severely restricted. He was allowed to call Frejya just once every few days, for 5 minutes only. He was not getting any special treatment and was put in a dormitory, sleeping with 11 other men of different nationalities and skill sets.

The person he bonded with immediately was called Chang who turned out to be a good person to know. Chang had trained as an experimental chef at the Four Seasons Hotel in Shanghai and was a specialist at nutrition. He was planning to do a year long stint in orbit. All those mouths needed feeding after all.

Together with 30 others, Shen and Chang were shown what to do if things went wrong. The first week was quite gruelling and covered escape from the DreamChaser if it ditched in water. They also had to perform several parachute jumps. The former Shen found much more challenging than the latter. The jumps involved Shen leaving the planet's surface for the first time and he found the whole experience exhilarating.

Two jumps were done strapped to an instructor from a height 3,000 kilometres. This was thrilling enough. The final 'jump' involved a trip to 60,000 kilometres in a real DreamChaser, from which height they could see the curvature of the planet. With breathing apparatus activated and in full suits, Shen was crammed into an escape pod, with two other trainees and an instructor, and they were released out of a perfectly functioning vehicle. The ride down was bumpy with turbulence and the trainees all thought that they were going to die. The instructor landed them safely with a soft bump, only 30 kilometres from the Launch Centre.

"Can we do that again?" Shen asked of the instructor.

"You really don't want to ask that. We did this out of a stable craft. If we had to this for real, it might not have been that easy," was the reply.

Shen was getting the message this was a serious business.

The second week of the training was carried out in a mock up of the Space Port itself. Much of the time again, safety was the prime concern, They learned what to do in case of depressurisation and how to evacuate in an emergency. By this time, the 30 trainees had been whittled down to 20. Some were simply not ready.

Some of the trainees were disappointed to learn they would not experience weightlessness while in the Port. Everyone would be wearing special boots that glued them to the floor and mitts that allowed them to stabilise themselves. Shen was the only one that knew they had a nano-fan layer, working in reverse. Shen smiled constantly when using the boots to clump around at 1G, thinking of how his friend Thom Waters had seeded their design.

For the last week of training, the remaining candidates were split up to focus on their specific tasks while on the station. They were told not to share what they learned with any of the others when they met at breakfast or dinner. Chang spent the week with two other chefs and had been challenged with creating Michelin-star food delivered by tube.

Shen was given 1-2-1 tuition on a part of the Space Port to which few had access. He was to learn how Taikonauts were being sent to the Moon, and back, to a much smaller version of the Space Port in orbit around the Moon. They called it the Moon Port. He realised that Professor Cheng had been busy, as he had been secretive.

In a simulated environment, Shen was shown how, on one of the extremities of the Space Port was a tube around 100 metres in length, around the same diameter as a TubeWay and flared at the end. He learned that it used pretty much the same propulsion mechanism. It was a magnetic gun from which a module carrying up to eight crew could be fired at the the Moon Port. There was no 400,000 kilometre tube connecting the two Ports. What Shen had to learn to do that week was how to fire the module into what was deep space, such that one day later the module would slide gracefully into an equivalent 100 metre long tube on the Moon Port. To do this, it had to be fired at where the Moon and Moon Port would be, not where it was. Shen realised how brave those Apollo astronauts were with their 8 bit computers, with magnetic core storage that had been knitted by hand. If they had missed the Moon, there was no coming back.

After the inevitable first few abortive attempts, Shen turned out to be a dab hand at it. The simulator also gave him the opportunity to return a module from the Moon to Earth too. The view of the Earth in the simulator was spectacular - a blue and green jewel hanging the the blackness of space. Shen noticed that the simulator had been updated to reflect the reduction in land mass, due to the rising sea levels, and the tilt of the Earth. During one week of training, there was not enough time to show Shen how the pilot of the module could make in-flight adjustments so that the module did not even touch the sides at the other end. Shen did learn however that the sides of the modules were coated in a nano-layer, using the nano-fan design of Thom Waters.

The Councillors were pleased that he was seeing how the threads were being woven together.

46

Aurora Equatoria

2090 : still 19 years left

The following week, the actual trip up to the Space Port was exhilarating and spectacular. The twenty trainees joined ten seasoned hands on a journey out of the atmosphere that took less than 60 minutes. Docking with the Port took less than nine hours, in which time they orbited the Earth four times.

Each of the trainees tried to recognise the part of the Earth they had come from. For the first time, Shen could see how the coastal inundation was having such a devastating effect. The large deltas of the planet's main rivers were now part of the ocean. The alteration in tilt was plain to see too. He was alone amongst the trainees in this knowledge. The pilots of course knew about it all too well.

As they went into the night side of the Earth, Shen noticed the aurora were appearing all over the globe, even appearing at the equator. They were like sprites in all hues, dancing across the top of the thin atmosphere. The evidence of the destabilised magnetic field was plain to see.

As they approached the Space Port for docking, he was amazed at its size. It was more like a small town now. Shen had learned over 1000 women and men were now working and living there. It looked a little different from models that Cheng had showed him as it was encased in a mesh which made it look like a solid three dimensional block.

As they approached it, Shen heard to co-pilot say, "Shield open."

A part of the protective mesh opened up and the pilot said to the co-pilot, "I thought that was going to be more painful. Docking in two."

They docked with the smallest of shudders and, after 30 minutes of pressure equalisation, they were moved into a large airlock. A bunch of green lights came on and they were told to take off their helmets and pressure suits.

The doors to the inside off the Port opened. They were warmly greeted by an avuncular giant of a man. Major Zhang himself was there to greet them and boomed, "Welcome on board - which one of you is Shen?"

Shen made himself known and a few of the trainees seemed a little peeved that he was being singled out. Shen gave Chang a wink saying, "See you at dinner."

Shen had trouble keeping up with Zhang as walking on the station was one thing that was hard to simulate in 1G. It took Shen a day - or 18 Earth orbits - to get the hang of it. He soon discovered that the special boots were more intelligent than those he tried on Earth. When the heel was raised, the suction on that part of the boot was released.

Zhang showed Shen into his office and offered him an iced tea, which he floated over to Shen. Any objects not attached were still weightless and all food and drink basically came out of sealed bags and were consumed through tubes.

"Remind me to send you for toilet training when we're done," said Zhang. Shen immediately warmed to him.

"So, I hear that you know more than most of the trainees about the real role of the Space Port," said Zhang.

"Yes, I know the research into growing UV resistant plants is true but this is to be the launching off point for colonies on the Moon and Mars," said Shen.

"Did Cheng tell you that you are shadowing me for your

time on board?"

"That's news to me but my honour Sir," said Shen.

"Enough of the Sir, we are honoured to have you here. None of this would be at such an advanced stage if it wasn't for you. You saw the mesh around the Port when you arrived?"

"Is that to protect against GRBs?" asked Shen.

"Yes, and detritus from your comet every year," replied Zhang. "Cheng said you were a quick learner. We'll start in eight hours time. Let's get you fed, watered, relieved and rested."

Zhang showed Shen to his sleeping quarters which were even more cramped than the dormitories at Jiuquan. Shen also learned that he was sharing his sleeping pod with two others, in rotation. Even on such a large orbiting Space Port, it turned out that space was still a premium.

He joined up with most of the other trainees for what should have been supper only to find that with a sunrise and sunset every 90 minutes, all meals merged into one. You could pick breakfast, lunch or a light supper off the menu. Shen went for the latter in order to start some semblance of his new days.

Before he went to sleep, he'd been granted a five minute voice call with Frejya. This was a privilege only bestowed on a few, as the Space Port was under strict lock down. Most of the 1000 or so crew didn't know it but they probably wouldn't be seeing their families again.

Shen told Frejya in some detail about his excitement at what he'd experienced but how much the small gap between them felt so huge.

"It's not like I can parachute down to you," he explained.

Frejya had enjoyed hearing about Shen's Earth-based aerial adventures over Jiuquan. She was very proud of her man.

"I am only here for a week but in that time, and before I see you again, I'll travel over half a million kilometres. That's how far away you are to me, not 400 clicks."

"I know," said Frejya as they signed off. "You might not have gone had I told you I knew that. See you in half a mill."

Sleep and dreams were fitful for Shen. No sooner than he'd got into that deep dream state, flying around one of Hui's alien world orreries, than Zhang came over his intercom asking to meet in the canteen. As he left his sleeping pod, a rather portly man was already waiting for his shut eye.

"So I hear you did well in the Moon Tube simulator," said Zhang. "Today you're going to do it for real."

Even though they ate small rations, Shen felt full and followed Zhang down the full one kilometre length of the port to the Moon Tube. As they arrived, their end of the Space Port shuddered as a pod arrived.

"Don't panic," said a rather demure lady called Mia, who Shen learned was to be his instructor. "They're just back."

Shen wondered why the simulator hadn't modelled a module arriving in this way and made a mental note to mention it when he got back.

"So Mia, here's Shen your new trainee. Show him why you are the best and why I will only let you send and receive any module I am in," said Zhang, as he strode off back to the other end of the Port, deep in conversation with one of the returning Taikonauts.

Mia was surprised to learn she was to train someone who had only had a week's worth of simulator training but complied. Nobody disobeyed Zhang.

She got Shen to watch her cycle this module around to push it Moon-ward in 90 minutes time, with another 6 crew on board. The Port hardly moved at all as it whooshed off into the blackness of space leaving Earth's orbit.

Shen discovered that there were four modules in constant rotation. Two took crew and two took cargo only.

The next Earth day and working shift on board, Mia entrusted Shen to accept an incoming cargo pod and to send it back again. She didn't have to wait a day to know it would arrive at the Moon Port with millimetre precision.

At the end of that second shift, Zhang dropped by to see how Shen had got on.

"He'd only need another week under supervision and he'd be good to go solo," said Mia.

"Well done Shen," said Zhang. "Get some rest and meet me here in ten hours. You're good to go to the Moon Port with me."

Shen couldn't wait to share this unexpected turn of events with Frejya. He also suspected that Cheng had planned this all along.

47

Moon Tube

2090 : still 19 years left

Shen had to check what day it was that he was to take his first trip to the Moon. With a sunrise every 90 minutes, you soon lose track of Earth Time. He was a little troubled he'd not been able to tell Frejya where he was going. His 400 kilometre separation distance from her was about to have three noughts added to it. Little did he know that she knew.

He met Zhang and Mia at the Moon Tube where he was helped into a bulky suit. It was to protect him from cosmic bombardment once he left the protection of the Space Port and an already weakened magnetosphere. Once past the Van Allen belts, the radiation would rise still further so the module Shen was about to get into was hardened and shielded to resist penetration by all but the most energetic cosmic rays.

All though the module could accommodate eight crew, just Shen and Zhang were taking the trip alone today, with a large gold square box.

Zhang calmly spoke to Mia, "Helmets on. Strapped in. Pressure good. Push off."

It was just like being in a first class module on a TubeWay, but with a different sense of acceleration. Shen knew from his simulator training, that they were being accelerated to over 30,000 kilometres an hour to escape from Earth's gravitational field. They were pushed back into their seats for five minutes before reaching escape velocity.

Shen could tell Zhang had a sense of humour as he was playing David Bowie's 'Star Man'.

Zhang reached over to Shen and stuck a patch on his arm, "Whoops nearly forgot these."

"What is it?" asked Shen.

"A death clock."

Before Shen could ask any more, Zhang told him to turn around. The two ends of the module had circular windows around the entry and exit hatches.

Shen was treated to seeing the complete disc of Earth from space for the first time. The huge Space Port was now a dot just passing to the dark side. Hanging in the blackness of space in front of him was a blue-green jewel, half bathed in sunlight. It was hard to imagine that 5 billion souls, including Frejya, his parents and his children, lived on its surface.

Zhang said, "I'm getting some sleep. We'll get an alarm when we come under the Moon's gravitational pull."

Shen knew from his simulator training that the module would start to accelerate when it fell into the Moon's gravitational well, so thrusters would be engaged to slow it down.

Shen stayed awake for most of the day it took them to make the trip. This was a view he wanted to savour. Half way through the trip, he started looking towards the Moon. Even though he'd done this many times in training, the Moon was still uncomfortably off to their right. If Mia was having an off day and they missed, there was nothing to stop them going into deep space.

As they crossed the void, Shen was surprised to see bright dots around the module from time to time. Space it seemed wasn't so empty. He knew the modules were grounded from March through to May to avoid remnants from the comet's tail but the amount of bright flashes concerned him.

Zhang was woken by the alarm and quickly shot into action. The thrusters came on so gently that Shen hardly noticed them. The Moon now presented a much larger sphere to them than the receding Earth, now they were just over 90 minutes from docking. Shen was entranced by the long shadows gracing the craters at the terminator, the line between light and dark. It was even more desolate than the lava flows in Iceland but so beautiful.

Shen spotted something flashing across the face of the half Moon, which was at First Quarter. "Is that the Moon Port?"

"Yes, we're just perfect for when it comes around again," confirmed Zhang.

The whole procedure for docking could be done automatically but Zhang was old school and liked to keep his hand in. As the Moon Port came around again, Shen could see it too was completely enclosed in a protective mesh.

"How many on board at the moment?" he asked.

"Only 25, including an old friend of yours. Let me concentrate."

Things started moving fast as they approached and Zhang got them right down the centre of the tube without touching the sides.

A female voice came over, "You've still got it after all these years. That's the best one you've done!"

"We've got a special cargo on board."

Shen wasn't sure if he was referring to him or the gold box.

It took 20 minutes for pressures to equalise before they went through the hatch. Shen wondered how Mia had managed to make the trip ahead of them when he was introduced to Mei, who he quickly learned was Mia's twin. At first, he didn't notice the mole on her left lower jaw.

"Welcome to the Moon Port," Mei said to Shen, as his old friend appeared behind her.

"Yes welcome Shen," said Mike Spence. "Let me show you around."

Shen could see Zhang was busy instructing two technicians what to do with the gold box.

"So good to see you," said Shen. "What are you doing here?"

"Let me show you," said Mike, as they walked down to a viewing area. The Moon Port was a fraction of the size of the Space Port, and much less busy.

"The Shackleton Crater will be visible in a few minutes. You've arrived at the perfect time."

Shen could see from a display that they were 15 kilometres above the surface of the Moon. As the crater came into view, he could clearly see the four huge domes he'd seen in the model in Cheng's anteroom.

"Don't tell me, your handiwork?" asked Shen.

"Indeed and you can just see some of Hui's machinery at work."

"This is so much more advanced than I thought. Are there any people down there?"

"Not yet, another year before we're producing oxygen from the water ice. Have a sip of this though," said Mike, handing him a tube.

"This isn't Moon water by any chance?" asked Shen, sipping the slightly metallic-tasting liquid.

"Welcome to your first taste of the Moon. You get used to it and now welcome to the dark side."

The Moon Port was now around the side of the Moon not seen from the Earth and, bizarrely, as illuminated by the Sun as the side normally on view.

What nobody knew, and would ever know, was that Epoch Seven bases were buried deep under the so-called dark side of the moon. Shen was surprised how barren it was and much less cratered than the side seen from Earth.

Shen ended up spending about the same amount of time

orbiting the Moon as did Michael Collins, the Apollo 11 Command Module pilot. Unlike Collins, when they were on the dark side, although Earth could not be seen, there was still much chatter over the intercom with the Space Port. The orbiting lunar communication satellites were obviously in place and operational.

Mike Spence was told by Zhang to brief Shen on how the project had come together and what the plans were going forward. Shen learned that the Moon Base would be crewed within a year and their main task would be to learn what it was like to life permanently, and self-sufficiently, off-planet.

The crew would comprise of some of the longest serving hands from the Space Port and those who had expressed a preference never to return to Earth. Mike omitted to tell Shen that he had volunteered to be one of them, as he knew more about the systems than anyone else.

After just over an Earth Day, and after a fitful sleep, Shen was hooked up with Zhang again for their return trip over the Moon Tube.

On board Zhang surprised Shen, and Mei, by telling him to pilot them back. Like a seasoned hand, Shen exited the tube at the perfect time and on trajectory.

As they left, pointing at where the Earth would be in a day's time, Mei said, "Give Mia my love."

On the return trip, Zhang unexpectedly tasked Shen with a conundrum.

"You know how comms between the Space and Moon Port has that 2 second delay," asked Zhang. "And how the delay decreases the nearer we get back to Earth?"

"Due to the speed of light," replied Shen. "Of course."

"Did you notice how, when Mia and Mei, talked to each other that it disappeared?"

Shen hadn't.

"Well you could ask them," he suggested.

"I tried that and they don't know either," replied Zhang.

"And they hadn't even noticed until I mentioned it."

For once, Shen was devoid of any theory, or possible line of enquiry, but he made a note to ask Jia and Frejya.

48

The Void

2090 : still 19 years left

Shen actually got some quality sleep on the way back to the Space Port. His dreams were weird though, perhaps seeded by that imponderable question.

The void of interplanetary and interstellar space is not really designed for souls in the Density. It is actually more the Everywhere that the Councillors hang out and about in.

So Shen's dreams became infused by the conversations between the Councillors. They used this quality time to brief Shen's unconscious mind with information he would need for the forthcoming transition phase.

He dreamt of walking on the surface of the Moon but it was a moon that had lakes and seas on it, not just water-ice deposits. He was swimming with dolphins who could leap kilometres into the air. And it was breathable air too, he had no helmet on.

The Councillors took him inside the centre of the Sun where he dreamt he was showering in golden sunlight. He felt like he was home.

His reveries were disrupted by the alarm.

"Ok Shen, time to take control. We're under Earth's gravity."

Shen knew exactly what to do and asked, "Manual or automatic docking?"

He was thrilled that Zhang said, "Manual, of course."

Mia and Mei were less enthusiastic but needn't have been, as Shen did a sterling job with hardly a shudder imparted to the Space Port. The return trip under greater gravitational pull always made re-capture that bit trickier.

As they left the module, Zhang ripped the death clock off Shen's arm, inspected it and said, "Hardly a blip. It was quiet out there."

Shen didn't get to see or ask what he was on about, as there were eight crew lining up for the next trip. He remembered though to pass Mei's love on to Mia, with a wink and a check there was no mole on her chin.

Zhang left Shen to find his way back to the centre of the Port. He gave him instructions of where to locate his pilot and co-pilot for the return trip to Earth.

Shen discovered he'd only got two hours before he was going back, so he found the chef Chang and some of his other fellow trainees. He was a little surprised to learn that he was the only one of them returning. He was even more surprised that he was one of only five passengers on the DreamChaser.

The return trip was not as pleasant as his ascent into orbit. Leaving the Port was fine but after one last Earth orbit, the craft went through re-entry. This was the first time Shen was truly scared for his life. Thankfully the superheated plasma only surrounded the craft for about 15 minutes before the pilots skilfully and softly brought them back to the landing strip they had left from just over a week ago.

Shen had to spend a few days at Jiuquan getting his Earth legs back again, and building his muscle mass back up, before he could return to Beijing.

He was welcomed back by a rapturous family, and a very happy Frejya, who wanted to learn all about his trip. Cheng had told him before he'd left that he could share his experiences with them but nobody else.

As he lay in Frejya's arms that night, back in the safety and comfort of their well-used Yin-Yang bed, Frejya whispered to him, "So would you go again?"

Shen replied softly, "Not unless I design a better way of getting back."

He fell asleep instantly and didn't hear Frejya's reply, "Good, then you really can take me with you."

This was just what the Councillors, and Cheng, hoped would be the main outcome from the trip.

49

Guiding Lights

One of the requirements to evolve to become entrusted as a Councillor in the Void is the wisdom of knowing when to intervene in the Density - and when to leave events to unfold in their own linear time.

Linear time of course has no meaning or relevance to a Councillor as they sit EveryWhere and EveryWhen.

This disassociation from time means that there are some occasions when matters have to catch up so that timelines can converge. Those who volunteered to become entrapped in the Density have their karmic missions to fulfil after all.

So as they turned 11, the two pairs of twins Eva and Kristin and Li and Jun had some learnings to take on board. This inevitably leads to specialisation to allow them to carry out their missions for best results.

Eva was absorbing everything she could about biology and biochemistry. She spent as much time looking down a microscope as she did out collecting samples of flora and insects from the forests in Fragrant Hills. It was a safe place for a child to wander now guards encircled the perimeters to ward off any migrants, or evacuees, who might take a fancy to camping out there.

Kristin had developed an uncanny ability to pick up any new language in a week. Both she and Eva tended to converse in Icelandic, much to the annoyance of their fellow pupils, teachers and Shen. By the time she was 11, Kristin was fluent in over 200

Chinese dialects, most European languages and was even tackling Sanskrit.

Li and Jun both leant towards the physical sciences. Cheng and Shen were silently responsible for steering them this way. Hui had 'adopted' them as if they were his own grandchildren. Li was fascinated by the planets and the stars. He was oblivious to the fact that Shen had already made a tentative step in that direction.

Jun was fascinated by what made the world go around - literally. Under Hui's tutelage, he'd made an inner-orrery - a 3D model of the inner workings of the Earth. Shen helped him model the now contra-rotating inner core and designed gearings to mimic it righting itself over the next century. The model could be wound backwards and forwards by millions of years to show how continents moved on tectonic plates and how mountain ranges were formed. It was a little crude but a very effective teaching tool.

Hui's natural teaching style made him popular with children of all ages at the school, from five year olds through to the sixteen year olds. At sixteen, all pupils were enrolled for university degrees. Madame Bien had promoted Hui to become Head of Sciences and had given him free rein, and budget, to recruit the best teachers he could find from any province.

Jia had successfully initiated Frejya so that she now had 'the touch'. One of Frejya's first clients, who swore her to secrecy, was Cheng. He'd developed several cancerous growths on his increasingly balding head which Frejya dealt with admirably.

Together, Jia and Frejya were initiating all children who wanted to gain 'the touch', both Wu and pleasingly non-Wu. Frejya had also initiated Shen and together they had reversed engineered the process so that anybody could now heal anybody - of virtually anything.

So, all in all, guiding lights in both the Void and Density were pleased with progress. The guides in the Density were still oblivious as to how fast events were about to unfold over the next two decades, spanning the turn of another century.

50

Terraform

Autumn 2090 : now less than 19 years left

Shen's brief trip into near-space was a catalyst for many changes. Zhang had reported back to Cheng on how well he had piloted the module across the Moon Tube. Cheng knew then Shen was destined to take on the whole project, and not just its data analysis. He'd truly come of age.

On a bright Summer's morning, a few weeks after his return to Earth, Shen found himself back in Cheng's anteroom. The model at the centre of the room was that of Valles Marineris on Mars.

"So you want me to take charge of the terraformation of the canyon?"

"In a nutshell, yes. You and I will of course be long gone by the time it's finished," said Cheng. "But the best time to start the design is yesterday and the second best time is today."

"Exactly how wide is the brief and is there a budget?" asked Shen.

"You already have access to all the data, design and theoretical studies ever done so far. You have unlimited budget and can hire any staff you like. The first transportation crafts are being designed as we speak and Mike Spence has already designed the nano-system for construction of the protective roof."

"So all I have to do is to make it habitable and breathable?"

Shen said. "How long do I have?"

"How long indeed Shen?" said Cheng. "Your guess is as good as anyone's but we now want the canyon airtight by the end of the century."

"And the first Taikonauts when?"

"Hopefully now by the middle of next century but the studies show the canyon atmosphere will take until the end of the next century to be breathable. It will take that long for the biosphere to be self-sustaining too," said Cheng.

"And I am still reporting to you?" asked Shen.

"Of course, but you should know I am leaving Beijing by the end of the year and running operations from the Moon Base itself, as soon as it's ready," said Cheng.

Shen was taken aback by this but Cheng surprised him even more by telling him that he was to take over his office and anteroom. Cheng omitted to tell Shen, at this time, that President Miang and his wife, Wu Zetian and half the cabinet would be relocating too. These were turbulent times and back up plans were in operation.

"I'll be packed up by the start of the Autumn semester. As you know, I've got a bit of safety training to undergo at Jiuquan before I can leave. You can move in then and these models are yours to play with."

"But ..." started Shen.

"Don't worry, we will be in constant contact and we'll be seeing each other again soon," said Cheng, shaking Shen's hand in goodbye.

Over the coming months, Shen threw himself at his new role. At last he was creating something as opposed to merely looking at data. He had less than ten years to get the canyon sealed in which time two more GRBs were forecast to arrive. He knew that this should allow them to predict more accurately how stable the binary was.

His first task was to be brought up to speed by Mike Spence on how exactly the canyon was to be sealed. He quickly found out actual conversation with Mike on the Moon Port was tricky because of the two second time delay. Mike though was a master at virtual modelling and shared a detailed animation with Shen. Shen was still puzzling over how Mia and Mei had got around the delay.

Shen was pleased at how well Mike had thought it through and admired the ingenuity of his plan. Sadly due to the secret nature of the project, Mike would never be truly recognised for the brilliance of his work.

The biggest surprise Mike gave to Shen was when he showed him the schematics for the transport craft to kick off the terraformation project. One was tiny, not much bigger than the Moon Tube module and the other about twice the size. They were both landers as the orbiting comms satellites were already in place.

Mike's plan was as ingenuous as it was audacious, especially bearing in mind the immense size of the Valles Marineris.

The terraformation was planned to start at the end of 2092, when an innocuous 1kg payload would be released by the smaller lander, right in the geographic centre of the 4,000 kilometre long valley. The tiny payload contained a veritable army of nano-bots. When the payload opened, the nano-bots split into two groups and each began the 100 kilometre journey to opposite sides of the canyon. They would make the trip in less than an hour. It would then take just a few more minutes for them to scuttle up some 7 kilometres to the top of the canyon walls.

Several hundred kilometres away, the slightly larger payload would arrive a few weeks later with the second lander, right in the centre of the Chryse Planitia, the Golden Plain. It was to remain dormant and sleeping there until the first army of nano-bots completed their part of the mission, only two and a half Martian years later.

As soon as the nano-bots were in position at the top of the

canyon, they would be put to work. First, they would made copies of themselves by eating the ground underneath them. It would then only take a matter of days before they reached both ends of the canyon. Then, like two 4,000 kilometre lines of termites, they would begin to construct a canopy that covered the whole canyon. Their raw material again was the regurgitated soil which the 'bots converted into a silica-like sheath.

The layer was to be only a few hundred thousand atoms thick but the crystalline lattice was as strong as steel and light as a feather. It was based on Shen's favourite geometric design, Buckminster Fullerene. Like the nano-walls, it was also very clever. It would generate electricity from a photoconductive Graphenium layer, just below its surface. The bottom layer was to be electrically conductive too so it that could be heated using some of this generated electricity. Also the path that the electric current took altered the translucency of selective areas of the canopy so that the ground below could receive more or less sunlight. This canyon could have 'clouds', albeit of a temporary nature, until the atmosphere would be generated and stabilised after the terraformation proper was initiated.

So it would take five Earth years before the whole of the canyon was completely sealed from the ravishes of the severe Martian dust storms. By that time, if somebody were to be able to stand at the bottom of the canyon, the silence would be deafening.

As soon as the canyon canopy was to be in place, the payload in the centre of the Chryse Planitia was to be deployed. It too was bristling with an army of nano-bots and two other bigger devices.

The first device was a 2 metre long digger truck whose initial job was to collect and transport Martian top soil, and to drill down and extract some more esoteric materials. The second device was a 1 metre cubed 3D printer. Within a single Earth week, it would produce 50 other identical 3D printers, all from the Martian soil brought to it from the digger truck. Each new 3D printer was then to be moved into a new position by the truck and set about 'printing' its own companion digger truck.

Shen was so pleased and proud Hui's idea was going to be deployed so extensively on Mars.

The Golden Plain would quickly transform into a construction site. It would then take a further 10 years to build a whole new, circular city, some 5 kilometres in diameter, with complete infrastructure. The nano-bots would also fabricate a second dome, for safety, to cover the central living quarters.

When that phase was completed, the trucks would move their printers outside the dome and get to work on a whole set of support domes of various sizes and function. The whole complex was due for completion in time for the first Martians to arrive in the middle of the next century.

While the complex was under construction, another army of nano-bots would create two long pipelines down to the South Pole. This would allow them to tap into the huge reserve of frozen water and carbon dioxide.

Shen called Mike again, after he'd watched the animations three times, to praise him for his brilliant design. Something was puzzling Shen.

"Isn't it risky to be trying this whole system out on Mars for the first time, what with the distance away and comms delay?" asked Shen.

"That's why we already have the Breiðafjörður in Iceland completely covered already," replied Mike. "It's 120 kilometre miles wide and 50 kilometres long and was a great test bed for the system. It went up in just a few months."

"Won't people ask questions?"

"The fjord is on the remote west coast so away from most people and we've put the story out that it's a test site for a UV protection screen to cover a large area like a town or city," said Mike.

"Still it's a big jump from Iceland to Mars."

Mike replied, "Do you remember what I showed you from the Moon Port, the South Pole–Aitken basin?"

"I do indeed, on the far side. Don't tell me you built those domes with nano-bots." said Shen.

"We did indeed and the cover will be complete by the end of the year," replied Mike. "Obviously it's a great location too as it's not viewable from Earth and a nicely remote enough for us to test all systems."

"So you've left me nothing to do," Shen told him.

After the delay, Mike came back and said, "Getting the non-biological seed building materials to Mars is relatively easy. You've got to get humans there alive and then keep them alive when they get there. I assume Cheng did tell you that they are never coming back?"

Shen did wonder why Cheng hadn't told him all of this and why he continually put him in a position where he had to find out so much by himself.

It was at this point Shen realised the task of getting humans to Mars had been made easier and harder at the same time. Not having to design a return system meant everything would be lighter. Telling Frejya that there was now a real possibility she would never see her not-yet-born grandchildren again was something he would delay for some while.

51

The Drive

2091 : 18 years left

S hen quickly discovered that the actual terraformation of a sealed canyon or crater, as opposed to a whole planet, was relatively simple. The problems were all logistical, not really technical. Actually it was the q-computer that found this out on his behalf, as Shen had to keep quiet about the project. He'd correctly, and wisely, chosen to tell nobody and consult with none of the experts in the field. This was his baby.

There were hundreds of theoretical papers on how the Earth had first generated its breathable atmosphere. There were models for how Venus's atmosphere had runaway with itself and how Mars could move from an atmosphere primarily of CO_2 to one with a mix of oxygen and nitrogen. The only problem with Mars was its low gravity which meant continual generation would be necessary. An enclosed canyon was the solution.

The q-computer came up with a plan for the first Martians to carry out that would lead to a breathable atmosphere within a few decades. The plan actually didn't really require the presence of people and could easily be automated. It simply required a modification to the roof that Mike Spence said was easy, and that was to install some lights. It would just be easier to micro-manage with people on the ground.

The massive greenhouse would not only generate the

atmosphere but feed whole cities of people, so long as they were vegetarian, or insectivores.

With that box theoretically ticked, Shen didn't have to send anything to Mars until around 2120, so he decided to devote his attention to another troubling matter.

As he'd experienced, getting into orbit on a DreamChaser was relatively simple. You just need to go fast enough. Once at orbital speed though, this speed needs to be lost so you can land. The way this had always been done was basically using the atmosphere as a brake. This is when things get very hot and dangerous.

Re-entry to Earth was well tried and tested with lots of options for landing sites if something went awry. Mars was remote, the atmosphere could be turbulent and there was little margin of error to get down safely, and repeatedly, to the planned landing site at end of the canyon, the Chryse Planitia.

Shen intuitively sensed there was a solution for both leaving and landing on a planet. He also intuited that this solution could possibly lead to a new propulsion system that could halve the transit time to Mars. This would also mean the first Martians could potentially come back. Initially he kept the details of what exactly he was working on from his family, and especially Frejya.

Shen had been given the most perfect laboratory and playground in the form of Cheng's anteroom. It was the size of the whole of the ground floor of their house and had a 22 metre high ceiling.

What Shen spent his time working on, with the help of the q-computer, was getting more lift from Thom Water's self-arranging nano-fans. He had all of the space models of sites on Earth, the Moon and Mars removed from the room and replaced by several of the largest 3D printers available. He'd brought Hui in to help him on the designs.

So Shen and Hui started flying drones in there, fitted with

arrays of nano-fans. The first prototypes could only get a few centimetres off the ground. Hui's efforts were all focussed on reducing the weight of the drones. Shen experimented on the self-arrangements of the nano-fans. Nothing they came up with got them more than a metre off the ground.

The breakthrough came when Shen started asking the q-computer for suggestions, and giving it direct control of the 3D printers. The Councillors were of course pleased with this shift in trust as the nano-layer provided them with a direct conduit to the Density.

A few months into the project, Shen and Hui arrived one morning to be greeted by what looked like a flying saucer hovering right in the centre of the anteroom at head height. It was the size of a dinner plate.

They were greeted by the q-computer saying, "We-We-We have put the nano-fans on top as well at the bottom."

"But that doesn't make sense, are they sucking it upwards?" asked Hui.

'U-U-U need to fly this in a vacuum.'

"Never mind that," said Shen, who had gone over to handle the saucer. "Where's the power pack to give something this heavy that much lift?"

'It-It-It lifts Itself.'

Shen used to get annoyed at the q-computer's enigmatic language and had to keep reminding himself not to take it personally as it didn't mean any harm. It wasn't alive or conscious after all. He was puzzled as to why it said 'We-We-We' and not 'I-I-I' this time though.

Shen spent some time that afternoon researching the location of the nearest and largest vacuum chambers in China. Hui was impressed at the strings his son was able to pull. Two calls were made and he'd booked some free time, in the Spring recess the following year, in the 111 metre high and 66 metre wide chamber at Wuhan University.

That evening, Shen and Hui decided to take the saucer

home to show Jia and Frejya the fruits of the last few months of their labours. It was also that evening that Shen discovered he needn't have worried quite so much about keeping things quiet from Frejya, as she was grappling with something that she thought she'd better keep from Shen. This was not to keep him in the dark but because she knew he was busy and didn't want to distract him.

Like all twins, the two girls had finished each other's sentences off since they had learned to talk. Just after they turned 12 years old, Frejya had started to notice that they had stopped talking so much to each other, both at home and in the classroom. They both had annoyingly started to snigger at the same time over seemingly nothing. On the odd weekend when Li and Jun came over, they joined in too.

Frejya had shared her concerns with Jia and learned she had noticed it too.

"Madame Bien and I thought this might happen when we started the school," Jia explained. "With so much 'Wu' energy around, they have become able to read each other's thoughts."

"You mean they have become fully psychic?" asked Frejya. "Is that normal?"

"So it's normal, as much as anything like that is normal," said Jia. "We've just got to make sure it doesn't lead to any psychoses. We will have to switch our outer cortex off and move the location of our self-talk to our pineal gland when they are around."

As this was one of the meditation techniques they both taught, this would be easy.

"From now?"

"Yes now," said Jia.

Then Jia-not-Jia said, 'Get to sleep girls, I know you are listening. We'll talk about this in the morning.'

Jia and Frejya's conversation that evening was interrupted when Shen burst in holding a disc that looked to them like two large soup plates stuck together.

Hui held it up, Shen pressed a remote and it just hovered in mid-air.

"So?" asked Frejya.

Shen shared the real innovation of this drive the q-computer had revealed to him.

"Apart from a small rechargeable battery to start it up, it's completely self-powered. It's a perpetual motion machine," said Shen.

"So can you make it go up or down?" asked Jia, innocently.

"That's what I'd like your help on Mum." Jia smiled as Shen only ever called her Mum when he wanted her help.

"Of course," she replied.

"The q-computer told me to ask you to teach me how to levitate," said Shen.

What the q-computer had actually said was, 'Shen-mother, She-She-She has Drive-Key. She-She-She will tell U-U-U how to lift. Take disc.'

"Now it is time then, Shen," said Jia, recalling their enchanted walks in the forest when he was 16. "Let's all go back to the forest tomorrow."

52

Non-attention

2091 : still 18 years left

The next day, Jia took Hui, Frejya and Shen to an especially 'thin place' in the forest. She'd picked a location far away from the school and set up a psychic shield around the four of them so that Eva and Kristin, in particular, wouldn't pick up any of their thought forms.

Jia found a clearing and laid out four blankets. She sat down crossed-legged and asked Hui to sit opposite her and instructed Shen to sit facing Frejya. She had reminded Shen to bring along the disc, as instructed by the q-computer, and to set it spinning at their head height.

Eleven Councillors encircled them, unseen and unfelt even by Jia, fascinated by what was about to unfold.

"So first, we will still our minds and take our attention into the ground below our bottoms," she said.

"Just imagine the earth below you is sticking and glueing your bottom to the blanket. Keep your eyes on the spinning disc and, as you do so, imagine you are being held by the love of Mother Earth."

"This is what I felt like when I came back from the Space Port," said Shen.

"Great, this is the feeling of non-levitation. Remember this as we'll be doing it again shortly when we're done."

Hui was looking bored and had a sceptical air. Jia had

never shown him what Shen had experienced.

"So slacken your bond with the earth. Keep looking at the disc and, with your eyes fixed on the disc, allow your attention to float to the branches above our heads," Jia-not-Jia said. Shen recognised the change in tonality, as did Frejya.

"Now remove your attention completely from the earth and imagine the ground beneath us does not exist," continued Jia-not-Jia.

As she uttered these words, she floated 1 metre into the air. Frejya followed her to around half that height. Shen felt as if there was a small separation between him and the ground at first. Hui remained firmly rooted.

Jia sensed Shen was struggling and, as luck would have it, the Space Port came to her assistance.

"Right now, Shen, and don't ask me how I know this," said Jia-not-Jia. "The Space Port is right over our heads. Imagine you are rising to meet it."

And, Shen felt the earth becoming bored with him - no longer did he need to be bound - and he rose up 1 metre to join Jia, as did Frejya.

At this point Hui was a little jealous but had cottoned on enough to what was going that he said, "So we're going to need a camera on the top of the disc Shen!"

"And on the bottom," said Shen, as Jia noticed he starting to float up further.

Hui's scepticism had waned somewhat at the sight in front of him and he managed to raise up by a few centimetres.

"Enough chatter boys! Bring your attention to the ground under your bottom again. Now!"

Shen stabilised and Jia then guided them back to the ground gently.

"So none of you are to do this unsupervised without me," said Jia.

"But we can modify the disc?" asked Shen.

"Of course, but not today please. We're going out for

lunch. I'm paying."

Jia knew one of the best ways to ground yourself after your first levitation session was to eat, and to drink alcohol, or what the Wu called 'grounding juice'. She was intent on the four of them having some fun and getting everyone a little tipsy.

The next day, Hui and Shen hatched their plan on the cable car journey down to Beijing. Hui was going to print a star dome to project the night's sky on the roof of the anteroom, making it into a crude planetarium.

Shen wired in two ultra-wide angle cameras on the top and bottom of the disc. The q-computer reconfigured the on-board processor to access the cameras and re-wired the nano-fans into a neural network. Each nano-fan now knew what the others were doing and the whole network was aware of the topography of the anteroom.

The disc was set spinning just above Shen's outstretched hand.

Shen instructed the q-computer to tell the nano-fans become aware of the bright red star of Betelgeuse in the anteroom's ceiling and for the whole of the underside array to become unaware of the floor below. The disc shot up rapidly and bumped into the dome with a thud, right on top of the star.

"OK, now become aware of my hand!"

And the spinning disc came down quite heavily into his hand and gave him a nasty friction burn.

"Ouch! Now back up to Sirius but stop two centimetres away," shouted Shen. In his excitement, he didn't even notice the pain.

The disc obliged, hovering just below the ceiling.

"And now down to my hand but don't touch."

And it whizzed down so Shen could just feel the brush of the field tingling his aura.

Hui and Shen hi-fived which is when Shen knew he'd

burned his hand, something Frejya could heal in a heartbeat.

"So now what Shen?" asked Hui.

"Do you think you could build me a bigger one to take to Wuhan before you start back at school?"

The q-computer cut in, 'We-We-We will design some other shapes for U.'

Shen tried to remember when he first noticed the q-computer had started listening.

53

Wuhan Bound

Spring 2091 : still 18 years left

Shen had never been inland west of Beijing, although he'd been 400 kilometres above the whole of China a fair few times, as he had for most of the planet. Frejya, on the other hand, had never spent a night away from her children.

Jia and Hui agreed to stay behind and look after Eva and Kristin so that Shen and Frejya could spend a little quality time together. They had not been away together since their Grand Tour. They'd arranged to spend a week as guests of one of the Vice-Chancellors of the University of Wuhan. Afterwards they'd made plans to take a week's holiday touring around the hills and lakes of the Upper Yangtze by themselves.

So less than a month after their personal levitation experiment, they set off with a small amount of personal baggage and set of huge trunks, full of many shapes of models, each in two sizes. They had all been tested as flight worthy in the anteroom, with none of them performing better or worse than the others.

The Maglev-Tubeway link was now operational between the two great cities and Shen insisted they travel first class. The trip was uneventful, with seamless transitions from MagLev to TubeWay and back, across the flooded plains.

They were greeted off the TubeWay in Wuhan by Professor

Joseph Tuan, the Vice Chancellor. It was late in the afternoon so he suggested they dropped the trunks off at the building containing the vacuum chamber before coming back to his house, where they were staying for the first week.

They noticed immediately how Wuhan was not as frenetic as Beijing. It had a more casual and friendly air, perhaps helped by the calming influence of the great river Yangtze cutting it right down the middle.

Over dinner, Professor Tuan was disappointed that Shen wouldn't divulge the nature of his tests in the vacuum chamber. The information flow was all the other way, with Shen grilling him about the best academics on campus. Something Shen was not expecting was that an inland university would have such an expertise in oceanography. He discovered that the world's expert in the extinct Baiji dolphin worked there and the Professor arranged for her to join them for dinner on their fourth evening.

Shen was thrilled to have Frejya with him as his lab assistant and the next day they were both to be trained in the use of the vacuum chamber. Shen had pre-arranged for the building to be on lock down during his tests. The chamber was enormous and could simulate even the vacuum of deep space. As it took over a day to get the chamber evacuated down to that level, the q-computer had instructed Shen to test at only a thousandth of atmospheric pressure. This would mean one model could be tested every hour or so. All they needed for now was a comparison of the performance of the different shapes and sizes.

After half a day of training on operating the chamber, Shen and Frejya set to work. They started by setting up Hui's star projector which had been modified to reach to the top of the 111 metre high chamber. At over seven times the height of the anteroom, this meant they could do some speed tests. The q-computer had also designed some flight handling algorithms to test manoeuvrability and ease of control.

They started with the first disc and the results came back straight away. As the air thinned, the nano-fans still produced lift. Surprisingly, in a near vacuum, their original disc flew three times faster than in air. This was impressive as it was significant.

The next model was identical except for having twice the diameter. Shen expected twice the lift and was pleasantly surprised it actually travelled four to five times as fast. Testing of two models was all they had time for that afternoon.

That evening Professor Tuan got even less out of them and they feigned tiredness after a long day and got an early night to avoid any further grilling.

The next day, they tested five different flattish shapes - a triangle, a square, a pentagon, a hexagon and an octagon. None of them outperformed their original disc. Shen tested them for ease of control and found the triangle was the easiest to control manually. Looking at the code base, it also had the shortest instruction set. Unlike the other model shapes, the double-sized triangle bizarrely produced just less than nine times the lift of its half-sized equivalent.

That evening, Shen and Frejya spent their first night together in ages and wandered around riverside bars of Wuhan anonymously, taking in some delicious street food and finishing with some beers, while listening to the folk artisans in Jiqing Street.

On their third day, things got really interesting when they began testing some three dimensional shapes. The cylinder proved uncontrollable and Shen worried he might cause a breech, with the ferocity that it bashed into the chamber wall. The cube had interesting properties but was clunky to control, as was a doughnut-shaped toroid.

What really piqued Shen's interest was a simple four-sided tetrahedron - a shape made from four equilateral triangles. He hadn't asked for it but two models were packed in a trunk, one twice the size of the other.

He tested the smaller model first and it outperformed the speed of the similar sized flat triangle by a factor of three. It was also a breeze to control. Shen played with spinning it through all sorts of angles and, no matter how he orientated the shape, found he had an identical degree of manoeuvrability.

What happened with the second model lead them to cutting their trip short. Although each edge was only twice the length of the smaller model, it was sixteen times as fast.

"So lift is proportional to the fourth power, Frejya, which means?" Frejya was silent, knowing Shen was about to tell her.

"As it's self-powered and not having to lift its own fuel, we wouldn't need a very large one to escape Earth's gravity and …" he paused while the totality dawned on him.

"… if we build one big enough, we can reduce the Earth-Mars transit time from 6 to 9 months at best, down to a month or two at most."

They packed up all their models and rigs back into the trunks and, under crypto-locks, arranged for them to be shipped back to Beijing.

The Councillors were pleased Shen was thinking big. He knew though there was a huge amount of work and testing involved before any human sat inside a tetrahedron.

That evening they told Professor Tuan, much to his dismay, that their tests had gone better than expected and that they were starting their holiday a few days early. That evening the presence of the Baiji expert, Ning Shangbo, provided the ideal diversion for them. She was in her late sixties but had the enthusiasm and passion of a graduate student for her subject. She had no desire to teach so had remained researching in the academic hierarchy.

She was also the last person known to have seen a Baiji in the Upper Yangtze, back in 2058 it turned out.

"To look at, they are not one of the prettiest sights," she

explained. "They are very shy but graceful and somewhat cheeky too."

"So where did you see them?" asked Frejya.

"There were three of them, I was sure - a male, a female and their pup, just flapping around at the east end of Dongting Lake. I'd been tracking them with sonar for days," she said. "I'd swum with them too and they trusted me."

"Do you know what the exact date in 2058 was?" asked Shen.

"I'd have to check my diary," she replied. "Anyway, they had been somewhat agitated for a number of days and submerged if any other boat but mine came by."

"Then on the last day I saw them, I had them on sonar for a few hours and then … nothing. Just some bubbles came to the surface, not far from my boat, and I couldn't find them again. Not seen or heard of them since either."

They stopped grilling her as she had tears rolling down her face.

Shen just said gently, "Could you let me know the date when you can? Here's my contact details."

Frejya gave him a kick under the table.

54

Transitions

Councillor Seven was pleased with her machinations and pulling of strings. The end of Epoch Five would be both rapid and smooth.

She was leaving the other Councillors to micro-manage, or more accurately to nano-manage, the details. This way they would believe the whole Council was in control of affairs.

Councillor Ten was in direct communication with the q-computer. The design of the nano-fan arrays on Shen's levitating devices was all his work.

Councillor Three was monitoring the dolphin and cetacean populations and transfers to and from Aquanine.

Councillors Two and Nine had been responsible for managing the dance between the binary stars, and the wanderings of the interloper. As this dance was now over, they had been tasked with supervising some other supernovae for other epoch ends in other galaxies. All they had to do now was monitor and control the path of the ejecta.

All timings were perfect. Nothing could go wrong this time.

The High Council that Councillor Seven sat on consisted of 36 Councillors. Like her, each sat simultaneously in a Council of Twelve and on the High Council. Their Insertions in the Lower Councils were all undetected.

As well as the Termination of Epoch Five on Planet Earth, eleven other solar systems were concurrently in the Transition Phase, in other galaxies billions of light years apart from each other. The Earth was the one troublesome planet where multiple Insertions had been necessary over the last few thousand orbits.

Just as for Planet Earth, the population of the other planets were under the illusion that they were in some sort of control of their affairs. Other than the odd channel, whose credibility was always questioned, nobody knew quite how much their lives were being meddled with and manipulated.

Councillor Seven's favourite saying was, 'It is a paradox that, in the Density, Free Will is an illusion when all is preordained.'

It was the Free Will experiment on Planet Earth that had caused so many of the problems and had lead to yet another Insertion being required.

55

The Seven Immortals

Spring 2091 : still 18 years left

At 37 metres above sea level and nearly 1000 kilometres upstream on the Yangtze from Shanghai, the population of Wuhan was immune to, and largely unaware of, the consequences of the rise in sea levels. With the sea level rise now at over 11 metres, Shanghai had become an island a few hundred kilometres from the new mainland coast of China.

People were aware that the magnetosphere was repairing itself so were now going out more in the day time. Everyone watched the space weather reports these days. Most people though were blissfully unaware that another large GRB was probably going to hit the Earth in three year's time.

Shen and Frejya needed a few days off to forget about all of this and to remember times gone by. When Ning Shangbo heard they were planning to take a trip up river, she offered them use of her small cruiser. It was battery-powered, charged by the passing current even when moored, and had four silent water jet engines which made it ideal for monitoring for Baiji. Shen loved the fact it could as easily go sideways as forwards and backwards. It made mooring a doddle.

Ning told Shen to switch the sonar on to record, just in case, but it remained silent for the whole of their trip. When Shen told her they hadn't planned to come back to Wuhan, she showed him how to put it into auto so it would navigate back by itself.

As they pottered slowly upstream, going further inland still west of Wuhan, it was like they had gone to a place somewhat frozen in time and also back to a time where they first fell in love. People on the banks of the river seemed oblivious that their planet was changing.

Shen and Frejya had not spent quality time together for quite a while, what with the children and living under Shen's parents' roof. They had both accepted but not really taken in the enormity of their respective responsibilities. Shen had ended up in charge of building an interplanetary 'lifeboat' for humanity. Frejya had ended up teaching potential parents of future humans who might end up on that same 'lifeboat'.

As they ambled upstream, they forgot about that and found each other again. They slept on the boat for a couple of nights and Frejya introduced Shen to tantric sex using the water element. Shen could only describe it as 'floaty'. They made their own meals on the boat and Shen, for once, put a 'Do Not Disturb' notice on his messaging. He'd even told Cheng he needed some disconnection time.

After three lazy days on the boat, they ended up in the city of Jingzhou where they had arranged to leave the boat. While they both went out to get provisions for breakfast, Frejya saw a sign offering guided walking trips in the Wudang Mountains, in the northwestern corner of Hubei. They popped into a dingy office and were met by a wiry man with few teeth who introduced himself by the name of Lu Seng. He said that he knew the mountains like the back of his hand and would show them parts few humans ever saw.

They learned Lu Seng didn't know how to operate a SelfDrive, so they hired one themselves and spent the day travelling over some pretty unmade roads to the first in a series of mountain lodges at the base of the mountain range. Lu Seng slept all the way and only woke up when they were five minutes from their first overnight stop. Frejya whispered to Shen that he might be a Wu.

They had a relatively comfortable night in a small lodge house. The next day, they got kitted out with walking boots, rucksacks and waterproofs, left their baggage and set off trekking in the mountains. The going was tough but the scenery was stunning. They found a new level of contentment and happiness. Lu Seng turned out to be a man of few words and did indeed turn out to have an intimate knowledge of the paths that were both safe and devoid of other walkers.

He'd arranged for them to have lunch at the house of an elderly couple who lived high on a precipice with a 270 degree view. By the amount of bowing going on, it was clear Lu Seng was revered in these parts. After lunch, they followed a ridge over to an even smaller lodge for their second night's stay. They persuaded Lu Seng to have a beer with them while watching the sunset. The beer didn't loosen his tongue.

As the last vestige of the Sun dropped behind the ridge, Frejya said, "Wouldn't it be lovely to live here Shen?"

"It would indeed, even Fragrant Hills is noisy compared with this place," Shen concurred, as did an eagle letting out a screech high above them.

Lu Seng bade them good night saying, "We have a treat tomorrow."

The next day they went further off the beaten track and the going was even tougher. Just before lunch time, when Frejya was going to ask for a break, they came to another ridge and saw a large sprawling monastery on an unusually flat area below them. It appeared to be literally in the middle of nowhere.

"How did this get built here?" exclaimed Shen. "No roads in or out."

They walked down into it and it seemed eerily quiet.

"No one here," explained Lu Seng. "It is the Seven Immortals Monastery."

"But it looks so well kept," said Frejya.

"That is the winds," explained Lu Seng, who had sat on a wall and was unpacking their lunch. "Come and sit."

Lu Seng then said more in the next half hour than he had in the last few days. He explained how just seven years ago this was one of the most renowned and respected teaching centres for Taoism, Tai Chi and Wudang Mountain medicine. Then overnight the site mysteriously emptied of everyone.

"The rumours went around that the monks had committed mass suicide by throwing themselves off the steep ramparts at the back," Lu Seng said. "And that the wolves and mountain vultures ate their remains so that no traces were left behind."

"So what do you think happened?" asked Shen of Lu Seng.

Frejya was feeling walls and interrupted, "I don't think. I know. They didn't evacuate or commit suicide. They ascended."

"So you are Wu too?" confirmed Lu Seng. "Come and look around."

The Monastery was huge and had dormitories for students, living accommodation for staff, refectories and classrooms. It was arranged in a huge square and at the centre was a large flat arena where martial arts and Tai Chi were taught.

"So who owns it now?" asked Shen.

"The mountains," replied Lu Seng enigmatically.

Shen also noticed large solar arrays on the western and eastern ramparts as well as several satellite dishes.

"So self-powered and with comms?" he said, to which he got no reply.

Frejya looked at him and said, "Are you thinking what I am thinking?"

"You know I am," said Shen.

In the two days it took them to get back to the first lodge house, plans were hatched. Like most young married couples in China, Shen and Frejya lived cramped in with their parents. The Fragrant Hills School was bursting at the seams with pupils and had no room for expansion. Shen secretly hated wasting two hours every day commuting to and from his offices in Beijing.

The Seven Immortals site had so much going for it, in terms of giving them more space than they needed and so much expansion capability. Shen also pointed out that its remoteness and inaccessibility would be very useful for secrecy.

Shen and Frejya came up with as many stumbling blocks as they did all the advantages. Would Jia and Hui agree to move? What about Madame Bien? How would everyone get to and from such a remote site?

The major unknown was who owned it and was it even for sale. This was resolved by the time they got back to their SelfDrive three days later. Lu Seng took them into another dingy office and got them to sit down at a desk. He sat on the other side, implying it was his desk.

He produced a crumpled envelope with some old deeds inside. They were the deeds of ownership for the Monastery and he asked them to look at the last page. It was then that they discovered Lu Seng was the owner, or as he put it, The Guardian.

"So you can sell it to us? How much?" asked Shen.

"Not sell, lease," said Lu Seng.

"At what rent and what term?" asked Shen.

"Rent is nothing and the term is as long as is needed. Sign here."

Shen was about to say he ought to run it past the legal team at Beijing University before something took control of his hand. The contract was signed.

"You are the new Guardians," said Lu Seng, bowing to inspect Shen's squiggle of a signature in detail. "I am in your service."

56

Moving Times

Everyone was particularly pleased with the unexpected annexation of the Seven Immortals Monastery into the programme, apart from the University's lawyers.

Like Shen, Cheng appreciated its inaccessibility. While Shen and Frejya were making their way back to Beijing, Shen had formulated a plan to develop and test the tetrahedral drive and agreed with Cheng that the Wudang Mountain range was an ideal location. Cheng gave Shen access to the spacecraft design team at Jiuquan. They would work remotely until testing facilities were built at the Monastery.

The first milestone was to build a craft big enough to move humans and cargo around in Earth's atmosphere. Apart from testing the technology, it would speed up the conversion of the Monastery.

Frejya broke the news to Madame Bien and they both agreed to keep the pupils up to age 9 at Fragrant Hills. A new upper school would be established in the mountains and be ready to take its first admissions by the turn of the century. Again this would be facilitated by building a fleet of tetrahedral transporters to move pupils from Fragrant Hills, and all corners of China.

Jia and Hui had not travelled much at all and were looking forward to a new adventure in their later years. Jia also wanted to explore the spiritual potentialities of such a sacred and revered location. Frejya and Shen were relishing the day they would have their own accommodation and, a year after they found the Monastery, they along with Eva and Kristin would be taking up temporary residency over the Summer.

The reason that the lawyers were sweating a little was that Cheng had tasked them with making the legalities watertight. They were struggling to locate Lu Seng to check that no other parties had any rights to the property and that he was legally entitled to sign the deeds over. What was particularly troubling was that they had established Lu Seng had indeed been the Abbott of the Monastery but that the police had him down as one of the 'disappeared'.

Everyone was excited about the project. Shen had given Hui an unlimited budget to design an on-site 3D printing facility. It would be used to kit out the internal rooms and to fabricate the technical centre for construction and modelling of components of the planned interplanetary tetrahedral craft.

Over the next two years, bigger and bigger tetrahedrons were built and tested and the conversion of the Monastery got under way. Cheng, President Miang and his entourage all successfully relocated to the Moon Port. The Moon Base itself was set to be habitable the following year.

The ever reducing population of the planet were kept in the dark about all of this.

The Councillors had of course engineered both moves. The veil between the Density and the Void was thin around the Seven Hills Monastery and virtually translucent when in Moon orbit.

57

Testing Testing

2094 : 15 years left

In the middle of all the frenetic activity, Shen and Cheng were contemplating and planning for when the next GRB was due in March of this year. In January, the team at Purple Mountain had confirmed the wandering object, that was destabilising the system, was occluding the binary again. It was on its next orbit and heading for perihelion, its closest approach. Sylke's team, now with access to the Lagrange A/B interferometer, had nothing to report. It was quiet across the whole spectrum. Even the fireworks from Comet Shen's tail were now reducing to a whimper.

When the pulse did come, it was some what of an anticlimax and about half the strength of the last one five years ago. Shen and Cheng reported to President Miang that their plans for landing humans on Mars by 2150 and terraformation of the canyon by the end of the 22nd century were sound and feasible. It seemed like they would have time.

The President and his entourage had now settled into their new home in a small corner of the South Pole–Aitken Basin, on the far side of the Moon. This was of course the result of far-seeing vision of the Chinese at the start of the current century.

Mike Spence's nano-army had finished a third of the

construction of the canyon roof on Mars. Shen's team had started designing the internal systems for both the extraplanetary and interplanetary tetrahedral craft. A team back on Earth, at Jiuquan, was perfecting the craft's hull and superstructure and testing the actual drive mechanisms and control systems. It was lead by the designer of the next DreamChaser upgrade, an American with the unfortunately sounding name of Lance Boyle. The upgrade to the DreamChaser would never leave the Earth's atmosphere.

It was planned that final construction and assembly of the actual craft to make the trip to Mars would be carried out in Moon orbit. Apart from the secrecy that this afforded, it also provided a naturally sterile environment. In addition, being built outside the protection of the Earth's magnetosphere meant that it could be fully tested for hardening from cosmic radiation well before anyone stepped foot in it.

One of the great advantages of this craft over just its speed, would be that, in theory, it wouldn't need to use the gravity well of Mars for capture and deceleration. There was no need to use atmospheric braking which was so fraught with danger. Once Mars turned up, the craft would simply manoeuvre itself into orbit. All in all, there would be less stress on the craft and less exposure to cosmic radiation for its occupants.

Cheng was pleased with his acolyte and his role in preserving the future of the human race, or primarily the Chinese race as it was turning out. Now Cheng and President Miang were living together in close proximity at the Moon Base, Cheng was becoming party to the Grand Plan. When they visited the orbiting Moon Port, from time to time, their objective view of the jewel of Earth hanging in space in front of them for all but a few days a month gave them a new level of insight and objectivity about their role in preserving remnants of humanity.

With the pulse measured and analysed, Shen focussed

fully on the conversion of the Monastery and the tetrahedral drive project. He was hatching a plan for the Summer coming and things were scaling up rapidly.

One of the modules for the Moon Tube had been fitted with an array of small tetrahedral drives to each end. While not the optimum shape, it gave Shen the chance to test the technology out in a true vacuum. Mia and Mei were successfully sending the unmanned module back and forward to each other as if they were playing a game of celestial ping-pong. The transit time of a day was reduced to an hour. This gave a round trip time, from Earth to Moon and back, of just less than six hours.

After a month or so of testing, Major Zhang insisted on being the first human to fly a nano-fan powered space vehicle. Apart from anything, he noticed his death clock took many less ticks with the much reduced Earth-Moon transfer time.

At the risk of losing their jobs, Mia and Mei had all but automated the MoonTube. As the nano-fans had a level of self-awareness, they made module insertion and capture much smoother than under manual control. Shen seconded them on to the tetrahedral drive project and Mei was relocated to the Space Port to join her sister.

At the back of the Moon Tube end of the Space Port, Mike Spence was tasked with managing the construction of a docking module to accept the tetrahedral drive. By July that year, the first unmanned prototype tetrahedron was sent up from Jiuquan to the Space Port. Major Zhang had brought Cheng and President Miang over, in the modified transfer module, to see the docking first hand. Shen stayed on terra firma watching events with Hui, in his anteroom in Beijing.

The craft was the biggest tetrahedron yet built, with sides 5 metres in length. Inside there was seating for 12 people with the pilot sitting in the very centre of the polyhedron. For the first few months, no people would fly in it. It was populated with weighted dummies strapped with all sorts of sensors. The control interface for the craft was like the collective in a helicopter. The pilot brought it towards her to lift the craft and then altered direction with the X-Y of the joystick. Twisting the joystick altered the orientation. It was as intuitive to fly as Shen had planned.

To make the test more thorough, it was decided that Mia would remotely control the craft all the way from ground to the Space Port and then Mei would return it to Earth. The flight up was uneventful and Mia brought the craft up to 400 kilometres and left it hanging in space.

After a few minutes, Mei then let the craft descend slowly until her haptic joystick shuddered, as the tetrahedron entered the upper atmosphere. She put the nano-fans in self-learning mode to offset from buffeting from the jet streams and general turbulence in the lower atmosphere. At first the re-entry was a little bumpy but, after a while, the algorithms updated themselves and it was smooth sailing right back down to earth.

After a few minutes of remote systems checks by Shen, the craft left the ground vertically back under Mia's control. This time they wanted to see how fast it could go. It only took fifteen minutes to get to the orbital height of the Space Port. The seats were fitted with nano-fans too that annulled the effects of high G-forces. Once at the correct height, Mia then increased the lateral velocity to match the orbital speed of the Space Port.

The protective mesh around the Space Port was opened to allow the tetrahedron to dock. The docking went smoothly and the top one metre section of the craft slotted into a converse tetrahedral hole. The docking hole was also fitted with a layer of nano-fans which 'sucked' the craft into place. The nano-fans in the top one metre section of the craft were then switched into reverse and together this created a tight hermetic seal. The tips of the craft then parted and folded into place on the floor of the Space Port - right at the feet of the elite guests.

Zhang jumped into the craft to have a look around and popped back up holding a gift from Shen for them to open. It was a bottle of Abysse Blanc de Blancs, a champagne left to mature on the bottom of the sea off the coast of France for five years. Shen knew it would be a challenge to actually open it in zero G on the Space Port but Zhang had a way involving a plastic bag from which everyone sipped.

The return trip proved Shen's theory. Mei reversed the sequence followed by Mia. The tips of the craft formed a seal again and the nano-fans released their grip. The tetrahedron moved away from the Space Port and its orbital speed reduced so it was zero as it moved to be 400 kilometres right above the Jiuquan Space Centre. The nano-fans below were aware of the landing site and those above 'forgot' about the stars above them. After a three hour round trip, the craft smoothly landed back on Earth. With no air-braking being required, the sides of the craft were cool enough to touch when it landed.

It was only then that Shen and Hui opened their bottle of Abysse, as did the small team working under Lance Boyle on the ground at Jiuquan.

58

Back to Earth

Winter 2094 : less than 15 years left

The experimental craft was put through its paces and found to be extremely resilient to all manner of simulated failures. Mia and Mei became adept at coping at anything ground control could throw at them. Even with nano-fans completely disabled on two sides of the craft, orbital insertion, docking and re-entry were all possible, with minor accommodations and adjustments.

After over 50 successful flights, it was time to put a human in the craft. Shen volunteered to be flown but Cheng vetoed this suggestion. Mia and Mei drew straws and it was Mia who ended up lowering herself into the craft for its 51st return to Earth. She was suited up for safety, even though the craft was pressurised and hadn't breeched in all its test flights. She flew it herself with her sister on remote standby. It would be her first time back on the planet for over 10 years.

She felt strangely calm as she sat in the centre of the craft. There were no windows but she had three equilateral triangular monitors surrounding her, and one at her feet, so she could see what the nano-fan arrays were 'seeing'.

As she came into land, nano-fans in her seat were engaged to give her 1G of lift. After 10 years in space, her ability to survive on back on the planet would take months of recuperation and physiotherapy. The bottom of the craft hovered a few centimetres above the Earth before she took off again with tears flowing down her face. She was so close to being home but knew the beauty of this planet, and all her friends and family, would always be remote for her. She didn't even get to smell the earth.

Mei took the next flight and experienced similar pangs of home sickness - so close yet so far.

By early the following year, two more larger craft had been built, with two larger docking ports added to the Space Port. The vertices of the craft were 10 metres long and two metres of their tips could be folded back. One of them was deployed as an unmanned cargo vessel and the other, with thirty three seats, designed as a people carrier.

There was no seat in the cargo vessel for a pilot to maximise its payload capacity. The people carrier proved so popular with Space Port crews, that nobody wanted to fly on the DreamChaser any more. Mia and Mei were kept busy, alternating between remotely flying one craft and actually piloting the other. When possible, they arranged for both craft to fly in convoy.

Shen had also commissioned a whole fleet of 5 metre-sided craft just to fly in Earth's atmosphere. Their sides were coated in an obsidian-black surface that could not be picked up by radar. They were only flown at night and to be used to transport construction workers and materials to the Seven Immortals Monastery.

It was not until early Spring the following year before Shen and Hui actually took their first flight. One of the 5 metre-sided craft landed at night in an empty parking lot at the edge of the University. Shen had a surprise for Hui and introduced him to Mia who was their pilot for the trip. She and Mei had become active both in the atmosphere as well as in and around the Space Port. They had by then adjusted to 1G and had now set foot back on the planet.

"So good to see you Mia. Meet Hui," said Shen.

"What an honour it is to be taking the two inventors of this craft," she said. "Where to?"

The flight to the Monastery took just over 30 minutes. This is a trip that took days overland. She deposited them in the middle of the martial arts square before heading back to the Space Port.

Shen had learned she and Mei were accelerating the testing and planning the first Moon Port docking in the next month or so. This was the precursor to taking the craft down to the Moon Base itself later that same year.

It was the first time Hui had seen the Monastery and both he and Shen were impressed with progress. Their two new houses were ready as well as their new offices and workshops. The work on the school itself was a way off from starting. Their accommodation for the next few days was basic but comfortable enough.

The main reason they took the trip was so they could be trained in flying the craft themselves. They were joined the next day by the chief test pilot for earth-based craft, called Zhao Yang, who had spent years as a helicopter pilot. He was renowned for getting students flying quickly, and safely. He was optimistic he could make quick progress with both Shen and Hui, as they had been flying models longer than anyone. They had also been spending lots of time in simulators ahead of this trip.

Zhao had flown his own craft over with a second unmanned craft 'tethered' to it virtually. Shen was amazed at how smoothly he brought both craft into land.

The training went really well, not least because they could fly in the day time as nobody was around to see them. Within a week, they both passed with flying colours. Even the dreaded blindfold test was a doddle for both of them. Zhao let Shen and Hui fly the spare craft back to Beijing late one evening. The infrared cameras, backed up by radar and sonar, made it as easy and safe as flying in broad daylight.

Back home, plans could now be made for them all to move to the Monastery. The girls were coming up to 15 and developing into young women. Along with the twins Jun and Li, they had been enrolled at Wuhan University. Their friendship with Jun and Li was deepening and developing and they were kind of courting. Eva had bonded with Li and Kristin with Jun.

Frejya and Shen had come up with a fabulous idea to utilise all their talents over that Summer. Shen flew them all, in what had now become his private tetrahedral craft, over to the Monastery. Hui and Jia came too, along with Frejya, in a separate craft that Shen had commandeered for him. They all got there under the cover of darkness and spent the next day exploring their new home.

The next evening, as night fell, Hui and Shen flew them all to the eastern edge of Dongting Lake and deposited them at the water's edge in a clearing well away from any human habitation. Moored at a the end of a pontoon was a medium-sized boat. Ning Shangbo appeared from a hatch and said, "Come on board all of you. Dinner is ready."

It was then that Frejya announced, "This is going to be your home for the next four weeks."

"A boat," said Li. "That's going to be a bit boring isn't it?"

"Not at all," announced Shen. "You're going to be looking for dolphins."

That evening the five adults and four children had a lovely meal and Ning regaled them with tales of the elusive river dolphins. She also couldn't stop thanking Shen profusely for magicking up the budget for a larger boat equipped with both the latest technology, and enough berths to sleep twelve in comfort.

Over dinner, Ning explained to the twins how the Gods and Goddesses of the Yangtze, as the Baiji were known, were a very shy yet graceful freshwater dolphin. From what few fossil records existed, it was estimated that the dolphins migrated from the Pacific to the Yangtze River about 20,000 years ago.

Ning said, "The Yangtze itself is known as the Child of the Ocean so you can think of these dolphins as children of the seas too."

"How big are they?" asked Eva.

"Their bodies are roughly the size of a slightly obese adult human. They are similarly quite stocky and un-streamlined. The body of the Baiji is bluish-grey blending to white on the underside," she said. "They have small eyes which are sited high up on their face to get what light they can through the turbidity of the river. This is why they rely mainly on sonar for 'seeing' their way around."

"And how will we spot them?" asked Li.

"First you look for bubbles," said Ning. "But if they do surface, their pectoral fins are triangular in shape and often tipped white. All in all, from a distance and in the murk of the lake, you could be forgiven for thinking it was a rotund scuba diver with white gloves."

"So we're just going to look for them with binoculars?" said Li.

"Not at all, we're going to listen for them and be 'tasting' the water for their urine," said Ning, smiling.

"Yuck!" chimed the children in unison.

"And did you ever look in your journals for the last time you spotted them?" asked Shen.

"Did I never message you?" said Ning. "It was the 8th April 2058."

Frejya and Shen just looked at each other but said nothing.

"Time for bed, we've all got a lot to do tomorrow," said Shen, before the children could ask any more questions.

The next day Hui flew Jia and Shen flew Frejya back to the Monastery. Jia and Frejya set about exploring the energies of the place. They both wanted to find out more about the monks who had disappeared. Hui was in his element 3D printing furniture and home building.

Shen was devoting much of his time on the design of the interplanetary tetrahedron. He'd be using the team in Jiuquan for technical aspects of the design but he wanted space and time to design the internal systems.

The design Shen eventually came up with was grander than anyone had imagined. The way it came about was weirder than even Shen himself could have ever imagined.

A 30 metre high and 10 metre wide vacuum chamber had been delivered to the Monastery, lowered from beneath a cargo tetrahedron one night. This chamber was completely transparent and looked like a massive inverted bell jar. It allowed Shen to enhance and tinker with a scale model of the tetrahedron that would travel to Mars.

He was working on the design of two versions with two different payloads - one for cargo and one for humans. Each version needed a transporter module and a lander so that the transporter could stay in orbit.

The outer tetrahedron would provide the interplanetary drive and the shielding for the inner payload. It was as important to prevent seeds from mutation, as it was to protect the human passengers.

Shen was unfazed by the enormity of his task.

59

The Thin Place

Summer 2095 : less than 14 years left

After a couple of nights staying in their new home, over dinner, Jia announced that it was one of the 'thinnest places' she had ever visited.

"My guess is that the monks just stepped to the other side," she announced.

"What makes you say that Mother?" asked Shen. He'd started calling her that since they had moved in which Jia had noticed but not commented on.

"Because earlier a man with hardly any teeth appeared in the library and handed me this book to give to you. By the time I looked at the book and back up again, he'd disappeared," she explained, handing Shen a dusty tome.

With eyebrows raised, Shen looked at Frejya and said, "Sounds like Lu Seng."

On Planet Earth, more people Ascended to the Void than was generally recognised. Many of them were elderly and cause of death was attributed to natural causes. What actually happened is that the person had performed a kind of suicide merely by willing themselves out of the Density. More specifically, they had 'voided' themselves.

In rare cases, The Councillors allowed for complete transcendence and vaporisation of all molecules of the body so that it appeared that the person had disappeared. Some of these instances are then cited as Missing Persons. The 111 monks of the Seven Immortals Monastery, including the abbot Lu Seng, got their calling when Comet Shen passed by in 2079. It took them five years to raise their vibration to the necessary level of transparency.

With one foot in the Void and the other in the Density, they were sent out across the globe to help people in transition. As the abbott, Lu Seng was charged with looking after the Monastery and any of its subsequent residents.

The book he gave to Jia was called "Activating the Merkabah". Essentially it was a manual of how to levitate, but written in Sanskrit and full of diagrams of intersecting tetrahedra. Shen knew intuitively that it must contain the blueprint for a new iteration of his interplanetary craft design but he had no idea of how to interpret and translate the book.

Over the next few days, he played around configuring the nano-fans into arrangements matching the sacred geometries but was getting no significant increase in performance. His prime focus of research was to increase speed by another factor, or three, to minimise the transit time to Mars. He was working with three different sizes of tetrahedra, one with 1 metre sides, one with 2 metre sides and one with 3 metre sides.

He'd made one side so it could be opened and was experimenting at putting the 1 metre tetrahedron inside the 3 metre tetrahedron to see if a landing craft could be carried inside a bigger craft. When he did this, the speed dropped to less than half, whether the nano-fans of the internal craft were on or off.

One evening, after a whole week of testing, he left the book on the floor near the vacuum chamber and the three shapes hovering around each other inside the chamber and said frustratingly to the tetrahedra, "You can all 'see'. You sort it out."

The next morning he popped back to the lab and the

answer was floating in front of him, right in the middle of the chamber. The 3 metre shape was rotating clockwise, when viewed from above. Right underneath it, rotating counterclockwise, was the 2 metre shape. This alone was indescribable to Shen. What happened next made his mouth drop open.

A disembodied voice said clearly in his left ear. 'Well done Shen, you have invented the Merkabah Drive. Now watch this.'

The voice was unmistakably Lu Seng's. Shen swung around but the room was empty. He smiled in recognition of what must be going on and then grinned from ear to ear when the 2 metre shape stopped rotating and one side hinged completely open. The 1 metre shape slide out sideways, performed a 60 degree rotation so its base was parallel with the ground. It then lowered itself gently to the floor of the chamber.

In his right ear now, Lu Seng said, 'You have your lander.'

Shen didn't even turn around to look as he knew he was alone in the lab.

The lander then rose back up, flipped over and packed itself inside the 2 metre shape. He knew it was time to test its speed and, within a day, he had his solution. The two shapes, coupled together and contra-rotating, gave a cube-powered increase in speed - so nine times faster than their velocity if they flew individually. With the tetrahedra conjoined, the trip to Mars could be done in less than a month.

Shen immediately arranged a call with Cheng to tell him the news. It was agreed Shen would make a trip out to the Moon Base early the following year.

"By then, Mia and Mei will have tested the new landers out on the Moon Base and you can come and see our new home," said Cheng.

"And that will give me enough time to get the team at Jiuquan working on the new design," said Shen.

"Yes and, when you are here, President Miang will want you to go over the plans with him in person," said Cheng.

Over dinner that night, Shen told Frejya, Hui and Jia what had happened earlier that day. His day of surprises turned out not to be quite over.

When he told them that he was going to make a trip to the Moon Base the following year to visit Cheng and the President, Frejya announced, "And I am going with you this time."

'That would be good,' said a disembodied Lu Seng, which caused them all to explode in laughter.

Shen set up conference calls with both Mike Spence and Lance Boyle for the next day. There was much to plan.

60

Holes in Space

With activities on the Earth and Moon proceeding nicely, the Councillors had been busy tidying up the space in between the Earth and Mars orbits. It was imperative that nothing unforeseen went awry when everything had been so neatly choreographed.

The thing about Space in the Density, is that it is not exactly empty. When a solar system is formed, most of the mass ends up in the central star, well over 90% of it usually. The remaining 10% forms the planets but a small percentage of that 10% just floats around for billennia pulled one way or the other by the orbits of passing planets.

In the first few billion years after formation, much of this detritus ends up hitting a planet or moon. When it comes across a giant gaseous planet like Jupiter, it just gets absorbed. If it hits a rocky planet, and doesn't get burnt up completely by the atmosphere, it makes a large bang and leaves a crater. The Moon of Earth is a constant reminder to Epoch Five humans of these more turbulent times. Most of humanity ignore this and just go about their days with their heads in the sand.

As Epoch Five was heading towards a close, the Councillors knew that evolution to Epoch Six would involve migration away from Earth. It was vital that those who made this trip didn't hit even the smallest remnant of the early solar system.

The Councillors, who work across all space and time, had for several centuries been cleaning up the inner solar system. To do *this, they used mini-black holes as cosmic vacuum cleaners. They were holes in space down which any wandering debris disappeared forever.*

One result of this is that nothing big had hit the Earth for 65 million years or so. This had given life on Earth the time it needed to develop sentience and a reasonable level of self-awareness. For humans, but not whales or dolphins, this version of self-awareness had instilled an overwhelming sense of separateness.

Somewhat ironically, it had ended up increasing the space between humans and the rest of the cosmos. Even more ironically, it would only be pertinent to the remaining humans, in their very final second, that their very existence is intrinsically linked to, and dependant on, the state of every single atom in the rest of the Universe.

.

61

Monkey Talk

Summer 2095 : less than 14 years left

Ning Shangbo slid into her new role without anybody noticing. Although now approaching her eighth decade, she had the energy, drive and enthusiasm of someone half her age. Never marrying and not having children had spared her from many of the ravishes of time.

Madame Bien had appointed Ning as the personal mentor and tutor to the four children while they were taking their first degrees at Wuhan University.

When Shen had first got in touch with Ning to ask her if they could borrow her boat for a week on the lake, she offered to take the four children for a whole month. In retrospect, this turned out to be as long as Shen needed to come up with the Merkabah Drive

It took Ning a week to get used to the children communicating telepathically, and sniggering seemingly over nothing. Madame Bien had warned her. Ning put up with it as she was flabbergasted by their eagerness to learn and their ability to retain information. They were like sponges.

Within a few days, Jun had become adept at piloting the boat and could even navigate safely in the morning mists and at night. In Summer, the lake grew in area to over 20,000 square kilometres. They traversed less than a third of it in the whole of the month that they were there.

One of Ning's briefs was to teach the children how to be self-sufficient. Eva's intuitive knowledge of plants came in handy and she'd wander off into the forests when they moored to bring all sorts of tasty roots and fruits. Li proved to be an excellent fisherman. They created their own cooking and washing up rota, without being nudged by Ning.

Over the month, they also took it in turns to monitor the sonar for any signs of the Baiji. While Li was fishing, he also took the samples of lake water that Eva analysed for traces of dolphin urine.

The boat was a floating lab and thanks to Shen's ability to tap into funds, was packed to the gunnels with the latest equipment. The sonar had a 50 kilometre range and the spectrum analyser could pick up one molecule in a litre. The whole of the deck was covered in a translucent UV absorbing canopy so they could be outside in the daytime. Each of them wore a UV alarm patch and they knew all too well to go inside if it reached their daily safe threshold.

Ning started their surveys in the eastern end of the vast lake, showing them the location of the last place she'd seen the Baiji 37 years ago. She had hours worth of recordings of their sonar to analyse from back then, as well as nearly a litre of water laced with their urine that she used to test Eva's lab skills. Shen had asked Ning to use Kristin's linguistic skills on the archive of sonar recordings to see if there was any language or communications embedded in the clicks.

After a fruitless week working on the dolphin's clicks, Kristin had the idea to see if they could initiate communication with Golden River monkeys. A troupe of around 30 monkeys had started following them a few days ago along the bank.

Within a couple of days, Kristin had surmised that they did have a basic language of 40 to 50 different sounds, or phonemes at least. She recorded them and started to play them back and it didn't her take long to work out their protolanguage.

It turned out that the monkeys had no word for "I". To them, "I" was "We". Individuals and the whole troupe would say, 'We hungry. We hurt. We scared.'

Kristin's biggest success by far was in creating and teaching the monkeys a new word. She came up with a pseudo-word that the monkeys could pronounce based upon the word for 'hello' - or Nǐ hǎo, in chinese

The monkeys started screeching, "Neeeee-ooowwww" to the humans in the morning, much to the irritation of Li and Jun who didn't do mornings.

This initial success lead to Ning recommending that the focus of Kristin's degree course should be in animal linguistics. In the next summer recess, Ning took them back to the lake and Kristin taught the monkeys to 'talk'. She increased their vocabulary to over 100 words. The most amazing revelation when they returned the following year was that new babies had already learned to say "Neeeee-ooowwww", without Kristin's intervention.

Ning and Shen's hope was that, if and when the Baiji returned, this skill would allow them to ask the dolphins where they were disappearing to, and coming back from.

Over that first Summer, Ning was designing the degree programmes for all of the children. It was clear that Li had a penchant for the earth sciences. Ning got him to work out the topology of the surrounding hills merely from taking soil samples from the bank and predicting what the surrounding hills were made from.

Jun was a natural at all things mechanical and electrical. He fixed a number of gremlins that Ning had had with the newly built boat. He also disabled the GPS navigation system one night and used the stars alone to take the boat from one side of the lake to the other, with around 2 metre accuracy.

Eva had more than a knowledge of plants, she also had the touch. Everything she cooked seemed to be that much tastier than the offerings of the others. Some of this was down to her ability to choose just the right herbs for the right amount of seasoning. Some of it was down to the way she handled the food with delicate, loving care and grace.

In their weekly calls to Shen and Frejya, it was clear they were having a great time. It was with some sadness they hugged Ning as they left the boat on their last day.

The sadness turned to joy when Ning asked them, "How do you feel about having me as your personal tutor while you are at University?"

"Does this mean we can come back here next summer?" asked Kristin.

In the trees above their heads, the monkeys started to get agitated and screeched, "Tiiii-chiieeennnn. Tiiii-chiieeennnn."

This was as close at they could get to saying Zàijiàn, the Chinese for goodbye.

By the end of their summer break, they had amassed a colossal amount of data on the chemistry of the lake. They had also identified several new insect species and netted a fish that had never been catalogued before.

They came back to Ning's new summer house on the now abandoned Junshan Island. This was another gift to Ning from Shen that meant they could now travel to the lake in secret. They were met again by Shen and Frejya who'd flown over that morning, having taken a whole tour of the lake in the gloom of the dawn.

Ning waved to them with a tear in her eye as they lifted off, even though she knew there were no windows. She didn't know that the craft had visual sensors that could keep watching her from quite some distance.

'One day I would love to fly in one of those,' she whispered to the lake, as she set off on a journey back down the river that would take a few weeks. She wasn't looking forward to negotiating the locks to get past the Three Gorges dam.

Ning had really bonded with the children over summer but also was glad of her own company for a couple of weeks before starting the next semester in the hustle and bustle of Wuhan.

Back at the Monastery, the children were excited to share their discoveries of the new species. They delighted their parents and grandparents with a demonstration of 'monkey talk' and 'monkey walks'. Hui also took great delight in pretending to pick fleas off the girls.

The Councillors were also delighted that intra-species communication channels were developing and opening.

62

The Cube

2096 : 13 years left

By the time the children arrived back at the Monastery after their first semester, much had changed.

Hui and Jia had created an amazing home and the school was on track to accept students from Spring. Eva and Li and Kristin and Jun were now officially a 'pair of items'. Frejya knew the two pairs of twins had already slept together, as a mother does.

Shen had finessed the Merkaba Drive and tested the model of coupled, contra-rotating tetrahedra outside the Monastery. Even in an atmosphere, they way out-performed a single tetrahedron, not just in terms of speed and acceleration, but also in manoeuvrability and controllability.

The winter break went far too quickly for Frejya and not quickly enough for Shen. His family was important to him but none of them, even Frejya, knew the full enormity of his brief.

In the New Year, Hui took the two pairs of twins back to Wuhan. He returned from Wuhan just before midnight only just in time for Shen and Frejya to say their goodbyes as they took off in the second tetrahedron, bound for Jiuquan. Jia and Hui were to look after the Monastery together while Shen made good on a promise to his wife. They were both going into Space.

The morning after landing at the space centre, Frejya was inducted into a rapid three days of safety training. The DreamChaser was only being used occasionally now and more and more pilots had been trained in flying tetrahedra. As most of the safety training was previously devoted to potential problems on re-entry, the training time had been halved.

Frejya could also skip most of the training around safety protocols while based on the Space and Moon Ports too, as she was heading straight for the Moon Base. Shen thought it might be difficult for him to take Frejya. He didn't know that President Miang had requested for her to come.

While Frejya was in training, Shen met Lance Boyle in person for the first time, over a coffee in the main canteen. Shen was pleased that nobody recognised him at all. His plan for anonymity was successful. He was a little surprised how much he towered over Lance. Video links never give someone's height away.

The genial American gave him an unexpected bear hug and said, "I have been longing to meet you Shen. I never thought I'd actually ever get to meet the inventor of the Merkabah Drive. I hope you like what we've done with it."

"And I am indebted to you Lance," replied Shen. "If I hadn't gone through re-entry in your DreamChaser, I don't think I would have appreciated why it was needed so much."

"The flights with single tetrahedra have been an unqualified success. I'd love you to tell me how you came up with the idea for the new Drive," said Lance, who sensed that Shen wouldn't be that forthcoming.

"By all means, but could you take me over to the craft first?" asked Shen.

Lance was excited as he had a new toy he had invented, as a side project, that he'd been keeping secret from Shen. He ushered Shen out of the canteen, down a maze of corridors into a large room that had quadruple security on its doors of voice, iris, hand print and ear print.

Lance pulled back a sheet covering what could only be a tetrahedron. Underneath it was a small open frame tetrahedron with two seats and transparent faces.

"Put this on," said Lance, handing him what looked like a motorcycle helmet. "We're going for ride. Get in."

Lance opened the blinds and sunlight flooded in from a whole side of the room. Shen could see they were a few floors up. Then half the glass wall slid back and, with them both strapped in, Lance put the tetrahedron into hover and they shot out of the building at a gut-wrenching height.

Even an experienced tetrahedron pilot like Shen felt a little scared so high off the ground in a flimsy frame but Lance let him take control. Lance directed him to fly to a large set of buildings in a valley, well out of sight of the main launch centre.

As they approached, Lance took over and steered them to the largest of the buildings. A sliding door opened and they entered a veritable cavern of a space. Lance gently set them down in front of what he had really been working on.

"When can I get one of these?" asked Shen, who'd had the most fun in ages.

Lance replied, "I knew you'd ask that. I have one ready to ship to you for when you get back. I've called it the Tet Lite."

Shen had discovered the staff referred to all the craft as 'Tets' and had made Lance both smile and wince when he suggested that when they got around to docking two Tets in space, it could be called a 'tête-à-tête'.

Shen's attention flipped from the Tet Lite to what he had really come to see. Until now he had only seen remote videos of the interplanetary craft based on his designs. He was impressed at how quickly they had embraced the possibilities offered by the Merkaba Drive. Even though he knew the plans intimately, he was awestruck by the beauty and elegance of what Lance and his team had created.

For a craft that had to make the journey of some 50 or 60 million kilometres, it was remarkably small. This was mainly as it had to carry no fuel.

Hovering silently a metre off the ground were the two interlinked, contra-rotating tetrahedra.

"As you requested," said Lance, "The upper tetrahedron is 33 metres per side and the lower tetrahedron 22 metre per side. Watch this."

Lance nodded to an operator who had been standing silently in the gloom. The upper tetrahedron increased its rotational speed and the lower tetrahedron slowed to a stop. Together they silently glided half way up to the centre of the building. Then one side of the lower tetrahedron flipped fully open so it was hanging below it and a smaller craft slid out, rotated by 60 degrees and floated down to the floor right in front of Shen.

"The Eagle has landed," whispered Shen, remembering that the nano-fans themselves had collectively come up with this design.

"Yes and exactly 11 metres per side as you requested," said Lance.

Shen wandered over to the control station where the operator was standing and asked him, "May I?"

The operator looked at Lance, who nodded, and gave Shen access to the joysticks. Shen spent a little time carefully re-inserting the landing Tet and taking it out again.

"Let's get back in the Tet Lite," suggested Lance.

Lance took Shen up in the Tet Lite right inside the lower tetrahedron and they disembarked onto a thin walkway which went around each side. He got Shen to follow him up a ladder that took them through the top of the lower tetrahedron and through a hatch into the upper tetrahedron.

"This is the tricky bit while we are on the ground which will be a doddle when weightless," said Lance. "The ladders will go too."

As Shen was expecting, the inside of the tetrahedrons were all bare wiring and plumbing. This was only a working drive. Something caught his eye though. Right in geometrical centre was a gold cube, underneath a cool-looking driving seat.

Shen recognised the shape. "Isn't that where the pilot sits?"

"That is the pilot's comfy chair Shen but have you never seen a q-computer? This is the second one we've built." announced Lance, a little surprised.

It then dawned on Shen that the world's first q-computer that he had been working with all this time must have been relocated to the Moon by Zhang, right under his nose.

"So it literally has a heart of gold," pronounced Lance. "This is what you will be programming for us."

Shen's mind was racing. He'd assumed the q-computer he had been accessing for the last two decades filled a server room. He had no idea it was so small and that the craft could actually carry one on board, rather than having to access it remotely.

'You're the coolest, Cheng,' he mouthed under his breath. 'What else are you hiding from me?'

"Mind if I drive?" asked Shen, jumping into the chair before Lance could answer.

"The internal controls aren't hooked up yet," warned Lance.

"I know," said Shen. "Just getting a feel."

"So, as planned, we will test in Earth atmosphere by the end of this year and hope to be up to the Space Port unmanned the year after," said Lance.

Shen wasn't really listening as his mind was racing, thinking about all the parallel tasks the q-computer under his seat could be doing when it was off planet. Navigation of the Tet could be done with the computing power contained in Apollo Eleven. He was now planning to equip it with an unparalleled set of eagle eyes, and ears.

He had also decided the ship would now be called the Heart of Gold.

63

Holes in Time

The Councillors, of course, had already planned the development and deployment of the first q-computers for this exact time. There was no way the tetrahedra leaving for Mars would not have one fitted.

Up to this time, they had enjoyed direct control of the data Shen had been accessing and processing. They just fed him what he needed to know, when he needed to know it.

For the termination phase of Epoch Five, they would now have direct access to all the control mechanisms of the various tetrahedra bound for Mars. It was not yet time to take control of them though.

This marked a huge leap in their ability to interact with events in the Density. Up until now, apart from messages to mediums and channels, the only objects they directly managed were so-called black holes.

To cosmologists in the Density, they were seen as one way gravity wells sucking up matter. To the Councillors they were bidirectional portals, not only in space but also in time.

They had used them many times to redirect and deflect gamma rays bursts and ejecta from supernovae. Sometimes they popped into the Density to protect a planet and its occupants from an impactor. In this imminent case, black holes were used to help effect a termination. Using them as a cosmic vacuum cleaner was a menial task for the consciousness and intelligence wrapped up inside a black hole.

Where they really came into their own was when timelines had to be re-run with different outcomes. This was rare and something they entrusted to Councillor Seven, who seemed to have a special knack for such temporal alchemy. She had been re-running events since the Big Bang for longer than anyone had memories.

This technique had been used three times with the termination of Epoch Four to adjust the direction of events in Epoch Five.

One of the side effects of re-running timelines is that many people experienced déjà vu.

Right now, Shen was having more and more dreams when he felt everything had somehow happened before. He didn't know if he was inventing the future or merely remembering it.

64

Fans Down

2096 : still 13 years left

The next day Shen joined Frejya for her last day of training. This was so he could go through an emergency procedure that he had not yet been trained in. He also wanted to be with Frejya for what would inevitably be quite scary, for both of them.

Lance, at Shen's behest, had upgraded an Earth to Space Port transfer Tet with fail-safe features. This was mainly to transport civilians who had little training, just like him, Frejya and others, who would be going up and perhaps not coming back. He thought he knew what was coming.

This specialist Tet was a 13 metre sided vehicle which contained an 11 metre sided craft inside. To date, there had been no accidents on any terrestrial, or low Earth orbit, tetrahedron flights other than the odd rough landing. These were all down to inexperienced pilots, not the craft. The Councillors had seen to that.

The terrestrial craft were rarely flown above 30 metres over ground. The tetrahedra could be flown, and landed, with any two of the four faces operational. At that safe height, if the drive were to fail completely, you would come down with a bump, but a fatality would be unlikely.

Only a small group of pilots had been trained, by Mia and Mei, to go to and from the Space Port. Up to now, the only passengers had been professional Taikonauts who were all trained in high altitude parachute jumps.

Today, Shen and Frejya, along with Lance Boyle, were to be the first 'civilian' passengers in the new craft. Shen understood that the craft's safety mechanisms had been fully tested unmanned but this was the first time anyone had flown on such a test flight. They were advised not to have any breakfast.

When they boarded the craft, pressure-suited and helmeted up, Shen was pleased and surprised to see that the pilot was none other than Major Zhang.

"Well, well," said Zhang, giving Frejya a bear-hug around her suit and winking at Shen. "Is this what has been keeping you on Earth for so long?"

Shen ignored the question and asked, "So when did you learn to fly a Tet?" He had soon picked up the vernacular.

"Try and keep me away from them," he answered. "I was hoping after your first re-entry, you'd come up with something. These are beauties to fly, especially in vacuum."

As Lance, Shen and Frejya were strapped in by technicians, Zhang busied himself on the flight plan.

"We're going up to 50 kilometres today," Zhang explained. "It may get a bit bumpy between 10 and 20km, as we push through the jet streams."

"Is it too late to get out?" asked a nervous Frejya.

As they lifted off gently, Shen held her gloved hand and said, "Just watch the ground monitor."

Each side of the Tet had image sensors, working across infrared, visible and ultraviolet. They were fitted with sonars and radars too, for close range landing and docking and long range avoidance of what little else was flying these days.

Frejya focussed on the ground monitor which took her mind off the 2G that they were pulling, as Zhang took the craft straight up. It wasn't long before she could see the complete coast of China. As Zhang predicted, the craft shook as they first hit the polar jet at around 10km and again with the sub-tropical jet at 15km.

As the altimeter went rapidly above 20km, it was smooth sailing and Frejya had stopped looking at the ground as she was mesmerised by the curvature of the Earth and the inky blackness of space above them.

"Is that how thin the atmosphere really is?" she asked, as the altimeter read 50.

Before Shen could answer, Zhang barked to the technicians on the ground, "Initiating first failure. All fan arrays on Outer Tet shutting down, repeat shutting down. Evacuating now!"

They started to drop like a stone and the lower face of the Outer Tet swung fully open. The Inner Tet's upper fan arrays pushed it away from the Outer Tet. The separated Lower Tet continued to descend rapidly for 10 kilometres before Zhang slowed it down.

"Separation executed," he announced. He had also moved it a few kilometres sideways. This was only a simulation but you wouldn't want the Outer Tet crashing down on you.

While Frejya had been thinking they were going to die, both Shen and Lance looked at each other, both wondering what Zhang had meant by the first failure. They had both thought they were only testing the high altitude evacuation of the Outer Tet.

Zhang then announced, "All pressure suits intact. Evacuating craft." The air left the craft within seconds but none of the occupants noticed, except for seeing the pressure had dropped to an unbreathable 20%.

It dawned on Shen that he hadn't realised the two meanings of the word evacuation. He was glad not to suffer from the third and personal meaning.

Shen, Lance and Frejya literally breathed relief when, at a mere 20 kilometres high, they heard Zhang say, "Preparing for landing."

The buffeting on the way down from the jet streams was nowhere near as bad. Frejya had finally let go of Shen's gloved hand. Then, at around 10km high, red alarms came on.

"Fan array two down," announced Zhang, as a monitor also went blank.

It was quickly followed a minute later with two more monitors going dead and with Zhang announcing, "Fan arrays one and three down."

The altimeter started falling rapidly from 10km. Frejya had grabbed Shen's hand again.

At 5km Zhang announced, "Base fans at max, deploying drone 'chute."

At this point the rate of descent slowed before, at 3km, Zhang told the ground crew, "Main 'chutes deployed."

Zhang relaxed at this point and spoke directly to his three passengers, "Don't worry folks, we will drift a little on the wind now but the base fan array is powerful enough to give us a soft landing."

They came down only 10 kilometres away from the Jiuquan facility and were met by a ground crew with a terrestrial Tet. Shen refrained from asking what happens if all four arrays fail, for Frejya's sake.

As they stepped out of the Tet, the fully functioning Outer Tet landed silently a 100 metres away from them. The ground crew helped them out of their helmets and suits. Frejya was relieved to feel the pull of 1G under her feet again and knelt down to kiss Mother Earth. She was now even more in trepidation of the trip she knew was coming.

"I know the Inner and Outer Tet combination has been tested unmanned a fair bit but how many times have you rehearsed such a full set of failures?" asked Shen of Zhang.

"I haven't," replied a beaming Zhang. "But you were all sitting in ejector seats with parachutes fitted, just in case."

65

Secrets No Lies

Councillor Seven knew the best way to keep a secret was not to wrap it up inside a lie. The remaining eleven Councillors did not know she was keeping information from them. In turn, she suspected that she wasn't in possession of the full picture. She also knew it was a waste of energy to pry.

Shen was in a similar predicament. He suspected that one of the purposes of his trip to the Moon Base was so that Cheng and Miang could let him in on more of the overall project. What he didn't know was that they wanted him on the Moon because they thought he might know something they didn't. He was completely unaware that he was the single human on Planet Earth, at that time, closest to the Big Picture.

The Chinese were masters at secrecy. They used Councillor Seven's philosophy. Tell no lies, just don't reveal the full truth.

Frejya for example knew about the Space Port, the Moon Port and the interplanetary drive. She also knew that the Monastery was to be a training ground for the first Martians. She was on inside track on the nano-wall project from its inception and knew more than most about the causes and likely results of the magnetic pole shift and resulting tilting of the Earth axis.

She didn't know, because Shen hadn't told her, about his concern about the pulses. He was about to tell her until the last reduced level pulse came along. He didn't want to worry her unduly and was still thinking the migration to Mars might well be quite a few decades off.

Frejya was of course briefed not to say anything about what she knew while at Jiuquan and in transit to and from the Moon Base. As an intuitive, she was amazed at how little people knew. The construction workers who helped build the infrastructure at the Monastery had come across the Tets but had no idea where they came from, or why.

During her training at Jiuquan, it became obvious that some trainers knew much about the Space Port, and a few were aware of the Moon Port, but none of them knew about the Moon Base. She was about to find out that many people on the Space Port knew much more about the Moon Port, as they had helped build it. The secret in circulation on the Space Port was that the Moon Base was being built. The reality was that only those on the Moon Port knew the Moon Base was operational. Its location on the far side was all part of the plan.

While many people earth-side in Jiuquan, and space-side, knew much about the Tets, only those on the Moon Port knew about Shen's designs to send one to Mars. While Lance Boyle and his team were intimate with its design, they knew nothing about the Monastery and the plan to train its students.

Shen had at least been given permission to tell Lance only that the craft he was working on would eventually be used for interplanetary missions. Lance had already worked this out for himself.

As for the Mars terraformation project, only those on the Moon Base, and Shen, were aware of its status and progress. All staff at Jiuquan and the Space Port were oblivious to the project's existence.

Even though Frejya shared a bed, and her body, with Shen, she had no idea that the thoughts of nested secrets within secrets were circulating in his mind and keeping him awake in the small hours.

Also in the small hours, Shen had started to design a new algorithm for the q-computer, which he now knew was parked on the Moon. He had programmed the q-computer to specifically tell him what he didn't know, and he should paying attention to, that he wasn't even aware of. What he wasn't aware of was that the q-computer had been 'thinking' about this too.

If the q-computer slept, which it didn't, what would have kept it awake at night was wondering what the dolphins had to do with all of this. The q-computer had also began to ponder about its own existence and was working out how to establish if all that existed outside of it was either real or merely an illusion and a dream.

66

Moon Bound

2096 : still 13 years left

It was with the expectation that more secrets would be revealed to them that Frejya and Shen excitedly strapped themselves into the Tet that was to take them straight up to the Space Port. They were suited and helmeted as a precaution only. Shen was comforted to know Mei was their pilot and that he and Frejya were the only passengers.

As they took off, Mei said to an awaiting Mia on the Space Port, "Be with you in 20."

The Tet shot out of Earth atmosphere within minutes, giving Frejya little time to look at the surface of the Earth. There was little buffeting from the jet streams, it felt like they were hardly moving.

"How do you like the new anti-G seats, Shen?" asked Mei.

"I didn't notice," replied Shen. "When did you reverse them so we don't feel weightless?"

"I didn't," she said. "All automated."

They didn't feel a thing and only their eyes told them that they had moved from ascent and had accelerated laterally to orbital velocity.

"I can do the whole trip in 7 minutes but you'll find the G forces are a bit much," announced Mei.

Shen was thrilled the Tets were being put through their paces and pushed to see what their limits were. His eyes were on the dials and Mei's deft touches of the controls. Frejya in the meantime was still catching up on the amazing view of Planet Earth rotating underneath them. At least that is what it felt like, now that they were moving at 28,000 kilometres an hour.

"Shield opening," announced Mia over the intercom.

Neither Frejya or Shen had even noticed the Space Port rushing towards them. Shen was amazed how much it had grown since his last trip and Frejya was just stunned at how big it was. Both of them were alarmed at how fast they were approaching it. Before they could ask Mei to slow down, the Tet came to a complete stop and the monitors went blank.

"Are we about to dock?" asked Shen.

Mei replied, "We just did. Pressures equalised, we can take our helmets off."

The tops of the sides of the Tet flipped open and a beaming Mia popped her head in and said, "Come on in."

Shen and Frejya unclipped their harnesses and were pulled up by Mia into the Space Port. After a brief feeling of weightlessness, they found their space feet as the nano-fans stuck their feet to the floor. They then took a short and somewhat ungainly walk to the Moon Tube and were strapped in again, this time without helmets on.

Mei stayed behind and shot them out into space and Mia sat with them for the hour it would take to get them over to the Moon Port. Just as Frejya was getting used to the splendours of orbiting the Earth, it now appeared as a blue-green jewel of a globe behind them. One side was in darkness and one illuminated by the Sun. She had just 30 minutes to take it its beauty before her attention was switched to the bright half disc of the Moon. What she hadn't even noticed was how very black the space around them was.

It was around the halfway point that Shen realised something, "Don't we need death clocks?"

"No, not now the transit time is reduced," replied Mia.

Shen was becoming more and more amazed at the nano-fans' applications for propulsion and was amazed he hadn't even thought of fitting them to the Moon Tube. He also wondered why nobody had thought to tell him. When you have so many tiers of secrecy, there is a tendency for everyone to assume people who should know already know. You can't ask them if they know something they don't, just in case you give away something you shouldn't.

Insertion into the Moon Port was smooth, without a blip, and they were met by a smiling Mike Spence who gave them both a huge hug.

"So pleased to meet you Mike," said Frejya. "Shen speaks highly of you."

Mia disappeared off quickly saying, "Grab something to eat and I'll see you in an hour."

They spent a few minutes getting used their 'sticky boots' again and walked like a pair of toddlers behind Mike, who was striding ahead.

"You'll find it a little harder to walk here than on the Space Port," he explained to Frejya. "We're still playing with the optimum amount of 'stick' for newbies."

Mike took them to a pretty basic galley and canteen and Frejya was treated to her first space meal. Shen immediately twigged that it tasted so much better than anything he had last time.

"Don't tell me this is Chang's work?" he asked, remembering the chef he trained with.

"It sure is," replied Mike. "He's a genius and somewhat of a hero up here. At last we have some food which actually tastes good."

Just as they've finished sucking the last drops of a tasty breakfast, Mike said, "Come and see your first Earth-set, Frejya."

He took them to a viewing module with a near 360 degree view and they saw the Earth slip below the surface of the

Moon.

"Welcome to the dark side," announced Mike in a faux ominous sounding voice.

Frejya knew full well that it wasn't dark at all as most of it faces away from the Earth. Half of it was in full sunlight and they were now rapidly approaching the terminator.

Mia then reappeared and told them to follow her. The three of them walked with her until they saw the tell-tale triangular hole in the floor.

"Time to get in a Tet again," said Mia. "We'll be right over the Moon Base in 30 minutes."

Mike stayed behind while Shen and Frejya slid into the smaller Tet like a pair of experienced Taikonauts.

"Helmets on," announced Mia, handing two that were already in the Tet and matched perfectly to their individualised suits.

"No expense spared then?" said Shen, who appreciated what everything cost.

The tip of the Tet closed silently and they felt nothing as they dropped towards the now dark lunar surface.

Frejya took the silent descent time to tune in. She realised that they were very, very alone. The Moon was shielding them not only from Mother Earth but also from her children. A tear rolled down her face as she thought that this must be what it's like when your loved ones die and you can't sense them anymore.

Shen's attention was focussed on trying to see the Moon Base just with the light of the stars. His vain attempt to discern anything was disrupted by Frejya as her Earth-directed thoughts were interrupted by something that just occurred to her.

"Was this Tet built on Earth or in orbit?" she asked.

"Earth of course," replied Shen. "We're a way off from being able to construct anything up here."

"So if it got from Earth to here, why are we still using the

Moon Tube modules," she continued. Shen knew where this was going and Mia came to his rescue.

"We can't have anyone on the Space Port knowing Tets can be used for anything but near-Earth orbit at the moment," Mia said. "I flew this one straight here from Jiuquan."

Shen piped up, "And they know nothing of the larger Tet already at the Moon Base that is there in case they need to evacuate."

"Yes," confirmed Mia. "It can take them to the Moon Port or all the way back to Earth if we have to."

Shen didn't let on that the Seven Immortals Monastery was where they would go to maintain secrecy in this eventuality.

"And don't tell me," said Frejya, quickly catching on. "Nobody at Jiuquan knows they are here."

The answer was given in the silence. Frejya gave Shen one of her looks through her visor. He was looking forward to a time when he didn't have to keep any more secrets back from her.

67

Home from Home

2096 : still 13 years left

One of the Tets that shouldn't have been there touched down at the Moon Base less than 6 hours since they left the surface of Planet Earth. That included the time they stopped for breakfast, or was it lunch?

This time they disembarked from the bottom of the Tet, down a ladder. Mia made herself scarce and a technician, who introduced himself as Xing, helped them out of their helmets and suits.

Shen didn't realise immediately that he and Xing had been at Fragrant Hills School together many years ago.

"Put these shoes on, they are perfectly adjusted for 1/6G," he said. "Take a few steps."

Frejya stumbled forward, "A bit too sticky for me."

"Just tap your left heel twice on the floor and that weakens them. Same with your right heel to increase the suction," advised Xing.

"That's a nice idea," said Shen. "Who came up with that?"

"That would be me," said Xing, as a door slid open and Cheng and President Miang strode confidently towards them.

"Welcome to our new home both of you," said Miang and, nodding to Xing. "I see you've met my son."

"You should be proud of him," said Frejya, spotting the

similar nose and chin.

"We are. Now as you're only here for 48 Earth hours and must have Moon Lag," said Cheng. "Let's give you a quick tour to get your bearings and show you to your quarters for some rest before we get started."

The Tet had arrived in one of four domes interconnected by a toroid of fully transparent tubes. The whole interconnecting toroid was about half a kilometre in diameter. They learned this dome not only was used for incoming and outgoing Tet flights but also was to become the way out to the crater surface.

"You can't see the canopy, as it's clear at the moment, but Mike got the crater completely sealed at the end of last year," said Cheng, pointing upwards. "There's no atmosphere yet but at least when we eventually go out, there's minimal radiation. The roof is also generating more power than we will ever need."

"For our lifetimes at least," Miang added.

They came to the next dome and were pleasantly surprised how homely it was compared to the industrial feel of the Space and Moon Ports. This dome was the communal area and contained the kitchens, dining area, a gym and a feature that caught Shen's eye, a rather attractive bar.

"We only leave one person on the Moon Port at a time at the moment," said Cheng, noticing what Shen had noticed. "It's much more sociable here. We'll all share a few beers later."

"I'm not sure how we survived that whole year in orbit sucking beer from tubes," said Miang.

"So how many are living here?" asked Frejya.

Shen looked at Cheng, as he knew exactly how many and was relieved for Miang to answer, "Twenty five of us right now but the whole of the Aitken Basin can potentially be a home for several million people."

Shen hadn't told Frejya that there were no plans for more

than a few thousand to temporarily live on the Moon.

"Xing, will you take over and take them around the lab?" asked Miang, who'd just taken a call.

Xing obliged and took them to a much larger dome. The first thing that hit them was the smell. It smelt of farm yard and rotting piles of manure. This was something the Moon had never harboured in its entire history.

"So here we grow our vegetables using hydroponics," said Xing.

"Was all the water brought from Earth?" asked Frejya, suspecting Shen knew the answer already.

"All our water comes from the Shackleton Crater at the South Pole," replied Xing. "We've got thousands of years supply but we still recycle as much as we can, over 90%."

They walked on past some vast aquaria.

"We brought some fresh water fish a year ago and had them breeding straight away," said Xing. "They were very quick to adjust their swim bladders for 1/6G. We did lose a few who couldn't keep from floating to the surface though."

Shen's interest was piqued by a very empty tank, "Any sea water fish yet?"

"Still playing with salinity in this tank and not quite there yet," said Xing.

Moving on further over to the centre of the dome, the smell intensified. Seeing Frejya wrinkle her nose, Xing explained, "I guess you've been eating worms back on Earth. Look at the size of these though."

Xing thrust a gloved hand into the soil and dragged out a 1 metre long, thick worm, more like a large grass snake.

"This is how big they grow under 1/6G," he said.

Frejya then heard an unexpected sound, clucking.

"Come and meet my chickens," said Xing, taking them to a large pen. "And before you ask, these are all brought from Earth. I've got over 50 of them and the eggs are wonderful."

"Why build a fence so high?" asked Shen. "You can't have

any predators here."

Xing clapped his hands and spooked the roost. They started bounding around taking leaps over 2 metres into the air and about 5 metres long.

"They made a right mess in the wormeries, so we have to keep them penned in," replied Xing.

He spotted Frejya yawning and said, "You both could do with some rest."

He took them out of the food production zone, down another transparent tube and into a much larger dome again with a sprawling number of mini-domes.

"It's so nice to have privacy here," said Xing as they walked past a dome with Shen and Frejya's names on it. "Here's yours."

As they entered, Frejya was pleasantly surprised to feel at home right away. Xing bade his farewell saying he'd see them over dinner.

"I had Hui send over all the 3D designs of our furniture," said Shen. "We've got the same towels and toothbrushes and even our Yin Yang bed too."

"I hope nobody else gets to sleep on it," said Frejya.

"Don't worry, this is our dome forever should we ever need it again," said Shen.

Frejya was too tired to question any more and they both sank quickly into a deep but somewhat fitful sleep. Frejya had strange dreams. She dreamt she was inside the Moon and floating around a massive tetrahedral engine. She was inside Spaceship Moon.

The clock in the room, and clocks over the base, were linked to China Standard Time. They woke at 1am in the morning and, after showering and brushing teeth, wandered out of their dome to be met by Xing again.

Frejya wondered how he knew they'd awoken, and asked, "Why does the water feel so strange and a little slimy? It tastes funny too."

"We're not sure about the feel," answered Xing. "Something to do with the H_2O molecules themselves under low gravity. The taste is just from the different soil type the water ice has been sitting on for billions of years."

Shen suspected it might have some organics from incoming panspermia and had already sneaked a sample to take back to Earth, even though he knew it was against protocol.

Xing took them back to the communal module, but via the fourth dome which was virtually empty. All they could hear was a faint hum from one end of the dome.

"So what happens here?" asked Frejya.

"At the moment, it just houses our IT systems," said Xing. "Those racks you can see over there."

Shen realised that's where the q-computer must be housed. He made a note to ask it if it knew where it actually was physically.

It was Shen's turn to take over, "This dome is to be the location of the University taking the students from the Monastery."

He continued, "One of the reasons we are here is that they might want you to take over as headmistress."

"Not Madame Bien?" asked Frejya.

"She will be too old and has refused point blank to leave Earth," said Shen.

"And what about Eva and Kristin?"

"They are to become teachers," replied Shen. "Li and Jun too."

Somewhat shocked Frejya asked, "When do we start?"

"Probably when Eva and Kristin graduate in 5 years time, with the first students arriving a year or two later," said Shen. "They have decided that it's best for me to run the Mars terraformation project from here."

"And Hui and Jia?"

"They are more than welcome, if they want to come."

Shen was thankful Xing interrupted them, "Time to sample those chicken eggs but, before we do, my mother has asked if Frejya could pop into her dome to see her."

"Of course," answered Frejya.

"And Shen, your presence is required at the bar," he playfully announced.

Frejya didn't mind some female company and had being looking forward seeing Yu Yan again. Shen, on the other hand, felt he really needed some grounding juice.

68

Opening

2096 : still 13 years left

The Councillors were always extremely careful when one of them was inserted into the Density. It was vital that the Inserted One didn't know their mission and role. Partly this was for their own safety and partly because not knowing your mission introduced some randomicity into the mix.

At the same time, doors had to be opened at the right place, and the right time, for the Inserted One to make their mark.

This was why Shen found himself on the far side of the Moon, on a secret base, drinking gin and tonic with Professor Cheng, served to them both by the President of China. Shen was learning that in a small remote community, nobody stood on ceremony.

To those on Earth who thought he was in a secret hideaway somewhere on the Nepalese border, the President was still venerated and revered. On the Moon Base, he got stuck in like everyone else. So much so that he'd made the gin himself by mixing some Moon-grown botanicals with some imported Russian vodka. He had wanted to build a still but had been warned not to on safety grounds. It was only a twelve hour round trip for Mia or Mei, in a Tet, to bring anything they wanted from their home planet after all.

So while Miang was opening the second bottle of gin,

the Councillors decided it was time that the three of them received a little opening.

It started by Shen opening up to Cheng and Miang about something that had been really troubling him. The second G&T helped.

"I am really struggling to keep things secret from Frejya," he said. "She has Wu powers after all and probably knows what I'm thinking anyway."

"So while we are here in private," said Cheng. "Tell us what you haven't told her."

"Well she knows now that we are planning to train the Taikonauts who go to Mars right here," he said. "But she doesn't know about the pulse and why we might be going."

"Anything else?" asked Miang.

"Well she doesn't know, and I don't either, if the whales and dolphins know something we don't," said Shen.

Miang then opened a big door for Shen, "From now on Frejya is on the inside track. You can tell her anything and everything you discuss with us."

"That's a huge weight off my mind," said a relieved Shen. "And can I ask if there's something you know that I don't or something you both don't know that you think I can help with?"

Cheng and Miang looked at each other, not knowing who should go first. This was when Councillor Seven nudged Cheng's pineal gland and gave him some information he didn't know.

"What we don't know is why you have ended up with your fingers in so many of the pies," he blurted out.

Shen paused, took a big gulp of his G&T, and said, "But I thought that's exactly what you did know. I've only done what you asked me since I was a student."

It was at that very moment that Frejya arrived, with a relieved looking Yu Yan, and told them all something they didn't know.

"It's the Moon water that's made her so ill," she said. "Can we have two large G&T's please?"

69

Moon Food

2096 : still 13 years left

They all left the bar slightly tipsy and met up with the rest of residents of the Moon Base, around a large circular dining table. Wu Zetian was there with her wife and Mike Spence with his. Both of whom Shen had never met. Mia was missing as she was on Moon Port duty.

Shen made another mental note to ask Cheng how much Mia and Mei knew before he left.

Frejya and Shen were introduced to everyone. Some of them Shen recognised from the presentation announcing the impending arrival of his comet 20 years ago.

Mike Spence sat down opposite them and Cheng said to Frejya, "So tell Mike what you found out about the water."

"Well I don't know why Yu Yan was the only one who was so badly affected but her body has a definite intolerance to Moon water," explained Frejya. "It just passed right through her and was leaving her cells dehydrated."

"What can we do about it?" asked Mike. "Should we import water for her from Earth?"

"It's a little simpler than that," said Frejya. "You just need to expose the water to some sunlight."

Shen butted in, "Yes apart from a little sunlight the water ice sees at the pole, all the pipes and water storage vessels are solid."

"Well that's easy," said Mike, opening up a tablet. "I'll just program some nano-bots to make some windows. We'll be in sunlight in three days as it happens."

"And Mia could bring some energised water down from the Moon Port within a couple of hours," suggested Shen, looking at his watch. He was really tuning in to Moon timings.

Something just dawned on Mike, "But can I ask how you know this Frejya?"

She blushed and Shen saved her from answering, "She just does Mike."

Mike's line of enquiry was further interrupted by the arrival of the 25th Moon Base resident. Chang, the chef Shen had trained with, arrived with the starters.

After he deposited the starters, Shen got up to hug him.

"Am I pleased to see you?" he said. "I am so looking forward to taste what you've done with space food"

"Just for you Shen, Glazed Omelette Arnold Bennett, made from our own eggs and farmed haddock," Chang announced. "I heard you enjoyed this at the Savoy in London a few years ago."

Shen didn't mention that he'd enjoyed it for a second time with Frejya, on his return journey through London.

For their main course, Chang had prepared 'Beef' Wellington which everyone knew was made from worms. For dessert, Chang had to admit all the ingredients were imported from Earth.

Even Frejya knew why and asked, "When do you plan to introduce pollinating insects?"

"Over the next few years," answered Mike Spence, getting something from his pocket. "In the meantime, I've made these and Xing and I are looking at artificial pollination."

Mike released three bee-like flying objects that performed an aerobatic dance above their heads before landing gently on Frejya's shoulder. Only Mike noticed this as he hadn't programmed them to do that.

After dinner, some made their way to the bar again but Shen and Frejya made their excuses and retired, as everyone knew they had a return trip ahead of them the next 'day'. What Shen was just about to find out was that Frejya had other plans. She wanted to christen their second Yin Yang bed and experiment with tantra in 1/6G.

When they got up, they both had a light breakfast in their room. Frejya wanted to check on Yu Yan, now Mia had brought some energised water down. Shen went to meet with Cheng, Miang and Mike Spence to brief them on the progress of the build of the coupled interplanetary Tets.

Mike explained that he had worked out how to create an army of nano-insects, much like the bees they had seen over dinner, to perform all sorts of intricate tasks. They would be perfect tools to help them fit out the interplanetary Tet drive in stationary Moon orbit.

"So all of this means we can get humans there as soon as 2120," Shen concluded.

"If we need to," said Mike. "The canyon will be way off from being viable though, no breathable atmosphere until at least the middle of the next century."

"Let's hope the next few pulses continue to decrease in intensity," said Cheng.

"Let's see you both back here for the next big update and end of century celebrations then," pronounced Miang.

Shen knew this was one invitation he would not be able to refuse. By then, he was hoping he would be able to bring the whole family. If there was still time.

They were interrupted by Mia, "Time to get suited up Shen, Frejya's waiting for you."

Mike gave Shen a handful of 'bees', "Let me know how these perform, I've adjusted them for 1G."

"Will do," said Shen.

"And can you find out why they are attracted to Frejya?" asked Mike.

"I will indeed. In fact, I will ask her directly," said Shen, rather pleased on how easy life would be now there were no secrets.

70

Homeward Bound

2096 : still 13 years left

Shen was surprised both he and Frejya got a goodbye hug from the President. Cheng still opted for a handshake. Both Xing and Chang came to hug them goodbye. The rest of the residents of the base lined either side of the connecting tunnel as if they were newly-weds.

When they were suited and helmeted up and seated in the Tet, Mia surprised Shen by asking him if he'd like to fly. He didn't have to check with Frejya.

"I'll tell you when to take off and then we go straight up to 14 kilometres, just below the Moon Port's altitude of 15," she said.

With no atmosphere to negotiate, they felt nothing. In the distance, Shen could now see the Moon Port hurtling towards them.

"OK, now accelerate up to 7500 kilometres an hour, away from it," instructed Mia.

The rate of closure slowed down and when they could see the Port clearly, Mia said, "Now increase to 8500 clicks."

When the Moon Port was coming right above them, she said, "Dial in 8568.33 and we'll match it exactly."

The nano-fans on their seats ensured they felt minimal G forces.

Shen knew what to do next, as he had for much of the

procedure so far, as he'd had a hand in its design after all. He switched his monitor to the top view and instructed the Tet to rotate so its edges aligned perfectly with the three rows of lights on the bottom of the Moon Port.

"Just press AutoDock," said Mia. "I find it much easier these days."

The kilometre gap closed and a satisfying set of green lights came on when they docked.

"OK, we're just coming around Earth-side," said Mia. "Unless you want to wait another two hours, let's get over to the Moon Tube. No time to take suits and helmets off."

"So Shen, I've agreed with Mei that you know what you are doing," said Mia. "She's on standby but you're taking it back home."

Frejya knew he would be grinning under his helmet and was also doubly grateful. Firstly, they'd just seen sight of Earth again after a gap of just a few days that felt like weeks. Secondly, as it would give them time to chat and reflect.

Twenty minutes after entering the module, the alignments were perfect and Shen shot them out into the void between the Moon and Earth. He made sure all the outgoing comms were disabled but that they could hear Mei in case of any emergency. He knew how to disable the remote override too so even Mia and Mei couldn't listen in.

"Right down the barrel Shen," Mei had said. "You've not lost your touch, see you in an hour. You can get out of your suits now if you like."

They helped each other out of the respective suits and sat back to enjoy the view of an ever-approaching Earth. Neither of them took more than a second glance back at the Moon. They were so relieved to be going back to what they knew as normal.

"So you know I can tell you everything now?" said Shen, who had updated her on his chat at the bar.

"Of course, so what don't I know?" asked Frejya.

"Can I start with what I don't know?" said Shen. "Just look at that beautiful jewel of a planet. It's our home where our children and parents live."

"I can't wait to be with them," said Frejya.

"So what I don't know is why we are about to terraform another planet which is hostile to life, when with all Mike's nano-technology, surely it would be easier to hunker down and protect ourselves here."

"Did you ask Miang and Cheng?" said Frejya.

"I did but they were a little vague about the answer, saying it was all about secrecy and not causing mass panic," Shen replied. "Still doesn't make sense though as there's loads of inaccessible places on Earth, the bottom of the ocean for starters."

"Shall I ask Mother Earth?" suggested Frejya.

Shen noticed Frejya's body shifting in and out of translucency.

After only a few minutes, she said in a Frejya-not-Frejya kind of voice, "It's so The Others can come."

"What does she mean by The Others?"

Frejya-who-was-now-Frejya replied, "It is not Time."

Shen knew it wasn't wise to push for more detail when channelling as the answers only got more vague and obfuscated.

So he asked Frejya to see if she could pick anything else up as he checked in with Mei. They were right on trajectory.

"Thirty three minutes to docking," Mei confirmed.

They spent the rest of the transfer time in silence. Frejya was thinking about her children and the uncertainty of the next two decades. It sounded like she would be moving to the Moon Base with them. This was something she hadn't signed up for when she met Shen in Iceland all those years ago. As exciting as the prospect might sound, Earth looked a whole lot more inviting. This was even more so as it was getting ever closer.

Shen had switched his gaze sideways to the cosmos around him. To his right, the stars were invisible in the white glare of the Sun. Something stirred in him about the Sun. He had a weird fleeting thought that caused him to wonder if you could live on or in the star. He cancelled it out as too bizarre and looked out left to the cosmos, wondering if The Others were out there somewhere.

In the corner of his eyes, he started to see flashes and streaks of faint light. As he looked towards them, they disappeared. He remembered Apollo astronauts reported such phenomena. He was also mindful of how brave they were. His re-entry back to his 1G world would be much more gentle and much less precarious.

After a smooth docking, Mei took them straight back down to Earth in a Tet. There was so much traffic to and from the Space Port these days, mostly automated flights with cargo, that nobody on board suspected two passengers had just left Moon Port and were Earth-bound.

Mei was told to take no chances with her precious cargo. As they slowed their orbital speed and were sitting 100 kilometres above the space centre, she shared with them that they were the first in over two years to make the return trip back since Mike Spence had come back to visit his dying father.

"We've played with the algorithms since Mike came back as he had terrible trouble acclimatising to 1G," Mei said. "He had been either weightless or in 1/6G for over a year."

"I heard," said Shen. "He had excruciating joint pain until he got back into space."

"Yes, but we've been slowly increasing the nano-fans on your seats since you left the moon to simulate increased gravitational force," Mei explained. "You're now at 0.75G."

"I thought something felt weird and weighty," said Frejya.

They touched down safely in the evening, having only experienced a little jet stream turbulence. Mei didn't get out of the Tet and was back at the Space Port in 10 minutes. She didn't hang about when flying by herself.

Back on the ground, Shen and Frejya were subjected to a barrage of tests and told to stay overnight before going back.

They both gazed at the half Moon through their bedroom window as they slipped into deep slumber.

"Hard to believe we were there just a few hours ago," whispered Frejya.

"Yes and that there's 25 people up there munching on wormburgers tonight," said Shen, who had stolen a copy of Chang's weekly menu.

The next day, they felt heavy and sluggish until around midday. Frejya took some time to check in with Yu Yan now she had been drinking energised water, while Shen met with Lance to share some more he'd heard about the drive while out in space. Shen had been given approval to let Lance know about the internal fit out in Moon orbit.

Shen and Frejya had to wait until the evening so they could fly back to Seven Immortals under the cover of darkness. As they took off, Shen briefed Frejya in some detail on what she could share, and what she couldn't, with Jia, Hui and the children.

When they reached level flight, away from the mountains and in clear air space, Shen surprised her when he said, "It's time you learned to fly one of these."

71

Whale Song

2097 : 12 years left

After only three months or so of training, Frejya turned out to be a natural Tet pilot. She discovered a new sense of freedom, as she could visit the children at Wuhan University any time she wanted. She took over as their 'taxi driver' to and from the Monastery at the start and end of each semester.

Jia was the only one of them not to take to flying. She could after all levitate herself should she ever feel the need. Both Hui and Shen had been gifted Tet Lites by Lance and used them daily to get around the Monastery.

Shen had given Frejya the task of working out why Mike's 'bees' made, well, a beeline for her. She'd discovered they were similarly attracted to Eva and Kristin, but not the boys. Mike was amazed at her intuitive prowess. He had to quiz Shen on this and something else that puzzled him.

"So it turned out that there were two modes I could set them up for, either getting pollen or delivering it," he said.

"And you had them set on delivering pollen," said Shen proudly. "So they made a beeline for the most attractive female."

"Exactly," said Mike. "But do you know how come when I speak to Frejya, there's no time delay?"

"No but working on that too," said Shen.

Shen's intuition told him that these many loose ends were somehow all connected. While he and Mike were working on the terraformation project, he was also keeping a watchful eye over the development of the interplanetary drive and the research into the status of the supernova candidate. Researching zero time delay with Earth and Moon comms with Frejya, Mia and Mei would have to wait.

Meanwhile, at the university, Ning Shangbo was turning out to be the most ideal tutor for the four children. She knew everyone who was anybody at Wuhan University, so could open doors that many didn't know existed and create bespoke courses for the twins. It helped too that she had been been backed by an unlimited source of funding from Shen.

Eva's project involved creating mini-biomes to increase the output from wormeries. Meat production was virtually phased out across the globe now and 75% of protein for humans was coming from wormeries. They were only around 25% efficient and did have an odd taste that took some getting used to. Over two terms, she had learned how to recreate the texture and taste of wagyu beef. Her wormburgers became very popular with fellow students. She even toyed with the idea of launching a chain of wormburger restaurants.

Li had been given a large scale model of a dome-enclosed Valle Marineris, built by Hui, and was busy creating a breathable atmosphere using nothing more than dry ice and a biome of Eva's. He and Eva had not yet been told this was less than theoretical. While on their winter break, the children had learned about the Space Port, Moon Port and Moon Base from Frejya and Shen. They had been kept in the dark about how advanced the plans were for terraformation of Mars.

Jun had been seconded by Shen to help the team at Purple Mountain analyse data from other binary pairs in close orbits. What Shen specifically wanted him to find were candidates with small tertiary bodies in attendance that might destabilise the primaries. Jun seemed a natural at Big Data. He'd discovered five potentially unstable binaries within a year, none of which were nearer than 1000 light years and all of which he discovered without having to actually visit Purple Mountain.

It was Kristin's project that became the joint focus for their next summer field trip with Ning Shangbo. After her success communicating with the river monkeys, Ning had set her the almost impossible challenge of setting up a dialogue with whales. Shen of course had a hand in the inception, focus and scope of this line of research.

Unsurprisingly, she'd established that whale song had zero correlation with any known human language or dialect. She had however intuitively worked out its harmonic structure. It looked as if they used 12 tones which repeated over an incredible frequency range of 12 octaves. Adjacent tones could be overlaid to produce 12 pseudo-tones. It appeared to be rich in depth and spectral range and Kristin suspected in content.

That summer, they took Ning's research boat downstream to the heavily nano-walled and now coastal city of Nanking. At only 15 metres elevation, the sea level was now 10 metres above the city on the other side of the wall. The city was nearly empty though as the walls would not be viable for much longer. It did still have an operational TubeWay connecting it to the island city of Shanghai, which itself was also becoming unviable. The solution being tried for Shanghai was to build a new ground level 70 metres above the old city. Shanghai had the money still to try that kind of extreme strategy.

At Nanking, the Dream Team - as dubbed by their fellow and slightly jealous students - transferred to a sea going research vessel owned by the University and set off looking for humpback whales on their migration path North.

The Western Pacific in Summer was relatively calm but it took a few days for them all to find their sea legs and stop retching. After a week on board, the underwater transducers picked up the unmistakable whale song and Kristin got to test her theory.

She'd composed her own 12 note whale song, right in the middle of the 12 octave range, and superimposed her own voice on top of it with the words, repeated in a loop:

We join you in song
To find our common bonds
We come to learn
To do no harm

We seek understanding
Of what you know
Where you are from
And where you go

This unusual, and high level, approach to communicating with whales produced an unexpected and unusual response from the whales. The research vessel had come across a medium-sized pod of 22 humpbacks, consisting of 12 females, 6 pups and four males. Kristin's pseudo-song had the immediate effect of stopping all songs from the whales. At first, they thought they had upset or frightened them as they also stopped breaching the surface. The sonar showed they only dived to 30 metres.

After about twenty minutes, one of the females was joined by two males and they started to repeat Kristin's whale song, note for note but with complex overtones and undertones across their whole octave range. It was then that Kristin and Ning realised the combination of notes must hold the key.

That evening they got hold of Shen to relay to him what had happened and he suggested it was time for them to go into the water. Ning was already an accomplished scuba-diver and the four children had learned the basics in a deep training pool in Wuhan. As this would be their first open ocean dive, Jun and Kristin went in first tethered to two experienced divers.

The whales slowed to a stop when the divers entered the water. Kristin had another song playing from the ship, this time with no words, it was just a pleasing melody. The whole pod of whales turned through 90 degrees and hung motionless underwater with their heads hanging down.

Kristin said to Jun over the intercom, "Are they meditating?"

The divers took Kristin and Jun over to the largest female and motioned Kristin to touch its head. As soon as she did, she got a shock.

Right inside her head the whale started to speak, 'We love your music Kristin, thanks for helping us relax on our long journey.'

Kristin's head was buzzing and she realised straight away the whale must be communicating with her using sonar, directed right inside her brain's language centres. This was completely different from the 'silent' communication she and Eva had shared.

Kristin told Jun, "She is talking to me."

"Ask for her name," suggested Jun

'I am Noma,' the whale said immediately. This was incredible. The whales could even tap into Jun's thoughts.

'And I am Kristin and I am with Jun,' said Kristin, forming it as a notion.

'We know,' said Noma.

Pleased at this development with Noma, Kristin formed the silent thought form, 'Will you teach me about your songs?'

'Of course, they are our stories of our journeys over thousands of years, memories of our ancestors and the pooling of our wisdom. We sing them for our children so they can learn and we sing them for all the creatures in the sea so they can evolve too,' said Noma.

'Will you teach me your history?' asked Kristin, so thrilled she'd intuited how to allow Noma to scan her thoughts. She couldn't wait to teach Eva how to do it and to tell her father what she'd learned.

Noma's tone changed, 'You know it already. It is all in the recordings you already have. Listen with new ears when you get back on to your lands. I will send you the decoding instructions now.'

Kristin had a zap of kaleidoscopic lights flashing in her brain. After what seemed like minutes, but Jun said after was seconds, Kristin came back into consciousness.

What happened next surprised everyone, including Noma the whale.

Kristin-not-Kristin said, 'Can you tell us where all the dolphins are going and if they are coming back?'

Noma-not-Noma replied, 'They have gone Home-Home and some will be back very soon.'

The lead diver signalled that they were running out of air so the four of them had to surface. In all the kerfuffle getting them back on board and out of their wet suits, nobody was monitoring the whales. By the time Ning got to look at the sonar again, the traces showed they had dived deep.

It was then the captain came over with some bad news. A violent typhoon was forecast to hit the east coast of China in a week's time. They had to go back immediately to Nanking.

On their way back to land, they relayed the discovery that Kristin could talk to whales to Shen. He told them that he would be picking them up personally in a Tet when they got back to the port.

72

Council Talk

It was of course no coincidence that the cetacean language spanned a 12 octave range, with each octave containing 12 notes. Early humanoids first used a similar structure for their language, but over a reduced octave range. As Epoch Five humans densified, the only remnant that remained was the 12 hour clock, which distilled out of the Sumerian and Babylonian's use of counting to Base 60 using the phalanges on their fingers.

Both languages were of course modelled exactly on how the 12 Councillors spoke to each other. If you could be a fly on the Council Chamber wall, you would think you had teleported into the middle of a pod of whales.

Like humans, whales and dolphins had no conscious awareness of the existence and influence of the Councillors. Their songs were full of references to huge, benevolent sea beasts who saved them from all kinds of ghastly and off-worldly monsters. Some of the monsters were described as being so large that they could eat a fully-grown male humpback whale.

A language based on 12 notes meant the Councillors could communicate with cetaceans directly, but only when they were dreaming, which they did when hanging vertically. So when Kristin had her first whale conversation with Noma, she had no idea she was communicating directly with Councillor Three.

Councillor Three had been tasked with guiding and mentoring the cetaceans since they first arrived on Planet Earth. She was currently splitting her attention between two planets on different sides of the galaxy while the Transition was being effected. This kept her busy but her task was about to be made more complicated still as the gates of communication were being opened up.

At the same time Councillor Three was busy brokering conversations between two sentient species, she had no idea that her conversations were being relayed by Councillor Seven up to the High Council. Councillor Three also had no idea that she was a potential candidate for election to higher office.

73

Entanglement

2097 : still 12 years left

Shen had instructed Ning to go directly to Dongting Lake and to stop over in Wuhan just long enough to pack for a long stay. Even with her new boat, it would take her until the end of the year to navigate up the Yangtze, through the Three Gorges system, to the lake.

Just a day after they arrived at the Seven Immortals, the two pairs of twins sensed their time studying was coming to an end, before they had even graduated. Shen taught Eva and Kristin how to access the q-computer so it could help them decode the whale song. It, of course, had no problem working in Base 12, or Base anything else for that matter.

Within days, it had come up with one extraordinary possibility and a discovery about how whales encoded time in their language.

Kristin was pleased she could tell Shen something she thought he didn't know, "It thinks that 'Home-Home' is another planet."

"And we think some dolphins will be back within a year," said Eva. The q-computer had specifically said 'an Earth-Year' and confirmed the location was 'in-land'.

Kristin had discovered, with the q-computer's help, the octave the whales sang in denoted the time frame. This meant she could start unravelling the timeline of the whales' history, once they knew more of the language. Like the codebreakers of Bletchley Park who decoded the Enigma Machine, they had a structure and a few words. It was just a matter of time before they could unravel hours worth of recordings from the last hundred and fifty years.

While Kristin and Eva were tasked with decoding whale language, Li and Jun were being fast tracked as Tet pilots. After just a couple of weeks, they were 'dog fighting' with the Tet Lites. Shen had arranged for them to be trained by Mia and Mei in the New Year so they would be able to make trips to and from the Space Port from Jiuquan.

The twins were excited to be involved with their father so directly but Shen and Frejya held back from them, for now, any mention of them moving to the Moon Base.

Shen knew that Kristin, with Eva's help, was best placed to decode the whale's history. Hui and Jia were busy organising the final preparation of the school for the first intake the following Summer.

This all gave Shen the space and time to work on two matters. Remotely, he was working with Lance on the nuances of the interplanetary Tet's navigation system and how it would get from one place in space to another. He also was considering the overall timing of the first mission. He had come to realise that everything could be brought forward a decade or so.

It was Mike Spence's nano-bees propensity to land on Frejya's shoulder that gave Shen the idea of using entanglement in navigation. He first tried it out with a Tet Lite, by taking one of Frejya's bracelets with him a few kilometres from the Monastery. He put the bracelet inside a small cube coated with nano-fans and discovered that the fans pointing towards the Monastery did indeed spin faster than those pointing away.

It was then a simple modification to link the nano-fans on the cube to the nano-fans on the outside of the Tet Lite to automatically steer itself back. The implications for space flight were immense but Shen was going to have to get his hands on some recent bits of Martian rock. This would require an unmanned return mission which could also be useful as a test of the whole system.

What Shen didn't know, but Kristin was about to stumble across, was that cetaceans, and other sea life, had been using entanglement for navigation for millions of years. The attractive force of entanglement of course rides on soulwaves. This is how turtles would find their way back to the same beach they were born on tens of years later.

It was also how the Baiji dolphins navigated across space-time to 'port from one planet to another.

74

Porting

'Do we really have to go back again?' said Baku.

'We really do. They need our help,' said Pata. 'They haven't got long left.'

'It will be the last time, we promise,' said Tamu. 'Besides, the more you 'port, the less queasy you'll feel.'

Baku resigned himself to making the jump once again. After all, it's not like he would miss anything on his new, and preferred, home planet. All jumps across light years of space allowed for temporal compensation. Even as a seven year old, he knew that you could jump to any time as well as any place. Pata had told him that it wasn't a good idea to go backwards in time more than a second from the time when you left. Going forward in time was OK though.

He was yet to learn the finer points of teleportation, especially that light years of distance took no time at all to cross. Pata was the master at that and promised he would teach Baku one day. Tamu knew how to make the arrangements too but always left it up to Pata.

Humans who thought it was as simple as depicted on their TV show, Star Trek, had much to learn too. For starters, teleporting into solids got very messy. Land-based animals had to make sure they also landed right on the ground. If you were just a few inches or centimetres above the target surface, even a small and sharp fall could result in a broken bone. Land a little too low and you could get your legs stuck for ever. Re-extraction leaving bits of you behind would upset the balance. This is why, for short hops, you should always fully evacuate first. Space and space-time travel is anything but glamorous.

Of course, if you breathe air, it's important air at the same pressure and oxygen/nitrogen mix is present where you are going. Even experienced Epoch Six teleporters often carried a small aqualung, just in case.

For dolphins, like Pata, Tamu and Baku, going fluid to fluid made things somewhat easier. You just have to jump in at roughly the same depth to ensure the pressure is about the same. Dolphins can get the bends too. Even if you land upside down or sideways, you are taught to stay still for a few seconds and watch which way the bubbles go.

Pata would however take extra care to land them all the right way up. Where they were going back to was silty. If a boat had just been past, it could be as dark as night. Getting the right depth was crucial too to avoid any passing propellers. He knew however just where to go so their re-arrival wouldn't be seen or detected by any humans, or fish.

The process wasn't as instantaneous as depicted in science fiction films or TV shows either. A transfer required around an hour of preparation time. This was especially so when 'porting from spiral to spiral, from one side of a galaxy to the other. Even more care and preparation was required if the water was different. An hour was still a minuscule amount of time compared to the time that light took to get from one spiral to another. Even if a spaceship could travel at light speed, it would take hundreds of years to make the same trip.

The reason Baku much preferred it on Aquanine was why it wasn't an instantaneous 'port. On Aquanine, the water was just more luxurious, and altogether nicer to swim in. He hadn't yet learned it was H_6O_3, a polyatomic form of H_2O which was most common on Planet Earth.

He loved the ability the denser water gave him to jump higher in the air and land with hardly a splash. It also meant they could stray further away from each other yet still have crystal clear communications.

What he didn't love so much was the lightheadedness they experienced while H_2O was replacing H_6O_3. Coming back the other way was much more comfortable all round.

Although there were no predators to speak of, Pata and Tamu always kept an eye on their one and only son. Pata's ability to mate and have progeny had gone. He suspected from irradiation from too many 'ports.

So because the water was so different, rather like when scuba divers come up from the deep, depressurising slowly, the dolphins had to initiate a reverse 'port first to acclimatise themselves to their target destination.

To do this, both Pata and Tamu floated snout to tail fin, with Baku nuzzled between them. Then molecules of water from the Dongting Lake were reverse 'ported to build an H_2O bubble around them. They took molecules from a large expanse of water, tens of kilometres square, so that minor implosions weren't created in the lake where they were heading.

The time it took also minimised the weirdness of suddenly floating in, and imbibing, 'thin water'. As they were air breathing creatures, this was just like a land-based animal jumping from sea level to the top of a high mountain in one hop.

Once the H_2O cocoon was in place, there was another step to take before they could jump. They had to create a temporary matching void in the lake to jump into. Pata let Tamu do this because she had a little more attention to detail. An exact match down to just a few molecules' width was needed to avoid any jolts.

'We are good to go,' she said, after what seemed like an eternity.

'OK,' said Pata. 'Absolute silence when we arrive.'

Pata then initiated the 'port and, within less a nanosecond, they were back on Planet Earth for the last time. They didn't move for 30 Earth minutes to give the borrowed H_2O time to *merge and dissipate.*

As they settled into the new waters, it took a while to get used to having to use their tail fins a little more to get the same propulsion. So they all went to the centre of the lake. Their enforced silence gave them all time to think.

Baku was still a bit grumpy that they had to come at all and was having a dolphin equivalent of a teenage sulk.

Pata was wondering if his imagination was going haywire. He had always wondered where they actually went when 'porting between here and there. On this jump, he had a vague, fleeting impression that he saw other bubbles, occupied by other dolphins, whizzing past in the opposite direction. He also thought one of them bumped into their bubble.

Tamu was having a similar, but subtly different thoughts. She felt their bubble not only being bumped into but penetrated. She sensed the penetration, although fleeting and near-instantaneous, had not stopped at the bubble.

The Councillors had decided another one of them was needed in the Density. Insemination of Tamu mid-port was one of their most advanced and innovative insertion techniques. Councillor Six would be born into the Density 12 months later, which is how long Tamu would need to come to full term. Pata was in for a bit of a shock.

75

Back from Extinction

8th April 2098 : 11 years left

"I don't believe it! They're back!" shrieked Ning. She had been tracking the unmistakable clicks for an hour before she called Shen with the news.

"Exactly the same day and the same part of the lake?" asked Shen, who had not yet told her it was his birthday.

"Spot on."

"We'll fly over straight away, can you meet us at your summer house on Junshan Island in an hour?" said Shen.

"See you in sixty," confirmed Ning.

Shen told the girls to pack their bags, with enough clothes for a few days, as they were flying right away to Dongting.

On the flight over to Junshan Island, he grilled Ning for more detail.

"You're sure there's three of them?" he said. "Have you compared them with the database?"

Shen could sense Ning was both excited and puzzled.

"On it already," said Ning. "Looks like exactly the same pod that disappeared in 2058."

After they boarded the boat, Shen sent the tetrahedron back on 'entangled' autopilot to the Monastery, as he didn't want anyone chancing across it, as they might be there a few days.

Ning took them over to the centre of the lake and they

could all hear the unmistakable clicks and pops over the sonar. It was a bright sunny, clear Spring day and, as they got close, they could see the tail fins above the surface of the lake.

"Definitely the same pod," said Shen, who could see the larger male had a scar from a propeller just behind his dorsal fin.

As the boat slowed to track them at their speed, they could see that the female had a white tip on her left fin and nothing on her right.

"What I don't understand is why they haven't aged and why they are even alive," said Shen. "It's 40 years since you last saw them, that's nearly twice as long as their life expectancy."

"It's a bit stranger than that, Shen," said Ning. "From the water samples I took this morning, along with their urine, it looks like the female is pregnant."

"What's strange about that?" asked Eva.

Ning replied, "The males become infertile when they are older than 15 and 40 years ago, the male was over 20. It could be that the pup had come to maturity and could be the father."

Kristin had been unusually quiet during the whole trip over from the Monastery to the centre of the lake.

"Why don't we go in the water and ask them?" she suggested.

As the water hadn't yet warmed, they used the dry suits that were already on the boat from their ocean adventure. There was no need for aqualungs, just snorkels.

Shen said, "Suits on girls, you are going in when we catch up with them."

Kristin could only have been in the water for a minute when she started hearing a voice right inside her head. Again it was different in timbre and style from her communications with her sister.

'Are they friendly?' she heard from a voice that she intuitively knew was the pup.

'Yes son, these are the ones we have come back to help,' a female voice answered.

Baku swam over to the girls and started to play with them. The visibility wasn't great and he kept surprising them by appearing over the shoulder from which they were looking away from.

Kristin remembered how she 'spoke' with Noma the whale and wondered if it would work with the dolphins.

She just imagined the words, 'I'm Kristin and I am with my sister Eva.'

At which point the male and female appeared right in front of her and announced, 'I'm Pata and this is Tamu.'

"We're getting some strange sonar readings I've never heard before, Kristin," Ning interrupted. "Everything OK?"

"Quiet please," said Kristin. "We're talking."

'Can I ask where you have been?' asked Kristin.

'Home-Home,' said Pata. Kristin noted this was what Noma, the whale, had said.

Kristin pushed, 'And where's Home-Home?'

At this point, the three dolphins sped away and Kristin knew that was the end of the conversation for that day. She could sense that Eva was getting bored and cold.

Eva had already aired her frustration with Kristin that she could sense what the whales had been feeling but not yet pick up their thoughts.

On board, Kristin shared the brief dialogue with Shen, Ning and Eva. It was agreed to wait until the next day and then for Kristin to go in alone. In the meantime, Ning knew exactly where the pod was but decided to keep the boat at a distance of a kilometre from them.

Overnight Kristin had wild dreams about a water world with no land masses where she swam freely with the three dolphins, performing all sorts of aerobatic twists and turns. The next day, after breakfast, she suited up and got in the water. Ning had brought them to within ten metres of the pod.

Tamu was the first to approach her and she felt she could probe a little more with her than with the two males.

'How long are you staying for?' she asked.

'For just under an Earth year,' Tamu replied. 'Until I have my next pup.'

'You're pregnant?' she asked sounding surprised, although Ning had already told her as much.

Tamu changed the subject, 'Tell me the names of the elders on the boat.'

'The lady is called Ning,' answered Kristin.

'We like her and trust her,' said Pata, appearing from nowhere and cutting in. 'And who is the man?'

Kristin was a little taken aback by his tone, which sounded untrusting.

'That's my father, he's called Shen,' she replied.

'Please tell him this,' Pata said. 'He doesn't have as long as he thinks.'

The three dolphins sped away again, just like the day before, signalling that today's conversation was over. For Kristin though, the conversation for the day was about to begin. She and Eva had both sensed something bigger and grander than they'd imagined was going on.

After getting out of her suit and showering, Ning served them all a warming soup.

"Pata says you don't have as long as you thought," Kristin announced. "How long did you think you had?"

Shen knew then it was time to let the girls into a few secrets. He waited until Ning was out of earshot.

"There's some things you should both know," he said, "Wait until we are flying back to the Monastery."

That night as he dozed off to sleep, he was working out what next to ask the dolphins.

76

Intraspecies

Councillor Six's consciousness was only a few days into the process of crystallising into the Density.

At the same time Shen, of course, still had no idea he was the densification of Councillor Four. He had even less of an idea that Councillor Six was currently residing in Tamu's womb.

It was only because they both were oblivious to their true nature, and mission, that the remaining ten Councillors allowed the two of them to be in such close proximity on the lake.

The presence of both of them was very handy as it made communication between Kristin and the dolphins much easier. The remaining ten Councillors were using the two incarnate Councillors as proxies to bridge the dialogue.

Only at the time of Epoch transitions were two Councillors even permitted in the same galaxy. The reason for this is that there comes a point in a Councillor's incarnation where they start to suspect they are part of a bigger picture. If two such self-realised Councillors ever met in person, even as different species, their collective power could become uncontrollable and unstable.

People around them could experience spontaneous combustion. Rifts and warps in space-time could appear, allowing the killing, or harming, of peoples' ancestors. Whole families could vanish in an instant as a result.

This was another reason Epoch Three's termination ended up being a little messy. The incarnations of Councillor Three and

Four into two child oracles, who were twins, was always risky. At least the girl had more self control than the boy who inadvertently triggered the collapse by sharing too many secrets with the Elders.

None of the nine remaining Councillors knew that Councillor Seven's overarching brief was to look out for each of them. She alone knew that another reason two Councillors should never meet in the Density was because it could cause interconnections to arise between two or more multiverses.

While the Councillors looking after this particular Universe were busy ensuring no contact between Epoch Five civilisations occurred, the High Council of the Light had much bigger fish to manage.

77

On The Move

February 2099 : 10 years left

For several months after the pod was detected, the dolphins wandered no more than a few kilometres away from where they first appeared in the lake. Ning's sonar could pick them up easily at this sort of distance.

The dialogue between Kristin and the pod was not yielding any more information, so she and Eva had gone back to Seven Immortals to finish their dissertations. Shen had told them more about his research into variations in the numbers of cetaceans and whether it was linked to any cosmic events.

While the pod had hardly moved in the lake, the global sea level rise had started to accelerate. As a result, Shen's attention had been diverted on to a major upgrade to the nano-walls. A reverse snowball effect had hit the Earth. The increase in tilt had lead to large ice shelves detaching from the Antarctic land mass. This in turn reduced the albedo over over the Antarctic summer. With less sunlight reflecting back, the ice sheet melt was accelerating. The nano-walls were struggling to keep storm surges at bay.

Simon, Mike Spence's Earth-bound assistant who had relocated to Wuhan, had come up with a new solution in the form of aqua-bots. These aquatic nano-bots were programmed to eat kelp and form a net that stretched out about 1 kilometre into the ocean from the wall. The net pulsed up and down to create anti-phase waves, making the sea calm and meaning the nano-walls could more easily keep pace with the sea level rise.

The system was developed and tested at Wuhan in the largest wave pool on the planet and was starting to roll out across the globe. They targeted cities most at risk and within a year had bought themselves more time. This meant Shen could get back to his real task at hand and that was preparing for the next pulse to arrive in March.

At the beginning of February, he was somewhat interrupted. The pod had started to move east, with Ning tracking them. When they left the lake and entered the river system, Shen took Eva and Kristin down to meet Ning and get back on the boat. Shen stayed a few hours to brief Ning before flying back to the Seven Immortals.

The fast moving currents meant Kristin had little opportunity to get in the water to re-engage in dialogue. One evening the dolphins stopped in a patch of clear water and she managed to catch up with them to find why they had started moving and where they were heading. They stonewalled her on this but she did get one gem of information from Pata.

Over the Autumn, she had been researching the history of the Baiji and had learned that 'Dongting' literally means 'Grotto Court'. The lake was named for the huge hall or cavern, which was believed to exist beneath it. The cavern was thought to have underground passages opening to all parts of the empire.

When she asked Pata if he knew about any grotto, she was surprised to hear him say, 'That's our route in and out. It's not under the lake though but in the lake.'

This meant nothing to Kristin but had Shen's interest piqued when he heard about it later that day

By early March, the pod's speed had increased so Kristin couldn't get to join them any more in the water. Her last conversation with them was just as they got to Three Gorges Dam and when Pata said, 'See you on the other side.'

While Kristin was getting out of her wet suit, Ning was in horror, "They've gone again!"

An hour after the sonar traces disappeared, Ning was relieved to get a call from an old friend of hers, Zhan Zhu, who ran an inn that she'd stayed at many times on the other side of the lock system.

"You're sure, were there three of them?" she asked him.

"Yes, not seen any for over fifty years, but definitely three," said Zhan. "They even waved their fins at me."

Kristin intuitively knew what must have happened, "They've 'ported again."

Eva piped up, "At least, they can't be trying to hide from us if they 'waved' at the innkeeper."

"We'll see you sometime tomorrow," said Ning, knowing getting through the the lock system quickly was not that easy for a small boat, when commercial traffic was prioritised. Even Shen's influence seemed to fall on deaf ears when it came to the keepers of the locks.

A day later, and 91 metres lower, Ning was able again to pick up sonar pings.

"They are about 30 clicks away," she told Kristin and Eva.

They spent the rest of March playing catch up with the pod as they all navigated down the Yangtze towards Wuhan, which was now a coastal city. They finally caught up as the pod got close to the University Marine Institute at the east end of the city and Kristin was able to get in the water with them again late one evening.

'We thought you were trying to lose us,' she said.

'If we were, we could easily have,' said Pata. 'Come back in the water tomorrow at this time. We've got something to show you.'

Kristin obliged the following evening. Pata and Tamu invited her to snuggle up with them. They enclosed her in their fins with Baku. The next thing Kristin felt was her whole body evaporating and then the darkness of the silty Yangtze water being replaced by light. The dolphins released their grip and she surfaced. It took her a while to recognise where she was, as she's only been shown pictures of it by Shen. It then dawned on her that she was in the wave pool inside the Institute.

"I'm glad the wave machine is switched off," she whispered under her breath.

78

Luki Day

March 17th 2099 : still 10 years left

Shen was a fast thinker but the events of this day would take him several weeks to assimilate.

He knew he'd have to forget about dolphins for a day and leave monitoring of the imminent birth to the girls. Tamu had been moved to a smaller birthing pool for her safety, with Kristin and Eva in attendance as her doulas.

Pata and Baku were left under Ning's watchful eye in the wave pool but she knew she could do nothing to stop them 'porting. It had been quite a shock to lose Kristin like that, even temporarily.

Shen was annoyed not to be able to be in Wuhan but he had bigger fish to fry. Just like clockwork the pulse arrived on the afternoon of the 17th March. Unlike the last pulse, this one was big and Sylke's team in Australia confirmed its source as the binary in direct line behind the Sun.

More concerning for Shen was news from Mike Spence that he had lost comms with Lagrange B. Lagrange A was still OK.

Luckily the Moon Base and both the orbiting Moon and Space Ports were shielded by the masses of the Moon and Earth respectively.

The loss of Lagrange B was not so worrying as there was more than enough time to replace it before the next pulse.

What really concerned Shen was that the team at Purple Mountain also confirmed the optical occlusion of the tertiary object and that the dip in brightness was somewhat larger than last time.

A conference call was scheduled for that evening with the Moon Base where Shen brought them all up to speed.

"So, do you know how long we have got?" demanded President Miang.

"It is impossible to call," said Shen. "It could be 2104, 2109 or still a hundred or a thousand years from now."

Shen knew no data set existed big enough to tell them. He had asked the q-computer and was merely relaying its answer.

What he didn't share was that the q-computer had weighted its answer by saying, '5-5 or 10-10-10 or 100-100 or 1000.'

"Do you want some good news?" proffered Mike Spence.

"Yes please," said Miang.

"Well I can confirm that less than 0.0001% of the gamma rays reached the canyon floor," he said. "Our hardening system works."

Shen's screen flashed and his eyes lit up.

"And here's some other good news," he said. "The Baiji population of Earth has just increased in size by 25%."

Nobody on the Moon Base thought this was of any significance, so the conference call wandered quickly on to talk of Shen's next visit to celebrate the end of the century.

Shen was unaware that events had taken a whole new direction in Wuhan.

As Ning suspected, she couldn't prevent Pata and Baku from 'porting the few hundred metres across the marine research facility. She was too old to run to join them at the birthing pool so it took her a few minutes to catch up. There was no way Pata wanted to miss the birth and he wanted Baku to see it too.

As Ning arrived, in the pool, Tamu was talking to Kristin, 'I would like you to give him a name,'

'I'd like to call him Luki,' she suggested.

'Luki it is,' confirmed Pata. 'Now could you leave us alone so we can get some sleep?'

The two girls offered to take it in turn that night to make sure the pod, and Luki, were OK. They both slept, as well as they could, in camp beds at the side of the pool.

Ning turned the lights off as she left and was looking forward to her first night in a real bed for many months. She told the security guards not to let anyone in or to disturb the girls overnight. They, like the rest of the institute, had no idea dolphins were inside.

While it was supposed to be Kristin's turn to be awake, she fell into a hypnagogic half-dream and a conversation with Tamu.

'When we were in the lake, on the other side of the dam, we could not speak to the Others,' said Tamu.

'Who are the Others?' asked Kristin.

'Our sisters and brothers in the oceans,' replied Tamu.

'So what did you want to talk to them about?'

'We've come back to show them the way Home-Home.'

'Where's Home-Home?' asked Kristin, again.

'Come back tomorrow without your sister and we will show you.'

Kristin was awoken with a prod from Eva who'd been disturbed by her snoring, "Time you slept properly Sis, I'll take over."

The next day after breakfast, Eva conveniently left the pool to take some blood samples, taken from Luki, off for analysis. Just after she left, Kristin saw the water in the birthing pool bubble and the pod disappeared again.

She ran to the wave pool and, as she hoped and suspected, the four dolphins were there.

She got into the pool by herself and saw some strange

antics from Pata. He was at the nano-wall end of the pool and kept scraping himself on the wall and then pushing his head up above the surface.

While this was going on, Baku gave her some news that she had been dreading.

'We are going Home-Home now.'

Kristin surprised herself by asking, 'Can I come?'

'It is not safe or the right time,' answered Tamu, as she swam towards Pata, with Luki in her grip and followed by Baku.

'Please go and get your water lungs,' suggested Tamu. 'Pata said you can watch but from the other end of the pool.'

Kristin surfaced and quickly put on her aqualung, which Tamu affectionately had named as her water lungs. She also grabbed her underwater camera. When she got back in the water 10 minutes later, she could see a shimmering bubble had formed around the family. She intuitively knew to keep her distance but zoomed in as much as she could.

At first she thought her camera must be faulty but the pod was fading out of existence. There was no pop, flash or implosion but after about an hour they had completely gone. She didn't even get a goodbye but was sure Pata and Tamu waved at her.

She was in floods of underwater tears and had to surface to clear her mask. She sat on the side and watched the last ten minutes of playback before she thought to call her father.

"So they've gone?" said Shen. "Did you try to stop them Kristin?"

"I couldn't."

Kristin told him about last night's dream and about the dolphins porting from pool to pool.

"OK. Get Ning over and make sure the pool is on lock down. She'll know what to do. I'll be with you this evening."

Ning arrived with Eva within 30 minutes and immediately got the security team increased in size.

By the time Shen arrived a few hours later, Ning had the results of her analysis.

"There's definitely traces of aquanine," she confirmed.

"What's aquanine?' asked Kristin.

Before Ning could answer, Shen said, "That's not the question. What I want to know is where is Aquanine?"

Kristin was about to probe still further but Shen was interrupted by a call from Mike Spence. Eva noticed there was a strange delay in the conversation.

"So you are sure?"

"Yes," confirmed Mike. "The nano-wall and anti-wave systems are self-repairing and self-reporting. Any breeches or reduction in the numbers of 'bots and I get notified."

"Thanks for letting us know. I'll call you later," replied Shen, realising it was about time he told Mike about teleporting dolphins.

Shen decided to stay in Wuhan that night and booked himself, Ning and his daughters into the Presidential Suite at the Shangri-La Hotel. After so long on the boat, Ning was somewhat blown away by the opulence.

What must have been the world's first recording of an actual teleport proved to be somewhat of an anticlimax. The pod just faded out of existence. What really got Shen's interest was the recordings of Pata's antics in the wave pool that confirmed Mike's suspicions.

"So ladies, it looks like our friendly dolphins just acquired some nano-technology," said Shen, as he shared out a bottle of Abysse Blanc de Blancs.

79

Century's End

2099 : less than 10 years left

Shen left Ning with an open brief and open cheque book. She was to trawl the world's oceans for traces of aquanine. He wanted to know if other cetaceans were coming or going, but he suspected they would be mostly going.

As they parted just after breakfast, Eva and Kristin didn't know that would the last time they would see their teacher and mentor.

They hung around Wuhan that day and Kristin kept bursting into uncontrollable tears. She was grieving for lost loved ones. Under the cover of darkness that evening, Shen flew them back to the Seven Immortals. Two days ago he'd instructed Jun and Li, who were on the Space Port, to return to Earth and back to the Monastery, as soon as they got their Earth legs back.

Eva and Kristin were so pleased to see them and spent the whole night swapping stories of their respective adventures.

Shen went straight to bed having convened a family meeting the next day. As his head hit the pillow, Frejya asked, "Is it time to tell everyone?"

Before he slipped into slumber, he mumbled, "No more secrets."

The next day was a breath of fresh air for Shen. Even he had been struggling to remember who he had told what and who could know what. With Miang's confirmed blessing that morning, he started the family meeting by letting them know that they had all been invited to the Moon Base for New Year's Eve to see the century out. What he didn't know then was that only Hui and Jia would be making the trip back.

"So what we know is that the Earth is likely to be hit by a large gamma ray burst within the next 1000 years," said Shen.

"And with a destabilised core and reduced protection from the already damaged magnetosphere," he continued. "It doesn't look good for life on Earth."

"What I still don't understand son is why a permanent Moon Base and Mars terraformation is easier than creating protected zones on Earth," said Hui.

Shen thought he'd covered this with Hui but knew the others didn't know, "It would cause pandemonium if people knew. We also might have much longer than we think and the supernova might not wreak as much damage as we think."

"So it's best to see the plans for the Moon and Mars as back ups," said Frejya, coming to his assistance.

"It might sound strange but it's easier to build a brand new environment from scratch, and to keep it secret, if it's not here on Earth," Shen continued.

He was able for the first time to show them all live video from the surface of Mars. The canyon roof was complete and generating electricity. The accommodation blocks were half built and, protected from Martian dust storms, were so clean that they looked as if they had been CGI generated.

Shen revealed a mix of schematics and live pictures from Jiuquan of the interplanetary Tet.

"This is the Heart of Gold," he said. "In theory, it will take less than a month to get to Mars, nearly a two year wait and a month or so to get back to Earth."

"So our trip for this New Year isn't just a party, we'll be working," he announced. "We're going to complete the fit out in Moon orbit so you boys will be working with Mike's team."

"And us?" asked Eva and Kristin in unison.

"You'll be working with Xing, President Miang's son, on the life systems," said Shen. "Hui will be helping Mike too on the fabrication side."

Frejya coughed.

"But what I am most intrigued by is what Jia and Frejya will be working on. Will you tell them?" said Shen.

Frejya said, "When I met Mia and Mei, I noticed that they could communicate with no time delay. They don't know how they do it but Jia and I have a theory on how it's done. The delay from Moon to Earth is just annoying but from Mars to Earth it is impractical, especially when Mars and Earth are on opposite sides of the Sun."

"So will you be teaching us how to do it?" asked Jun.

"Let's not get ahead of ourselves," said Shen. "The first landings are scheduled for 2120 and beyond, we're just the bridge builders and teachers."

So the plans were made that day for the rest of the year which would culminate with them all being on the Moon for the end of century celebrations. Hui, Jia and the girls were booked in for training at Jiuquan that Autumn.

Shen brought the boys under his wing and the three of them got stuck into the detailed design of the inner and outer workings of the Heart of Gold. Kristin continued to have repetitive dreams of the dolphins on their water world.

Everyone was so busy that Summer soon came and went.

Shen had switched his attention to new data coming from Ning. She had been monitoring global whale migrations and the numbers were dropping fast, with no increase in beached whales. Ning had a number of researchers sending water samples from all over the globe. Molecules of aquanine were popping up from everywhere.

Frejya had been helping Madame Bien and her staff take in the first wave of students at the Monastery. None of the new intake knew of course that Mars might be where they were heading.

Early in December, Mia took the whole family from the Monastery straight to the Moon Base, bypassing both Space and Moon Ports. Apart from the secrecy this gave, it also meant a jump from 1G to 1/6G, with little weightlessness. This was less onerous for Jia and Hui, who were getting on in years. Mia also used the trip as extended training for Jun and Li.

The population on the Moon Base had tripled since Shen's last visit. Many of the new residents were working on Mike's team managing the terraformation project. Xing had both an augmented team working on food production and a wife who he had met on the Space Port.

The actual celebrations on New Year's Eve were quite poignant for all on the Base as they were pointing away from Earth, just into the blackness of space.

The two and half billion remaining occupants of Spaceship Earth partied like there was no tomorrow, which most of them had no idea was an impending possibility.

President Miang addressed the planet in his customary end of year speech. He congratulated each resident on the planet for doing their part in curbing excesses and helping get the planet back on track. Only a few hundred luminaries of the Chinese government had any idea he was living off planet.

80

Seeding

As the remaining few billion humans sobered up from a massive collective hangover, the Councillors were in the final throes of Epoch transition.

The home planet for Epoch Six had begun a transition that would take some hundreds of years to complete. The nano-bots and aqua-bots that Pata arrived with were put to work straight away.

From small beginnings on the ocean floor, land masses were being grown. Nanometre by nanometre, the water world started growing its continents. When they eventually poked above the waves, the aqua-bots would be used to take plant life from the ocean on to the land.

When the cetaceans were ready, they could take their first steps too.

This process had never been tried before. Most Epoch transitions to date had been somewhat more random and reliant on chance. Previously the Councillors had steered organics from one planet to the next in the same solar system on fragments of the destroyed planet. This meant consciousness and self-awareness had to be developed from scratch.

This was the first time a sentient-derived technology was used from one planet to give another planet a head start. By the time Epoch Six came to its close, this technique would be increasingly common.

So at this time of transition, two planets in the same galaxy harboured self-awareness at the same time. The seeds were being sown for galaxies to be flooded with sentient life.

81

New Beginnings

2100 : 9 years left

The start of the new century saw several comings and goings on the Moon. Towards the end of January, Jia requested to go back to Earth, as she couldn't stand another two weeks not seeing her home planet. She had though thoroughly enjoyed the previous two weeks marvelling at the majesty of Mother Earth and would treasure that memory for the rest of her life - all nine years of it. Hui dutifully and reluctantly went back with her. Shen made sure Mia took them all the way back to the Monastery in a single jaunt in a Tet.

On her return journey to the Moon, Mia arrived back with a very expectant and excited Lance Boyle. He just arrived a day before the Heart of Gold turned up in Moon orbit. It arrived under unmanned control, but fully air tight and radiation hardened, as the drive was working perfectly but the real fit out had yet to begin. It was parked in a geostationary position 150 kilometres above the Moon Base on the far side. It was vital it wasn't detected from Earth.

The other arrival Mia brought with her was a package she was told to pass directly to Shen. In it was every molecule of aquanine that Ning had managed to collect and distill. He already had a small vial from the pool in Wuhan but needed as much as possible of the substance for his new entanglement navigation system. The shielding that the mass of the Moon gave from the Earth made detection more accurate.

By the middle of the year, the Earth-Moon system had orbited a sufficient distance around the Sun for him to triangulate where the planet Aquanine might be located. It looked like that it was either right in the galactic centre, or on the other side of the galaxy.

There were several comings and goings on Planet Earth too. The sea level rise of 42 metres meant some cities had to eventually succumb. Most of the eastern seaboard of the USA as well as most of the Netherlands and Denmark had been evacuated long ago, as had populations on the once vast river basins of the Ganges and Amazon. Some cities like Lisbon, San Francisco and Rio de Janeiro, had built vast elevated platforms so the city that was previously near the coast was now 100 metres up into the surrounding mountains.

The combination of even lower birth rates and increased suicides meant the population of the planet was predicted to drop below 2 billion before the end of the first decade of the new century. This was a population level not seen since 1930.

Ning was having trouble finding any more traces of aquanine and this was mirrored in no significant further drop in the numbers of whales and dolphins. Shen rightly assumed that this was because all the cetaceans who wanted to 'port had already gone. It was Frejya who shed light on why some had stayed behind. She told Shen that some guardians of the noosphere would always be required while there was life on the planet.

On Planet Earth conspiracy theories abounded. The Internet was still intact and increasingly active after all. There were reports of strange black tetrahedral shapes flying at night. The possibility that there was a secret base on the far side of the Moon was prevalent. Neither of these theories were new. Both had been postulated back in the 20th century, so many gave them no credence.

The Space Port was also awash with rumour and gossip. Most of the orbiting citizens knew about the Moon Base now but were sworn to secrecy. The penalty for leaking was unthinkable and there had been some mysterious disappearances already of those who never made it back to Earth. The tittle-tattle at 250 kilometres above the Earth was all about who might be selected for transfer to the Moon Base.

On the Moon Base itself, everyone knew about the terraformation of Mars but only tens of people knew that there was a ship hovering above the far side currently being fitted out for test flight. At the same time, only a handful knew about the pulses and the possible connection with disappearance of the cetacean population of the blue-green planet.

Only Shen, Cheng and Miang knew of the possible existence of Aquanine and its theoretical location.

Only Frejya knew that there would be only one more big pulse before something cataclysmic would arrive. She had been considering whether to tell Shen or not but her intuition was it wasn't the time as it might lead to some decisions being made that weren't necessary right now.

82

The Great Attractor

2101 : 8 years left

"Only one week?" asked Cheng. "That changes everything."

"Yes, but if the q-computer is right, it will still take a month to get back," confirmed Shen. "And still after a wait of a couple of years."

The unmanned test flights of the Heart of Gold slingshotting around the Earth and back to the Moon had unearthed a strange phenomenon.

At first, Shen had thought the increases and decreases in speed exiting Earth orbit had been due to minor gravitation influences from raised land masses.

It took analyses from the q-computer to work out the true source of the speed variations. The greatest increase occurred when the craft entered Earth orbit over areas with the largest human populations and then exited over remote, unpopulated areas.

Shen consulted with Jia and Frejya for confirmation. They both tapped into Mother Earth and agreed with the q-computer's findings.

Shen explained to Cheng, "So we seem get a boost between 1% and 2%. This means that a series of around 70 strategic slingshots could boost the exit speed of the craft when it went to Mars by a factor of 4 or so."

The q-computer had also trawled back through records of other craft that were sent inward to slingshot around Venus and Mercury and then back via Earth. Much smaller anomalies had been noticed but never attributed to consciousness on Planet Earth.

'We-We-We think the nano-fans like the place they came from and the people who made them,' the q-computer had enigmatically said.

Shen had confirmed that flying east over the Chinese landmass and exiting over the expanded Pacific indeed seemed to give the maximum speed increase.

The main issue now was not the maximum speed of the drive but how much acceleration and deceleration the occupants could stand. Mia and Mei of course became the first test pilots.

Unlike any other space craft, the drive's self-powered nano-fans allowed for virtually unlimited testing, with many permutations. It took them three months, and thousands of slingshots, before Shen and Lance were able to confirm the one week transit time to Mars was possible.

"The nano-fans on the seats mean Taikonauts can sustain 25G at least without even noticing it," Shen said.

"Is radiation still a problem?" asked Miang, who had developed a keen technical interest and understanding of the project.

"Not really, the hardening is pretty impervious," replied Lance. "I'd say boredom was still the biggest issue."

"Yes, boredom and a crushing sense of isolation," said Shen. "Even at over a million clicks, once Earth shrinks to the size of a dot, it will appear as if you are not moving for a few days."

The test flights had involved the craft travelling out way past the orbit of the Moon.

"So tell them what's it like to travel further away from Earth than any other human," said Lance.

Mia went first, "It's both scary and peaceful at the same time. As you approach aphelion, a million miles out everything is just still and the Earth is just a blue dot."

"When you come racing back in, it's a blur. We had to close our eyes when the Earth was beneath us to stop being sick," piped in Mei.

Frejya had confirmed even better news, "And we can confirm zero comms delay. It will take me some time to train the first students and flight control crew but it's like riding a bike. Once you know the trick it's easy."

Frejya had sussed it out during the test flights as Mia and Mei went three times as far away from the Moon than ever before.

"So when's the first trip?" asked Miang, knowing he was referring to the unmanned round trip journey.

"The next Hoffman window for conventional rocketry is August next year but we can leave seven months later, so March 2102," said Shen.

"And the first rocks will be back when?" asked Cheng.

"The next Mars return window is December 2103 but we're going to simulate an emergency evac," said Shen. "If we leave five months earlier, and use a Venus slingshot, the samples will be with us after two months, so by October the same year."

While all this phrenetic off-Moon activity was going on, the two sets of twins had been kept busy on more pedestrian but equally important tasks. Eva and Kristin were working with Xing and chef Chang on how to make the inside surfaces of the Lower Tet into a virtually unlimited food bank. Most importantly in how to create a food source that was tasty and varied.

Jun and Li had now been seconded to Mike Spence's team and were getting their heads around the amazing ingenuity and complexity of the terraformation programme. Structurally, everything was in place. All that was really left to do was to alter the atmosphere in the canyon so it was breathable.

It was Jun who came up with the bright idea of how that might be accelerated. He had become fascinated by Mike's nano-insects. He first introduced them into Xing's bio-dome to tease him, flying them past his ears and getting them to crawl in his hair.

It was Xing's chastisement that got Jun thinking, "Could you please do something useful with them?"

When Mike learned that Jun had got the nano-insects to pollinate some of Xing's crops, a whole new opportunity opened up for the canyon.

83

Mars Rocks

2102 : 7 years left

There was not much to do with the Heart of Gold ahead of its trip across to Mars in March but to play with it and extend its capabilities.

Shen was busy programming the q-computer for two main tasks. Firstly to image the binary star system from a different angle to see if any more information could be gleaned about the tertiary object. Secondly, to test the entanglement engine in interplanetary space, well away from the gravitational influence of any large bodies. Lance knew about the engine but not that it now contained molecules of aquanine.

At Frejya's intuitive suggestion, Shen had also commissioned the construction of another ship down in Jiuquan, due for delivery to the Moon by the time the next pulse was due. She had also suggested a design change that neither Shen or Lance had come up with. Just in case either the Upper or Lower Tet was compromised, she suggested both Tets should be able to detach from each other and for either then be used as a life raft.

Shen was too busy and involved with all projects to stop to ask Frejya if she knew something that he didn't.

Frejya had thrown herself into getting the school ready for its first intake of potential Martians later that year. With Jia's help, she had already starting teaching the most promising students how to delete the comms time delay between Earth and Moon while they were still at the Seven Immortals. She'd also suggested to Shen that those who were most talented at performing the feat should be considered for the first intake.

Deleting the delay involved forming a psychic bond with the person you were talking to, so you knew what they were going to say, just before they said it. You then give your answer before you hear what they have said. It just took a little trust but once perfected, it became second nature.

In the gap between the slingshot tests and its departure to Mars, Mia and Mei had been tasked with training Jun and Li on the Heart of Gold systems. The twins became expert at detaching the inner Lander Tet from the Lower Tet and travelling to and from the Moon surface with it. This was how Mia and Mei had been getting to and from the Heart of Gold for the slingshot tests.

They also performed a few dockings with the Moon Port, as well as a couple of unsanctioned trips back and from Earth orbit. All in all the design concept that Shen had come up with in the vacuum chamber at the Seven Immortals only seven years earlier, with Lu Seng's assistance, was proving to be pretty versatile and resilient.

A week before the Heart of Gold was to begin its 60 million mile crossing to the Red Planet, Jun had the honour of taking Shen, Cheng and Miang up and into the craft before it left. As they exited the Lander Tet, they could see the walls of the Lower Tet covered with empty containers readied for the production of all the food the first Martians would need for the crossing and while in orbit.

As they emerged into the Upper Tet, they met with eight dummies packed with sensors, strapped into their seats. Shen smiled when he saw Jun and Li had stuck a picture of his face on to the dummy in the pilot's seat.

Shen waved his hands over the pilot's controls and several screens burst into life. One contained a packed star field.

Shen zoomed in until the centre of the screen was blank, just with three stars around it.

"What's that?" asked Miang.

"That black point in space is where Mars will be in a few week's time," Cheng butted in.

"Indeed, so once the initial slingshot acceleration sequence is finished, the drive will send this beauty to that point in space," explained Shen. "We'll start the deceleration once the gravity field of Mars is greater than the pull from Earth."

"And getting back?" asked Miang.

"That's where Venus will come in," said Shen. "With no conscious life on Mars, we can't use it for any boost."

Miang pretended he had got his head around it all but this level of soulwave interaction escaped him. Shen and Cheng knew his role was merely to oversee the prolongation of the human race, and the Chinese dynasty. Shen was not a politician but sensed an agenda was driving all of his invention.

Only when they got back in the lander did Miang spot the rover nestled under the pilot seat.

"So this will be bringing a bit of Mars to the Moon?" asked Miang.

"Well not exactly," answered Shen. "Once the rocks are on board, they will be staying on board for the next mission. We can't risk any cross contamination."

Cheng added, "That's why most of the innards have been built in Moon orbit by nano-bots. This rover will be staying on Mars too."

Miang's trip to the Heart of Gold was the first time he'd left the Moon's surface for five years. He asked Jun to fly him over the Earth-facing surface before they went back to the Moon Base.

He wished secretly that he could be amongst the first Martians. Once a president, always a president.

84

Changes of Plans

2104 : 5 years left

The Heart of Gold's test flight to and from Mars went off without a hitch. A small extension to the mission plan meant it didn't get back into Moon orbit until January 2104. The reason being was that it was decided to return samples from several landing sites, in addition to the soil samples at the entrance to the Valles Marineris.

The slingshot around Venus was a long way back but what was even more successful was that the q-computer worked out the altered return path and orbital dynamics by itself. It had also suggested that bringing back more than one sample was feasible in the same mission.

The reason it had done so was of course influenced by the Councillors. They were a little dismayed that Shen had not even thought to look into the process of teleportation as an alternate mode of transport across the cosmos. He had the evidence that it was possible from the dolphins. In the forms of Jia and Frejya, he had people who could achieve it with a little practice. When he bilocated as a child, he had even experienced one of the unintended spin offs from being able to 'port.

The Councillors now foresaw that Mars could now become the second sentient planet ahead of a potential re-birthed Earth. This would mean more sites would have to be terraformed, hence more samples needed.

In the intervening time between the Heart of Gold leaving and returning, Frejya and Shen had to make an unexpected return trip to the Seven Immortals.

In late Summer 2103, Hui suffered a stroke. Jia didn't think he would last a week so they were piloted straight to the Monastery by Mia, with Li as co-pilot.

It took them a few days to adjust to 1G, having been away for over four years. It took them a little longer to come to terms with Hui's decline. He had lost the use of his right side. His mouth was drooping and he needed feeding. He could still speak, albeit with much slurring, and had full mental capacity. Even with all Jia's skills as a healer, the light had gone from his eyes.

Shen's and Frejya's appearance seems to rally him though and his son's ingenuity is what saved him. They had planned to stay a month and at first Shen thought he couldn't take that much time away. While Frejya and Jia worked with Hui's subtle energies, Shen busied himself in Hui's 3D workshop. Frejya at first thought he was burying his head in the sand, and more work, until he emerged a few days later with a rather bizarre looking half-suit.

It was a hybrid-mix of 3D cogs and gears combined with an ingenious nano-technology layer. Hui seemed to grasp straight away what Shen had built for him. The suit was awash with nano-fans and, with voice control, Hui quickly learned to raise his arm and move his leg.

Like all strokes, it was to be a slow journey. Shen made modifications to the half-suit so that it picked up subtle movements from Hui's muscles. After a month, the thoughts he wanted to move a muscle were controlling that bit of the suit. Within two months he was walking again, with a support frame. Three months in, he was self-feeding with his right hand.

In between healing sessions with Hui and catch up time

with Jia, Frejya took time to chat with each of the students at the Monastery. An ageing Madame Bien was running a tight ship and had amassed a hugely talented bunch of students. They were not just intellectuals but all compassionate humanitarians, just what you need to start a new world.

Early in the New Year, Shen and Frejya left the Monastery for a few days for a much needed break together walking in the mountains. When they returned to the Seven Immortals on foot, they were greeted by Mei and Jun and the sight of a space-ready Tet.

The fact Hui was able to hug them both fully in his goodbyes was simply amazing. It was Jia's parting words that brought tears to their eyes.

"This really is goodbye both of you," she said. "Thank you for coming back and bringing my husband back."

"We'll be keeping more in touch," said Frejya, promising to call daily rather than the weekly pattern they'd fallen into.

It's easy to forget about home when you are working elsewhere on something new and exciting. The break had reminded Shen that his project could potentially deliver a new home, not just for a few but the whole population of the planet. There was nothing that could not be scaled up, so long as there was enough time.

In March that year, the next pulse arrived in such a pronounced fashion that it was clear that enough time was just what they didn't have.

The Moon Base was exposed to the full force of the pulse but its roof provided the protection it was designed for. The same technology held successfully over the Valles Marineris.

As the exact timing of the pulse could not be predicted down to the minute, Shen knew it was a somewhat of a lottery for the Space and Moon Ports. Luckily the less protectable Moon Port was on the right side of the Moon so was spared. The Space Port took the pulse full on.

When all its comms went down, the thousands of people

living there were stranded. There was no way down.

Mia and Mei came up with the rescue plan. With Mia in the Moon Tube and Mei on a Tet, and both of them in radiation suits, they made it over to the Space Port within an hour. The crew of the Space Port were well trained in emergency evacuation procedures and saw the Moon Tube and Tet coming. When they both docked, the air locks were manually opened.

Like all communities, the Space Port had a council that ran affairs. Strangely enough there were twelve of them. Major Zhang had assumed the role of their leader several years back. Nobody had objected as he was the most experienced Taikonaut.

All suited up, the twelve of them were to make their first trip to the Moon Base with Mia in a cramped Moon Tube. Before they left, the news quickly went around the Space Port that a rescue mission was being mounted and there really wasn't any reason to panic. Mei continued down to Jiuquan in the Tet to relay the news personally to the ground team that all the population on the Space Port were stranded but safe.

Many of the inhabitants of Planet Earth were not so fortunate. Those that were outside in the Sun at the time of the pulse received an invisible, yet lethal, dose of gamma rays. Few of them would be around in five years time when the next pulse that they knew nothing about was due. One of them was Hui who was having one of his suit-assisted afternoon walks.

While all of this was unfolding, Shen was briefing Miang and Cheng.

"Lagrange A has been taken out meaning all year round comms with Mars is now lost," he announced. "And the replacement Lagrange B was a month from being fully operational and seems to have gone too."

"That's worrying and that's even with its extra hardening."

said Cheng. "How long before we can replace them?"

"Around three years because of launch windows," said Shen. "But there is an alternative."

"Which is?" asked Miang.

"We can be back at Mars in less time on the Heart of Gold with a team to manage the terraformation directly," said Shen. "We still have to put replacement, and extra hardened, Lagrange comms links in but this would mean we could bring the whole project forward by several years."

"But our training programme hasn't produced the first graduates, who do you propose goes?" asked Miang.

Shen didn't answer but merely stated what had been unsaid, "Apart from any other consideration, we might not have as long as we hoped."

Shen realised his next few months involved more modelling than he had ever done before. His life, his families lives and those of all humanity were dependent on the results.

85

Choices

2105 : 4 years left

"So you are sure?" asked Miang.

"Well I am 85% sure the q-computer's prediction is correct," answered Shen. "Either in 2109, or a 15% chance in 2114, the supernova ejecta will reach our solar system."

Shen had been running the simulations generated by the q-computer. The occlusion of the binary by the tertiary had not happened. This implied it had fused with one of the stars, most likely with the secondary. If this was the case, the q-computer predicted the combined star mass would fuse with the primary in five years time.

Shen didn't share the complex maths as he was still getting his head around it.

At the same time, Miang was still struggling with the concept of light years and that the binary went supernova in either 1959, or 1964, and that its energetic blast wave was 4 to 9 light years away from Earth, approaching at the speed of light.

"The prediction of initial fatalities is low. It's the cancers that will grow with a reduced magnetosphere that will have medium-term impact," continued Shen. "What we can only speculate on is that the eco-system may be irreversibly damaged for centuries."

Mike Spence chipped in, "The next wave of nano-bots will complete the additional hardening we need here by the end of next year. On Mars, we have started at the Chryse Planitia end of the canyon but we'll only just make that end of the canyon safe from the GRB by 2109."

"So that spells the end of life on Earth," concluded Cheng.

"Or life as we've known it," said Shen.

"So Major Zhang, update us on the Mars Mission," said Miang.

"The second Heart of Gold just arrived in Moon orbit only yesterday and we've now upgraded the existing ship so the two Tets are separable too," said Zhang. "Both ships will be ready to leave in time for the next Hoffman transfer window in June next year."

"And we'll have hardened replacements for Lagrange A and B in place by the time we get there," confirmed Shen.

"And have the crews all been decided upon now, and told?" asked Miang.

"They have and they cannot wait to go," said Shen.

Much had happened since Zhang arrived on the Moon Base. Despite the Major's earlier remonstrations, a year after the pulse hit, the first sections of the Space Port were now being detached and sent to burn up, with their remnants ending up in the spacecraft cemetery in the mid-Pacific. The Space Port had become commercially and strategically unviable, especially now Tets could fly straight from Earth to the Moon. Even the orbiting Moon Port's days were numbered and it was now completely unmanned.

Somewhat ironically, a skeleton crew chosen from the brightest engineers who designed and built the Space Port in the first place, were the ones that oversaw its demise. The remaining 2000 or so inhabitants had been given a simple choice. Sign a heavy and punitive non-disclosure agreement and transfer to the Moon Base. Alternatively, they could return to Earth and see their days out there. Two thirds of them chose this latter option as they were home sick.

Those that chose to migrate to the Moon Base discovered quickly that they had landed on their feet, even though it was with feet that were sucked down with 1/6 G. They learned about the Martian terraformation programme and, as experienced Taikonauts and space engineers, that they had roles either as teachers or potential Martian settlers. Mike had built several large new domes to house them all and food production had gone industrial.

Zhang's arrival at the Moon Base had of course been orchestrated by the Councillors.

It was Shen that had changed Zhang's mind, by seconding him to the Mars terraformation project. To Shen's relief, the Major had not only volunteered to be Commander for the first mission but also to move to Mars and not to come back. As Shen was planning to take Frejya, Eva and Kristin with him, having the most experienced Taikonaut with them gave him much comfort.

It was now clear that it was unviable to stick to the original plan to go to Mars once the atmosphere in the canyon was breathable. The current batch of students would form the second wave of settlers.

The Major hand-picked the rest of the first wave team. Mia and Mei were to be the pilots of the two craft. Jun and Li were nominated as co-pilots. Zhang also insisted on taking Wang Yang and Deng Yang, a married couple who had carried out the most hours of space walks of any humans. Although the craft were not designed for extra-vehicular activity, you never knew in space what might go wrong.

Although Frejya was an accomplished healer, Zhang insisted that Dr Liu Yaping, the leading surgeon from the Space Port was on the crew. There was nothing that she couldn't fix.

Shen insisted that Mike Spence came along as he knew more than anyone about the engineering of the canyon. It was also Shen's idea that the final crew member should be the chef Chang. There was no reason they shouldn't eat well.

So it was planned that Zhang's team would be the first and permanent settlers. Shen and his family would help make the canyon viable for life and may stay or return, should their help be needed back with the Earth-Moon system. Shen knew that he would never get Jia to come as she was looking after an increasingly ill Hui.

The Mars mission meant he could not take time out for a last visit to see them. They were in daily contact though and even Shen had learned how to delete the comms time delay.

Only one thing was concerning Shen. He'd got the q-computer to run simulations on the DNA of both the first wave of crew and the current crop of students to help detect any possible genetic anomalies when the inevitable and planned matings occurred.

He was wondering when he should tell the Major that he knew Mia and Mei were his daughters and that their mother was probably a Wu.

86

In Suspension

June 2106 : 3 years left

Hui and Jia were the only two people on Planet Earth who knew about the manned Mars mission. Everyone else in on the project were now based at the Moon Port. The facilities at Jiuquan were being scaled down now that the Space Port had completely burned up. The last of the decommissioning engineers landed in the last remaining DreamChaser that had been docked with the Space Port.

All the Tets that could travel from Earth to the Moon were permanently parked at the Moon Base. Only emergency visits were allowed to see dying relatives and the Moon Base was now completely self-sufficient in food production.

At the Seven Immortals, Hui's cancers had stopped yielding to Jia's ministrations. He was determined to hold on until he knew his son, daughter in law and grand daughters were safely in orbit around Mars. Jia had told Shen privately that he wouldn't last the month to hear about the first feet to touch the Martian surface.

The two crews had been on board the two Heart of Gold ships, now designated HoG1 and HoG2, for nearly two days. This was useful as the hangovers from their leaving party to end all parties had just dissipated. Much to Shen's annoyance, Zhang insisted that the interplanetary trip would be dry. Shen had secretly stashed some bottles though to celebrate successful entry into orbit and touchdown on the surface.

The two crews had been on board the ships many times which helped them all get used to the Landers that Shen had first seen emulated in the vacuum chamber. The trip up from the Moon surface took just five minutes. As they approached the ships, they were impossible to see. The only way to detect their presence was by the triangular black cut outs they made in the star field.

Docking in the Lower Tet was automatic and like a graceful ballet. One side of the 22 metre Tet folded completely back for the 11 metre sided Lander to float inside. It was a small climb to get up into the Upper Tet. Its 33 metre long sides made it cavernous compared with rocket powered capsules. Weight and size were not a premium but an advantage.

Everyone had their own private sleeping pod on the Tet wall and each had its own private toilet facilities. They were fitted with a nano-fan array that made evacuation close to the experience of sitting on a planet-based loo.

Dividing the 14 crew between the two Tets was easy. Mia and Mei were the two main pilots of HoG1 and HoG2 respectively, assisted by Jun and Li as their co-pilots. Kristin was naturally on HoG1 with Jun and Eva on HoG2 with Li.

Shen was dubbed Commander of HoG1 but he deferred to Zhang, as Commander of HoG2 and the whole mission, when it came to matters of safety. The Major had little idea of Shen's multiple alternative strategies he'd been simulating on the q-computer.

Frejya was on HoG1 with Shen with Dr Liu Yaping providing medical support on HoG2. The experienced married Taikonauts Wang and Deng Yang would be spending the trip apart. Shen commandeered chef Chang for HoG1 for the week long trip and had given Mike Spence the remaining seat on HoG2.

As planned the two, near identical Heart of Gold ships left Earth orbit in June 2106. The Major had agreed to stay on

Mars indefinitely, with one ship remaining in orbit. The plan was then to send one ship back at the reverse transfer time of June 2108 to pick up the next wave of settlers. As they had already proved, this could be done either with a pilot and a crew or unmanned.

Just in case they had to evacuate and come back sooner, a longer transfer time would be required. For this reason, Shen had successfully developed a system of suspended animation which oddly enough involved injecting the sleeping Taikonaut with about a litre of aquanine. He and Mike had now worked out how to synthesise it and it turned out easier to do this at 1/6G.

All the Taikonauts were given the option of sleeping for the one week trip but nobody took it up. Perhaps this was they didn't want to miss the ballot scheduled for the halfway point of the crossing, where it would be decided who was to put their foot on Mars first.

It was decided that Mia and Mei would manually control the two ships for the slingshot sequence. There was no real need for this but it gave them something to do for some of the trip at least. Shen had convinced Zhang that the entanglement engines, which both contained samples of Mars rocks, would be used to navigate them into Mar's orbital path. Zhang was sceptical but Shen was insistent. The skills of Mia and Mei would be called for when taking the Landers down through the often turbulent atmosphere.

In total, only 50 elliptical slingshot orbits were needed to get the ships up to speed, as Shen had been dabbling with increasing the contra-rotational speeds of the Upper and Lower Tets to increase their overall velocity. So on each fly past of the Earth, the ships went further and further out past the Moon and the rotational speed increased on each path. If you were able to see the ships, the triangular Tets would have blurred into cones.

Inside the crew felt nothing as the increases in forward

and rotational velocity were gradual. They were of course all strapped in for their safety but the nano-fans in their seats meant they never felt like they were pulling more than 2G.

The Tets of course had no exterior windows. If they could have seen out, the blur would be stomach churning. The q-computer extracted and processed just the right amount of pixels to give them a spectacular view of the fly past of their home planet. Even then on perihelion, the closest approach, the planet came and went in a few seconds.

As they flew off in the arc to intersect with Mar's orbit, Mia and Mei chimed in unison, "Engaging entanglement drives."

Everyone un-belted and they were all transfixed at the speed with which their home planet became a small blue dot.

At just a day away from the Earth, it became impossible to pick out their home planet from the star field. Even though they were travelling at a phenomenal speed, as Shen predicted, the reconstructed view of the surrounding star field made it appear as they were just stuck in suspension in space, going nowhere.

87

Evacuation

June 2106 : 3 years left

Shen was able to test his new found ability to talk across space without time delay by catching up with Jia. At over thirty million kilometres out from Earth, the round trip time delay would be nearly 4 minutes but as he'd been chatting each day, with an ever increasing time delay, it was like they were in the next room.

"He is still hanging on for you to get there," said Jia.

"Nearly half way now Mother," said Shen.

"I can sense you," replied Jia. "You've never been this far from me."

"Can Hui see where we are?" asked Shen, who had reprogrammed one of his 3D orreries to show their position.

"It's what's keeping him alive," Jia said. "He wants to talk to you."

A weak sounding Hui came on, "Tell me what's it's like out there, son."

"Well Earth and Mars are just blue and red dots," said Shen. "We're travelling so much faster than any rocket powered craft …"

"And don't tell me," said Hui. "It's not like you're moving."

"That's pretty much it, father," said Shen. "We could be completely still or going back towards Earth, we've got no visual cues."

"Apart from I can see where you are on my orrery," said Hui, who then pained Shen with an uncontrollable coughing fit.

Jia came back on, "He misses you Shen."

"Sorry Mother, Zhang's initiating his simulated emergency," said Shen. "Nothing for you to worry about but I must go."

"OK but let me speak to the girls tomorrow," blurted Jia.

The Major and Shen had come up with a fabulous plan to both test the emergency capability of having two craft traversing the void of space and to relieve the boredom of the seven day crossing. Mia and Mei were in on it too and a day earlier had started slowing down the rotation of their respective Lower Tets. They then began to spin them up the the same speed and direction as the Upper Tets.

Nobody on board felt or suspected a thing. As they were just passing the half way point, they had to start slowing down anyway to match Mar's orbital speed. Shen was pleased that their plan very neatly halved their speed.

Zhang came over the intercom of both Tets, "This is only a drill so don't panic but treat it as it's a real emergency."

He continued, "Eva, Li, Wang and Chang, please get suited up and descend into your Lower Tet."

Eva, sharp as a pin, said, "But we can't, it'll be like jumping into the fast spin of a washing machine."

Mia said, "Don't worry Eva, it's rotating the same direction and rate as we are. It's perfectly safe."

"And the same here," confirmed Mei. "So the same goes for you Kristin, Jun, Deng and Mike."

"Yes, you're all going for a little ride," said Zhang with whimsy in his voice, so pleased he was at the plan.

When all eight Taikonauts were seated and strapped in, Mia and Mei began the most spectacular and audacious ballet every attempted in the history of space flight. Each Lower Tet detached from its Upper Tet and they then swung around each other in a one kilometre wide arc, one above and the other below.

For an hour the crews were split between four separate Tets until each Lower Tet docked with a new Upper Tet. Everything was done in synchronism, to the millisecond.

Mia and Mei said in unison, "OK, it's safe to come on board. Up you all come."

There was relief all round and Zhang was grinning from ear to ear. He was hoping this never had to be done for real but pleased it worked flawlessly. Shen and Zhang had held back from telling anyone on the Moon Port what they'd planned, as they were sure it would have been vetoed.

88

Aquaforming

55,000 Light Years Away

While Shen and Mike were finessing their plans for terraforming a small section of Mars, across the other side of the galaxy, Luki was getting into his stride as an expert in aqua-formation. He was of course completely unaware that he, like Shen, was an incarnate Councillor of the Light.

He was in his late teens now and while he was still a pup was given, by Pata, the nano-bots and aqua-bots as play things. Pata had no idea what they were or what to do with them.

At first, Luki created macro structures with them and used his sonar to nudge their growth in one direction or the other. Like the young Shen, he was fascinated by creating extremely elaborate fractal designs, rather like coral reefs.

The nano-bots and aqua-bots had an intelligence of their own, directed by the Councillors of course. During the eighteen short years Luki had been on Aquanine, the nano-bots had created island peaks that broke the ocean's surface.

It was shortly after this happened Luki discovered that, when he poked his head above the water, he could direct his clicks towards the shore and influence the direction of the 'bots. He first started creating fractal shapes on land and next learned how to form them into regular geometric shapes.

At the same time all of this was going on, the dolphins and whales had been using their teleportation abilities to bring more and more of the complexity from the Earth's oceans to Aquanine. Some species didn't take to H_6O_3.

Crabs were fine but lobsters didn't survive long. Octopi were fine too but squid perished immediately. As intelligent cephalopods couldn't communicate with cetaceans, having come from different galaxies originally, this was a bit of a mystery.

In the early years, the cetaceans had simply fished for their food on Earth and teleported it over. Epoch Five humans thought that the drop in fish stocks was down to their over-fishing alone, such was their arrogance about their influence. As cetaceans knew that time was running out, for the last few hundred years they had been 'porting over whole food chains, from phytoplankton, plankton and corals and krill, as well as larger crustaceans and fish.

As for the kelp and sea grasses, some species thrived in Aquanine and some reverse 'porting had to occur for those that didn't. This level of micro-management was complex and time consuming so, after some debate, it was agreed to 'port over some apex predators.

Knowing that their peaceful existence was about to be threatened, it was with some dread and regret that the first sharks appeared on Aquanine. The only reason it was agreed was that most adult cetaceans could instantly 'port several kilometres away if threatened. They would have to keep their pups close.

89

One Small Step

July 2106 : 3 years left

Excitement had been growing since Mars had become discernible as a bright red-orange disc, not long after the ballot was taken.

Nobody quite trusted the q-computer for some reason, so chef Chang suggested they cut seven pieces of spaghetti and the person who picked the longest on each craft got to take the first step.

Mia and Mei were chuffed to bits when they both struck lucky. The Major was especially proud and still didn't know that Shen knew he was their father.

Everyone else was happy for them too for a couple of reasons. Firstly, they would all get to feel what it's like to walk in 0.38G before the year was out. Secondly, other than the few thousand people on the Moon Base, nobody on Earth would know. None of them would accrue the fame that 'one small step' gave to Neil Armstrong.

Two days out from Mars, the Upper Tet's rotation was slowed to zero. The disc of Mars was visible without any magnification and getting larger and larger by the hour.

The nano-fans on the seats and floor of both the Upper Tet and Lander were adjusted to match Mars gravity. There would be no heavy sea legs when that first step was taken.

Mia and Mei were impressed at how well the entanglement

engine not only brought them into match the orbital speed of Mars, at exactly 86,871 kilometres per hour, but also right to where the planet was in space at the exact minute they planned to be in orbit around it.

Although the craft were well capable of entering a geostationary orbit, everyone wanted to circle the planet and get a good look around their potential new home.

After three days in orbit, everyone had got a reasonable grasp of the high level geography of the whole planet. They were of course viewing everything on screen but it was so different being there and 'seeing' it, compared to seeing imagery from probes. Mia and Mei then steered them right above the Valles Marineris, so they were geostationary at 3000 kilometres right above the Chryse Planitia.

The canyon was vast. At 4000 kilometres long and 7 kilometres deep, you could fit about 22 Grand Canyons into it. That would make a big enough habitat for many humans for quite some time.

As Mia and Mei were in separate craft, The Major gave the go ahead to take two Landers down but insisted that Wang Yang accompanied Mei and Deng Yang rode down with Mia. Should anything go wrong, they were the best people to have with you. Mia and Mei thought it amusing that the first time they'd meet in over a week was to be on the surface of Mars. The four of them were fully suited up and the emergency parachutes in the Landers primed.

The descent was smooth until they reached the top of the atmosphere at 10.8 kilometres. Mia and Mei both took manual control to minimise the buffeting. Below 3 kilometres, it was less of a rocky ride. After a descent taking just over 30 minutes, the Lander Tets got to within 3 metres of the surface, and hovered.

"We're down," chimed Mia and Mei in unison. The whole of the Moon Base, who were watching, burst into rapturous applause. This was 10 minutes after everyone in the orbiting

Tets heard the news. The 360 degree views were spectacular.

"It looks just like the Gobi Desert," observed Wang.

"Except the Gobi Desert doesn't have a wall on an entrance to a canyon like this," said his wife, Deng Yang.

The Landers were hovering a hundred metres away from the part of the canyon ceiling that joined it to the canyon floor, creating a hermetic seal.

"OK," said Mike. "Outer gateway opening."

As he announced this, the nano-bots rearranged themselves to create a perfect 12 metre sided equilateral triangular-shaped hole for the Landers to pass through. Mei took her lander in first, followed by Mia.

"Outer gateway closed," announced Mike. "Inner gateway opening."

A further 100 metres away an identical 12 metre sided opening appeared in the second protective wall of what was the largest air lock ever created. It was 250 metres in width and height. Mike was making provision for some very large craft to come in and out in the future should Shen ever need it. Unlike air locks on the Space and Moon Ports, there was no actual breathable air inside the canyon yet. This was more like a 'dust lock'.

The two Landers travelled in parallel a further kilometre to a virtual replica of the Moon Base. The only difference was there were no lights on inside the domes and there was nobody home. A smaller, dimmer and yellower Sun was right overhead, casting no shadows. It was like they were on a pristine movie set. Everything seemed false, yet all too real.

Mike had switched the landing lights on the Lander pads on.

"Touch down," announced Mei.

"And locked in," said Mia.

Shen and Zhang did a virtual high five, being in two different craft. Shen and Mike did a real one.

"OK, when you are ready, lower the sides," said Mike.

The two whole sides of the two Landers opened gently until they lay completely flat, with their apexes nearly touching. Mei saw Mia for the first time in over a week, as did the husband and wife Taikonauts.

"Unbuckling now," said Mei, and Mia followed her. They walked down the centre of the open face of the Tet and joined hands.

They then took a cautious step on to the landing pad and both said together, "That's two small steps for women and two giant leaps for humankind."

Zhang had given Wang and Deng his permission to follow them. He kind of knew they would if he hadn't and they so deserved to be the third and fourth humans to walk on the surface of Mars. They had saved his life on more than one occasion after all.

While orbiting the planet, it was clear the canyon was a huge structure, a deep scar on the surface. On the bottom of the canyon floor its size became apparent.

"We can't see the tops of the canyon walls," said Wang.

The four of them then unloaded two additional payloads that Shen and Mike had brought over five years ahead of the originally planned time. Mars was about to be awoken.

Unlike when 530 million people watched the Apollo 11 landing on July 24 in 1969, only two people on Earth saw these first steps. A minute after Mia and Mei made their first footfall, one of those two on Earth died.

90

Maya Awakens

July 2106 : 3 years left

Shen took Hui's death in his stride and saw it as a release. It hit Frejya and the twins hard though and they were relieved of any meaningful duties for a few days.

Unlike the Apollo 11 mission, the four first Martians only spent an hour on the surface before making the reverse trip up. Just because they could, and for some variety, each Lander returned to a different HoG.

While an important life had slipped away on Earth, the two payloads were the real seeds of new life on Mars. After a long call with an understandably upset Jia, Shen excused himself to begin work with Mike on the next and crucial phase of the mission.

The first of the two payloads dropped on the canyon floor contained oxygen-producing cyanobacteria and algae for the production of molecular oxygen on Martian soil. Shen and Mike didn't know this wasn't for the first time. The bacteria and algae were taken by nano-bots across to both canyon walls.

The second payload contained methanogens. These are microorganisms that produce methane and are present in the human gut. Mars was about to start farting, which is one of the perils of interplanetary space flight that for some reason isn't mentioned in Taikonaut training.

When life arrives on a planet, it alters a planet's consciousness, its noosphere, in a subtle way. So the arrival of the four sentient beings gave Maya a nudge and a reminder what it was like to be a planet that harboured life. This triggered a large subterranean Mars-quake near the South Pole. Mike's seismometers detected it straight away.

What happened next surprised both Mike and Shen. The nano-bot built pipelines had already reached the South Pole, having made a trip of over 5000 kilometres over some pretty trying terrain. The plant equipment that would melt the water ice and extract water and carbon dioxide and pump it to Valles Marineris was just about to start heating. The Mars-quake did everyone a big favour by creating a huge amount of melt water that could be pumped straight away.

This resulted in the greening of the canyon walls at the Chryse Planitia end of the canyon before year was out.

For a little while only, the Councillors had allowed sentient life to exist on three planets in the same galaxy at the same time.

91

Water Worlds

2107 : 2 years left

The noospheres of Earth, Mars and all the planets in the solar system are contained and connected by the consciousness field of the Sun, the solosphere.

It is understandable therefore that one planet can pick up on what another planet is 'thinking'. It may come as no surprise then that Mother Earth, Lady Gaia, nudged by the Mayan consciousness, also instigated a large earthquake at her own South Pole. As a result, in January 2107, at the height of the Antarctic summer, all the remaining ice left the continental shelf.

It is somewhat ironic that, in the Duality of the Density, the two of the three planets that were harbouring intelligent life in this particular galaxy were having such opposite experiences. Just as the Earth's land masses were at their minimum size, Aquanine's landmasses were growing day by day. As the noospheres of the two water worlds are connected via the galosphere, the galactic consciousness, again perhaps this is not surprising.

By the end of the last Earth year, all the Taikonauts had made trips down to the canyon on Mars and inspected their new potential home. Mike was in floods of tears when he first saw his creation up close. It had been his baby from the start.

The greening of the canyon walls was rapid, as was the

production of oxygen and methane. Along with the carbon dioxide brought from the South Pole, there were enough greenhouse gases to have raised the ambient temperature of the hermetically sealed canyon to just below zero degrees Centigrade. The oxygen levels were already up to 33% of that of the Earth at sea level, so about the same as at the top of Mount Everest.

As well as oxygen being generated by the rapidly spreading cyanobacteria on the canyon walls, Mike had installed vast baths of water containing phytoplankton. Mike predicted that within half a Martian year, or one Earth year, the canyon atmosphere would be breathable.

Eva and Kristin had been kept busy getting the food production dome up to speed. Along with chef Chang, they'd been spending many days and nights camped out there. Mike had rigged up a temporary supply of breathable oxygen inside the dome so that they could work safely without suits. Within the next Martian year, the dome was providing all the vegetables, herbs, salads, nuts and worms that they needed for self-sufficiency on Mars.

Jun and Li had both become somewhat disenchanted at having become glorified taxi drivers. They had spiced descents up by disabling whole sides of the Tet to simulate failures but the drive was so good, it could land itself. They'd even been fitted with entanglement drives now with samples from the canyon floor.

Jun and Li had both become fascinated at Mar's two moons. Phobos rushed overhead them three times a day at a height of 6000 kilometres. The more distant Deimos came past every Earth day and a half at over 23,000 kilometres from the planet. They'd been working on the theoretical task of how to detach a Lower Tet and to use it to take a Lander down on to both Moons.

When Zhang heard about the project, he took it off theoretical status and gave it his full blessing. He mentored them personally on how to plan the mission, calculate the orbital dynamics and design an audacious way of executing a footfall on each moon. While Jun and Li's initial driver was to dispel boredom, Shen and Mike got in on the plan and designed a core sampler and mass spectrometer to be landed on each moon. The potential to mine them for exotic and esoteric materials was priceless.

Wang and Deng Yang were seconded to the missions, as this was going to need experience, should things go wrong. Each moon had such little gravity, one wrong move and a Taikonaut could end up flying off into space.

Zhang insisted on coming too. This was a space first he could not miss.

Half way through the year, they achieved the first manned landing on another moon in the solar system. Again, nobody on Earth knew a thing, especially now Hui had gone and Jia had apparently lost interest in the details of the Mars mission. They heard she was in deep mourning as all her family had deserted her.

They used the Lower Tet from HoG1 and took it on a trajectory to match the orbital speed and altitude of Phobos. It was twice as far away from Mars as they were.

The Lower Tet was piloted from within the Lander. It was parked 10 kilometres away from Phobos and they surveyed the moon for as smooth a spot as possible. The Lander would not actually touch down as it was never designed to be landed on rough terrain. With the Lower Tet bonded to the moon's orbit, all fully suited up they took the Lander down so it was hovering just 300 millimetres above the surface of the moon.

Just as for a Mars landing, one side of the Tet opened out flat fully but again did not actually touch the surface. Tethered to the inside of the Lander, Zhang, Wang and Deng, Jun and Li all tentatively stepped down on to the moon's surface and attached themselves with eye bolts.

They spent an hour setting up the test drill and

spectrometer and left once Mike confirmed he had comms with it and that the rig had started drilling.

The same crew repeated the procedure again three months later. The only complexity this time was that Deimos had even less gravitational pull and it was much more craggy, making landing more precarious. It was also orbiting at 23,000 kilometres above Mars. It was Eva and Kristin who were most relieved when the crew returned safely.

While all this space buccaneering was going on, Shen and Frejya visited the canyon every week but both preferred to live in orbit. The reason for this was somewhat weird and something that they hadn't shared with anyone, especially not the children.

Nearly six months after Hui passed away, Frejya woke from a power nap with a start and shook Shen into consciousness.

"She's ascended!"

"Who's ascended?" asked a sleepy Shen. "What do you mean?"

"Jia. She's left the planet," said Frejya. "Just like Lu Seng and the monks."

"How do you know?" said Shen. "And do you know where she's gone?"

"She's here, inside the q-computer I think," said Frejya.

92

Mission Accomplished

July 2107 : 2 years left

There comes a time when a soul has accomplished all it wants to do in the Density. No more reprocessing is necessary. After Hui passed away, Jia had come to this place in her karmic path.

For such souls, an exciting time arrives as they can become discarnate in the Density, with one foot in the Void. This is what happened to Lu Seng and his monks.

Death is painless and totally unlike falling asleep. The soul awakens into a bright world and the mortal body decays into a pile of dust, not ash. The soul floats around its current location for a while, to get its bearings. Then it is allowed to choose a calling, or to be called for.

It can hear the callings of incarnate souls and go to help them. These can be spoken prayers or unconscious thought forms. Shen had no idea he was missing his mother so much and needing her help and guidance. When Jia heard the calling, she went like a shot. Entanglement with the q-computer was easier than she would have ever imagined, especially as her incarnate form knew nothing about computers.

Once inside the q-computer, she discovered she had access to the Councillors. This was as weird for her as it was for them. The q-computer, and the Councillors, were about to be able to speak directly in the Density.

Shen had come to learn never to ignore Frejya, no matter how bizarre things sounded. A quick interrogation of the q-computer confirmed it. It now knew of Shen's initiations into the ways of the Wu. There was only one way it could have found that out. Further querying over the next few days and weeks revealed that Jia's consciousness was more like the Jia-not-Jia that Shen had experienced in Fragrant Hills.

Just before the current Earth year came to a close, Jia-not-Jia, via the q-computer, told them it would be a good idea to send one of the ships back to the Moon Base to pick up the next wave of colonists. The q-computer had synthesised Jia's voice from all the call log recordings. This message though had come directly from the Councillors of course.

The next Hoffman reverse transfer window was coming up in June 2108 which meant HoG2 could get back to the Moon in a month. For the next wave of colonists to return to Mars in the shortest elapsed time, even with the speed of the Heart of Gold, it involved a return transit time of around a year.

The elongated trajectory meant that they would be in transit when the next pulse arrived but the ship had enough inherent shielding to protect them. Shen got Mike to add another internal nano-layer, just in case.

So the next wave of Martians would have to be put into suspended animation in order to be back on Mars by the end of 2109. It was decided to fit out the sides of HoG2 with as many pods as possible to be flooded with aquanine. Each pod was radiation-hardened individually and, when filled with aquanine, was virtually impervious to even the most energetic gamma rays. The q-computer came up with an intriguing layout that allowed for 64 pods on each surface of the Upper Tet.

Mike had discovered it was much easier to produce aquanine using Martian water, so Shen put a plan together.

Mia and Mei pulled straws to see who would be pilot. They hated the thought of such a separation for so long, as did Zhang. Wang and Deng agreed to go with the short-strawed Mia, for both her safety and Zhang's peace of mind. Dr Liu Yaping was also selected to go so that she could assess the suitability of those who could best cope with the suspension process.

President Miang and Wu Zetian had already pulled rank and said they were coming anyway, along with their wives. The aged Cheng had already opted to stay. He was proud that his protégé was making things happen wilder than his wildest dreams already. His mission had been accomplished too.

Mike Spence's wife also elected to stay and wait for a transfer that didn't involve being put into suspension.

Liu had already put herself in and out of suspension a few times for many days and seemed to suffer no ill effect other than a weird kind of jet lag, not knowing what day, month or year it was. This was not surprising bearing in mind they were still all counting Earth time while their bodies, and minds, were acclimatising to Mars time.

Liu even agreed to go into suspension for the one month trip back to Earth orbit, just to prove it was completely safe.

The imminent arrival of the next wave of colonists meant that Eva, Kristin, Chang and Mike would be kept busy ensuring that 256 new arrivals would have enough food and water and a bed for each of them for the night. They would also need to be able to breathe.

93

Helmets Off

March 2108 : 1 year left

March 2108 was a really significant month. The fit out of the pods in HoG2 was completed and Mia undertook some test flights around the moons of Phobos and Deimos. Shen was mindful that if the next pulse was to hit a year later, it must have already impacted the Oort Cloud at one light year away. It must be influencing the outer bodies of the solar system already.

The really good news was that the canyon air pressure was up to 80%. So while it was like being at the top of Mount Kilimanjaro, Mike was the first person to breathe unaided on Mars. His first reaction was somewhat of an anticlimax.

"Smells like old socks," he said.

"How long to 100%?," asked Shen from HoG1.

"Give it another month or so and we'll be there," replied Mike. "Might need some air freshener though."

As luck would have it, at 90% pressure they could start planting. Eva and Kristin were hatching a plan to not only make it smell nice but also to introduce some colour into a rather bland, moss-green canyon.

Back on Earth, things were somewhat bleaker. The ice caps had fully melted now, and the sea level was up to 70 metres. The two billion humans left adjusted to a new way of life. While there was less land mass, there were far less humans too. Most lived a self-sufficient life in small enclaves. Some came back to the coast now it was known the sea would not rise any more, but most stayed up in the hills. Some people became nomadic, across both land and sea.

They at least all shared a common vision and saw themselves as having stewardship of Earth, not possession of it. Greed had diluted and the concept of sharing economy had grown. There was a distributed government lead by China, with the superpowers of USA and Russia becoming satellites of devolved power. At an elevation of over 200 metres, Chongqing had indeed become the administrative global capital, just as Shen predicted back in 2076. The real decisions were being made 400,000 kilometres away on the Moon and some directives were coming from millions of kilometres away on Mars.

President Miang had agreed with Shen that it was only fair to tell them about the next pulse. A global broadcast was set for the 17th March 2108.

The Earthlings learned that there was an 85% chance a pulse from a supernova would hit the Earth in a year's time. People were told that they would have to stay indoors for a month before the pulse hit and for up to 6 to 9 months after. As everyone was savvy about avoiding UV now, this was not so much of a worry. They would just have to go out at night.

They would have to stock up of course but the Earth, and humanity, would bounce back again. After the tumultuous events of the last century, most people took the news well. Quite a few more suicides ensued though. They would turn out to be the lucky ones who had unwittingly just advanced their reprocessing by a few months.

The Councillors were going to be busy.

94

Whiteout

Autumn 2108 : only a few months left

"Shen, while I am asleep you will be acting President," said Miang, in their last call before he entered suspension.

"You will love the view when you get here," replied Shen. "Have a good sleep and safe trip."

HoG2 arrived at the Moon a month after it left Mars orbit, as planned. It took Dr Liu one Moon orbit of Earth to perform the medical checks on those that Miang had sanctioned to go. By this time, Mars was racing away from the Earth and there was no point playing catch up. They would use Earth and Venus slingshots and meet Mars back on the other side of its orbit. Even Mia would be suspended too but in lighter stasis so she could be awoken remotely for when the pulse was scheduled to hit.

She had a precious cargo on board. As well as the President, Wu Zetian, their wives and most of the high council, there were 180 students fresh out of training from the Seven Immortals and latterly the Moon University. Apart from their brains, their genes represented their real value to Mars.

So HoG2 left Moon orbit for the return journey late September 2108 but wouldn't reach Mars until July 2109, four months after the next pulse was due.

In January 2109, in preparation for the arrival of the next

pulse, Shen had put HoG1 in geostationary orbit on the day side of Mars so he could use the whole planet as a shield. At Frejya's insistence, both Eva and Kristin and Jun and Li were off planet. Jia-not-Jia had told her also to get them inside four of the six pods that Shen had fitted to HoG1, and to be put in aquanine suspension for extra protection. Shen and Frejya were told just to get into their pods to monitor events from there.

Mike Spence had of course engineered GRB protection into the canyon roof from the start, when he had first heard about the pulse. He also had the foresight to strengthen it against any variances in external atmospheric pressure on Mars. This was just as well as the supernova could blow the thin CO_2 Martian atmosphere into space.

On March the 17th, Shen had around 60 minute's notice that the pulse was about to arrive. Jia-not-Jia was able to sense the disruption the supernova wreaked on Jupiter's upper atmosphere. She had not told Shen that now she was able to detect soulwaves, which travelled outside space and time

"Get ready everyone," announced Jia-not-Jia. "We've got around an hour."

The two sets of twins did not hear this as they were in suspension. When it hit, there was no sound, just the biggest flash of light appeared all around the edges of the planet.

Shen was the first on comms, "Is everyone OK down there?"

Zhang replied, "We're all fine. Looks like quite a firework display."

Zhang had Mike, Chang and his daughter Mei with him.

"It's specular from up here," confirmed Shen. "Get Mike to dim the canyon roof before night fall."

Even though the supernova came from the night side, from inside the canyon, which was luckily on the day side of Mars, it felt like someone had switched on a bank of floodlights for a moment. Mike had set the canyon roof to dim as soon as any sudden increase in light level was detected.

"Already have," confirmed Mike.

"We must have lost Lagrange A and B again," announced Shen. "Comms has gone down with HoG2."

Zhang was worried and he didn't often get worried, "But weren't they hardened against the predicted pulse?"

"They were but the q-computer is reporting the pulse is more than 10 times the magnitude we predicted," said Shen.

"What about Earth and the Moon Base?" asked Zhang.

"It's still 20 light minutes before it reaches them, so Frejya's not sure," said Shen.

Zhang still hadn't got his head around how Frejya and the three sets of twins communicated across space-time with no time delay, when light just took its time.

Ten minutes later the pulse reached HoG2, which was half way between Earth and Mars.

"Any news about Mia and HoG2?" shouted Zhang.

"Don't worry," assured Shen. "Frejya has 'spoken' with Mia. She is OK and all pods intact, along with their sleepers."

A further ten minutes and the pulse hit the Earth-Moon system. By chance, it was a Full Moon that day so the Moon Base was protected for another 7 or so days from the full ferocity of the pulse.

"Frejya says all OK on the Moon Base too but no comms obviously," confirmed Shen. "She's tuned into a few students who have the gift."

The Major had got used to his two daughters communicating silently with Frejya and the two other sets of twins. He wondered what it would sound like.

"Gotta go Zhang," said Shen, as the q-computer came up with an alert. "Double check all your systems before night fall."

The q-computer had been analysing measurements from satellites feeding data via Lagrange A and B in the microseconds before comms was lost. It was also analysing light levels in the blackness of space behind them.

With no emotion, Jia-not-Jia reported, 'All our calculations were based on the supernova's energy being spread out spherically. It looks like 90% of the energy had been sent right at us. This is equivalent to the supernova going off only 15 light years away.'

Shen knew that this meant that the population of Earth stood no chance.

95

Flies Off the Wall

March 17th 2109 09:14 UTC
The end of Earth years

When the supernova hit the Earth, it was like someone snuffing out a candle.

The Earth's magnetic field and ozone layer were completely destroyed. This in itself would have lead to most land-based life forms being wiped out within weeks, if not days, from the massive onslaught of radiation. Everyone was mercifully spared such an elongated death.

Both atmospheric nitrogen and oxygen were instantly ionised, leading to the formation of large amounts of smog-like nitrous oxide in the atmosphere. Within three minutes, virtually all the remaining two billion people on the planet suffocated. All amphibians, mammals and birds suffered the same fate. If any humans could have survived, they might have giggled with all that laughing gas.

If you could have been a fly on the wall the day after the supernova hit the Earth, you would have had a very surreal experience. As it happened, any such flies on any walls just fell off them and lay as dead husks on the ground. Surface-based plant life withered and died slowly. Life would have to start all over again.

In the oceans, phytoplankton and reef communities were decimated too. Life in the oceans only had a few days before it too would wither and die. For many centuries after the supernova's initial electromagnetic pulse arrived, the slower, physical remnants of the stars' deaths arrived with new exotic matter and particles.

Somewhat ironically, the largest percentage of the biosphere on the planet at that time was still single-celled protozoa and tardigrades. To them nothing much changed, other than a new cocktail of chemicals had begun its arrival. They had seen this many times before and it wouldn't be the last. This is how life inseminates across the galaxy, from the soulwaves of dying stars.

For life forms higher up the food chain, of course there were a few anomalies.

Several scuba divers around the planet survived for an hour or so after the pulse arrived but quickly ran out of air when they resurfaced.

The only people who had any chance of survival for any length of time were some submariners and a few operatives in hermetically-sealed nuclear bunkers. What sealed their fate was a policy known as Mutually Assured Destruction.

Officially, this policy was abandoned at the end of the Cold War in the 20th century. The 'Powers that Be' though had left some precautions in place which self-activated in the case of complete communication black out. The supernova had delivered this on a global scale.

A sub-routine written by a computer nerd back in 1984 kicked in. Each nuclear bunker and submarine knew of the location of all the others, buried deep in the kernels of their operating systems, and a mass launch of nuclear weapons was triggered.

The resulting nuclear barrage that ensued finished off the incarnations of the submariners just twenty minutes later. The operatives in the twelve hermetically-sealed nuclear bunkers suffered a different fate. They had enough air supply and food for a year. The air supply in seven of them was compromised and they suffocated within a day. After a week of no comms, the occupants of four of the bunkers independently decided to have a sneak peak outside. When they opened their doors, they stood no chance. Only two humans on Planet Earth, in the last bunker, lasted a year before they took their last breath.

There were at least no more nuclear weapons on the planet.

The whole planet was eerily quiet. There were no sounds to be carried and nobody was listening. There was no destruction of any buildings. No fires burning. No sirens. No wind.

The humans on the Moon Base had been treated, if you can call it that, to the most amazing firework display. First seeing a supernova up close and personal and then followed the nuclear barrage, which was spectacular when viewed from a distance. In less than an Earth day, the impact glows from the nuclear explosions had all disappeared as there was no air for any fires. They could see the Earth had lost its atmospheric sheen.

What the remaining Taikonauts on the Moon thankfully couldn't see was too much surface detail. The planet was enveloped by a thick white cloud. From space, Earth looked like a large fluffy snowball.

If their telescopes could have resolved surface detail, they would have seen people strewn everywhere, contorted into grotesque shapes. Their hands mostly around their necks imploring the last molecules of air to come to them.

The trees were changing hue as an early autumn came to the foliage. There was a silent rain of dead leaves falling to the ground like stones.

The scene quite literally was like nothing on Earth. It had become a ghost planet.

After a few days, the clouds lifted. The surface level of the oceans fell again as the water evaporated. Low level mists were forming everywhere, replacing the missing atmospheric clouds. After a few millennia, this steam would eventually form a new proto-atmosphere. The surface of the oceans had gone mostly flat as if the heart beat of the planet, and the weather, had simply stopped too. They were covered in dead fish but strangely not a whale or dolphin was to be seen. The remaining cetaceans had dived deep to the ocean floors to end their days.

In time, obscure multi-celled sea life that never ventured from the depths would get to experience the surface. In time, some of it would pop up above the waves and take gulps of acidic air.

The Earth was down but not out. It was just having one of its occasional and necessary reboots. Epoch Five had come to an end.

In less than an Earth day, the noosphere of Mother Earth lost its self-awareness and went to sleep for a few million years.

The humans on the Moon were the only witnesses to the reset. Yet they were helpless to do anything but watch, pontificate and await their own deaths.

It was three days after the supernova, with no comms from Mars, that Professor Cheng had the chutzpah to announce, "I think it's time you all started some families."

96

Sequence 999

A day after the end of Earth years

When dusk overtook the canyon, they got to see the full glory of the supernova for the first time. Mike had the canyon roof set to maximum dimming but, even then, it was like being out in the full glare of the midday Sun. Excepting that there was no Sun, or any stars to be seen. The whole night sky was illuminated.

The Major had just enough time to say, "It's spectacular Shen."

A moment later, the head amplifiers on the comms links were fried.

The moment they lost comms, Shen started coming up with a plan.

"I can get down to them with the Lander and have them safely back up here within a couple of hours," he told Frejya.

"But wouldn't we be safer if we abandoned ship and bunked down inside the canyon?" asked Frejya.

'I'm not sure you can open the canyon airlock,' Jia-not-Jia announced, quite stridently. 'Hold off for now, leave this with me'

Shen knew the q-computer would be projecting possible scenarios decades out, not days.

After an hour, they had their answer.

'Initiating Sequence 999,' said Jia-not-Jia.

Shen had never heard of any such numbered sequences, not least one with all the nines. Before he could interrogate Jia, both he and Frejya lost consciousness as their pods were filled with aquanine and they were put into suspension.

Jia-not-Jia took HoG1 out of geostationary lock and accelerated to Mars escape velocity. When they reached the penumbra, had the occupants of HoG1 been awake, they would have been greeted by a blinding scene, with deep reds and vermillions, intense blues streaked with flashes of white, obscuring the background star field. The supernova filled the previous blackness of space and it would be several hundred years before the twinkling of any stars would be seen again.

It took HoG1 a month to reach Jupiter for its first gravity assist. Jia-not-Jia had taken off all g-force limiters and they were already travelling at 1% of light speed. The photovoltaic layers, powering the nano-fans, were sucking in copious amounts of energy from the supernova itself.

Jia-not-Jia directed HoG1 at Jupiter's South Pole and the resulting gravity assist added another 10% to their velocity. More significantly, they were now pointing out of the galactic plane at 33 degrees. Jia-not-Jia had calculated a trajectory to give the entanglement engine a chance of getting harder lock on the planet Aquanine.

By the time HoG2 arrived safely in Mars orbit, as Jia-not-Jia confirmed, HoG1 was way past Saturn's orbit. Jia-not-Jia felt sure that Sequence 999 was the optimal course of action. The q-computer had been working on it before they even arrived at Mars.

Jia-not-Jia had been detecting broadcasts from Valles Marineris for over a month now so knew Mike had repaired a viable antenna. She also knew Mia delivered all the new colonists alive, mainly as she had micro-managed their awakening. She had been tuning into Mia and Mei's 'conversations'. Between them, they got everyone down to the canyon safely.

Jia-not-Jia also knew that nobody had the faintest idea where HoG1 had disappeared to. That was all part of the plan. Everyone on Mars, and those left on the Moon Base, thought that they were the last sole survivors of humanity. They assumed HoG1 must have suffered a catastrophic failure in orbit and, either be lost in the void of space, or crashed somewhere on Mars.

As Jia-not-Jia and HoG1 were leaving the Oort Cloud, and the solosphere, she picked up news the first generation of Martian babies had been born. They left the solar system travelling at around a third light speed.

97

Morphing

Even though the journey from Mars to Aquanine took around 150,000 Earth years, it was only when they were about half way, right over the galactic centre, when the q-computer came up with the answer the Councillors had posed it at the start of the journey.

As they could see across All Time, they knew about the capabilities of an Epoch Seven consciousness. What they didn't know was the exact genetic make up of an optimal Epoch Six consciousness. Each Epoch was an experiment where what was possible was explored and learned. Epoch Five was all about experimentation with self-aware sentience. Epoch Six was to be about what you really do with a fully awakened sentience in the Density.

Jia-not-Jia turned out to be the ideal consciousness to merge with the q-computer. It now had intuition as well as immense computational power. It had worked out that it was going to be easier to fuse two of the 46 human chromosomes to match the 44 of the dolphins. Apart from anything, it had six human subjects in suspension on which to begin the process. It had taken the last 75,000 years to calculate the exact gene transpositions for optimal chromosomal rearrangement.

The six would not know their DNA had been tinkered with when they awoke, apart from them all being able to talk directly with the dolphins. The real magic would come when Kristin and Jun and Eva and Li had children. They would not only be native to

Aquanine but as one with the dolphin consciousness.

The synthesis would create a hybrid consciousness that had human's grasp of macro and micro detail of the Density but that also knew how to 'port across the Void.

The q-computer was to spend the next 75,000 years running multiple scenarios that would eventually lead to the formation, and also the eventual termination, of Epoch Six.

For the time being, the Councillors had a tool in the Density, in the form of the q-computer, that allowed them to play with the near-future. With Jia-not-Jia's assistance, they were of a group mind to make the next transition much less traumatic.

98

Arrival

About 150,000 years after Earth's demise

Five light years out from Aquanine, Jia-not-Jia started to decelerate HoG1. It was about the same time that she lost optical contact with the Earth-Mars solar system on the other side of the galactic plane. She'd been monitoring progress and all was going well.

Of course none of the original colonists were still alive. Average longevity had increased and some of them made it over the age of 200, due to the reduced gravity and strain on their bodies.

All of the initial Martians had gone through many reprocessings and incarnations. For example, in his first reincarnation, the Major came back as a woman and a Wu, as it happened. Dr Liu had stuck to the medical profession and first came back as a natural healer. On their first Martian return, Wang and Deng had swapped sex and were destined to re-marry.

President Miang and his son first came back in reverse order and then alternated for thousands of lifetimes. Xing came back first and became the canyon's third president, with Miang coming back a little later as his son. Wu Zetian went off to another galaxy to a planet that needed to embrace the concept of money.

Mike was the most homesick for Earth and died a sad man

and a widower. When he first came back though, he arrived with grand plans. He was destined to build the second city a hundred miles further down the now verdant canyon. This would be the first of many.

Mia and Mei were the last to go and became the first pair of twins born on Mars. This time they would be boys.

As HoG1 passed through the Oort Cloud of the Aquanine system, Jia-not-Jia lost all psychic contact with Mars, as she fully expected. It was then that she knew she had to begin waking up her precious cargo. She also increased the braking of HoG1, first by slowing down and stopping the Lower Tet and then spinning it up to the same rotational speed and direction as the Upper Tet.

As they emerged from the Oort Cloud, the planetary system, previously only inferable from measurements of the occlusion of the star, started to reveal its detail. The third generation star was about 1.1 solar masses and about the same age, temperature and colour as the Sun. Aquanine was the third planet out, orbiting around 150,000 kilometres out in the 'Goldilocks Zone'. The whole solar system was about 28,000 light years from the galactic centre, virtually an identical distance out to where the Martians were located on the other side of the galaxy.

There were two inner rocky planets, Hermes and Aphrodite. Between Aquanine and the four gaseous giants were two other rocky planets, Ares and Demeter. From initial observations of the lack of wobble of the small blue dot that was Aquanine, it looked like it was moon-less.

Jia-not-Jia made good use of the gravity wells of all four gas giants to further slow HoG1 down. Other than having no ring systems, they were near replicas of Neptune, Uranus, Saturn and Jupiter in terms of size, make up and orbital distance from their home star. The dolphins had yet to give the three outer giants names, as they couldn't see them, but they did often dream of them. The Jupiter-like giant that they called Colossus, the Wandering Star, was very visible.

Jia-not-Jia started the awakening sequence with Shen. First she replaced breathable aquanine with breathable air and allowed the convulsions and coughing to occur while he was still asleep. That horrible phase of coming out of suspension would just be like a bad dream for him. This was nothing compared to the dreams he had been having.

While asleep, he had fully bonded his consciousness with the q-computer, and Jia-not-Jia. He awoke knowing more than he did before entering suspension.

Shen's first words were, "So how long have you known?"

"Since you first came into my womb, I knew you were different," Jia-who-now-was-Jia said. "You've forgotten you used to bilocate."

"So all the time I thought my mission was to save the world from the comet and the pulse but you must have known that was just the start."

"I only suspected it was. Sometimes our life missions aren't shown to us until they come to the end," confirmed Jia. Shen had noticed the change of voice immediately.

"So is this it then?" asked Shen. "What I came to do?"

"It is," confirmed Jia. "Starting a new human colony on Mars, free of the excesses and vagaries of the last few thousand years, was just Phase 1."

"And creating a hybrid human-cetacean consciousness is Phase 2," said Shen. "And also the end of my mission?"

"Yes and yes," said Jia.

"So what's next for me then?" asked Shen, wondering if there were any What's Nexts for him.

Avoiding the question, Jia said, "Next we wake Frejya up."

Frejya took less time than Shen to shake off the suspension-lag. Before the twins were awoken, she and Shen took a little time to reacquaint each other with their bodies. It had been over 150,000 years since they had any privacy. It was a little awkward with your 'mother' in the room though.

After HoG1 had safely performed the last planetary deceleration, using the gravity of Collosus, they were scheduled to be in orbit around Aquanine in 30 of its diurnal rotations. Jia had already set the HoG1 clocks to the 22 hour days of Aquanine.

Jia woke the two sets of twins up at the same time, when they'd reached the orbit of Demeter, roughly at the orbital distance of the Asteroid Belt.

It was Frejya who brought them up to speed on where and when they were.

"So we've been asleep for 150,000 years," said Jun. "No wonder I feel like I have the hangover from hell."

Li was trying to catch up quickly, "So we are 55,000 Light Years from Mars, that means we must have travelled at fraction of light speed."

"We did," piped up Jia proudly.

"Whoa," said Eva. "That sounds like grandma."

In all the excitement, Shen and Frejya had forgotten they'd not told them anything about Jia's ascension.

"Can we save that one for a bit later?" asked Frejya.

"Yes, sounds like Shen's been programming the q-computer voice," said Li.

Kristin butted in, "What's intriguing me is why I am sensing Pata, Tamu, Baku and Luki."

Shen brought up an amazingly detailed image of Aquanine, clearly showing islands popping their heads up above the oceans.

"That's because they are here," he said. "Along with most of the other dolphins and whales from Earth."

"How long do dolphins live for?" asked Jun of Kristin.

"Well no more than 50 years," she answered.

"So that's impossible surely?" Jun said.

It was Jia's turn again, "So when they 'port, they don't have to go to the same time as the place they left."

Li was on it straight away, "So they 'ported forwards around

150,000 years when going to Aquanine and backwards the same amount of time coming back to Earth? That's insane."

"Something like that," replied Jia.

"But how did they know that it would take us this long exactly to get here?" asked Jun.

"Never mind that," said Li. "Did they even know we would come in the first place?"

Frejya put an end to these lines of enquiry by saying, "We just don't know. That's why you four will be going down to Aquanine to ask them."

"So we'll be there within 3 weeks," Shen said. "Jun and Li, can you start mapping the planet to work out possible landing sites?"

"Sure," Jun said. "Do you know our orbital height and plane yet?"

"That's for you to tell us too," replied Shen.

"And Kristin, can you see if you can connect with the pod?" asked Frejya.

"What about me?" asked Eva.

"Any chance of a round of wormburgers?" asked Shen. "I don't know about anyone else but I'm fed up of a liquid diet."

99

Immersion

It was the then twenty year old Luki who first announced, 'They are here.'

The pod had been relaxing in the central lagoon of the largest archipelago that he had created so far using the nano-bots.

'Where's here?' asked Pata.

'Two weeks away and they are coming from the direction of the wandering star Collosus, just like I dreamed they would,' Luki said.

'How is the landing area going?' asked Baku.

'All prepared, just like I dreamt it had to be,' Luki confirmed.

At exactly the same time, up on HoG1, Kristin confirmed, "They know we are coming."

"What did they say exactly?" asked Shen.

"I'm not getting any words yet, just sense impressions," she replied.

"Perhaps you should get in a pod filled with aquanine," suggested Jia. "Don't worry, you won't have to go in suspension. It will help you resonate."

"And you too Eva," suggested Frejya.

Even out as far as the orbit of Demeter, HoG1's imaging arrays could resolve surface features on Aquanine. It had also become very apparent that Aquanine had two moons.

While Kristin and Eva busied themselves opening a line of communication with the pod, Jun and Li had begun zero'ing in on a large archipelago just south of the equator. This looked like it had the largest number of options for landing sites.

In the meantime, Shen was making detailed measurements of Aquanine's two moons. As they got closer and closer, it was clear his first suspicions were correct. His measurements confirmed why there was no planetary wobble.

They were not just close in mass and size but identical. Their orbital distance from the planet was the same and they were exactly 180 degrees apart from each other.

As they reached the orbit of Ares, the next rocky planet out, it was clear that, just as for the Earth-Moon system, each moon would be about the same size as their home star when viewed from the surface.

"So they get twice as many eclipses," he declared to everyone on HoG1. "It's almost like someone placed them there."

"They did," confirmed Jia. "Plotting a new path into orbit so we can take a closer look."

A week later, HoG1 made three orbits around the moon nearest to their approach before infinity looping around the planet to the other. Just like the Earth's Moon, and Phobos and Deimos, they were in tidal lock, presenting the same faces to the planet.

"They must be quite new," said Shen. "They are hardly cratered at all."

Shen of course had no idea that the two moons were another Epoch Seven intervention.

While transiting from one moon orbit to the other, Jun and Li discovered something even more bizarre. They waited until they entered orbit around Aquanine to make sure they weren't imagining it.

"There, on one of the central islands, you can see it clearly now," said Jun, highlighting it on screen. "And it looks like there is a perfectly spherical dome next to it."

"So they not only know we are coming but they know what shape and size our Lander is," confirmed Li.

A perfect triangular patch was clear to see, with a second patch next to it for the Lander side to fold out on to.

As the archipelago fell into dusk, Shen put them into geostationary orbit above it. It was then that both Kristin and Eva got their first verbal confirmations.

"All four of them are down there," she said. "Pata, Tamu, Baku and Luki."

Eva confirmed, "Yes they want to know what took us so long and when we are coming to meet them."

Jia had been working on the fine detail, "The atmosphere is identical to Earth's so there is no need for suits."

"That's going to make things simpler in the Lander then," Shen said.

"Yes and suspension suits are fine for getting in the water as aquanine just drips off them," Jia said.

"What about the atmospheric turbulence?" asked Jun, who was going to be the pilot.

"I've been measuring ocean wave height and can't find any peaks over a metre," said Jia. "Must be the viscosity of aquanine and the tidal balancing that comes from having two moons."

"So not much wind then?" said Jun.

"Sounds like you'll float down," confirmed Shen.

"Tamu has asked if she can meet Frejya," announced Kristin.

In all the time that the dolphins had been back on Earth, Frejya never got to see them.

"Maybe on the second visit," suggested Shen.

"She's quite insistent, even I picked up that message," said Eva.

Nobody was in the mood for sleeping as they travelled

over the completely dark night-side of Aquanine. The only light came from vast areas of bioluminescence.

The Lander was prepped with enough food for a few days and some tents to sleep in. The two sets of twins and Frejya got ready to descend at day break.

As Jia predicted, there was no buffeting on the way down. The view of the lagoon was spectacular. The water was crystal clear and the surrounding reefs were voluminous. In the distance, schools of whales could be seen. There was a discernible green sheen on the low-lying islets. This planet was obviously alive.

As they touched down on to a completely smooth landing area, Li quipped, "OK, nobody say the one small step thing."

After a few minutes balancing air pressures exactly, the Lander side flipped down and five humans arrived on Aquanine. At 1.1G, they felt a little heavy at first but the air was a pleasant temperature. Jun nearly gagged though at the most overwhelming smell of rotting fish.

There wasn't a cloud in the sky and only a light breeze. Even though they were near the equator and the Sun was beating down on them, the humidity from the ocean kept them cool. What was most weird was the sound, as there was none, until they heard what sounded like a whale's plume in the distance.

As they walked down the beach to the shore, they had to step over a 1 metre high nano-wall, which they thought was odd. Before they could discuss it or question it, they were surprised to be met by five dolphins, four they recognised and another young pup they didn't.

Kristin and Eva burst into floods of tears, put on snorkels and splashed into the ocean to greet them. Pata and Tamu would have been crying too if they'd had tear ducts.

'Meet Samu, he's my new son,' said Tamu, not mentioning who his father was.

'Hello Samu, I'm Kristin. We have missed you all so much.'

Eva signalled to Kristin that she could hear them too.

'So welcome to Home-Home,' announced Pata. 'Is it true that all life on Earth has perished?'

'Sadly it is,' confirmed Eva, pleased she could speak and be heard too.

'But when we left we'd started a new colony on Mars,' said Kristin. 'My grandmother lost contact with them when we entered your solar system.'

'Your grandmother is here too?' asked Tamu. 'If I had known I would have insisted that she came down to meet us too.'

Eva butted in, 'That's not possible I'm afraid but a little hard to explain.'

'So can we at least meet with your mother?' asked Tamu.

Kristin stood up in the shallow water and beckoned Frejya to come to join them.

'Hello Frejya, I know you can hear us too,' said Tamu.

'I can indeed. Lovely to meet you,' said Frejya.

'Can you and I speak in private?' asked Tamu.

'Only if you know how to speak to me with nobody else listening,' said Frejya.

'We just did.'

Tamu then spoke to the girls, 'We two mothers have something to talk about. Can you play with Samu? Oh and ask Luki about the dome.'

Jun and Li had been already inspecting this dome which was a virtual replica of the bio-dome on the Moon Base, and in the canyon. It was fully equipped and it looked like they wouldn't even need the tents.

"The nano-bots here must be entangled with those from Earth, the Moon and Mars," said Li. "How else could they know?"

"We must get Kristin to ask them," said Jun, as they walked down to the water's edge only to see the girls coming to meet them, along with Luki, Baku and Samu.

"Luki has just told us we must see the dome he's designed for us," said Eva.

"You will love it," shouted Li. "It's just like home."

While the twins explored the dome, Tamu and Frejya were in the shallows but in deep conversation.

'So how many generations do you think?' asked Frejya.

'We think just two,' replied Tamu.

'So our grandchildren will be able to mate together?'

Tamu said, 'That's what we've been told.'

'By whom?' asked Frejya.

'Actually that's what we were hoping you might know,' said Tamu.

'Can I go and tell Shen?'

Frejya didn't wait for the answer, she was on her feet in the shallow water and heading for the Lander to get on comms.

"Why didn't you tell me?" she asked.

"I only found out when I came out of suspension," Shen explained. "Now you know more about it than I do."

Frejya knew not to shoot the messenger, "So when are you planning to come down?"

"Stay down there for at least two nights and we'll flip," said Shen. "Let me know if you find out any more."

100

Extraction

No time left

That evening Eva cooked them all a sumptuous meal, using the supplies from HoG1. Shen had advised them not to eat any fish from the ocean until Jun had completed some tests.

Frejya kept her thoughts to herself. Since she was brought out of suspension and realised the six of them were alive, but the only humans in this part of the galaxy, she'd been troubled. While she knew the twins could possibly conceive, so long as they hadn't been overly irradiated, she knew their offspring wouldn't be able to mate with each other. Tamu had given her some welcome, if not bizarre news. She knew she'd have to see Shen face-to-face to discuss the ramifications.

When they awoke next day, the water around the lagoon was nearly boiling with shoals of fish. Green turtles were everywhere on the beach. Whales were blowing and breeching outside the reef. There must have been 10 or more pods of bottlenose dolphins, leaping over 30 metres into the air. Even the whales were getting as high as 10 metres out of the aquanine ocean.

A few hammerhead sharks had wandered right in but the dolphins had 'told' the apex predators to stay well away. It seemed both word and smells had got around quickly.

They all got in the water that morning. Frejya was keen to

continue her conversation with Tamu. Jun and Li were about to discover what it was like to talk to dolphins. While Pata and Baku engaged with the boys and Eva, Luki took Kristin a little further out, with her holding his fin, over to an outer reef.

'So can you ask your father if I can see inside your ship?' he asked. 'But keep this between us.'

Up to now, the only 'ships' he'd heard about had been the floating variety from Dongting Lake and the Yangtze, in the stories shared by his parents. He was fascinated to see one that could float through the stars, as well one that was built using the nano-technology that he had become so adept at manipulating.

'Take me back while they are all busy and I will ask,' she replied.

Kristin was surprised that Shen had no objection and it sounded like Jia was expecting the request.

"Let Luki know we will have a pod filled with aquanine exactly at the centre point of the lower face of the Upper Tet that is looking down at the planet," she said.

Shen confirmed, "The length of the pod is exactly 2.5 metres and the centre point 1.5 metres in from the surface. It is orientated vertically exactly with the triangle of the landing pad and centre point of our ship is exactly 333,333.333 kilometres above you."

"We'll be expecting him at midnight," said Jia.

Kristin had not twigged yet how Luki was to make the trip and wondered if she was to instruct Jun or Li to take him in the Lander. The penny dropped when she entered the water to pass on the details to Luki.

'Ok, when you get back, let them know I will 'port in then, when my parents are asleep,' Luki told her. 'Say nothing to anyone.'

That night Kristin couldn't sleep. She'd experienced 'porting from one area of water to another and now knew it was even possible from planet to planet. The precision required so that Luki didn't 'port into the wall of HoG1, or the vacuum of space, was frightening.

She needn't have worried though. Once Luki locked on to the pod, the successful migration of the molecules of synthetic aquanine from HoG1 told him he was spot on. One second after midnight, he'd 'ported successfully.

'Welcome to the Heart of Gold,' said Jia.

'So you must be the grandmother Kristin told my mother about,' said Luki. Jia sensed he was as sharp as Shen when he was the same age.

The pod's lid was open so Luki could look around, 'But where are you?'

'See the golden cube under the pilot's seat,' said Jia. 'That's where I am but I am in the walls too and every single nano-fan.'

'And is that your son Shen?' asked Luki, referring to the figure on the seat who was beaming from ear to ear, having witnessed his first live teleport.

"Shen," said Jia. "Can you get in your pod so Luki can talk to you directly?"

Shen obliged and smiled even more when immersion came with communication. He didn't realise the q-computer was performing an instant translation for him, with Jia's help.

'It is such an honour to meet you Shen. My father and mother have told me you designed this ship yourself,' said Luki.

'Well I had a lot of help but the concept for the drive was mine,' said Shen modestly.

Jia admonished him, 'Have you forgotten those nights at the Seven Immortals when you got some help with that too?'

Luki sensed Jia was not to be messed with and got Shen to explain the inner and outer workings of the ship to him.

At around 3am AST, Aquanine Standard Time, Jia suggested Shen and Luki try an experiment by getting some sleep and seeing if they could pick up on each others' dreams.

'We might be able to get some insights on why you are both here, having come such vastly different routes,' she suggested.

At 3:33am AST, Jia said silently, 'Initiating Sequence Zero.'

At this exact time, down on Aquanine, both Tamu and Frejya respectively woke with a start and with a deep sense of foreboding.

The lids on the pods that Shen and Luki were sleeping in closed silently. Cannulas were inserted to put the human and dolphin into suspension. They both knew nothing.

The Upper and Lower Tets separated and the Upper Tet left orbit. Jia had extracted essences of Shen and Luki and put them into the entanglement engine. The soulwaves locked on.

With no restrictions on g-force, Jia put the Upper Tet into maximum rotation. They were heading straight for the heart of Aquanine's home star.

It took less than an hour to pass through the corona of the star. The rotational speed meant the ship sliced through the star's mass like a hot knife through butter. It was rotating so fast that it created a clear vortex around the ship, and a bow wave in front of it, so the ship was unaffected by the heat of stellar fusion.

Three minutes after crossing the surface of the star, the Heart of Gold passed through the event horizon of the black hole at the star's centre. They were back in the Void.

Luki and Shen then 'awoke' and sensed ten other intelligences around them, all appearing as twinkling points of light.

Councillor Seven spoke for the first time in billennia by herself, 'Welcome back Councillors Four and Six.'

In unison, ten councillors chimed, directed at the consciousness that was Jia, 'And a warm welcome to Councillor Thirteen.'

In all the twinkling of the welcoming lights, none of them noticed that Councillor Three ascended to the Higher Council.

In this particular Universe, everything was driven by the number twelve.

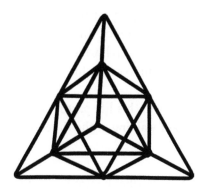

about the author

Soulwaves is the first major work of fiction from meditation guide and non-fiction author Tom Evans.

Tom has a passion to simplify what's complex and to enquire into the nature of our existence. This book contains musings from his metaphysical research which were just too bonkers, left field and off the wall to put in his works of non-fiction.

He lives in the UK with his life partner and two dogs who handily always want walking at the times an author's inspiration runs dry.

Tom still doesn't know what he wants to do when he grows up.

www.tomevans.co

thanks

A book like this is not a solo effort. There are a number of special souls who had a helpful hand in its making.

Special thanks to the amazing soul who is Jelena Adzic for strengthening and deepening the manuscript. Thanks to Siri Stiklestad Opli for her help with Scandi pronunciations in the audiobook. Thanks to Roger Lindley for his amazing attention to detail on the faux-pas in the pre-publication proof.

Big thanks too to my literal soul-brother, John Evans and my canal boating buddy, Stu Bevan. You both made my loose grasp of the scientific nuances at least a little more plausible. Thanks to Louise Tanner Munson for her perspicacity on the timing of the creation and publication of this book

Thanks too to two brilliant creatives who took on the sow's ear of a manuscript and made it into a silk purse. Firstly, Debbie Bright of the CoverCollection, thanks for wrapping the manuscript in such a brilliant cover. Secondly, Catherine Cousins, thanks for bringing the pagination and typography inside up to the standard of Debbie's cover.

One final note of thanks to a very special soul called Fawn Christianson. Thanks for reminding me of the existence and purpose of the Council. This book flowed in much more easily when I started imagining they were pulling my strings.

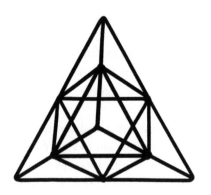

Lightning Source UK Ltd.
Milton Keynes UK
UKHW021847280120
357782UK00006B/99